Regency Rogues

Regency Rogues:

Outrageous Scandal

ANNIE BURROWS

MILLS & BOON

First Published in Great Britain 2019
By Mills & Boon, an imprint of HarperCollins*Publishers*
1 London Bridge Street, London, SE1 9GF

REGENCY ROGUES: OUTRAGEOUS SCANDAL © 2019
Harlequin Books S.A.

In Bed with the Duke © 2016 Annie Burrows
A Mistress for Major Bartlett © 2015 Annie Burrows

ISBN: 978-0-263-276763

0819

MIX
Paper from
responsible sources
FSC™ C007454

This book is produced from independently certified FSC™ paper to ensure responsible forest management.

For more information visit: www.harpercollins.co.uk/green

Printed and bound in Spain
by CPI, Barcelona

IN BED WITH
THE DUKE

Once again, my thanks to the Novelistas for constant support, brainstorming when necessary, and cake.

Chapter One

'Vile seducer of women!'

Gregory winced and pulled the quilt up over his ears. What kind of inn was this? Surely even travellers to such a Godforsaken backwater shouldn't have to put up with deranged females bursting into their rooms and screeching at them before breakfast?

'Oh! What wickedness!'

Pulling the quilt up round his ears clearly wasn't a strong enough hint that deranged females weren't welcome in his room. For the voice was definitely getting louder. Coming closer.

'What is the world coming to?'

Just what he'd like to know, he thought resentfully, dragging his eyelids open and seeing the owner of the strident voice standing right over him, jabbing a bony finger at his face.

'How could you?' the bony-fingered, screeching woman shouted into his face. *Right* into his face.

Enough was enough. He knew that public inns were of necessity frequented by…well, by the public. But surely even here a man was entitled to some privacy? At least in his own bedchamber?

'Who,' he said, in the arctic tone that normally caused minions to shake in their shoes, 'let you into my room?'

'Who let me into your room? Why, I let *myself* in, of course.' She smote her breast theatrically. '*Never* have I been so shocked!'

'Well, if you will invade a man's chamber what can you expect?'

'Oh!' the woman cried again, this time laying the back of one hand across her brow. 'Was *ever* there such a villain? Truly, your soul must be stained black with depravity if you can treat the seduction of innocence with such levity!'

Seduction of innocence? The woman must be fifty if she was a day. And *she'd* invaded *his* room. Nothing innocent about that.

'And as for you!' The screeching woman's finger moved to a point somewhere to his left side. 'You… you *trollop!*'

Trollop? There was a trollop in his bed as well as a hysterical woman standing next to it?

A brief foray with his left foot confirmed that, yes, indeed there was another pair of legs in his bed. A slender pair of legs. Belonging, he had to suppose, to the trollop in question.

He frowned. He wasn't in the habit of taking trollops to his bed. Nor any other kind of woman. He always, but *always*, visited theirs. So that he could retire once he'd reduced them to a state of boneless satiation and get a peaceful night's sleep at home. In his own bed. Where he heartily wished he was now. For there wouldn't be a strange woman in his bed if he'd stayed at home. Nor, which was more to the point, would *anybody* be daring to stand over him screeching.

'How could you repay me by behaving like this?' The hysterical woman was still ranting. 'After all I have done for you? All the sacrifices I have made?'

Her voice was rising higher and higher. And getting louder and louder. But even so there seemed to be a sort of fog shrouding his brain. He couldn't for the life of him pierce through that fog to work out why there was a woman in his bed. He couldn't believe he'd hired her. Because he had never needed to hire a woman. So how did she come to be here?

How, for that matter, did *he* come to be here?

And how was he to work it out with that harpy shrieking at him?

He put his hands over his ears.

'You ingrate!'

No use. He could still hear her.

'Madam,' he said coldly, removing his hands from his ears, since ignoring her in the faint hope that she might go away wasn't working. 'Lower your voice.'

'Lower my voice? *Lower my voice?* Oh, yes, that would suit you just fine, would it not? So that your vile misdeed might be covered up!'

'I have never,' he said in outrage, 'committed *any* vile misdeed.' Nor used the kind of language that more properly belonged on the stage.

He pressed the heels of his hands to his temples. His throbbing temples. How much must he have had to drink last night to wind up in bed with a trollop he couldn't remember hiring and be parroting the vulgar phrases of a woman who seemed intent on dragging him into some kind of…*scene*?

'Get out of my room,' he growled.

'How dare you order me about?'

'How dare *I*?' He opened his eyes. Glared at the screeching woman. Sat up. 'No. How dare *you*? How dare you walk into my room and address me in that impudent manner? Fling accusations at me?'

'Because you have seduced my own lamb! My—'

Indignation had him vaulting out of the bed.

'I am no seducer of innocents!'

The woman shrieked even more loudly than before. Covered her eyes and stumbled towards the door. The *open* door. Where she had to push her way through a crowd of interested bystanders. Who were all peering into his room with a mixture of shock and disapproval.

Except in the case of a plump girl he recognised as the chambermaid. She was gazing at him round-eyed and slack-jawed.

At which point he realised he was stark naked.

With a low snarl he stalked across the room and slammed the door shut on the whole crowd of them.

Then shot the bolt home for good measure.

He had a brief flash of his nurse, clucking her tongue and quoting that proverb about shutting the stable door after the horse had bolted.

No horse. He shook his head. A horse was about the only thing that *didn't* appear to have wandered into his room while he lay sleeping.

Sleeping like the dead. Which made no sense. How had he managed to get to sleep at all? When he'd decided to rack up here for the night he'd suspected he wouldn't be getting a wink of sleep. Other, similar inns in which he'd stayed had made a restful night wellnigh impossible. If it wasn't travellers in hobnailed boots tramping up and down the corridor at all hours, or coaches rattling into the inn yard with their guards blowing their horns as though it was the last trump, it was yokels with lusty voices bellowing at each other in the tap. Over which his room was always inevitably situated.

Although this chambermaid had brought him to a room right up in the eaves. So the noise wouldn't have been an issue. Had he been so exhausted after the events of the past few days that he'd slipped into a state resembling a coma?

It wasn't likely. And it didn't explain the muzzy feeling in his head. That felt more as though he'd taken some kind of sleeping draught.

Except that he'd never taken a sleeping draught in his life. And he couldn't believe he'd suddenly decided to do so now.

He rubbed his brow in a vain effort to clear his mind. If he could only recall the events of the previous night.

He concentrated. Ferociously.

He could remember having a brief wash and going down for dinner. And being served with a surprisingly good stew. The beef had melted in his mouth. And there had been cabbage and onions and a thick hunk of really good bread to mop up the rich gravy. He remembered congratulating himself as he'd come up the stairs on stumbling across an inn that served such good food.

After that—nothing.

Could the overseer and his accomplice have attacked him on the way upstairs? Had they followed him and sneaked up on him, intent on getting revenge? He felt the back of his head but didn't find any lumps or cuts. No sign that anyone had struck him with a blunt instrument. It was about the only thing they *hadn't* used.

They certainly hadn't hesitated to use their boots when they'd managed to knock him to the ground.

Not that he'd stayed down for long. A feeling of satisfaction warmed him. He flexed the fingers of his right hand, savouring the sting of grazed knuckles. It was one thing practising the science in a boxing saloon, where due deference was always given to regular customers, quite another to rise triumphant from an impromptu mill with a brace of bullies who had neither known who he was nor fought fair.

But, still, that didn't answer the question of why this harridan had burst, shrieking, into his bedroom, nor the female he'd apparently taken to his bed without having any recollection of so much as meeting her.

He turned slowly, wondering just exactly what sort of female he had found in such a ramshackle inn, in such a dreary little town.

He took a good look at the girl, who was sitting up in the bed with the covers clutched up to her chin.

Contrary to what he'd half expected she was a pretty little thing, with a cloud of chestnut curls and a pair of huge brown eyes.

Which was an immense relief. He might have lost his memory, but at least he hadn't lost his good taste.

Prudence rubbed her eyes. Shook her head. She'd never had a dream like this before. Not as bad as this, at any rate. She had sometimes had nightmares featuring her aunt Charity, for despite her name her mother's sister was the kind of cold, harsh woman who was bound to give a girl the occasional nightmare, but never—not in even the most bizarre ones that had invaded her sleep when she'd been feverish—had her aunt spoken such gibberish. Nor had she ever had the kind of dream in which a naked man invaded her room. Her bed.

He'd stalked to the door and shut it, thankfully, though not before she'd realised that the landlord was staring at her chest. Her *bare* chest.

Why hadn't she checked to see if she was naked before sitting up? And why *was* she naked? Where was her nightgown? Her nightcap? And why wasn't her hair neatly braided? What was going on?

The naked man by the door was ruffling his closely cropped light brown hair repeatedly, as though his head hurt. And he was muttering something about horses and gravy.

Naked.

Man.

Her stomach lurched. She had a clear recollection of snuggling up against that man a few minutes ago. He'd had his arms round her. It had felt…lovely. But then she'd thought it was all part of a pleasant dream, in which someone was holding her, making her feel safe for once. Loved.

Instead he'd probably…

She swallowed. Heaven alone knew what he'd done to her.

And now he was standing between her and the door. The door he'd just bolted.

Don't come near me. Don't turn round. Don't turn round.

He turned round.

Looked at her searchingly.

Appeared to like what he saw.

Started walking back to the bed.

She opened her mouth to scream for help. But the

only sound that issued from her parched throat was a sort of indignant squeak.

She worked her tongue against the roof of her mouth, desperately trying to find some moisture so that she could call for help.

Though from whom? That landlord? The man who'd just taken a good look at her breasts?

Aunt Charity? Who'd come in here and called her a trollop?

Although…it didn't look as though she needed to call for help just yet. The man was standing still. Fists on his hips. Glaring down at her.

Glaring down from a face she suddenly recognised. Now that she was actually looking at it. And not at those broad, bare shoulders. Or the bruised ribcage. Or the… Well, she'd never seen a naked man before. She couldn't help looking at *that*. Even though she knew she shouldn't.

But anyway, now that she was looking at his face she knew she'd seen it before. Last night. In the dining room.

He'd been sitting in the corner, at a table all on his own. Looking dangerous. And it hadn't been just the bruise to his jaw, or the fact that one eye had been swelling and darkening, or that he'd had the grazed knuckles of a man who'd clearly just been in a fist fight. It had been the cold atmosphere that had surrounded him. The chill emanating from steel-grey eyes that had dared anyone to try and strike up a conversation, or walk too closely past his table, or serve him with anything that didn't meet his expectations.

She hadn't noticed him observing her. But he must have been doing so. He must have somehow known she was in a room on her own and followed her up here, and then…

But at that point her mind drew a blank.

He hadn't handled her roughly—that much she knew. Because she didn't feel the slightest bit sore anywhere. Though perhaps she hadn't put up much of a struggle. Perhaps she'd known it would have been useless, given the size of the muscles bulging out all over that huge, great body…

'It won't work!'

'Pardon?' The word just managed to crawl over her teeth.

'This—' The big, dangerous, naked man waved his arm round the room. Ended up pointing at her. 'This attempt to compromise me.'

Compromise? What an odd choice of word. Besides, if anyone was compromised it was her.

She tried clearing her throat, in order to point this out, but he'd whirled away from her. Was striding round the room, pouncing on various items of clothing that lay on the floor. He bundled them up and threw them at her.

'Get dressed and get out,' he snarled. And then, for good measure, he drew the hangings around the bed, as though to blot out the very sight of her.

Which at least gave her the privacy to scramble into what turned out to be the clothes she'd been wearing last night. Clothes which had been scattered all over the room as though they'd been torn off in a frenzy and dropped just anywhere.

Which wasn't like her at all. She was always meticulous about folding her clothes and placing everything she might need upon rising close at hand. It was a habit ingrained during the first dozen years of her life, when the ability to move out of a billet at a moment's notice might have meant the difference between life and death.

Still, she wasn't going to dwell on that. If ever there was a time to make a swift exit then that time was now. She needed to get decently dressed, as fast as was humanly possible, and out of this room before the gigantic, angry, naked man changed his mind about letting her go.

She untangled her chemise and pulled it on over her head. Reached for her stays. And considered. It would take some time to wriggle it into a comfortable position and do up all the laces. Better just to get her gown on and get out of here.

When she peeped out through the bed hangings she saw that he was sitting on a chair, stamping his feet into a pair of scuffed, rather baggy boots.

Which reminded her. Shoes. Where were her shoes?

There. Right by the door. Next to each other, although one was lying on its side.

She grabbed her stays and waited until the man— the no longer naked man, since he'd pulled on some breeches and a shirt—reached for his second boot. He didn't look like the kind of man who'd sacrifice his dignity by hopping after her. So as he started easing his foot down the leg of that boot she made a dash for the door.

As quickly as she could, she thrust her feet into her shoes, and went to open the door.

It wouldn't budge.

She tugged and tugged at it, but no matter how hard she pulled, or how frantically she turned the handle, she simply couldn't get it open.

And the man must have got his second boot on. Because she could hear him walking across the room. He was coming in her direction.

In panic, she dropped her stays so she could tug at the handle with both hands. But she wasn't quick enough. He'd come right behind her. Was reaching up. Over her head.

And drawing the bolt free.

The bolt. In her panic to escape she'd forgotten all about the bolt.

'Allow me,' said the man, opening the door and making a mockingly courteous gesture with one hand.

Before putting the other on her back.

And shoving her out onto the landing.

The beast. The rude, nasty, horrible man! He hadn't even let her pick up her stays! Not that she really wanted to be seen running round an inn with her stays in full view in her hands.

But still— Her lower lip trembled. If she'd had a drop of moisture in her parched body she was sure tears would have sprung to her eyes.

She rubbed at them, but got no relief. The gesture only made the landing spin, and then sort of ripple— the way the surface of a pond rippled when you threw in a pebble.

And there was something else odd about the landing. It all seemed to be the wrong way round. True, she hadn't spent much time exploring the place when they'd arrived, but it had been such an odd little space, up under the eaves, that it was bound to have stuck in her mind. The owner of the inn had made clever use of his attics, fashioning three rooms around three sides at the top of his property, with the head of the stairwell and a broad landing taking up the fourth side. Last night, when she'd come up the stairs, she'd had to go right round the narrow gallery which bordered the stair-well to reach her room. But now she was standing right next to the staircase, which meant she hadn't been in *her* room just now.

But his.

Why had she been in his room? Could she have stumbled, sleepily, into the wrong room last night?

No…no, that wasn't it. She distinctly recalled starting to get ready for bed and her aunt coming in with a drink of hot milk.

A sound from inside the room she'd just shared with a total stranger made her jump out of her skin.

She shouldn't be loitering here. Who was to say he wouldn't change his mind and drag her back inside?

With legs that felt like cotton wool, she made her way round the gallery. She passed the door to the room where her aunt and her… She shook her head. She still couldn't think of her aunt's new husband as her uncle. He was no relation of hers. It was bad enough having to share her home with him, let alone address the old skinflint as though he was family.

She stumbled to a halt in the doorway that stood open. *This* was her room. She was *sure* this had been her room. The bed was just where it should be. And the washstand. And the little dormer window with the seat underneath on which she'd knelt to peer down at the view. She'd been able to see along the road that led to the market square. Even from this doorway she could just spy the top of the market cross.

But—where were her things? Her trunk should be just there, at the foot of the bed. Her hatbox beside it. Her toiletries, brush and comb should be on the washstand.

Confused, she tottered round the landing to the back of the house, to the room her aunt and the vile Mr Murgatroyd were sharing. There was nothing for it. She'd have to intrude, even though they might be— she shuddered—*embracing*, which they tended to do with revolting frequency.

She braced herself and knocked on the door. When there was no reply she knocked again, and then gingerly tried the handle. The door opened onto an empty room. No luggage. No personal clutter on the washstand or dresser.

As if they'd gone.

She blinked a couple of times and shook her head. This must all be part of the same nightmare. That was it. In a minute she'd wake up, back in… Back in…

She pinched her arm—hard.

But nothing changed. She was still standing on the landing at the top of an inn, in a little town whose name she couldn't remember. After waking up in bed with a naked man.

It couldn't be happening.

Her aunt and her new husband must be downstairs. Paying the bill. That was it. They couldn't have abandoned her. They just *couldn't* have.

Her heart fluttering like a butterfly trapped in a jam jar, she turned away from the empty room and ran down the stairs.

Chapter Two

'We run a respectable establishment,' said the land-lady, glaring at Gregory as she folded her arms over her ample bosom.

'Really?' If this was what passed for a 'respectable' establishment, he hated to think what she considered *un*respectable. *Dis*respectable. He gave himself a mental shake. Why couldn't he think of the word for the opposite of respectable?

'So we'd be obliged if you'd pay your shot and leave.'

'I haven't had my breakfast.'

'Nor will we be serving you any. We don't hold with putting our guests through the kind of scene you caused this morning.'

'I didn't cause any kind of scene.'

Why was he bandying words with this woman? He never bandied words with *anyone*. People did as they were told or felt the force of his displeasure.

'Well, that's not what my Albert told me,' said the landlady. 'Came to me with tales of guests complaining they'd been woken up by screaming women in the halls, naked girls in rooms where they didn't ought to be, and—'

He held up one imperious hand for silence. Very well, he conceded there *had* been a scene. In which he'd become embroiled. Now that he came to think of it, did he really want to break his fast here? The last meal he'd eaten under this roof, although palatable, had ended with him sinking into a state of oblivion so profound it appeared a band of criminals had attempted to perpetrate some kind of…of crime against him.

Dammit, he'd thought his mind was getting clearer. He'd managed to summon up words like palatable and perpetrate. Why, for heaven's sake, had he been unable to come up with another word for crime?

It felt as though someone had broken into his head and stolen three-quarters of his brain. When he'd first awoken he'd likened it to the kind of haze that followed a night of heavy drinking. A state he disliked so much he'd only very rarely sought the form of release that alcohol promised. And then only when he'd been young enough to know no better.

And the landlady was still standing there, hands on her hips now, glaring past him at the state of his room as though expecting to see the naked girl he'd ejected the moment she'd put on her clothes. That sounded wrong. As though he'd only tolerated her in his room while she was naked. What he'd meant was that of course he wouldn't have thrown her out until she was dressed. That would not have been a decent thing to do.

While he was standing there, wondering why his thoughts were in such a muddle when he was used to making incisive decisions about complex issues in the blink of an eye, the landlady's eyes narrowed and her nostrils flared. He followed the direction of her fixed stare to see what had put that disgusted expression on her face. And spied a stocking. A lady's stocking. Dangling from the mirror over the washstand. Looking for all the world as though it had been thrown there during an explosion of frenzied undressing.

He stalked across the room, wrenched it from the mirror and shoved it into his pocket, feeling…cheated. If he really had torn that girl's clothing from her in a burst of passion so overwhelming he'd thrown her stockings clear across the room, then he ought to be able to remember it. Remember being so out of control that he'd not only scattered her clothing all over the room but his own, too.

He shivered in distaste at the recollection that his shirt had spent its night on the floor. A floor that was none too clean.

'I will be down directly,' he said, coming to a sudden decision to shake the dust of this place from his shoes. As he'd had to shake the dust from his shirt a short while ago.

The landlady gave him one last basilisk stare before very pointedly stepping over the stays that lay on the floor by the door through which she exited.

He strode to the door and slammed it shut after her. Picked up the stays. Glared at them. Wondered for a moment why he felt such reluctance to leave them lying exactly where they were.

Because he didn't want any trace of himself, or whatever had happened here, lingering after he'd gone, he decided. Which was why he thrust them into the one meagre little valise he'd brought with him. Then he went to the washstand and rolled up his shaving kit, tossed it into the valise with the stays and the rest of his things.

Not that the stays were his.

And who was likely to look in his valise and imply that they were?

Nobody—that was who. Not once he'd returned to where he belonged. Which he planned to do as soon as possible.

He paid his bill downstairs at the bar, rather than calling for the landlord to come and attend to him. The sooner he'd done with this place, the better. He needed to get outside and breathe fresh air. Perhaps even find a pump under which to douse his head with cold water. He certainly needed something to clear his head.

Instead of calling for someone to bring his gig round to the front of the inn, he decided to go and fetch it himself. Because there was bound to be a pump in the yard at the back. Or at least a trough for the horses.

He had to pause on the threshold when the spring sunshine assaulted his eyes. It seemed incredibly bright after the darkness of the inn.

When his eyes adjusted to the daylight he saw that there was indeed a pump in the stable yard. And that next to it were two people. One was an ostler. The other was the girl. The girl from the night before—or rather this morning. Heaven alone knew what had happened the night before.

She was inching backwards, round the pump. While the greasy-haired ostler was stalking her. Leering at her.

He frowned. Surely if she was plying her trade at this inn she ought not to be taking evasive action. Or looking so scared. She should be smiling coyly, attempting to wheedle as high a price from the ostler as he could afford to pay.

Come to think of it, she shouldn't have clutched the sheets to her chest, or dressed so hurriedly, or scrabbled at the door in what had looked like desperation to get away from him earlier, either.

'Hi, there. You! Ostler!'

The ostler suspended his pursuit of the girl. Recognising him as a customer, he pushed his hat to the back of his head with a grubby forefinger and shambled over.

'Leave that girl alone,' Gregory found himself saying. When what he'd meant to say was, *Harness up my gig.*

The ostler gave him a look that was very much like a sneer. 'Want to keep 'er to yerself, do yer?'

The girl was looking round the yard wildly, as though for a means of escape. The only way out of the yard was through an archway. To reach it she'd have to get past both him and the lecherous ostler.

'That is none of your business,' he replied. 'I want my gig. And I want it now.'

'Oh-ar,' said the ostler, apparently remembering what his job here actually was. He shot the girl a look that made her shudder as he went past her and into the stable.

Once the ostler had gone into the stable Gregory turned to look at the girl. She was pressed up against the far wall of the stable yard, as though trying to disappear into the plaster.

It didn't make sense. Well, nothing about this morning made sense. But the girl's behaviour, above all, was perplexing.

He didn't like it. He didn't like not being in complete control of any situation. He didn't like the feeling of stumbling about in the dark.

He'd thought all he wanted to do was get away from this inn and back to normality. But the mystery of this girl, and how she'd come to be in his bed when she clearly wasn't a professional, was plaguing him.

He'd never be at rest until he knew what had really happened here last night. He wanted answers. And the girl would have those answers.

He stalked towards her. And as he did so she pressed even deeper into the plasterwork, her eyes widening with alarm. He supposed she must fear the consequences of having perpetrated—ah, there was that word again—whatever deception it was she'd attempted last night. As well she might. When she'd attempted to perpetrate whatever it was she'd been attempting to perpetrate she'd picked the wrong man.

He came to a halt a scant foot from her, wondering how best to make her abandon any loyalty she might feel towards her accomplices and put her faith in him, instead. Only then would she tell him what he wanted to know. Which was how the deuce had they managed to penetrate his disguise and what would be their next move?

The answer came to him when the ostler led his gig out of the stable, giving the girl a knowing, triumphant grin as he hitched the reins to a ring in the wall. If she wasn't a whore yet she would be one by tonight, that look said. Willing or unwilling.

His whole being rejected the notion of abandoning any woman to such a fate. No matter what she'd tried to do to him.

Besides, he had his reputation to think of. Somehow

the screeching woman with the bony fingers must have worked out who he was.

Or been informed.

Ah, yes, that would explain everything. Even the confusion and panic on the girl's face. It would be just like Hugo to drag some unsuspecting third party into one of his pranks and leave them to pay the price.

And the devil of it was that Hugo knew *he* would do his utmost to hush it all up. That he would never let the family name be dragged through the mud.

'Once I have left this inn yard in that gig…' he pointed it out to the quaking girl '…you will be completely at that man's mercy.'

Her eyes flicked wildly from the gig to the ostler, who was ambling in their direction, and to him. Only once she was looking at him did he continue.

'You would do better to come with me. I will keep you safe.'

She didn't look as though she believed him. Her inference that he might not be telling the truth was an insult so grave she might as well have spat at him.

Drawing himself to his full height, he bit out, 'I give you my word.'

Something about his demeanour, or maybe the approach of the ostler, must finally have managed to convince her, because she nodded her head before shooting past him and clambering up into the gig.

The ostler's face fell. And *he* actually did spit. At the pair of them as they swept past him and out into what passed for the high street in this scruffy little town.

The girl had wrapped her arms around herself in a protective gesture the moment he'd climbed into the driver's seat. And he was so angry with her that for a while he didn't bother to reassure her that she really was safe with him. How dared she insinuate that he was the kind of man who told lies?

Though, to be fair, these last few days he *had* been somewhat economical with the truth.

But never—not under any circumstances—would he harm a helpless woman. Not even an *un*helpless woman. Oh, blast it all. There went his vocabulary again. There was no such word as unhelpless, was there?

The approach of a farm cart from the opposite direction caused him to abandon his vain attempt to find a suitable word to describe the girl sitting next to him. He needed all his concentration to get his vehicle past the cart in the narrow confines of the lane. Particularly since the farmer's horse appeared to annoy the one harnessed to his own gig. What with preventing his bad-tempered nag from biting the gentle, rather stupid mare belonging to the farmer, and convincing it that it really *did* need to progress further down the lane, even though it looked as if it would be better sport to make the farmer's horse back his cart into the wall, he had his hands—and his mind—completely full.

They were right out in the countryside, with the little town of Much Wapping far behind them, before he decided to speak to the girl again.

He found he was looking forward to coaxing her into speaking. The only word that had so far passed her lips had been huskily spoken. Like a velvet caress.

Velvet caress? Good grief, what was the matter with him that he was coming up with such bizarre ideas?

Anyway, he shouldn't have to coax her into speaking again. Females, in his experience, were never silent. Not for as long as this anyway. Not unless they were planning something. He gave her a sharp look. She still had her arms wrapped around her middle. Her fingers tucked under her armpits. It struck him that she didn't look merely defensive any longer. She looked cold.

Cold. Of *course* she was cold. She wasn't wearing a coat. Or a bonnet. Her rust-coloured gown was made of good quality kerseymere, but a brief glance at her feet revealed an expanse of bare skin between the tops of her sturdy shoes and the hem of that gown. And it might be sunny, but this early in the year it wouldn't be really warm until perhaps the middle of the afternoon. If then. She needed to put something else on. But she hadn't any luggage, had she?

Frowning, he cast his mind over what to do for her. It would be pointless to offer her the one stocking he had in his jacket pocket. She needed more than one stocking. She needed a coat.

He could lend her his own coat… But, no. It would swamp her. Even his jacket would probably come down to her knees. Though that, actually, might not be such a bad thing. She could tuck her hands inside the sleeves.

He couldn't just stop where they were and offer her his jacket, though. The lane was so narrow that if any other vehicle came from either direction they wouldn't be able to pass. But from now on he'd look for a place where he could safely pull over.

Before very much longer he spied a gate leading into a field, which gave him the chance to pull the gig off the road a little. He put on the brake, removed his gloves and swiftly unbuttoned his coat.

Just as he was leaning forward, with his left arm out of one sleeve, about to remove his right arm from the other, the girl gave him a hefty shove in the side. She caught him so off balance that he tumbled right out of the seat, landing between the gig's nearside wheel and the gatepost.

Dammit, why hadn't he seen that coming? Women were never as defenceless as they looked. *Obviously* she was going to try and steal his horse and gig the moment he let down his guard.

And *why* had he let down his guard? All she'd had to do was shiver and look a bit pathetic and he'd promptly forgotten the way they'd met. All he'd been able to think of was shielding her. Just the way he'd wanted to shield her from that repulsive ostler.

Well, no longer. He surged to his feet on a wave of absolute fury. He might despise the bad-tempered nag harnessed to the ramshackle gig he normally wouldn't have permitted in any of his stables, let alone take out onto a public road, but it was currently his only means of transport. And he was *not* going to relinquish it to a slip of a girl! He'd climb back into the driver's seat and wrest the reins from her hands. And then—

And then nothing. Because she wasn't in the driver's seat, whipping the horse into a gallop and leaving him standing in the lane. On the contrary—she'd scrambled out of the gig while he'd been picking himself up and was currently running away as fast as she could.

Back towards Much Wapping.

Her accomplices must still be there. Hang it all, why hadn't he thought of that? She must have been loitering in the stable yard awaiting them.

Well, he wasn't going to let her get back to them and…and do whatever it was she was planning to do. He'd had enough of stumbling about in ignorance. Of being chivalrous, and merciful, and all the rest of it. He

was going to drag her back and shake the truth out of her,
if that was what it took. For only by discovering the truth
would he stand any chance of regaining the upper hand.

Prudence ran as fast as her legs could carry her.
Though her shoes chafed against her bare feet and her
legs still didn't feel as though they quite belonged to her.

But she wasn't going to be fast enough. She could
hear the man's feet pounding down the road behind her.
Getting closer and closer.

She wasn't going to be able to outrun him. She had
to find another way to stop him. But what?

Just then she stumbled and half fell to the ground,
which was littered with large chunks of jagged rock.
Chunks of rock which looked as though they had come
away from the dry stone wall that flanked this side of
the lane.

She grabbed one. Turned. Faced the big, angry man
who was planning to… Well, she didn't know what he
planned to do with her once he caught her, but from the
look on his face it wasn't anything she'd like.

In a sort of wild desperation she flung the rock at
him as hard as she could.

To her surprise—and his—it caught him on the forehead.

He went down like a… Well, like a stone. Prudence
stood rooted to the spot. Stared in horror at the blood
which was trickling down his face.

The ungainly sprawl of his limbs.

His total stillness.

What had she done? She'd only meant to show him
she meant business. To stop him pursuing her.

Instead she'd…she'd *killed* him!

Chapter Three

She ran to where he lay, sprawled on his back in the dirt, blood streaming across his forehead and into his hair. She dropped to her knees beside him. She couldn't believe she'd felled him like that. With one little stone. Oh, very well then, with a large chunk of rock. She pressed her hands to her mouth. He was such a big man. So full of life and strength. It was unnatural to see him lying so still.

And then he groaned. She'd never heard such a welcome sound in her life.

'Oh, thank God! You aren't dead.' She was almost sobbing.

He opened his eyes and shot her a cold, disbelieving look.

'No thanks to you,' he growled, then raised one hand to the cut and winced. He drew his hand away and held his fingers before his eyes, as though he couldn't believe he really was bleeding without seeing the evidence as well as feeling it.

She reached into the pocket of her skirt for something to dab at the wound. But there was nothing. She had no handkerchief. Her chemise was of fine lawn, though.

Its material would be as good. She hitched up her skirt and started tugging at her chemise.

'What,' asked the man warily—which wasn't surprising since she'd well-nigh killed him, 'are you doing?'

'I'm trying to tear a piece from my chemise,' she said, still desperately trying to rip the fabric that was proving more resilient than she'd expected.

'Why?' He looked baffled now, as well as wary.

'To do something about that cut on your head,' she said.

'The cut *you* caused by throwing a rock at me?'

'That's the one.'

'Wouldn't you rather get another rock and finish what you started?' he enquired mildly.

'No! Oh, no—I never meant to hurt you. I didn't think my aim was that good. Actually...' She sat back on her heels. 'My aim *wasn't* that good. Because I wasn't aiming at your head. I was just throwing the rock in your general direction, so you'd understand I wished you to leave me alone.'

'Why?'

While she'd been attempting to explain he'd been fishing in his own pockets and found a large, pristine white silk square which he handed to her with a sort of flourish.

'Thank you,' she said, taking it from him and applying it to the cut. 'Why what?'

'Why were you running away? Why didn't you just steal the gig? Or can you not drive?'

'Yes, I can drive. Of course I can drive. It just never occurred to me to steal your gig. I'm not a thief!'

He quirked one eyebrow—the one that wasn't bleeding—as though in disbelief. 'Not a thief?' he repeated dryly. 'How fortunate I feel on receipt of that information.'

She put her hand around the back of his head to hold it still, so that she could press down hard on the cut. 'Yes, you are fortunate,' she said tartly. 'I could have left you lying in the road for the…the next gang of thieves to come along and finish you off!'

'Well, that would have made more sense than this,' he said, making a vague gesture to his forehead.

She couldn't be sure if he meant her trying to stanch the flow of blood, or the fact she'd caused his injury in the first place.

'You had no reason to run off,' he said, a touch petulantly for a man who looked so tough. 'I told you I wouldn't harm you. But,' he said, drawing his brows down and narrowing his eyes with what looked like suspicion. 'I suppose you were desperate to get back to Much Wapping to collect your fee.'

'Fee?' She withdrew the handkerchief, noting with some relief that the bleeding was slowing already. 'I don't know what you mean.'

'It's no use playing the innocent with me. Hugo put you up to this, didn't he?'

'Hugo? I don't know anyone by that name.'

'A likely story. If you were not attempting to get back to Much Wapping and claiming your reward, why were you running away?'

'You scared me,' she admitted. 'When you started undressing.'

'Undressing? I was not undressing.' He frowned. 'Not precisely. That is, I *was* removing my coat, but only so that I could lend you my jacket. You looked cold.'

'Your…your jacket?' She sat back on her heels. The handkerchief slid from the man's brow to the ground on which he was still lying, glaring up at her. 'Because I looked cold? But… But…'

She pressed her hands to her mouth again for a moment. Looking back on his actions in the light of that explanation, it all looked very, very different.

'I'm so sorry. I thought… I thought…'

'Yes,' he said grimly. 'I can see what you thought.'

'Well,' she retorted, suddenly angered by the way he was managing to look down his nose at her even though he was flat on his back and she was kneeling over him. 'What would *you* have thought? I woke up in bed naked, in a strange room, with no idea how I came to be there. Aunt Charity was screaming at me, you were wandering about the place naked, shouting at me, too, and then I went to my room and it was empty, and Aunt Charity had gone with all my things, and the landlady called me names and pushed me out into the yard, and that man…that man…' She shuddered.

'I told you,' he said, reaching for the abandoned handkerchief and pressing it to his brow himself, 'that I would keep you safe. Didn't you believe me?'

'Of course I didn't believe you. I'm not an idiot. I only went with you because I was so desperate to get away from that dirty, greasy stable hand. And because at least *you* didn't seem…amorous. Even this morning, when we woke up together, you didn't seem amorous. Only angry. So I thought at least you'd spare me *that*. Except then you took me out into the middle of nowhere and started undressing. And I… I didn't know what to think. It's all like some kind of nightmare.' She felt her lower lip tremble. 'None of this seems real.' Her eyes burned with tears that still wouldn't quite form.

'No,' he said slowly. 'None of this seems real.'

And then he sat up.

Her instinct was to flinch away. Only that would look terribly cowardly, wouldn't it? So she made herself sit completely still and look him right in the eyes as he gazed into hers, searchingly.

'Your eyes look strange,' he said, reaching out to take hold of her chin. 'I have never seen anyone with such tiny pupils.'

For such a large man his touch was remarkably gentle. Particularly since he had every right to be angry with her for throwing that rock. And actually hitting him with it.

'My eyes *feel* strange,' she admitted in a shaky voice. The touch of his fingers on her chin felt strange, too. Strange in the sense that she would have thought, given all that had passed between them so far, she would want to recoil. But she didn't. Not in the slightest. Because for some strange reason his fingers felt pleasant. Comforting.

Which was absurd.

'My head is full of fog. Nothing makes sense,' she said, giving her head a little shake in a vain attempt to clear it of all the nonsense and start thinking sensibly again. It shook his fingers clear of her chin. Which was a pity.

No, it wasn't! She *didn't* want to take his hand and put it back on her face, against her cheek, so that she could lean into it. Not one bit.

'It is the same for me,' he said huskily.

'Is it?' That seemed very unlikely. But then so did everything else that had happened today.

'Yes. From the moment I awoke I could not summon the words I needed.'

Words. He was talking about words. Not wanting to put his hand back on her face.

'They seem to flit away out of reach, leaving me floundering.'

'It is my aunt and uncle who've flitted out of *my* reach,' she said bitterly. 'Leaving me floundering. Literally. And my legs don't seem as if they've properly woken up yet today.'

'And you really haven't heard of anyone called Hugo?'

Just as she shook her head in denial her stomach growled. Rather loudly.

He looked down at it with a quirk to his lips that looked suspiciously like the start of a smile.

'Oh, how unladylike!' She wrapped her arms around her middle.

'You sound as hungry as I feel,' he said, placing his hands on his own stomach. 'I didn't have any breakfast.'

'Nor me. But until my stomach made that noise I hadn't thought about being hungry,' she found herself admitting. 'I'm too thirsty.'

'I'm thirsty, too. And foggy-headed. And I don't feel as though my limbs want to do my bidding, either. I'm generally held to be a good whip, but I'm having real trouble controlling that broken-down hack that's harnessed to the gig. And what's more...' He took a breath, as though coming to a decision. 'I don't recall a thing about last night. Not after dinner anyway. Do you?'

She thought for a bit. Today had been so bizarre that

she hadn't done anything more than try to work her way through it. And that had been hard enough, without trying to cast her mind back to the day before.

'I went up to my room directly after dinner,' she said. 'I remember starting to get ready for bed, and Aunt Charity bringing me some hot milk which she said would help me sleep...'

A coldness took root in her stomach.

'After that,' she continued as a horrible suspicion began to form in her mind, 'I don't remember anything until I woke up next to you.'

'Then it seems clear what happened,' he said, getting to his feet and holding out his hand to her. 'She drugged you and carried you to my room.'

'No. *No.*' She shook her head as he pulled her to her feet. 'Why would she do such a horrid thing?'

'I wonder if *she* knows Hugo,' he mused. Then he fixed her with a stern look. 'Because if Hugo *isn't* behind this...' he waved his free hand between the pair of them '...then we're going to have to find another explanation. You will have to have a serious think about it on the way.'

'On the way where?'

He hadn't let go of her hand after helping her up, and she hadn't made any attempt to tug it free. So when he turned and began to stride back to the gig she simply trotted along beside him.

'On the way to Tadburne,' he said, handing her up into the seat. 'Where we are going to get something to eat in a respectable inn, in a private parlour, so that we can discuss what has happened and what we plan to do about it.'

She liked the sound of getting something to eat. And

the discussing of plans. But not of the private parlour. Now that he'd let go of her hand she could remember that he was really a total stranger. A very disreputable-looking stranger, in whose bed she'd woken up naked that morning.

But what choice did she have? She was hungry, and cold, and she had not the means to do anything about either condition since Aunt Charity had vanished with all her possessions. She didn't even have the small amount of pin money she was allowed. It had been in her purse. Which was in her reticule. The reticule she'd last seen the night before, when she'd tucked it under her pillow for safekeeping.

Oh, why hadn't she thought to go to the bed in that empty room and see if her reticule was there? At least she'd have a few shillings with which to… But there her mind ran blank. What good would a few shillings be at a time like this?

But at least she would have had a clean handkerchief.

Though it wouldn't have been clean now anyway. She'd have had to use it to mop up the blood. And then, if she'd needed one for herself later, she'd have had to borrow one from him anyway.

Just as she was now having to borrow his jacket, which he'd stripped off and sort of thrust at her, grim-faced.

'Thank you,' she said, with as much penitence as she could muster, and then pushed her arms gratefully into sleeves that were still warm from his body. Which reflection made her feel a bit peculiar. It was like having his arms around her again. The way they'd been before she'd woken up.

Fortunately he shot her a rather withering look,

which brought her back to her senses, then bent to retrieve the coat that had fallen into the road when she'd pushed him off the seat just a short while since.

'To think I was concerned about my *name* being dragged through the mud,' he muttered, giving it a shake. 'You managed to pitch me into the only puddle for miles around.'

She felt a pang of guilt. Just a small one. Because now not only was his eye turning black around the swelling he'd already had the night before, but he also had a nasty gash from the stone she'd thrown, spatters of blood on his neckcloth, and a damp, muddy smear down one side of his coat.

She braced herself for a stream of recrimination as he clambered back into the driving seat. But he merely released the brake, took up the reins, and set the gig in motion.

His face was set in a fierce scowl, but he didn't take his foul mood out on her. At least she presumed he was in a foul mood. Any man who'd just been accused of indecency when he'd only been trying to see to a lady's comfort, and then been cut over what must already be a sore eye, was bound to be in a foul mood.

'I'm sorry,' she said, after they'd been going for a bit. Because she felt that one of them ought to say something.

'For what, exactly?'

Oh. So he was the sort of man who sulked when he was angry, then, rather than one who ranted.

'For throwing the rock. For hitting you when normally I couldn't hit a barn door.'

'You are in the habit of throwing rocks at barn doors?'

'Of course not! I just meant… I was trying to apologise. Do you have to be so…so…?'

'You cannot think of the word you want?'

'No need to mock me.'

'I didn't mean to. It was an observation. I have already told you that I am struggling to find the words I want myself this morning. And, like you, none of this seems real. I suspect that when whatever drug we have both been given wears off I shall be rather more angry about the rock and your assumptions about me. But right now all I can think about is getting something to drink.'

'A cup of tea…' She sighed. 'That would be heavenly.'

'A pint of ale.'

'Some bread and butter.'

'A steak. With onions.'

'At breakfast?'

'Steak with onions is always good.'

She shuddered. 'I don't know about that. My stomach doesn't usually wake up first thing. I don't normally eat much before noon.'

'I don't bother with a break at noon. I'm usually out and about. Busy with estate business when I'm in the country. Or in my office with my secretary when I'm in town.'

'You have a secretary? What kind of business are you in?'

Did she imagine it, or did he look a little hunted?

'Never mind what business I'm in,' he said, rather defensively.

Oh, dear. Last night Aunt Charity had remarked that he was just the kind of disreputable person she'd been afraid they might encounter in such an out-of-the-way tavern. That he was probably a highwayman. Or a housebreaker. Though surely housebreakers didn't have secretaries? Still, the fact that he didn't want to answer any questions about his background made it more than likely that he was some sort of scoundrel.

But not a complete scoundrel. A complete scoundrel wouldn't have given her his jacket. Wouldn't have rescued her from the ostler or offered to buy her breakfast, either. No—a complete scoundrel would have left her to fend for herself. Climbed into the gig and driven away. If not the first time then definitely the second time, after she'd thrown a rock at him.

She rubbed at her forehead. He looked so villainous, and yet he wasn't acting like a villain. Whereas her aunt, who made a great display of piety at every opportunity… Oh, nothing made sense today! Nothing at all.

'I have just realised,' he said, 'that I don't even know your name. What is it?'

'Prudence Carstairs,' she said. 'Miss.'

'Prudence?' He gave her one sidelong glance before bursting out laughing.

'I don't see what's so funny about my being called Prudence,' she objected.

'P…Prudence?' he repeated. 'I cannot imagine a name *less* suited to a girl whom I met naked in bed, who gets chased around horse troughs by lecherous ostlers and throws rocks at her rescuer. Why on earth,' he said, wiping what looked like a tear from one eye, 'did they call you *Prudence*? Good God,' he said, looking at her in sudden horror as a thought apparently struck him. 'Are you a Quaker?'

'No, a Methodist,' she said, a touch belligerently. 'Grandpapa went to a revival meeting and saw the light. After that he became a very strict parent, so naturally my mother named me for one of the virtues.'

'Naturally,' he said. 'But why Prudence in particular?'

'Because it was the one virtue it was impossible for her to attain in any other way,' she retorted, without thinking.

'And did she feel she *had* attained it, once you grew old enough for her to discern your personality? I suspect not,' he observed. 'I think you are just like her.'

'No, I'm not! *She* ran off with a man she'd only known a week, because his unit was being shipped out and she was afraid she'd never see him again. Whereas *I* have never been dazzled by a scarlet jacket or a lot of gold braid. In fact I've never lost my head over *any* man.'

'Good for you.'

'There is no need to be sarcastic.'

'No, no—I was congratulating you on your level head,' he said solemnly, but his lips twitched as though he was trying to suppress a smile.

'I don't think so.'

'So,' he said, ignoring her retort. 'Your mother ran off with a soldier, I take it, and regretted it so much that she gave you a name that would always remind her of her youthful folly?'

'She did no such thing! I mean, yes, Papa was a soldier, but she never regretted eloping with him. Not even when her family cut her out of their lives. They were very happy together.'

'Then why—?'

'Well, doesn't every parent want a better life for their child?'

'I have no idea,' he said.

He said it so bleakly that she stopped being angry with him at once.

'And I have no patience with this sort of idle chatter.'

What? She'd hardly been chattering. All she'd done was answer the questions he'd put to her.

She'd taken a breath in order to point this out when he held up his hand to silence her.

'I really do need to concentrate for a moment,' he said brusquely. 'Although I am familiar with the area, in a general sort of way, I have never travelled down this road.'

They had reached a junction to what looked like a high road.

'I think we need to turn left,' he muttered. 'Yes, I'm almost sure of it.'

He looked to the right, to make sure nothing was coming, before urging the horse off the rutted, narrow lane and out onto a broad road that looked as though it saw a lot of traffic.

'So how come,' he said, once they were trotting along at a smart pace, 'you ended up falling into such bad company? If your mother was so determined you would have a better life than she did how did you end up in the power of the termagant who invaded my room this morning?'

'That termagant,' she replied acidly, 'happens to be my mother's sister.'

'You have my sincere condolences.'

'She isn't usually so—' She flared up, only to subside almost at once. 'Actually, that's not true. Aunt Charity has never been exactly easy to get along with. I did my best. Well, at least at first I did my best,' she confessed. 'But eventually I realised that she was never going to be able to warm to me so it didn't seem worth the effort.'

'Why should she not warm to you?'

He looked surprised. As though there was no earthly reason why someone shouldn't warm to her. Did that mean *he* had?

'It was all to do with the way Mama ran off with Papa. The disgrace of it. I was the result of that disgrace. A constant reminder of it. Particularly while my father was still alive.'

'He sent you back to your mother's family while he was still alive?'

'Well, not deliberately. I mean…' Oh, why was it so hard to explain things clearly? She screwed up her face in concentration, determined to deliver the facts in a logical manner, without getting sidetracked. 'First of all Mama died. And Papa said that the army was no place for a girl my age without a mother to protect her. I was getting on for twelve, you see.'

'I *do* see,' he grunted.

'Yes… Well, he thought *his* family would take me in. Only they wouldn't. They were as angry over him marrying a girl who "smelled of the shop" as Grandpapa Biddlestone was that his daughter had run off with a sinner. So they sent me north. At least Mama's family took responsibility for me. Even though they did it grudgingly. Besides, by then Aunt Charity had also angered Grandpapa Biddlestone over her own choice of husband. Or at least the way he'd turned out. Even though he was of the Methodist persuasion he was, apparently, "a perpetual backslider". Though that is neither here nor there. Not any more.'

'By which you mean what?'

'He'd been dead for years before I even reached England. I cannot think why I mentioned him at all.'

'Nor can I believe I just said, *By which you mean what.*'

'It doesn't matter that your speech isn't very elegant,' she said consolingly. 'I knew what you meant.'

The sort of snorting noise he made in response was very expressive, if not very polite.

'Well anyway, Grandpapa decided I should live with Aunt Charity until my father could make alternative arrangements for me, since she was a woman and I was of an age to need female guidance. Or that was what he said. *She* told me that Grandpapa didn't want the bother of raising a girl child who couldn't be of any use to him in his business.'

'And why didn't your father make those alternative arrangements?'

'Because he died as well. Only a couple of years later.'

'That makes no more sense than what I originally thought,' he said in disgust.

'*What* did you originally think?'

'Never mind that,' he said tersely. 'I need to concentrate on the traffic now that we're approaching Tadburne. This wretched animal—' he indicated the horse '—seems to wish to challenge anything coming in the other direction, and I need to keep my wits about me—what little I appear to have remaining this morning—if you don't want to get pitched into the road.'

She could understand that. She'd already noted that

he was having increasing difficulty managing his horse the nearer they drew to the town she could see nestling in the next valley.

'However,' he said, 'I should like you to consider a few things.'

'What things?'

'Well, firstly, why would your own aunt—your own flesh and blood—drug you, undress you, and deposit you in my bed? And, worse, abandon you in that inn after removing all your possessions, leaving you completely at the mercy of strangers? Because, Miss Prudence Carstairs, since you deny having any knowledge of Hugo and you seem to me to be a truthful person, then I feel almost sure that is what happened.'

Chapter Four

'You are wrong,' Prudence said. 'Aunt Charity is a pillar of the community. Positively steeped in good works. She couldn't have done anything like that.'

Though why could she recall nothing after drinking that warm milk?

He made no answer.

It must have been because he was negotiating a tricky turn before going under the archway of an inn. The inn was, moreover, right on a busy crossroads, so that traffic seemed to be coming at them from all directions. It was concentration that had put the frown between his brows and made his mouth pull into an uncompromising line.

It wasn't because he disagreed with her.

Of course he was wrong. Aunt Charity couldn't possibly have done what he said.

Yet how else could she have ended up in bed with a stranger? Naked? She would never, ever have gone to his room of her own accord, removed every stitch of clothing, flung it all over the place, and then got into bed with him.

And the man denied having lured her there.

He brought the gig to a halt and called over an ostler.

Well, no, he hadn't exactly denied it, she reflected as he got down, came round to her side and helped her from the seat. Because she hadn't accused him of doing any luring. But from the things he'd said he seemed to think *she'd* been in some kind of conspiracy against *him*. And he was also unclear about what had happened last night after dinner. Claimed to have no recollection of how they'd wound up in bed together, either.

So what he was saying was that someone else must be responsible. Since she wasn't. And he wasn't.

Which left only her aunt.

And uncle.

Or this Hugo person he kept mentioning.

'Come on,' he said a touch impatiently.

She blinked, and realised she'd been standing still in the bustling inn yard, in a kind of daze, while she struggled with the horrid notion he'd put in her head.

'Well, I want some breakfast even if you don't,' he said, turning on his heel and stalking towards the inn door.

Beast!

She had no choice but to trot along in his wake. Well, no acceptable choice anyway. She certainly wasn't going to loiter in another inn yard, populated by yet more greasy-haired ostlers with lecherous eyes. And she *did* want breakfast. And she had no money.

When she caught up with him he was standing in the doorway to what looked like the main bar. Which was full of men, talking and swigging tankards of ale. It must be a market day for the place to be so busy and for so many men to look so inebriated this early.

'Stay here,' he growled, before striding across to the

bar. 'I want a private parlour,' he said to the burly man in a stained apron who was presiding over the bar. 'For myself and...' he waved a hand in her direction '...my niece.'

His *niece*? Why on earth was he telling the landlord she was his niece?

The answer came to her as soon as she looked at the burly tapster and saw the expression on his face as he eyed their appearance. Bad enough to have been called a trollop by the landlady of the last inn she'd been inside. At least if people thought she was this man's niece it gave an acceptable explanation for them travelling together, if not for the way they were dressed.

'And breakfast,' her 'uncle' was saying, as though completely impervious to what the burly man might be thinking about his appearance—or hers. 'Steak, onions, ale, bread and butter, and a pot of tea.'

The burly man behind the bar looked at her, looked over the rowdy market-day crowd, then gave a sort of shrug.

'Well, there ain't nobody in the coffee room at present, since the Birmingham stage has just gone out. You're welcome to sit in there, if you like.'

'The coffee room?'

Her muddy-coated, bloodstained companion looked affronted. He opened his mouth to make an objection, but as he did so the landlord's attention was snagged by a group of men at a far table, all surging to their feet as though intending to leave. They were rather boisterous, so Prudence wasn't all that surprised when the burly man came out from behind the bar to make sure they all paid before leaving. Her newly acquired 'uncle', however, looked far from pleased at being brushed aside as though his order for breakfast was of no account. He must be really hungry. Or spoiling for a fight. Things *really* hadn't been going his way this morning, had they?

Some of the boisterous men looked as though they were spoiling for a fight, too. But the burly landlord dealt with them deftly, thrusting them through the doorway next to which she was standing one by one the moment he'd extracted some money from them. She wouldn't be a bit surprised to learn that he'd been in the army. He had that look about him—that confidence and air of authority she'd seen fall like a mantle over men who had risen through the ranks to become sergeants. She'd heard such men talk about opening taverns when they got out, too...

Her suppositions were rudely interrupted by a couple of the boisterous men half falling against her on their way out, knocking her against the doorjamb. She decided enough was enough. It was all very well for her *uncle* to stand there looking indignant, but it wasn't getting them anywhere. Ignoring his command to stay where she was, she threaded her way through the tables to his side and plucked at his sleeve to gain his attention over the uproar.

'Can we go into the coffee room, please...er... Uncle?' she said.

He frowned down at her with displeasure.

She lifted her chin. 'I'm really not feeling all that well.' In fact the hot, crowded room appeared to be contracting and then expanding around her, and her head swam unpleasantly.

The frown on his face turned to a look of concern. 'You will feel better for something to eat and that cup of tea,' he declared, slipping his arm round her waist. 'I am only sorry we cannot have complete privacy, because what we have to discuss will of necessity be rather...'

'It certainly will,' she muttered, rather shocked at how good it felt to have him supporting her into the coffee room, when not half an hour since she'd been trying to escape him. 'Perhaps,' she suggested as he lowered her gently into a chair, 'we should discuss things right now, before anyone comes in.'

'We will be able to think more clearly once we've had something to eat and drink,' he said.

'How do you know? Have you ever been drugged before?'

He quirked one eyebrow at her as he drew up a chair next to her. Then leaned in so that he could speak quietly. 'So you *do* accept that is the case?'

She clasped her hands in her lap. 'Couldn't there have been some sort of mistake? Perhaps I stumbled into your room by accident?'

'And tore off all your clothes and flung them about in some sort of mad fit before leaping into my bed? It isn't likely. Unless you are in the habit of sleepwalking?'

She flushed as he described the very scenario she'd already dismissed as being completely impossible. Shook her head at his question about sleepwalking.

'Then what other explanation can there be?'

'What about this Hugo person you keep asking if I know?'

'Yes,' he said grimly. 'I still wonder if he could somehow be at the back of it. He has good reason to meddle in the business that brought me up here, you see. Only...'

He rubbed his hand over the back of his neck, looking troubled. Then shook his head.

'Only he isn't a bad lad—not really. Only selfish and thoughtless. Or so I've always thought.'

'Always? You have known him a long time?'

'Since his birth,' said Gregory. 'He is my cousin. My nearest male relative, in point of fact. Ever since he left school I have been attempting to teach him all he needs to know should he ever have to step into my shoes. He couldn't have thought it through. If it *was* him.'

'But how on earth could he have persuaded my aunt to do such a thing? Let alone my uncle?'

'He might have put the case in such a way that your aunt would have thought she was acting for your benefit.'

'My *benefit*? How could it be of any benefit to…to humiliate me and abandon me? Anything could have happened. If you were not the kind of man who…that is if you were not a… I mean…although you don't look it… I think you are a gentleman. You could easily have taken advantage of me. And you haven't. Unless… Oh! Are you married?'

'No. Not any more.'

'I am so sorry. I did not mean to make you uncomfortable by mentioning a topic that must surely cause you sorrow.'

'It doesn't.' He gave a sort of grimace. Then explained, 'My wife has been dead these eight years.'

'Oh, that's good. I mean…not that she's dead, but that it is long enough ago that you are past the worst of your grief. But anyway, what I was going to say was that perhaps you are simply not the sort. To break your marriage vows. I know that even the most unlikely-looking men can be doggedly faithful…'

His gaze turned so icy she shivered.

'Not that you look like the *un*faithful sort,' she hastily amended. 'Or the sort that… And anyway you have been married, so… That is… Oh, dear, I do not know what I mean, precisely.'

She could feel her cheeks growing hotter and hotter the longer she continued to babble at him. But to her relief his gaze suddenly thawed.

'I think I detected a sort of compliment amongst all those observations,' he said with a wry smile.

'Thank goodness.' She heaved a sigh of relief. 'I mean, it is not that I *intended* to compliment you, but…'

He held up his hand. 'Just stop right there, before you say anything else to embarrass yourself. And let me bring you back to the point in question. Which is this: perhaps your aunt thought to put you in a compromising position so that she could arrange an advantageous match for you.'

'An *advantageous match*? Are you mad?' She looked at his muddy coat, his blackened eye, the grazes on his knuckles.

And he pokered up.

'Although,' she said hastily, in an attempt to smooth down the feathers she'd ruffled by implying that someone would have to be mad to consider marrying the likes of *him*, 'of late she *has* been growing increasingly annoyed by my refusal to get married. On account of her wanting a particular member of her husband's family to benefit from my inheritance.'

'Your inheritance?'

Oh, dear. She shouldn't have blurted that out. So far he had been behaving rather well, all things considered. But once he knew she would come into a great deal of money upon making a good marriage it was bound to bring out the worst in him. He had told her he was no longer married. And, whatever line of business he was in, acquiring a rich wife would be a definite asset.

Why hadn't she kept quiet about it? Why was she blurting out the answers to all his questions at all?

She rubbed at the spot between her brows where once she'd thought her brain resided.

'You don't think,' he persisted, 'that your aunt chose to put you into *my* bed, out of the beds of all the single men who were at that inn last night, for a particular reason? Or that she chose to stay at that particular inn knowing that I would be there?'

She kept on rubbing at her forehead, willing her brain to wake up and come to her rescue. But it was no use.

'I don't know what you mean!' she eventually cried out in frustration. 'We only stopped there because one of the horses went lame. We were supposed to be pushing on to Mexworth. Uncle Murgatroyd was livid when the postilions said we'd have to put up at the next place we came to. And Aunt Charity said it was a miserable little hovel and she'd never set foot in it. And then the postilion said she could sleep in the stable if she liked, but didn't she think she'd prefer a bed with sheets? And then they had a rare old set-to, right in the middle of the road...'

'I can just picture it,' he put in dryly.

'The upshot was that we didn't have any choice. It was sheer coincidence that we were staying at the same inn as you last night. And I'm sure my aunt wouldn't have wanted to compromise you into marriage with me anyway. She made some very derogatory remarks about you last night at supper. Said you looked exactly the sort of ruffian she would expect to find in a dingy little tavern in a town she'd never heard of.'

He sat back then, a thoughtful expression on his face.

'How much money, exactly, will you receive when you marry?'

Or was it a calculating expression, that look she'd seen?

She lowered her eyes, feeling absurdly disappointed. If he suddenly started paying her compliments and… and making up to her, the way so many men did when they found out about her dowry, then she would…she would…

The way she felt today, she'd probably burst into tears.

Fortunately he didn't notice, since at that moment a serving girl came in with a tray bearing a teapot, a tankard and a jug. He was so keen on getting on the outside of his ale that she might have thrown a tantrum and she didn't think he'd notice.

She snapped her cup onto its saucer and threw two sugar lumps into it before splashing a generous dollop of milk on top. She removed the lid from the teapot and stirred the brew vigorously.

'What will happen,' he asked, setting down his tankard once he'd drained it, 'to the money if you don't marry?'

'I will gain control of it for myself when I am twenty-five,' she replied dreamily as she poured out a stream of fragrant brown liquid. Oh, but she was counting the days until she need rely on nobody but herself.

She came back to the present with an unpleasant jerk the moment she noticed the pale, unappealing colour of the brew in her cup. She'd put far too much milk in first. Even once she stirred it it was going to be far too weak.

'And in the meantime who manages it for you?'

'My trustees. At least…' She paused, the teaspoon poised in mid-air as yet another horrible thought popped into her head. 'Oh. Oh, *no*.'

'What? What is it you've thought of?'

'Well, it is probably nothing. Only Aunt Charity remarried last year. *Mr Murgatroyd.*'

She couldn't help saying the name with distaste. Nothing had been the same since he'd come into their lives. Well, he'd always been there—right from the first moment she'd gone to live with her aunt. But back then he'd just been one of the congregation into which her aunt had introduced her. She hadn't disliked him any more than any other of the mealy-mouthed men who'd taken such delight in making her life as dreary as possible. It hadn't been until he'd married her aunt that she'd discovered how nasty he really was.

'He persuaded my trustees,' she continued, 'that he was a more proper person to take over the management of my money once he became the husband of my guardian.'

'And they agreed?'

'To be honest there was only one of them left. They were all older than my grandfather when he set up the trust in the first place. And the one who outlived him wasn't all that…um…'

'Capable?'

'That's a very good word for it.'

He looked into his tankard with a stunned expression. 'I always thought drink addled a man's brains. But this ale appears to have restored my intellect. That's the first time since I awoke this morning that I have been able to come up with an appropriate word.'

'Good for you,' she said gloomily, then took a sip of the milky tea. Which wasn't strong enough to produce any kind of restorative effect.

'And your uncle—this man your aunt has married—is now in charge of handling your inheritance? Until such time as you marry? Do I have it correct?'

'Yes.'

He set his tankard down on the table with a snap. 'So when shall I expect him to come calling? Demanding I make an honest woman of you?'

She shrugged. 'I would have thought he would have done so this morning, if he was going to do it at all. Instead of which he left the inn, taking all my luggage with him. You'd better pour yourself another tankard of ale and see if it will give you another brilliant idea, Mr—' She stopped. 'You never did tell me your name.'

'You never asked me for it.'

'I told you mine. It is only polite to reciprocate when a lady has introduced herself.'

He reared back, as though offended that she'd criticised his manners.

'A lady,' he replied cuttingly, 'would never introduce *herself*.'

'A gentleman,' she snapped back, 'would not make any kind of comment about any female's station in life. And you still haven't told me your name. I can only assume you must be ashamed of it.'

'Ashamed of it? Never.'

'Then why won't you tell me what it is? Why are you being so evasive?'

He narrowed his eyes.

'I am not being evasive. Last time we came to an introduction we veered off into a more pressing conversation about bread and butter I seem to recall. And this time I…' He shifted uncomfortably in his chair. 'I became distracted again.' He set down his tankard and pressed the heels of his hands against his temples, closing his eyes as though in pain.

'Oh, does your head hurt? I do beg your pardon. I am not usually so snappish. Or so insensitive.'

'And I am not usually so clumsy,' he said, lowering his hands and opening his eyes to regard her ruefully. 'I fear we are not seeing each other at our best.'

He'd opened his mouth to say something else when the door swung open again, this time to permit two serving girls to come in, each bearing a tray of food.

Prudence looked at his steak, which was smothered in a mountain of onions, and then down at her plate of bread and butter with a touch of disappointment.

'Wishing you'd ordered more? I can order you some eggs to go with that, if you like?'

She shook her head. 'I don't suppose I could eat them if you *did* order them, though it is very kind of you. It is just the smell of those onions…' She half closed her eyes and breathed in deeply. 'Ohhh…' she couldn't help moaning. 'They are making my mouth water.'

He gave her a very strange look. Dropped his gaze as though he felt uncomfortable. Fumbled with his knife and fork.

'Here,' he said brusquely, cutting off a small piece of meat and depositing it on her plate. 'Just a mouthful will do you no harm.'

And then he smiled at her. For the very first time. And something inside her sort of melted.

She'd never known a man with a black eye could smile with such charm.

Though was he deploying his charm on purpose? He certainly hadn't bothered smiling at her before he'd heard she was an heiress.

'Are you ever,' she asked, reaching for a knife and fork, 'going to tell me your name?'

His smile disappeared.

'It is Willingale,' he said quickly. *Too quickly?* 'Gregory Willingale.'

Then he set about his steak with the air of a man who hadn't eaten for a se'ennight.

Thank goodness she hadn't been fooled by that charming smile into thinking he was a man she could trust. Which, she admitted, she had started to do. Why, she hadn't talked to anyone so frankly and freely since her parents had died.

Which wouldn't do. Because he had secrets, did her *uncle Gregory*. She'd seen a distinct flash of guilt when he'd spoken the name Willingale.

Which meant he was definitely hiding something.

Chapter Five

Perhaps his real name wasn't Gregory Willingale at all. Perhaps he was using an alias, for some reason. But what could she do about it anyway? Run to the burly bartender with a tale of being abandoned by her aunt and left to the mercy of a man she'd never clapped eyes on until the night before? What would that achieve? Nothing—that was what. She already knew precisely what people who worked in inns thought of girls who went to them with tales of that sort. They thought they were making them up. At least that was what the landlady of the last inn had said. Before lecturing her about her lack of morals and throwing her out.

Earlier this morning she'd thought the woman must be incredibly cruel to do such a thing. But if Prudence had been the landlady of an inn, with a business to run, would *she* have believed such a fantastic tale? Why, she was living through it and she hardly believed it herself.

She cleared her throat.

'So, Mr Willingale,' she said, but only after swallowing the last of the sirloin he'd shared with her. 'Or should I call you *Uncle* Willingale? What do you propose we do next?'

Her own next step would depend very much on whatever *his* plans were. She'd only make up her mind what to do when she'd heard what they were.

'I am not sure,' he said through a mouthful of beef. 'I do not think we are in possession of enough facts.'

Goodness. That was pretty much the same conclusion she'd just drawn.

'Though I do think,' he said, scooping up a forkful of onions and depositing it on her plate, 'that in some way your guardians are attempting to defraud you of your inheritance.'

'Thank you,' she said meekly. 'For the onions, I mean,' she hastily explained, before spreading them on one of the remaining slices of bread and butter, then folding it into a sort of sandwich.

'You're welcome. Though how abandoning you in a small hostelry in the middle of nowhere will serve their purpose I cannot imagine. Surely the disappearance of a wealthy young woman will not go unnoticed wherever it is you come from?'

Since her mouth was full, she shook her head.

'It might not be noticed,' she admitted, as soon as her mouth was free to use it for anything other than eating. 'Not for a very long time anyway. Because we were on our way to Bath.'

'Bath?'

Why did he look as though he didn't believe her?

'Yes, Bath. Why not? I know it isn't exactly fashionable any more, but we are far from fashionable people. And I did tell you, didn't I, that Aunt Charity had been trying to get me to marry…? Well, someone I don't much care for.'

'A relative of her new husband?' he said grimly.

'Yes.'

'And then she suddenly changed her tack, did she? Offered to take you somewhere you could meet a young man you might actually like?'

'There's no need to say it like that!' Though she *had* been rather surprised by her aunt's sudden volte-face. 'She said she would rather see me married to anyone than have me create talk by moving out of her house to set up home on my own.'

'My mental powers are growing stronger by the minute,' Gregory said sarcastically, sawing off another piece of steak. 'Do go on,' he said, when she glowered at him over the rim of her teacup. 'You were about to tell me why nobody will be raising a hue and cry.'

'I have already told you. Aunt Charity finally saw that nothing on earth would induce me to marry…that toad. So she told everyone she was going to take me to Bath and keep me there until she'd found me a match, since I had turned up my nose at the best Stoketown had to offer.'

'Stoketown? You hail from Stoketown?'

'Yes.'

'And your aunt claimed she was taking you to Bath?'

'Yes.'

He laid down his knife and fork. 'You are not very bright, are you?'

'What? How *dare* you?'

'I dare because you were headed in entirely the wrong direction ever to end up in Bath. You should have gone in a south-westerly direction from Stoketown.

Instead you had been travelling in completely the opposite direction. Wherever it was your guardians were planning to take you, it most definitely wasn't Bath.'

'I don't believe you. That cannot be true.' Though why would he say such a thing if he didn't think it?

'Would you like me to ask the landlord to bring us a road map?' he asked her calmly. 'He probably has one, since this inn is on a staging route.'

'I've had enough of landlords for one day,' she said bitterly. 'The less I have to do with the one of this tavern, the better.'

'So you believe you were not headed in the direction of Bath?'

She turned her cup round and round on its saucer for a few moments, thinking as hard as she could. 'I cannot think of any reason why you should say that if it weren't true,' she said pensively. 'But then, I cannot think of any reason why Aunt Charity should claim to be taking me there and actually be taking me in the opposite direction, either.'

'Nor why she should give you something that would make you sleep so soundly you wouldn't even wake when she carried you to the room of the most disreputable person she could find, undressed you, and put you into bed with him? Aha!' he cried, slapping the tabletop. 'Disreputable. *That* was the word I was searching for.'

'Do you have to sound so pleased about it?'

'I can't help it. You have no idea how irritating it has been, not being able to come up with the words I want,' he said, wiping the gravy from his plate with the last slice of her bread.

Her bread. The bread *she'd* ordered.

Though, to be fair, he had shared some of his own

meal with her. If he had taken the last slice of her bread, at least he'd made up for it by sharing his steak and onions.

'I wasn't talking about that,' she protested.

'What, then?'

'I meant about the conclusions you have drawn.'

'Well, I'm pleased about them, too. That is that things are becoming clear.'

'Are they?'

'Yes.' He finished the bread, picked up his tankard, emptied that, and sat back with a satisfied sigh. 'I have ruled Hugo out of the equation. You,' he said, setting the tankard down on the tabletop with a sort of a flourish, 'are an heiress. And villains are trying to swindle you out of your inheritance. First of all they told everyone they were going to take you to Bath, and then set off in the opposite direction. Where exactly they planned to take you, and what they planned to do when they got there, we may never know. Because one of the horses went lame and they were obliged to rack up at The Bull. Where they were shown to rooms on the very top floor.'

He leaned forward slightly.

'There were only three rooms on that floor, if you recall. Yours, mine, and I presume theirs?'

She nodded.

'Your aunt saw me, reached an unflattering conclusion about my integrity on account of my black eye and travel-stained clothing, and decided to make the most of what must have looked like a golden opportunity to dispose of you. You have already admitted that you believe your aunt gave you some sort of sleeping draught.'

'Well, I suppose she might have done. I didn't think it was anything more than hot milk at the time, but—'

'How they managed to administer something similar to me is a bit of a puzzle,' he said, cutting her off mid-sentence. 'But let us assume they did. Once I lay sleeping heavily they carried you to my room, safe in the knowledge that there would be no witnesses to the deed since we were isolated up there.'

She shuddered. She couldn't bear to think of Mr Murgatroyd touching her, doing who knew what to her while she was insensible. Oh, she hoped he'd left the room before her aunt had undressed her. At least she could be certain he hadn't done *that* himself. Aunt Charity would never have permitted it.

'Then, in the morning,' Gregory continued, 'they set up a bustle, pretending to search for you. They must have summoned the landlord and dragged him up all those stairs, attracting a crowd on the way so that they could all witness you waking up naked in my bed.'

'There is no need to look so pleased about it. It was horrid!'

His expression sobered.

'I beg your pardon,' he said. 'But you see I have led a very dull, regulated sort of existence until very recently. Suffocatingly boring, to be perfectly frank. And I had come to the conclusion that what I needed was a bit of a challenge. What could be more challenging than taking on a pair of villains trying to swindle an heiress out of her inheritance? Or solving the mystery of how we ended up naked in the same bed together?'

She wished he wouldn't keep harping on about the *naked* part of it. How did he expect her to look him in the eye or hold a sensible conversation when he kept reminding her that she'd been *naked*?

She had to change the subject.

'Pardon me for pointing it out,' she said, indicating his black eye and then the grazes on his knuckles, 'but you don't look to me as though you have been leading what you call a dull sort of existence.'

'Oh, this?' He chuckled as he flexed his bruised hands. 'This was the start of my adventure, actually. I'd gone up to Manchester to deal with a…ah…a situation that had come to my attention. I was on my way… er…to meet someone and report back when I…' He looked a bit sheepish. 'Well, to be perfectly honest I took a wrong turning. That's why I ended up at that benighted inn last night. So Hugo *couldn't* have done it!' He slapped the table. 'Of *course* he couldn't.' He smiled at her. 'Well, that's a relief. I shan't have to hold him to account for what has happened to you. I don't think I could have forgiven him this.'

His smile faded. He gave her a look she couldn't interpret, then glared balefully at his empty tankard.

He took a deep breath. 'I'm going to take you to the place where I've arranged to meet him. Straight away.'

She wasn't at all sure she liked the sound of that.

'Excuse me, but I'm not convinced that is the right thing to do.'

'I beg your pardon?' He looked completely stunned. 'Why should you not wish to go there?'

'I know nothing about it, that's why.' And precious little about *him*, except that he had recently been in a fight and was being downright shifty about what it had been about.

Oh, yes—and she knew what he looked like naked.

'It is a very comfortable property in which a relative of mine lives,' he snapped. 'A sort of aunt.'

She gave an involuntary shiver.

'You need not be afraid of her. Well…' He rubbed his nose with his thumb. 'I suppose some people *do* find her impossible, but she won't behave the way your aunt did—I can promise you that.'

'I would rather,' she said tartly, 'not have anything to do with *any* sort of aunt—particularly one you freely admit is impossible.'

'Nevertheless,' he said firmly, 'she can provide you with clean clothes, and we will both enjoy good food and comfortable beds. In rooms that nobody will invade,' he said with a sort of muted anger, 'the way they did at The Bull. And then, once we are rested and recovered, I can contact people who will be able to get to the bottom of the crime being perpetrated against you.'

'Will you? I mean…thank you very much,' she added doubtfully.

If he really did mean to take her to the home of a female relative who lived in some comfort, even if she *was* a touch difficult to get on with, and contact people on her behalf to right the wrongs done her, then it was the best thing she could think of.

It was just that coming from a man with a black eye and bruised knuckles it sounded a bit too good to be true.

He shot her a piercing glance. 'Don't you believe me?'

'I am sorry,' she said, a touch defiantly. 'But I am having trouble believing *anything* that has happened today. But if you say you mean to help me, then I shall…' She paused, because she'd been brought up to be very truthful. 'I shall *try* to believe you mean it.'

'Of course I mean it. Your guardians picked the wrong man to use as their dupe when they deposited you in my bed. I will make them rue the day they attempted to cross swords with *me*.' He flexed his bruised, grazed hands.

'Did you make *them* rue the day as well?'

She'd blurted out the question before she'd even known she was wondering about it. She looked up at him in trepidation. Only to discover he was smiling. True, it wasn't what she'd call a very *nice* sort of smile. In fact it looked more like the kind of expression she imagined a fox would have after devastating a henhouse.

'Yes, I made a whole lot of people sorry yesterday,' he said.

She swallowed. Reached for the teapot.

Something about the way she poured her second cup of tea must have betrayed her misgivings, because his satisfied smile froze.

'I don't generally go about getting into brawls, if that's what you're afraid of,' he said.

'I'm not afraid.'

He sighed. 'I wouldn't blame you if you were. Look…' He folded his arms across his chest. 'I'll tell you what happened, and why it happened, and then you can judge for yourself.'

She shrugged one shoulder, as if she didn't care, and took a sip of her tea. This time, thankfully, it had much more flavour.

'It started with a letter from a man who worked in a…a manufactory. In it he described a lot of double-dealing, as well as some very unsavoury behaviour towards the female mill workers by the foreman, and he asked the owner of the mill whether he could bear having such things going on in his name. He couldn't,' he said, with a decisive lift to his chin. 'And so I went to see if I could get evidence of the wrongdoing, and find a way to put a stop to it.'

So he was employed as a sort of investigator? Which explained why he had a secretary. Someone who would help him keep track of the paperwork while he went off doing the actual thief-taking. It also explained why he was reluctant to speak of his trade. He would have to keep a lot of what he did to himself. Or criminals would see him coming.

She took a sip of tea and suddenly saw that that couldn't be the right conclusion. Because it sounded like rather an exciting sort of way to make a living. And he'd said he had lived a dull, ordered existence. She sighed. Why did nothing make any sense today?

'I soon found out that it wouldn't be possible to bring the foreman to trial for what he was doing to the women under his power, because not a one of them would stand up in court and testify. Well, you couldn't expect it of them.'

'No,' she murmured, horrified. 'So what did you do?'

'Well, Bodkin—that's the man who wrote the letter— said that maybe we'd be able to get the overseer dismissed for fraud if we could only find the false ledgers he kept. He sent one set of accounts to…to the mill owner, you see, and kept another to tally up what he was actually making for himself. We couldn't simply walk in and demand to see the books, because he'd have just shown us the counterfeit ones. So we had to break in at night, and search for them.'

'Aunt Charity said you looked like a housebreaker,' she couldn't help saying. Though she clapped her hand over her mouth as soon as she'd said it.

He frowned. 'It's funny, but I would never have thought I'd be keen to tell anyone about Wragley's. But you blurting out things the way you just did… Perhaps it's something to do with the drug we were given. We can't help saying whatever is on our minds.'

'I…suppose that might be it,' she said, relieved that he wasn't disposed to take her to task for being so rude. 'Although…' She paused.

'What?'

'Never mind,' she said with a shake of her head. She didn't want to admit that for some reason she felt as though she could say anything to him. 'You were telling me about how you tried to find the second set of books?'

'Oh, yes. Well, long story short, we found them. Only the night watchman saw the light from our lantern, called for help and came after us. It was touch and go for a while, but eventually we got clean away,' he ended with a grin.

So even if he wasn't a professional thief-taker, he certainly enjoyed investigating crime and seeing villains brought to book. A man who could speak of such an adventure with that look of relish on his face would be perfect for helping her untangle whatever it was that Aunt Charity and Uncle Murgatroyd thought they'd achieved last night.

Someone who could fight for her. Defend her. And he was certainly capable of that. She only had to think of all those bulging muscles. The ones she'd seen that morning as he'd gone stalking about the bedroom, stark naked and furious.

Oh, dear, there was that word again. The one that made her blush, since this time it wasn't just her own nudity she was picturing but his.

She pushed it out of her mind. Instantly it was replaced by the memory of him handing her his jacket. And that after she'd almost brained him with a rock.

Which helped her come to a decision.

'I should like you to make Aunt Charity and Uncle Murgatroyd sorry, too. Because I think you are right. I think they *are* trying to take my money. Trying to make me disappear altogether, actually. If it was them who put me in your room—'

'Who else could it have been?'

'I know, I know. You're clearly very good at working out how criminals think. It still isn't very pleasant to accept it. But...' She drew a deep breath. 'Very well, *when* they put me in your room,' she said, although her stomach gave a little lurch, 'they probably did take advantage of the way the rooms were isolated up there— particularly after they saw the way you looked and behaved at dinner. I do think they believed that of all the men in that place you looked the most likely to treat me the worst.'

'For that alone I should break them. How dare they assume any such thing?'

And that was another thing. He had a vested interest in clearing his own name, too. Now that she'd heard the lengths to which he'd gone to right the wrongs being done to the women at that mill, she felt much better about going to the house of which he'd spoken. They would need somewhere to go and hatch their plans for... not revenge. Justice. Yes, it was only justice she wanted.

'So you will help me track them down and make them pay?'

Make them pay? 'I most certainly will,' he said.

He would set his people on their trail. He would

tell them it was their top priority. From what Prudence had told him so far, he wouldn't be surprised to learn they'd actually been heading for Liverpool. Possibly with a view to leaving the country altogether, if her uncle had actually swindled her out of all her money. On the off-chance that the case was not as bad as all that, he'd make sure his staff found out everything about their business dealings, too, and gained control of any leases or mortgages they had. He would throw a cordon around them so tight that they wouldn't be able to sneeze without his permission.

And if it turned out that they *had* stolen Prudence's inheritance, and hadn't had the sense to get out of the country while they could, then he would crush them. Utterly.

Just then the door opened and the landlord came in.

'Next coach's due in any time now,' he said without preamble. 'Time for you to make off.'

Gregory deliberately relaxed his hands, which he'd clenched into fists as he'd been considering all the ways he could make Prudence's relatives pay for what they'd done. 'Bring me the reckoning, then,' he said. 'I am ready to depart.'

He turned to see Prudence eyeing him warily.

'Hand me my purse, would you, niece? It's in my pocket.'

She continued to stare at him in that considering way until he was forced to speak to her more sternly.

'Prudence, my purse.'

She jumped, but then dug her hand into one of the pockets of the jacket he'd lent her. And then the other one. And then, instead of handing over his purse, she pulled out the stocking he'd thrust in there and forgotten all about. She gazed at it in bewilderment.

Before she could start asking awkward questions he darted round the table, whipped it out of her hand and thrust it into his waistcoat. And then, because she appeared so stunned by the discovery of one of her undergarments that she'd forgotten to hand him his purse, he decided he might as well get it himself.

It wasn't there. Not in the pocket where he could have sworn he'd put it. A cold, sick swirl of panic had him delving into all the jacket pockets, several times over. Even though it was obvious what had happened.

'It's gone,' he said, tamping down the panic as he faced the truth. 'We've been robbed.'

Chapter Six

'Ho, robbed, is it?' The landlord planted his fists on his ample hips. 'Sure, and you had such a fat purse between you when you come in.'

'Not a fat purse, no,' said Gregory, whirling round from his crouched position to glare at the landlord. 'But sufficient. Do you think I would have asked for a private parlour if I hadn't the means to pay for it?'

'What I think is that there's a lot of rogues wandering the highways of England these days. And one of them, or rather two,' he said, eyeing Prudence, 'have fetched up here.'

'Now, look here…'

'No, *you* look here. I don't care what story you come up with, I won't be fooled, see? So you just find the means to pay what you owe or I'm sending for the constable and you'll be spending the night in the roundhouse.'

There was no point in arguing. The man's mind was closed as tight as a drum. Besides, Gregory had seen the way he'd dealt with that bunch of customers in the tap. Ruthlessly and efficiently.

There was nothing for it. He stood up and reached

for the watch he had in his waistcoat pocket. A gold
hunter that was probably worth the same as the entire
inn, never mind the rather basic meal they'd just consumed. The very gold hunter that Hugo had predicted
he'd be obliged to pawn. His stomach contracted. He'd
already decided to go straight to Bramley Park rather
than wait until the end of the week. But that was *his*
decision. Pawning the watch was not, and it felt like the
bitterest kind of failure.

'If you would care to point me in the direction of
the nearest pawn shop,' he said, giving the landlord a
glimpse of his watch, 'I shall soon have the means to
pay what we owe.'

'And what's to stop you legging it the minute I let
you out of my sight? You leave the watch with me and
I'll pawn it if you don't return.'

Leave his watch in the possession of this barrel of
lard? Let those greasy fingers leave smears all over
the beautifully engraved casing? He'd rather spend the
night in the roundhouse.

Only there was Prudence to consider. Spending a
night in a roundhouse after the day she'd had... No, he
couldn't possibly condemn her to that.

'I could go and pawn it,' put in Prudence, startling
them both.

'That ain't no better an idea than to let *him* go off and
not come back,' said the landlord scathingly.

He had to agree. She was sure to come to some harm
if he let her out of his sight. He'd never met such a mag-
net for trouble in all his life.

'You do realise,' he said, folding his arms across his
chest, and his gold watch to boot, 'that I have a horse

and gig in your stables which would act as surety no matter which of us goes to raise what we owe?'

The landlord gave an ironic laugh. 'You expect me to believe you'd come back if I let either one of you out of my sight?'

'Even if I didn't return you'd still have the horse.' Which would serve him right. 'And the vehicle, too. I know the paint is flaking a bit, but the actual body isn't in bad repair. You could sell them both for ten times what we owe for breakfast.'

'And who's to say you wouldn't turn up the minute I'd sold 'em, with some tale of me swindling and cheating you, eh? Trouble—that's what you are. Knew it the minute I clapped eyes on yer.'

'Then you were mistaken. I am not trouble. I am just temporarily in a rather embarrassing state. Financially.'

Good grief, had he really uttered the very words he'd heard drop so many times from Hugo's lips? The words he'd refused to believe any man with an ounce of intelligence or willpower could ever have any excuse for uttering?

'What you got in that case of yours?' asked the landlord abruptly, pointing to his valise.

Stays—that was the first thing that came to mind. And the landlord had already spied the stocking Prudence had extracted from his jacket pocket.

'Nothing of any great value,' he said hastily. 'You really would be better accepting the horse and gig as surety for payment.'

The landlord scratched the lowest of his ample chins thoughtfully. 'If you really do have a horse stabled here, I s'pose that'd do.'

Gregory sucked in a sharp stab of indignation as the

landlord turned away from him with a measuring look and went to open one of the back windows.

'Jem!' the landlord yelled through the window. 'Haul your hide over here and take a gander at this sharp.'

Gregory's indignation swelled to new proportions at hearing himself being described as a 'sharp'. He'd never cheated or swindled anyone in his life.

'It's horrid, isn't it?' said Prudence softly, coming to stand next to him. 'Having persons like that—' she jerked her head in the landlord's direction '—doubt your word.'

'It is indeed,' he replied. It was especially so since, viewed dispassionately, everything he'd done since entering this inn had given the man just cause for doing so.

'Though to be fair,' she added philosophically, 'we don't look the sort of people *I* would trust if I was running this kind of business.' She frowned. 'I put that very clumsily, but you know what I mean.' She waved a hand between them.

'Yes,' he said. 'I do know exactly what you mean.'

He'd just thought it himself. Her aunt had marked him as a villain the night before just because of his black eye. Since then he'd acquired a gash, a day's growth of beard, and a liberal smear of mud all down one side of his coat. He'd been unable to pay for his meal, and had then started waving ladies' undergarments under the landlord's nose.

As for Prudence—with her hair all over the place, and wearing the jacket she'd borrowed from him rather than a lady's spencer over her rumpled gown—she, too, now looked thoroughly disreputable.

Admirably calm though, considering the things she'd

been through. Calm enough to look at things from the landlord's point of view.

'You take it all on the chin, don't you? Whatever life throws at you?'

'Well, there's never any point in weeping and wailing, is there? All that does is make everyone around you irritable.'

Was that what had happened to her? When first her mother and then her father had died, and one grandfather had refused to accept responsibility for her and the other had palmed her off on a cold, resentful aunt? He wouldn't have blamed her for weeping in such circumstances. And he could easily see that bony woman becoming irritated.

He wished there had been someone there for her in those days. He wished there was something he could do for her now. Although it struck him now that she'd come to stand by his side, as though she was trying to help *him*.

To be honest, and much to his surprise, she had succeeded. He *did* feel better. Less insulted by the landlord's mistrustfulness, at any rate.

'We do look rather like a pair of desperate criminals,' he admitted, leaning down so he could murmur into her ear. 'In fact it is a wonder the landlord permitted us to enter his establishment at all.'

Just then a tow-headed individual poked his head through the open window.

'What's up, Sarge?'

'This 'ere *gent*,' said the landlord ironically, 'claims he has a horse and gig in your stable. Know anything about it?'

As the stable lad squinted at him Gregory's heart

sped up. Incredible to feel nervous. Yet the prospect that Jem might fail to recognise him was very real. He'd only caught a glimpse of him as he'd handed over the reins, after all.

Prudence patted his hand, as though she knew exactly what he was thinking. Confirming his suspicions that she was trying to reassure him all would be well.

'Bad-tempered nag,' Jem pronounced after a second or two, much to Gregory's relief. 'And a Yarmouth coach.'

Yes, that was a close enough description of the rig he'd been driving.

'Right,' said the landlord decisively. 'Back to work, then.'

Jem withdrew his head and the landlord slammed the window shut behind him.

Gregory resisted the peculiar fleeting urge to take hold of Prudence's hand. Focussed on the landlord.

'So, we have a deal?' he said firmly.

'I suppose,' said the landlord grudgingly. 'Except now I'm going to have your animal eating its head off at my expense for the Lord knows how long.'

'Fair point. How about this? If I'm not back within the space of one week from today, with what we owe for the meal we've eaten, plus the cost of stabling the horse, you can sell the beast and the...er...Yarmouth coach.'

'One week from today?' He narrowed his eyes. 'I s'pose that'd do. But only if you put something in writing first.'

'Naturally. Bring me pen and paper and you may have my vowels.'

The landlord screwed up his face and shook his head, indicating his reluctance to let them out of his sight even for the length of time it would take to fetch writing implements. Instead, he rummaged in his apron pocket and produced what looked like a bill and a stub of pencil, then slapped both on the table.

As Gregory bent to write the necessary phrases on the back of the bill he heard the sound of a coaching horn. Closely followed by the noise of wheels rattling into the yard. Then two surprisingly smart waiters strode into the coffee room, bearing trays of cups and tankards.

The landlord swept Gregory's note and the pencil back into his pocket without even glancing at them, his mind clearly on the next influx of customers.

'Get out,' he said brusquely. 'Before I change my mind and send for the constable anyway.'

Gregory didn't need telling twice. He snatched up the valise with the incriminating stays with one hand, and grabbed Prudence's arm with the other. Then he dragged her from the room against the tide of people surging in, all demanding coffee or ale.

'Come on,' he growled at her. 'Stop dragging your heels. We need to get out of here before that fat fool changes his mind.'

'But…' she panted. 'How on earth are we going to get wherever it is you planned to take me without your gig?'

'Never mind that now. The first thing to do is find a pawn shop.'

'It will be in a back street somewhere,' she said. 'So that people can hope nobody will see them going in.'

'It isn't a very big town,' he said, on a last flickering ray of hope. 'There might not even be one.'

'If there wasn't the landlord would have said so,' she pointed out with annoyingly faultless logic.

Condemning him to the humiliating prospect of sneaking into some back street pawn shop. After all the times he'd lectured Hugo about the evils of dealing with pawnbrokers and moneylenders.

'And I don't see why you have to walk so fast,' she complained. 'Not when we have a whole week to raise the money.'

'We?' He couldn't believe she could speak of his possessions as though they were her own. As though she had some rights as to how he should dispose of them. '*I* am the one who is going to have to pawn *my* watch.'

'I'm sorry. I can see how reluctant you are to part with it. But you know I don't have anything of value.'

'Not any more,' he fumed. 'Thanks to you.'

'What do you mean, thanks to *me*?'

'I mean that *you* had my purse. Which contained easily enough money to last until the end of the week. I can't believe how careless you are.'

'Careless? What do you mean? Are you implying it's *my* fault you lost your purse?'

'Well, you were wearing my jacket when those oafs jostled it out of the pocket.'

'What oafs?' She frowned. 'Oh. You mean when we came in here?'

He could see her mind going over the scene, just as his own had done the moment he'd realised the purse wasn't where he'd put it.

'So,' she added slowly. 'You think that is when the purse went missing, do you?'

'When else could it have gone?'

'How about when you fell out of the gig?'

'You mean when you pushed me out of the gig?'

They were no longer walking along the street but standing toe to toe, glaring at each other. Though what right *she* had to be angry, he couldn't imagine. He was the one who was having to abandon every principle he held dear. She was the one whose fault it was.

Yet she was breathing heavy, indignant breaths. Which made her gown strain over her bosom.

Her unfettered bosom.

Since her stays were in his hand. At least they were in his valise, which was in his hand.

'Right,' she said, and drew herself up to her full height and lifted her chin.

He probably ought to warn her to pull his jacket closed. She could have no idea how touchable and tempting she looked right now.

Tempting? No. She wasn't tempting. She was *not*.

No more than she'd been when she'd moaned in ecstasy at the flavour of his steak and onions. There was still something the matter with his brain—that was what it was. Some lingering after-effect from the drug. It explained why he'd spilled out almost the entire story of his adventure at Wragley's. And why he kept on being afflicted by these inconvenient, inappropriate surges of lust.

Though part of it *was* down to her. The way she looked all wild and wanton in the grip of anger, so much more alive and vital than any other woman he'd ever known. The way she openly stood up to him in a way nobody had ever dared before.

Though he'd even found her appealing when she'd looked drugged and dazed and helpless. Helpless, she aroused his protective instincts. Angry she just aroused…more basic instincts.

'Right,' she said again. And with a toss of her head turned round and strode away from him.

'Where do you think you are going?' The insufferable wench was obliging him to follow her if he didn't wish to lose sight of her.

'I'm going,' she tossed over her shoulder, 'to sort out the mess you have plunged us into.'

'Mess *I* have plunged us into? You were the one who got robbed—'

'You were the one who left the purse in my pocket, though, once it became an outside pocket after you removed your coat.'

'I—' Dammit, she was correct. *Again.* He should have kept hold of the purse himself.

'In my defence,' he pointed out resentfully, 'I had just suffered a stunning blow to the head.'

'Trust you to bring that up,' she said, rounding on him. And then, taking him completely by surprise, she reached up and snatched off his hat.

'You don't mind me borrowing this, do you?'

'For what, pray?'

'To collect the money.'

'Collect the...what?'

She didn't seriously mean to go begging through the streets, did she? That would be worse by far than anything that had happened to him yet.

'Yes, I do mind,' he said, reaching round her to retrieve his property.

But she twitched it out of his reach. And slapped his hand for good measure. And carried on walking down the street towards the market square.

'Prudence,' he warned her. 'I cannot permit you to do this.' It was unthinkable. If anyone ever found out that he'd been seen begging… The very thought sent cold chills down his spine.

'*Permit* me?'

If he thought she'd looked angry before it was as nothing compared to the way she looked now. She came to an abrupt halt.

'You have no say over anything I do,' she said, poking him in the chest with her forefinger. A habit she'd no doubt picked up from that bony aunt of hers. 'I shall do as I please.'

'Not with my hat, you won't.'

He made a move to get it back. But she was still too quick for him, nimbly leaping out of his reach with the agility of a professional fencing master.

'Prudence,' he snapped. 'Don't you realise you can be arrested for begging?'

'Begging?' She gave him a disbelieving look over her shoulder. 'I have no intention of begging.'

Well, that was a relief. But still… 'Then what *do* you plan to do? With my hat?'

'It's market day,' she said, as though the statement should be self-explanatory. And then added for his benefit, as though he were a total simpleton, 'People expect entertainers to come to town on market day.'

'Yes. But you are not an entertainer. Are you?'

'No,' she said indignantly. 'But I do have a very fine singing voice.'

'Oh, no…' he muttered as she made for the market cross with his hat clutched in her determined little fingers. 'You cannot mean to perform in the street for pennies, surely?'

'Well, do you have a better idea?'

'Yes.'

'Which is…?' She planted her hands on her hips and pursed her lips again.

Dammit, nobody *ever* questioned his decisions. If he said he had an idea people always waited to hear what it was, with a view to carrying out his orders at once. They didn't plant their hands on their hips and look up at him as though they didn't believe he had ever had a plan in his life.

'I see no reason,' he said, affronted, 'why I should tell you.'

'Just as I thought,' she scoffed. 'You haven't a plan. Except to pawn your watch and then go crawling back to that nasty landlord, with your tail between your legs, in order to retrieve a horse you despise and a gig that you have trouble steering.'

'I do not!'

He was a notable whip.

Normally.

'And I have no intention of crawling. I *never* crawl.'

'Really?'

She raised one eyebrow in such a disdainful way it put him in mind of one of the patronesses of Almack's, depressing the pretensions of a mushroom trying to gain entrance to their hallowed club.

'Really,' he insisted.

'So, how do you propose to treat with the landlord?'

'Once I've pawned my watch—'

'Look,' she said, in the kind of voice he imagined someone using on a rather dim-witted child. 'There will be no need for you to pawn that watch. Because I intend to rectify the situation *I* have caused by being so *careless* as to lose the purse you entrusted to my keeping without informing me you had done so. If it *was* actually there when you draped your jacket around my shoulders,' she said with an acid smile. 'For all I know you dropped it at The Bull. A lot of things went missing there. Why not your purse?'

'Because I distinctly recall paying my shot there—that's why.'

'Well, then. It's clearly up to me to make amends,' she flung at him, before mounting the steps of the market cross and setting his hat at her feet.

'Not so fast,' he said, striding after her and mounting the steps himself.

'You cannot stop me,' she said, raising one hand as though to ward him off. 'I will scream,' she added as he reached for the open edges of his jacket.

But she didn't. Not even before she realised that all he was doing was buttoning it up.

'There,' he growled. 'At least you no longer run the risk of being arrested for indecency.'

She clapped her hands to her front, glancing down in alarm. While he stalked away to seek a position near enough to keep watch over her, yet far enough away that nobody would immediately suspect him of being her accomplice.

Once he'd found a suitable vantage point he folded his arms across his chest with a glower. Short of wrestling her down from the steps, there was no way to prevent the stubborn minx from carrying out her ridiculous threat. Let her sing, then! Just for as long as it took her to realise she was wasting her time. They'd never get as much money from what amounted to begging as they would by pawning his watch.

And then she'd have to fall in with his plans, meek as a lamb. A chastened lamb. Yes, he'd wait until the citizens of Tadburne had brought her down a peg, and then he'd be…magnanimous.

He permitted himself a smile in anticipation of some of the ways in which he could be magnanimous to Miss High-and-Mighty Prudence Carstairs while she cleared her throat, lifted her chin, shifted from one foot to the other, and generally worked up the nerve to start her performance.

The first note that came from her throat wavered. He grimaced. If that was the best she could do they weren't going to be here very long. He'd pull her down off the steps before the locals started pelting her with cabbages, naturally. He didn't want a travelling companion who smelled of rotting vegetables.

Prudence cleared her throat and started again. This time running through a set of scales, the way he'd heard professional singers do to warm up.

By the time she'd finished her scales the notes coming from her throat no longer squeaked and wavered. They flowed like liquid honey.

Prudence hadn't exaggerated. She did indeed have a fine singing voice. In keeping with the husky, rather sensuous way she spoke, she sang in a deep, rich, contralto voice that might have earned her a fortune in London.

Blast her.

Every time he looked forward to gaining the advantage she somehow managed to wrest it back.

So why did he still find her so damned attractive?

Oh, Lord, if Aunt Charity could see her now! She'd be shocked. Horrified. That a Biddlestone should resort to singing in a public street… Although, had Aunt

Charity not abandoned her in The Bull, there would have been no need to do any such thing. Or if Mr Willingale hadn't lost his purse and chosen to blame *her* instead of shouldering it like a gentleman.

No, she mustn't get angry. Anger would come out in her voice and ruin her performance. One of the singing teachers she'd had intermittently over the years had told her always to think pleasant thoughts when singing, even if the ballad was a tragic one, or it would make her vocal cords tense and ruin her tone.

So she lost herself in the words, telling the story of a girl in love with a swain in the greenwood. She pictured the apple blossom, the rippling brook and the moss-covered pebbles about which she was singing.

She would *not* look at Mr Willingale, whose expression was enough to turn milk sour. Or at least not very often. Because, although it was extremely satisfying to see the astonishment on his face when she proved that not only could she sing, she could do so to a very high standard, it made her want to giggle. And nobody could sing in tune when they were giggling. It was worse than being angry, because it ruined the breath control.

Far better to look the other way, to where people were starting to take note of her. To draw near and listen. To pull out their hankies as she reached the tragic climax of the ballad and dab at their eyes.

And toss coppers into the hat she'd laid at her feet.

She did permit herself to dart just one triumphant glance in Mr Willingale's direction before launching into her next song, but only one. There would be time enough to crow when she could tip the shower of pennies she was going to earn into his hands.

She'd show him—oh, yes, she would. It had been so

insulting of him not to trust her to pawn his watch. He'd looked at her the way that landlord had just looked at him. How could he think she'd run off with his watch and leave him there?

He'd assumed she would steal his gig, too, earlier, and leave him stunned and bleeding in the lane.

He was the most distrustful, suspicious, insulting man she'd ever met, and why she was still trying to prove she wasn't any of the things he thought, she couldn't imagine.

Why, she had as much cause to distrust *him*—waking up naked in his bed like that.

Only honesty compelled her to admit that it hadn't been his doing. That was entirely down to Aunt Charity and her vile new husband. There really could be no other explanation.

She came to the end of her second ballad and smiled at the people dropping coins into Mr Willingale's hat. How she wished she had a glass of water. Singing in the open air made the voice so dry, so quickly. Perhaps she could prevail upon Mr Willingale to fetch her some? She darted a hopeful glance in his direction. But he just grimaced, as though in disgust, then turned and strode off down a side street.

He had no intention of helping her—not when he was opposed to her plan. The beast was just going to leave her there. Probably hoping she'd become nervous once he was out of sight and run after him, begging him not to leave her alone.

Well, if he thought she would feel afraid of being alone in the middle of a strange town then he didn't know her at all. Why, she'd been in far more dangerous places than an English town on market day.

Though then she'd been a child. With her parents to protect her. Not to mention the might of the English army at her back. Which was why she'd never felt this vulnerable before.

Not even when she'd realised her aunt had abandoned her at The Bull. Though that had probably been largely due to the fact that she'd been numb with shock and still dazed from the sleeping draught at that point this morning. But now she was starting to think clearly.

What was to become of her?

She had no money. Only the few clothes she stood up in. And no real idea where she was or where she was going. In just a few short hours she'd become almost totally reliant on Mr Willingale. Who'd just disappeared down that alley. For a second, panic gripped her by the throat.

But she was not some spineless milk-and-water miss who would go running after a man and beg him not to abandon her to the mercy of strangers. She was a Carstairs. And no Carstairs *ever* quailed in the face of adversity.

Defiantly, she lifted her chin and launched into her third ballad.

Chapter Seven

Prudence had hardly got going when a trio of young men emerged from a side street and sauntered in her direction. She could tell they were trouble even before they pushed to the front of the crowd who'd gathered to hear her sing.

She did her best not to display any sign of nervousness. But it was difficult not to feel anxious when one of them pulled out a quizzing glass, raked her insolently from top to toe, and said, 'Stap me, but I never thought to find *such* a prime article in *such* an out-of-the-way place.'

She carried on singing as though she hadn't heard him.

One of his companions, meanwhile, turned to look at the farmer standing next to him. With a supercilious sneer he pulled out a handkerchief and held it to his nose. The yokel turned a dull, angry shade of red and shuffled away.

The three young bucks had soon had the same effect on all her audience. By the time she'd reached the end of her song they'd all dispersed. Leaving her alone on the steps of the cross.

Time to leave. Her voice was past its best anyhow. What with having nobody to bring her a glass of water...

She darted the bucks a smile she hoped was nonchalant as she bent to pick up the hat.

'Allow me,' said the one with the quizzing glass, snatching it from the ground before she could get to it. He smirked at his companions, who chuckled and drew closer.

'Thank you,' she said, holding out her hand in the faint hope that he'd simply give her the hat. Though she could tell he had no intention of doing any such thing.

'Not much to show for your performance,' he said, glancing into the hat, then at her. 'Hardly worth your trouble, really.'

The others sniggered.

'It is to me,' she said. 'Please hand it over.'

He took a step closer, leering at her. 'Only if you pay a forfeit. I think a hatful of coins is worth a kiss, don't you?'

His friends found him terribly amusing, to judge from the way they all hooted with laughter.

He pressed forward, lips puckered as though to make her pay the forfeit.

She backed up a step. 'Absolutely not,' she protested.

'A kiss for each of us,' cried the one who'd driven the farmer away with his scented handkerchief.

All three were advancing on her now, forcing her to retreat up the steps until her back was pressed to the market cross.

'Let me pass,' she said, as firmly as she could considering her heart was banging against her ribs so hard.

'If you are going to give my friends a kiss just for letting you pass,' said the ringleader, 'I should demand something more for the return of your takings, don't you think?'

The look in his eyes put her forcibly in mind of the greasy ostler from The Bull. And when he leaned forward, as though to follow through on his thinly veiled threat, her whole being clenched so hard she was convinced she was about to be sick.

'You will demand *nothing*, you damned insolent pup,' said someone, in such a menacing growl that all three bucks spun round to see who was trying to spoil their fun.

It was Mr Willingale. Oh, thank heavens.

'I will take that,' he said, indicating the hat.

Miraculously, they didn't argue, but meekly handed it over and melted away, muttering apologies.

Or perhaps it wasn't such a miracle. He'd looked disreputable enough last night for her aunt to select him to act as the villain in her scheme. With the addition of a day's growth of beard and a furious glare in those steely grey eyes he looked as though he might easily rip three slender young fops to ribbons and step over their lifeless corpses without experiencing a shred of remorse.

She forgot all about her determination to prove she didn't need him to look after her as she stumbled down the steps and flung her arms round his neck.

'I've never been so glad to see anyone in my life,' she sobbed. 'I thought you'd gone! Left me!'

'Of course not,' he snapped, standing completely rigid in the circle of her arms. As though he was highly embarrassed.

'Oh, I do beg your pardon,' she said, unwinding her arms from his neck and stepping hastily back.

'That's quite all right,' he said gruffly, patting her

shoulder in an avuncular manner. 'You had a fright. Here,' he said then, tipping the small change from the hat into her hands. 'Your takings.'

Then he clapped the hat back onto his head and tipped it at an angle that somehow magnified the aura of leashed power already hanging round him.

A tide of completely feminine feelings surged through her. Feelings he'd made it very clear he found embarrassingly unwelcome. She bent her head to hide the blush heating her cheeks, pretending she was engrossed in counting her takings.

Fourpence three farthings. Better than she'd have thought, considering her audience hadn't looked all that affluent.

'Well?'

His dry, sarcastic tone robbed her of what little pleasure she might have felt at her success if he hadn't already made her feel so very awkward, and foolish, and helpless, and...*female*.

'Well, what?'

'Do you have enough to pay the landlord for our breakfast?'

'You know very well I haven't.'

'So we shall have to pop my watch after all.' He grimaced. 'I can't believe I'm using such a vulgar term. I suppose I must have caught it from Hugo. He is always being obliged to "pop" something or other to "keep the dibs in tune", or so he informs me.'

'Not necessarily.'

'What do you mean?'

'Well, we have this,' she said, jingling her coins.

'Oh, please,' he huffed. 'We've already established you've hardly made anything there.'

'It's enough to buy some bread and cheese,' she pointed out. 'Which will keep us going for the rest of the day. We have a week before we have to pay the landlord what we owe him. A week in which to raise the money some other way.'

'That's true,' he said, with what looked suspiciously like relief.

'And if all else fails, or if we run into any other difficulties, we will have your watch in reserve.'

'And knowing you,' he muttered, 'we are bound to run into more difficulties.'

'And what is that supposed to mean?'

'Just that you seem to have a propensity for stumbling from one disaster to another.'

'I never had any disasters until I met you.'

'That is not true. We would not have met at all had you not already been neck-deep in trouble. And since then I have had to rescue you from that ostler, *and* your penury, *and* your foolish attempt to evade me, and now a pack of lecherous young fops.'

For a moment his pointing all this out robbed her of speech. But she soon made a recovery.

'Oh? Well, I do not recall asking you to do *any* of those things!'

'Nevertheless I have done them. And what's more I fully intend to keep on doing them.' He halted, frowning in a vexed way at the clumsiness of the words that had just tumbled from his lips. 'That is,' he continued, 'I am going to stick to your side until I know you are safe.'

'Well, until we reach wherever it is that your dragon of an aunt lives and you hand me over to her, I reserve the right to…to…'

'Be mean and ungrateful?'

'I'm not ungrateful.' On the contrary, she'd been so grateful when he'd shown up just now and sent those horrible men packing that she'd fallen on his neck and embarrassed him. Embarrassed herself. In fact she suspected that half the reason she was suddenly so cross with him again was because she was ashamed of appearing clingy and weepy. Right after vowing she wasn't going to rely so totally on him.

'Of course I'm grateful for everything you've done,' she said. 'But that doesn't give you the right to...to... dictate to me.'

'Is that what I was doing? I rather thought,' he said loftily, 'I was making helpful decisions which would keep you from plunging into further disaster.'

'Oh, did you indeed?'

All of a sudden his manner altered.

'No, actually, I didn't,' he said, rubbing the back of his neck with one hand. 'You are quite correct. I *was* being dictatorial.'

'What?'

'Ah. That took the wind out of your sails,' he said with a—yes—with a positive *smile* on his face. 'But, you see, I am rather used to everyone doing as I say without question. You are the first person in a very long while to argue with me.'

'Then I expect I will do you a great deal of good,' she retorted.

'I shouldn't be a bit surprised,' he replied amiably. 'Just as being in my company will be an improving experience for *you*. Because you,' he said, taking her chin between his long, supple fingers, 'are clearly used to having your every whim indulged.'

'I am *not*,' she objected, flinching away from a touch that she found far too familiar. And far too pleasant.

'You behave as though you have been indulged all your life,' he countered. 'Pampered. Spoiled.'

'That is so very far from true that…' She floundered to a halt. 'Actually, when my parents were alive they did cosset me. And Papa's men treated me like a little princess. Which was what made it such a dreadful shock when Aunt Charity started treating me as though I was an unwelcome and rather embarrassing affliction.'

Just as Gregory had done when she had rushed up to him and hugged him. That was one of the reasons it had hurt so much. He'd made her feel just as she had when she'd first gone to live with Aunt Charity, when everything she'd done had been wrong. She'd already been devastated by having lost her mother, being parted from her father, and then being spurned by both grandfathers. But instead of receiving any comfort from Aunt Charity she'd been informed that she had the manners of a hoyden, which she'd no doubt inherited from her morally bankrupt father.

'I suppose it must have been.'

They stood in silence for a short while, as though equally surprised by her confession. And equally bewildered as to how to proceed now they'd stopped quarrelling.

'Look,' said Prudence, eventually, 'I can see how difficult you are finding the prospect of parting with your watch.'

'You have no idea,' he said grimly.

'Well, then, let us consider other options.'

'You really believe we have any?'

'There are always other options. For example, do we

really need to redeem your horse? I mean, how far is it, exactly, to your aunt's house?'

'Exactly?' He frowned. 'I couldn't say.'

'Guess, then,' she snapped, barely managing to stop herself from stamping her foot. 'One day's march? Two?'

'What are you suggesting? *Marching?*'

'I don't see why not. We are both young—relatively young,' she added, glancing at him in what she hoped was a scathing way. 'And healthy.' *He* most certainly was. She'd never seen so many muscles on a man. Well, she'd never seen so *much* of a man's muscles, to be honest, but that wasn't the point. 'And the weather is fine.'

He placed his hands on his hips and gave her back a look which told her he could rise to any challenge she set. And trump it.

'We *could* cut across country,' he admitted. 'I don't believe it is all that far as the crow flies.'

'Well, then.'

'There is no need to look so smug,' he growled.

'I beg your pardon,' she said, although she couldn't help smiling as she said it. 'It is just that, having grown up in an army that always seemed to be on the move, I am perhaps more used than you to the thought of walking anywhere I wish to go, as well as having more experience of adapting to adversity than you seem to.'

There—that had been said in a conciliating manner, hadn't it?

'What do you mean by that?'

'Well, you said yourself that your life has been rather dull and unpredictable up to now. Obviously I assume I am more used to thinking on my feet than you.'

'Ah.' He gave her a measured look. 'Strange though

it may seem, I do not regard my time with you as being one of unalloyed adversity, exactly. And thinking on my feet is...' He paused. 'Exactly the kind of challenge I was looking for when I set out. So, instead of regarding the loss of my horse as a problem, I agree— we *could* look upon it as the perfect excuse for taking a stroll through what looks to be a rather lovely part of the countryside.'

Now he was catching on.

'And having a picnic?' she suggested. 'Instead of having to eat in yet another stuffy inn.'

'A picnic...' he said, his eyes sliding to her takings. 'We would only need to purchase a bit of bread, some cheese, and an apple or two.'

'And what with it being market day,' she added, 'there will be plenty of choice. Which generally means bargains.'

'I shall take your word for it,' he muttered.

'You won't have to. Until you have seen an army brat haggle over half a loaf and a rind of cheese you haven't seen anything,' she informed him cheerfully.

And then wished she hadn't. For he was looked at her in a considering manner that had her bracing herself for some kind of criticism. Hadn't Aunt Charity always said that her life in the army was not a suitable topic of conversation—indeed, forbidden her ever to mention it?

'Then lead on,' he said, picking up his valise in one hand and crooking his other arm for her to take. 'And haggle to your heart's content.'

She let out her breath in a whoosh of relief. And took his arm with pleasure. She couldn't remember the last time anyone had allowed her to be herself, let alone appeared to approve of it.

It felt as if she were stepping out of an invisible prison.

Morals, Gregory decided some time later that day, could be damned inconvenient things to possess. For if he didn't have so many of them he could be making love to Miss Prudence Carstairs instead of engaging only in stilted conversation.

He'd been thinking about making love to her ever since she'd flung back her head and started singing. That rich, melodious voice had stroked down his spine like rough velvet. And had made him see exactly why sailors leaped into the sea and swam to the rock on which the Sirens lived. Not that she'd been intentionally casting out lures, he was sure. For one thing she'd been covered from neck to knee by his jacket, whereas the Sirens were always depicted bare-breasted.

Ah, but he *knew* that her breasts were unfettered beneath his jacket and her gown. He had her stays in his valise to prove it. Which knowledge had given him no option but to take himself off for a brisk walk while reciting the thirteen times table. Fortunately he'd just about retained enough mental capacity to keep half an eye on her, and had made it to her side before those three drunken young fops had done more than give her a bit of a fright.

He'd have liked to have given *them* a fright. How dared they harass an innocent young woman? A woman under *his* protection? He could cheerfully have torn them limb from limb.

Though who, his darker self had kept asking, had

appointed *him* her guardian? To which he had replied that he'd appointed himself. And he knew of no higher authority.

Besides, what else was he to do after the way she'd rushed to him and hugged him and said she'd never been so pleased to see anyone in her life? Nobody had ever been that pleased to see him. He hadn't known how to react. And so he'd stood there, stunned, for so long that eventually she had flinched away, thinking he hadn't liked the feel of her arms round him.

Whereas the truth was that he'd liked her innocent enthusiasm for him far too much. Only his response had been far from innocent. Which put him in something of a dilemma. She wasn't the kind of girl a man could treat as a lightskirt. For one thing she came from the middling classes. Every man knew you didn't bed girls from the middling classes. One could bed a lower class girl, for the right price. Or conduct a discreet affair with a woman from the upper classes, who'd think of it as sport.

But girls from the middling class were riddled with morals. Not that there was anything wrong with morals, as a rule. It was just that right now he wished one of them didn't have so many. If only Prudence didn't hail from a family with Methodist leanings, who called their daughters things like Prudence and Charity. Or if only he wasn't fettered by his vow to protect her. Or hadn't *told* her of his vow to protect her.

Or if only she hadn't gone so damned quiet, leaving him to stew over his own principles to the extent that he was now practically boiling over.

What was the matter with her? Earlier on she'd been a most entertaining companion. He'd enjoyed watching her haggle her way through the market. She'd even induced many of the stallholders to let her sample their wares, so that they'd already eaten plenty, in tiny increments, by the time they'd left the town with what they'd actually purchased.

But for a while now she'd been trudging along beside him, her head down, her replies to his few attempts to make conversation monosyllabic.

Had he done something to offend her?

Well, if she thought he was going to coax her out of the sullens, she could think again. He didn't pander to women's moods. One never knew what caused them, and when they were in them nothing a man did was going to be right. So why bother?

'How far?' she suddenly said, jolting him from his preoccupation with morals and the vexing question of whether they were inconvenient encumbrances to a man getting what he wanted or necessary bars to descending into depravity. 'How far is it to wherever you're planning to take me?'

'Somewhat further than I'd thought,' he replied testily. When people talked about distances as the crow flies, the pertinent fact was that crows *could* fly. They didn't have to tramp round the edges of muddy fields looking for gates or stiles to get through impenetrable hedges, or wander upstream and down until they could find a place to ford a swiftly running brook.

'So when do you think we might arrive?'

He glanced at the sky. 'It looks as though the weather is going to stay fair. It should be a clear night. If we keep going we might make it some time before dawn tomorrow.'

She made a noise that sounded suspiciously like a sob.

'Prudence?' He looked at her. Really looked at her for the first time since they'd left the outskirts of town. 'Prudence, you aren't crying, are you?'

She wiped her hand across her face and sniffed. 'No, of course not,' she said.

'Of course not,' he agreed, though she clearly was. Which gave him a strange, panicky sort of feeling.

There must be something seriously wrong for a woman like Prudence to start weeping. A woman who'd been abandoned by her guardians, left to the care of a total stranger, had thought up the notion of singing for pennies with which to buy provisions so he could keep back his gold watch for emergencies, and then gone toe to toe with him about how to spend money she was proud of having earned herself—no, that wasn't the kind of person who burst into tears for no good reason.

Was it?

'Look, there's a barn over there,' he said, pointing across the rise to the next field. 'We can stop there for the night if you like,' he offered, even though he'd vowed only two minutes earlier not to pander to her mood. After all, it wasn't as if she was crying simply to get attention. On the contrary, she looked more as though she was ashamed of weeping, and was trying to conceal her tears behind sniffles and surreptitious face-wiping.

'You will feel much more the thing in the morning.'

'Oh.'

She lifted her head and pushed a handful of wayward curls from her forehead in a gesture that filled him with relief. Because when they'd first set out she'd done so at regular intervals. Without a bonnet, or a hairbrush to tame her curls, they rioted all over her face at the slightest provocation. But as the day had worn on she'd done so less and less. She'd been walking for the last hour with her head hanging down, watching her feet rather than looking around at the countryside through which they were trudging.

'Well, I don't mind stopping there if *you* wish to rest,' she said.

She was drooping with exhaustion, but would rather suffer in silence than admit to weakness.

All of a sudden a wave of something very far from lust swept through him. It felt like…affection. No, no—not that! It was admiration—that was all. Coupled with a completely natural wish to put a smile back on that weary, woebegone face.

As they got nearer the barn he started casting about in a very exaggerated manner. Tired as she was, she couldn't help noticing the way he veered from side to side, stooping to inspect the ground.

'What are you looking for?' She turned impatiently, as though getting inside that barn was crucial.

'A rock,' he said.

'A rock?' She frowned at him. 'What on earth do you want a rock for? Aren't there enough in your head already?'

'Oh, very funny,' he replied. 'No, I was just thinking,' he carried on, with what he hoped was an expression of complete innocence, 'of giving you some practice.'

'Practice?'

'Yes. You claimed you weren't able to hit a barn door when you threw that rock at me. I just thought that now we have a barn here for you to use as target practice you might like to…'

'In the morning,' she said, her lips pulling into a tight line, 'I may just take you up on your generous offer of using this poor innocent building as target practice. For now, though, all I want to do is get inside, get my shoes off and lie down.'

So saying, she plunged through the door, which was hanging off its hinges, and disappeared into the gloomy interior. Leaving him to mull over the fact that, in spite of deciding that coaxing a female out of the sullens was beneath him, he'd just done precisely that.

With about as much success as he'd ever had.

Chapter Eight

The barn was almost empty. It looked as though the farmer had used up most of last year's crop of hay over the winter. Though there was enough, still, piled up against the far wall, to provide them with a reasonably soft bed for the night.

Clearly Prudence thought so, because she made straight for it, sat down, and eased off her shoes with a little moan of relief.

His own progress across the barn was much slower. She was too tempting—in so many ways.

'Miss Carstairs…' he said.

Yes, that was a good beginning. He must not call her Prudence. That had probably been where he'd gone wrong just now. He'd called her Prudence when he'd thought she was crying, and then he'd started trying to think of ways to make her smile, rather than ignoring her poor mood. He had to preserve a proper distance between them, now more than ever, or who knew how it would end? With him flinging himself down on top of her and ravishing her on that pile of hay, like as not. Because he was too aware that she had nothing on beneath her gown. That her breasts were easily accessible.

He'd tell her that he had her stays in his valise and beg her to put them back on in the morning—that was what he would do.

Though that would still leave her legs bare. From her ankles all the way up to her... Up to her... He swallowed. All the way up. Whenever he'd caught a brief glimpse of her ankles today that was all he'd been able to think of. Those bare legs. And what awaited at the top of them.

Now that she'd removed her shoes, her feet were bare, too. Whatever he did, he must not look at her toes. If thoughts of her breasts and glimpses of her ankles had managed to work him up into such a lather, then seeing her toes might well tip him over the edge. There was something incredibly improper about toes. A woman's toes, at any rate. Probably because a man only ever saw them if he'd taken her to bed. And not always then. Some women preferred to keep their stockings on.

Just as he was thinking about the feel of a woman's stockinged leg, rubbing up and down his bare calves, Prudence flung herself back in the hay with a little whimper. And shut her eyes.

All his good resolutions flew out of the door. He strode to her bed of hay. Ran his eyes along the whole length of her. Not stopping when he reached the hem of her gown. His heart pounding, and sweat breaking out on his forehead, he breached all the barriers he'd sworn he would stay rigidly behind. And looked at her naked toes.

'Good God!'

Her feet—the very ones he'd been getting into such a

lather about—were rubbed raw in several places. Bleeding. Oozing. He dropped to his knees. Stretched out a penitent hand.

'Don't touch them!'

He whipped his hand back.

'No, no, of course I won't. They must be agonisingly painful.' Yet she hadn't uttered one word of complaint. 'Why didn't you tell me you were getting blisters, you foolish woman?'

'Because…because…' She covered her face with her hands and moaned. 'I was too proud,' she muttered from behind her fingers. 'It was my idea to walk wherever it is we are going. When I haven't walked further than a mile or so since I was sent to England. And I *boasted* about being young and healthy. And I *taunted* you for not thinking of it. So how could I admit I wasn't coping?'

'Prudence,' he said gently, immediately forgetting his earlier vow to address her only as Miss Carstairs, and removing her hands so that he could look into her woebegone little face. 'You would have struggled to get this far even if you'd had stockings to cushion your skin. Those shoes weren't designed for walking across rough ground. It would have been different if you had been wearing stout boots and thick stockings, but you weren't. You should have said something sooner. We could have…'

'What? What could we possibly have done?'

He lowered his gaze to her poor abused feet again. And sucked in a sharp breath. 'I don't know, precisely. I…' It seemed as good a time as any to explain about the stocking she'd found in his pocket. 'If I'd had both your stockings I could have given them to you. But I didn't. There was only the one this morning…'

She looked up at him as though she had no idea what he was talking about. He'd been trying to explain that he wasn't the kind of man who kept women's underthings about his person as some kind of trophy. It made him even more aware of the immense gulf separating them. Of his vast experience compared to her complete innocence.

Though not the kind of experience that would be of any use to her now. He had no experience of nursing anyone's blisters. Of nursing anyone for any ailment. 'They probably need ointment, or something,' he mused.

'Do you *have* any ointment?' she asked dryly. 'No, of course you don't.'

'We could at least bathe them,' he said, suddenly struck by inspiration. 'There was a stream in the dip between this field and the next. I noticed it before, and thought it would come in handy for drinking water. But if it is cool that might be soothing, might it not?'

'I am not going to walk another step,' she said in a voice that was half-sob. 'Not even if the stream is running with ice-cold lemonade and the banks are decked with bowls of ointment and dishes of strawberries.'

He took her meaning. She was not only exhausted and in pain, but hungry, too.

'I will go,' he said.

'And fetch water how?'

He put his hand to his neck. 'My neckcloth. I can soak it in the water. Tear it in half,' he said, ripping it from his throat. 'Half for each foot.'

She shook her head. 'No. If you're going to rip your neckcloth in two, I'd much rather we used the halves to wrap round my feet tomorrow. To stop my shoes rubbing these sores even worse.'

She was so practical. So damned practical. *He* should have thought of that.

'I have another neckcloth in my valise,' he retorted. See? He could be practical, too. 'And a shirt.' Though it was blood-spattered and sweat-soaked from his exploits at Wragley's. He shook his head. How he detested not having clean linen every day. 'Plenty of things we can tear up to bind your feet.'

As well as her stays.

He swallowed.

'Why on earth didn't you say so earlier?'

'I would have done if only you'd admitted you were having problems with your shoes. I could have bound your feet miles ago, and then they wouldn't have ended up in that state,' he snapped, furious that she'd been hurt so badly and he hadn't even noticed when he was supposed to be protecting her.

Though how was he to have guessed, when she hadn't said a word? She had to be the most provoking female it had ever been his misfortune to encounter.

'You weren't even limping,' he said accusingly.

'Well, both feet hurt equally badly. So it was hard to choose which one to favour.'

'Prudence!' He gazed for a moment into her brave, tortured little face. And then found himself pulling her into his arms and hugging her.

Hugging her? When had he ever wanted to hug anyone? Male or female?

Never. He wasn't the kind of man who went in for hugging.

But people gained comfort from hugging, so he'd heard. And since he couldn't strangle her, nor ease his frustration the only other way that occurred to him, he supposed hugging was the sensible, middling course to take. At least he could get his hands on her without either killing or debauching her.

Perhaps there was something to be said for hugging after all.

Prudence let her head fall wearily against his chest. Just for a moment she could let him take her weight, and with it all her woes—couldn't she? Where was the harm in that?

'You've been so brave,' he murmured into her hair.

'No, not brave,' she protested into his shirtfront. 'Stubborn and proud is what I've been. And stupid. And impractical—'

'No! I won't have you berate yourself this way. You may be a touch proud, but you are most definitely the bravest person I've ever met. I don't know anyone who would have gone through what you have today without uttering a word of complaint.'

'But—'

'No. Listen to me. If anyone is guilty of being stupidly proud it is I. I should have swallowed my pride at the outset and pawned the watch. I should have done everything in my power to liberate that horse and gig from the stable so you wouldn't have to walk. I will never forgive myself for putting you through this.'

'It isn't your fault.'

'Yes, it is. Oh, good grief—this isn't a contest, Prudence! Stop trying to outdo me.'

'I'm not.'

'Yes, you are. Even when I admit to a fault,' he said, as though it was an immense concession to admit any such thing, '*you* have to insist your fault is greater.'

'But I *feel* at fault,' she confessed.

It was easy to maintain her pride when he was being grumpy and aloof, but so much harder when he was trying to be kind.

'It was my fault you lost all your money.' She'd known it from the start, but had been so angry when he hadn't scrupled to accuse her of carelessness that she'd refused to admit it. 'It was my fault you got into this...this escapade at all. If my aunt and her new husband, whom I refuse to call my uncle, hadn't decided to steal my inheritance...or if you hadn't had a room up on our landing...'

'Then we would never have met,' he said firmly. 'And I'm *glad* we have met, Miss Prudence Carstairs.'

Her heart performed a somersault inside her ribcage. She became very aware of his arms enfolding her with such strength, and yet such gentleness. Remembered that he'd put them round her of his own volition.

And then he looked at her lips. In a way that put thoughts of kissing in her head.

'Because before I met you,' he said, with a sort of intensity that convinced her he meant every word, 'I have never admired or respected any female—not really.'

What would she do if he tried to kiss her? She had to think of something to say—quickly! Before one of them gave in to the temptation to close the gap that separated their faces and taste the other.

What had he just said? Something about never admiring a female before? Well, that was just plain absurd.

'But...you were married.'

He let go of her. Pulled away. All expression wiped from his face. Heavens, but the mention of his late wife had acted upon him like a dousing from a bucket of ice water. Which was a *good* thing. If she'd let him kiss her or, even worse, started kissing him, who knew how it would have ended? A girl couldn't go kissing a man in a secluded barn, on a bed of sweet-smelling hay, without it ending badly.

'Instead of sitting here debating irrelevancies, I would be better employed going to that stream and soaking my neckcloth in it,' he said in a clipped voice. Then got to his feet and strode from the barn without looking back.

A little shiver ran down her spine as she watched him go. It was just as well she'd mentioned his wife. It had been as effective at cooling his ardour as slapping his face.

It was something to remember. If he ever did look as though he was going to cross the line again she need only mention his late wife and he'd pull away from her with a look on his face as though he'd been sucking a lemon.

Had he been very much in love? And was he still mourning her? No, that surely didn't tie in with what he'd just said about not respecting or admiring any female before. It sounded more as though the marriage had been an unhappy one.

Gingerly, she wiggled her toes. Welcomed the pain of real, physical injury. Because thinking about him being unhappily married made her very sad. It was a shame if he hadn't got on with his wife. He deserved a wife who made him happy. A wife who appreciated all his finer points. Because, villainous though he looked, he was the most decent man she'd ever met. He hadn't once tried to take advantage of her. And he had been full of remorse when he'd seen what her pride had cost her toes. And when she thought of how swiftly he'd made those bucks who'd been about to torment her disperse...

She heaved a great sigh and sank back into the hay, her eyes closing. He might have admitted to breaking into a building, but that didn't make him a burglar. On the contrary, he'd only broken the law in an attempt to redress a greater wrong. He might not have the strict moral code of the men of the congregation of Stoke-town, and her aunt would most definitely stigmatise him as a villain because of it, but his kind of villainy suited her notion of how a real man should behave.

She must have dozed off, in spite of the pain in her feet, because the next thing she knew he was kneeling over her, shaking her shoulder gently.

'You're exhausted, I know,' he said, with such gentle concern that she heaved another sigh while her insides went all gooey. 'But I must tend to your feet before we turn in for the night. We should eat some supper, too.'

She struggled to sit up, pushing her hair from her face as it flopped into her eyes for the umpteenth time that day. He knelt at her feet, holding a wet handkerchief just above the surface of her skin, as though loath to cause her pain.

And though he looked nothing like a hero out of a fairytale, though he had no armour and had put his horse up for security, at that moment she had the strange fancy that he was very like a knight in shining armour, kneeling at the feet of his lady.

Which just went to show how tired and out of sorts she was.

'Don't worry about hurting me,' she said. 'I shall grit my teeth and think of— Oh! Ow!'

'Sorry, sorry,' he said, over and over again as he dabbed at her blisters.

'I wish I had a comb,' she said, through teeth suitably gritted. 'Then I could tidy my hair.'

'You are bothered about your *hair*? When your feet are in this state?'

'I was trying to distract myself from my feet by thinking about something that *would* normally bother me. Trying to think of what my usual routine would be as I prepare for bed of a night. My maid would brush my hair out for me, then plait it out of the way...'

But not last night. No, last night she'd had to rely on Aunt Charity's rather rough ministrations. Because she'd said there was no need to make her maid undergo the rigours of a journey as far as Bath. Even though Bessy had said to Aunt Charity that she wouldn't mind at all, and had later admitted to Prudence that she thought it would be rather exciting to travel all that way and see a place that had once been so fashionable.

Why hadn't she seen how suspicious it was for her aunt to appear suddenly so concerned over the welfare of a servant? Why hadn't she smelled a rat when Aunt Charity had said it would be better to hire a new maid in Bath—one who'd know all about the local shops and so forth?

Because she couldn't possibly have guessed that Aunt Charity had been determined to isolate her—that was why. So that there wouldn't be any witnesses to the crime she was planning.

Prudence sucked in a sharp breath. It was worse than simply taking advantage of the opportunity that being housed in that funny little attic in The Bull last night had provided. Aunt Charity and that awful man she'd married had made sure there wouldn't be any witnesses to what she now saw was a premeditated crime.

'Did I hurt you?'

'What? No. I was...' She shivered. 'I was thinking about my maid, Bessy.' She paused. Up to now she'd been too busy just surviving to face what her aunt had tried to do. But her mind had been steadily clearing all day. Or perhaps the pain of Gregory tending to her feet was waking her up to the unpleasant truth.

'I'm afraid you will have to make do with my clumsy efforts tonight,' he said. Then reached up and twined a curl round one finger. 'Though it seems a kind of sacrilege to confine all this russet glory in braids.'

'Russet glory!' She snorted derisively. 'I never took you for a weaver of fustian.'

'I am not. Not a weaver of anything.' He leaned back on his heels. His eyes seemed to be glazed. 'But surely you know that your hair is glorious?'

The look in his eyes made her breath hitch in her throat. Made her heart skip and dance and her tummy clench as though she was flying high on a garden swing.

Oh, Lord, but she wanted him to kiss her. Out of all the men who'd paid court to her—or rather to her money—none had ever made her want to throw propriety to the winds. And he hadn't even *been* paying court to her. He'd been alternately grumpy and insulting and dictatorial all day. And yet... She sighed. He'd also rescued her from an ostler and a group of bucks, forgiven her for pushing him out of his gig and throwing a rock at him. Even made a clumsy sort of jest of the rock-throwing thing.

A smile tugged at her lips as she thought of that moment.

'So you accept the compliment now?'

'What? What compliment?'

'The one I made about your hair,' he breathed, raising the hank that he'd wound round his hand to his face and inhaling deeply.

'My hair?'

Why was he so obsessed with her hair? It must look dreadful, rioting all down her back and all over her face. A visible reminder of her 'wayward nature', Aunt Charity had always said. It was why she had to plait it, and smooth it, and keep it hidden away.

He looked at her sharply. 'If not that, then why were you smiling in that particular way?'

'I didn't know I was smiling in any particular way. And for your information I was thinking of something else entirely.'

'Oh?' His face sort of closed up. He let her hair fall from his fingers and bent to dab at her feet again.

Good heavens, she'd offended him. Who'd have thought that a man who looked so tough could have such delicate sensibilities? But then she hadn't been very tactful, had she? To tell him she'd been thinking of something else when he'd been trying to pay her compliments.

'I was thinking,' she said hastily, in an effort to make amends, 'of how funny you were, searching about for rocks for me to throw.'

He shrugged one shoulder, but didn't raise his head.

'How very forbearing you have been, considering the abuse you've suffered on my account.'

He laid her feet down gently in the hay. 'That is all I can do for them for now,' he said, and scooted back.

Looked at his hands. Cleared his throat. Scooted another foot away.

Which was both a good thing and a bad. Good in that he was determined to prevent another scene from developing in which their mouths ended up scant inches apart. Bad in that... Well, in that he was determined to prevent another scene from developing in which they would be tempted to kiss.

No, no, it was a *good* thing he wasn't the kind of man to attempt to take advantage of the situation. They were going to have to spend the night together in this barn, after all. And if they started kissing, who knew how it would end?

Yes, it was a jolly good job he was maintaining some distance between them.

It would have been even better if she'd been the one to do so.

'We had better eat our supper before the light grows too dim to see what we're putting in our mouths,' he said, opening his valise and taking out what was left of the provisions they'd bought in Tadburne Market.

'We know exactly what we have for supper,' she said wearily. 'About two ounces of cheese and the heel of a loaf. Between the two of us.'

'If it were only a few months later,' he said, spreading the brown paper in which their meagre rations had been wrapped on the hay at her side, 'I might have found strawberries growing by the stream.'

'Strawberries don't grow by streams,' she retorted as he flicked open a penknife and cut both the cheese and the crust precisely in half. 'They only grow in carefully tended beds. Where they have to be protected from frosts over winter with heaps of straw. Which is why they're called *straw*berries.'

He raised his head and gave her a level look. 'Black-berries, then. You cannot deny that blackberries thrive in the wild.' He picked up the sheet of brown paper and its neatly divided contents and placed them on her lap.

From which he'd have to pluck his own meal. One morsel at a time.

She felt her cheeks heating at the prospect of his hand straying over her lap. Felt very conscious that her legs were totally bare beneath her skirts.

She picked up her slice of cheese and nibbled at it. What had they been talking about? Oh, yes…blackberries.

'Some form of fruit would certainly be welcome with this cheese.'

'And with the bread,' he added. 'It's very dry.'

'Stale, I think is the word for which you are search-ing,' she said, having tried it. 'But then, what can you expect for what we paid?'

No wonder the baker had let them have so much for so little. She'd been so proud of her skills at haggling. But they weren't so great, were they? This bread was clearly left over from the day before.

'I had a drink at the stream,' he said, after swallow-ing the last of his share of their supper. 'So I am not too thirsty. But what about you?'

'I think I can just about manage to get the bread down. Though what we really need is a pat of butter to put on it. And then about a gallon of tea to wash it down.'

'This will not do,' he growled. And then, before she had any inkling of what he meant to do, he'd swept the

brown paper to one side, hauled her up into his arms
and was carrying her across the barn.

'What are you doing?'

And what was *she* doing? She should by rights be
struggling. Or at least demanding that he put her down.
Not sort of sagging into him and marvelling at the
strength of his muscular arms.

'I'm taking you down to the stream so that you can
have a drink. And dip your feet into the water. I don't
know why I didn't think of it before,' he said crossly. 'I
must be all about in my head. Dipping a handkerchief
in the stream and then dabbing at your blisters...' he
sneered.

'I daresay you were attempting to observe the pro-
prieties,' she said kindly. 'For this isn't at all proper, is
it? Carting me about like a sack of grain?'

'Proper? There has been nothing "proper" about our
relationship from the moment I stretched my foot out in
bed this morning and found you at the other end of it.'

Naked, at that, he could have added.

In the gathering dusk he strode down the field in the
direction of the water she could hear babbling along its
channel. Without giving the slightest indication that he
was doing anything out of the ordinary. He wasn't even
getting out of breath.

Whereas her own lungs were behaving most errati-
cally. As was her heart.

'And what we're about to do is highly *im*proper, Prudence, in case you need reminding.'

She looked at his face, and then at the stream, in bewilderment.

'Watching me bathe my feet in the stream? You think
that is improper conduct?'

'No,' he said abruptly, and then set her down on a low part of the bank, from where she could dangle her feet into the water with ease. 'It's not the bathing that's improper. It's what is going to happen after I carry you back to the barn.'

'What?' she asked, breathless with excitement.

No, not excitement. At least it shouldn't be excitement. It should be maidenly modesty. Outraged virtue. Anything but excitement.

'What is going to happen after you carry me back to the barn?'

'We are going to have to spend the night together,' he bit out. He rubbed his hand over the crown of his head. 'All night. And, since it promises to be a cold one, probably clinging to each other for warmth.'

'We don't need to cling,' she pointed out, since the prospect appeared to be disturbing him so much. 'Hay is very good at keeping a body warm. I can remember sleeping in a barn a couple of times when I was very little and we were on the march. Papa made me a sort of little nest of it.'

He gave her a hard look. 'If you were still a little girl that might work. But you are a full-grown woman. And there isn't all that much hay, Prudence. It is more than likely we *will* end up seeking each other's warmth. And, unlike last night, which neither of us can remember, I have a feeling we are going to recall every single minute of tonight. You will know you have slept with a man. You will never be able to look anyone in the eye and claim to be innocent. Tonight, Prudence, is the night that your reputation really will be well and truly ruined.'

Chapter Nine

'Oh, my goodness!' said Prudence as her feet slid into the ice-cold water. She didn't know whether it was the shock of it, or something else, but suddenly everything had become clear. 'That was what they were after.'

'What *who* was after? *What* was it they were after?'

'You know,' she said, shuddering at the sting of the water on her raw feet. 'My aunt and that man she married.'

'I don't follow,' he said, sitting down on the bank beside her.

'No, well…' she said wearily. 'That's because I haven't told you everything.' But there wasn't any point in keeping her revelation to herself. He was in it with her now—or would be after tonight—up to his neck.

'I told you I was due to come into an inheritance?'

'Yes.'

'Well, it is not totally without stipulations. The money comes from my grandfather, you see, and he was livid, apparently, when Mama ran off with Papa. He'd already refused consent to their marriage—not only because they hadn't known each other for five minutes, but also because Papa was a soldier. A man who saw nothing wrong with drinking alcohol, or gambling, or any number of things that Grandpapa regarded as dreadful sins.

'Not that Papa was a dreadful sinner—I won't have you thinking that,' she explained hastily. 'It was just Grandpapa was so terribly rigid in his views. Anyway, he cut Mama out of his will. But then when I was born, and Mama wrote to inform him of the event, he put me in it instead. *She* was still disinherited, but he said that it wasn't right to visit the sins of the fathers on the children. And just in case I turned out to be as great a sinner as either of them, there was this…stipulation.

'The money wasn't to come direct to me upon his death but was to be held in trust. Either until I married *"a man of standing"*, I think was the exact term. Or, if I hadn't married such a paragon by the time I was twenty-five, then I could have it without strings, to use however I wish, but only if I am found to be *"of spotless reputation".*'

'In other words,' he said slowly, 'all your aunt had to do was blacken your name and…'

'Yes. Mama's portion—or rather mine, since Mama didn't feature in the will at all, and I never had any brothers or sisters who lived more than a few days— would go directly to Aunt Charity.'

'Villainous,' he hissed.

'Yes,' she agreed, drawing her feet out of the water and pulling her knees up to her chin.

Wrapping her arms round her lower legs, she gazed across the stream to the ploughed fields on the opposite bank, blinking determinedly whenever the chill breeze stung her raw flesh.

'And it isn't just what happened this morning. Or last night. Aunt Charity and I have been at war, subtly, for years. I can see it all now...'

She shook her head, the furrows blurring as tears misted her vision.

'I thought she was just a cold, strict sort of woman, and I made allowances for the way she was because I could sort of understand how she might resent me for being thrust upon her when she obviously hadn't a maternal bone in her body. But I think it was worse than that. Of late I've felt as though she has been doubling her efforts to make me feel bad about myself. Always harping on about my *"falling short"*, as she termed it. And punishing me for the slightest fault.'

She turned to him and searched his face for his reaction.

'But what if it wasn't that at all? What if she was trying to make everyone think I was a terrible sinner? So that she'd have the excuse to say I didn't fulfil the terms of the will?'

He opened his mouth to say something, but thoughts were tumbling into her head so fast she simply had to let them out.

'It's true that at one time—about the time Papa died and I knew I was never going to get away from her—I was...well, a bit of a handful. No, I must be honest. I was downright rebellious for a while. I told her I hated her and everything she stood for. But as it drew nearer to my birthday nothing seemed to bother me so much. Only a few more months, I thought, and then I will be free. Only a few more weeks, now...'

She shook her head.

'But she still looked at me as though I was a problem

she had to work out rather than a real person… Oh, I'm not explaining it terribly well, am I?'

'No,' he said thoughtfully, 'I think I see only too well.' He sighed. 'For I have been guilty of seeing my young cousin Hugo in that light,' he said.

He plucked at some strands of grass. Tossed them into the stream and watched them float downstream.

'I have shown him scant sympathy whenever he comes to me with his troubles. The last time I refused to bail him out of his difficulties he accused me of having a mind like a ledger. Of not understanding what ordinary people have to go through. And he was right. I *did* regard him as nothing more than a financial drain. And an intolerable nuisance.'

'Yes, but you wouldn't have gone out of your way to destroy him, would you? You're not that kind of man.'

He reached out and touched her arm, just briefly, as though her declaration of faith in him had meant something to him.

'I didn't think my aunt was that kind of person, either. But her husband…' She shuddered. 'I wouldn't put anything past him. As soon as they married there stopped being any money for the things I'd taken for granted before. It started with fewer trips to the dressmaker. When I questioned him he accused me of vanity. And since I already thought he was a terribly pious and unpleasant sort of man I just thought he was trying to *improve* me. But then there were things like… Oh, he wouldn't let me have a fire in my room unless it was actually snowing outside. That sort of thing. And I'm sure there isn't anywhere in the Bible that says you have to go cold to prove how virtuous you are.'

He drew in a sharp breath. 'It is possible that he has

squandered your inheritance—have you thought of that? And this is his attempt to cover it up?'

She thought for a bit. Then shook her head. 'If it is, he's gone a very strange way about covering anything up. Surely my disappearance will eventually cause no end of talk? Especially since it looks as though they mean to explain it away by accusing me of improper conduct,' she finished bitterly.

'And me,' he growled. 'If anyone asks where you have gone, they will drag my name into it.'

'I don't see how they can. They don't know it,' she pointed out.

'*I* will know it,' he growled. 'I will know that somewhere people are accusing me of…debauching an innocent. Well, your aunt and uncle picked the wrong man to play the villain of the piece. I won't let them get away with it.'

'Good,' she said, turning to gaze up at him. 'Because you are not a villain. Not at all.'

He might look like one, with his bruised face, his harsh expression, and his dishevelled and muddied clothing. But she knew how he'd come by the mud, and the bruises. At the time he'd told her about his adventure in the mill she'd half suspected he might have made some of it up, to try and impress her. But that was before he'd rescued her from those drunken bucks simply by looking at them with that murderous gleam in his eyes. Before he'd carried her to this stream just so she could soothe her feet in its ice-cold water. And had listened to her as though her opinions had merit.

'So far as I'm concerned,' she said, reaching up to touch the deep groove between his brows, 'they picked the *right* man.'

'What?' His eyes, which had been glaring off into the distance as though he was plotting a fitting revenge on her guardians, focussed on her in bewilderment.

'I know that you will put all to rights, somehow— won't you?' For that was what he did. 'Or at least you will do your very best.'

'How can you possibly know that?' He fidgeted and turned his head away.

'Because that is the kind of man you are. Completely upright.' And not in the way the male members of Stoketown Chapel were upright. Not one of them would break into a warehouse at dead of night to steal a set of false ledgers in order to uncover a fraud. They'd be too scared of what other people would think of their actions.

She might have been mistaken, because it was growing too dark now to see clearly, but she rather thought her last comment might have caused him to blush.

'Time to turn in for the night,' he said gruffly. Then bent to put his arms around her and got to his feet.

Just as before, the ease with which he carried her filled her with admiration. Admiration spiced with a series of totally feminine responses. Because this time he was carrying her to a bed they were going to be sharing.

As though he shared the tenor of her thoughts, he came to a complete halt just before entering the barn and stared into the gloom at the far end. Where they were about to make a bed in the pile of hay.

'This is going to be damned awkward,' he grated, before turning sideways to slide through the drunken excuse for a barn door.

And then he stopped again.

And cleared his throat.

Though she could scarcely hear it over the thunder of her heartbeat.

'Right, this is what we're going to do,' he said. 'I'm going to use my valise for a pillow, then spread my jacket over some of the hay. That is if you don't mind taking it off.' He glanced down at the row of buttons, then at her face, then into the gloom again, his jaw tightening.

'I don't mind at all,' she said. In fact excitement fizzed through her at the prospect of undressing in front of him. Even if it was only his jacket he'd asked her to remove. And she would still be wearing her modest kerseymere gown. 'Hay is very prickly,' she added hastily. 'It is a very sensible notion to use your jacket as a barrier.'

'Sensible,' he repeated, suddenly breaking into a stride that took them all the way to the back of the barn. 'I will use my coat to cover us, as another barrier against the hay. I shall pull it over the top of us both.'

'A very practical notion,' she said.

One of his eyebrows shot up. 'Really?' He pulled it down. 'I mean, naturally. Eminently practical. So,' he said, 'you will remove my jacket while I will divide up the hay, and so forth, to make our bed.'

Our bed. The words sent a flush to her cheeks. And, by the feel of it, to other parts she ought never to mention.

'I give you fair warning,' he said gruffly, 'that if it gets really cold, in spite of all the hay, I shall put my arms around you and hold you close.'

Her heart skipped a beat. But that beat sank to her pelvis, where it set up a low, insistent throb.

'Will you?' Was that really her voice? All low and husky and breathy?

'Yes. But I swear, on my honour, that I shall do nothing more.'

'I know.' She sighed.

'How can you possibly know?'

'I have told you already—I know what kind of man you are.' And she wasn't sure why she'd forgotten it, even for those few exhilarating seconds when he'd been standing there talking about taking her to bed. Wishful thinking, she supposed.

'How can you? We only met this morning. Can you stand for a few moments if I set you down?'

'Yes,' she said. 'And that question only goes to prove what I was saying. You are still going out of your way to tend to my comfort. A lot of men wouldn't bother. They wouldn't try to reassure me that my virtue would remain unsullied, either. In fact, I think a lot of men—' most men, from what she'd seen of masculine conduct so far '—would turn this situation to their own advantage.'

'Oh?' He bent to pick up his valise and held it before him like a shield while she unbuttoned the jacket he'd lent her. As she slid it from her arms he turned swiftly and buried the valise under a mound of hay.

'Yes, indeed,' she said as he turned back and took the jacket from her outstretched hand. He dropped it onto the makeshift mattress quickly, as though it was burning his fingers.

'I have told you all about my fortune,' she said. 'Other men have paid court to me to get their hands on it. You could, at any time today, have started to pressure me into marrying you under the pretext of saving my reputation, and then the money would have been yours. As my husband. But you haven't.'

'Perhaps I am not a marrying kind of man—had you thought of that?'

'No. For one thing you have looked at me once or twice as though you were thinking about kissing me. And you said that thing about my hair.'

'Hmmph,' he said, swinging her into his arms again and setting her down gently onto the makeshift bed.

'For another,' she said as he reared back and began stripping off his coat. 'You have already been married.'

'Perhaps that is what has put me off ever getting married again,' he said bitterly, before coming down beside her and whisking the coat over them both.

'Is it?' She watched through lazily lowered lids as he reached for the hay, pulling bunches of it up and over them until it really did feel as though they were lying in a sort of nest. 'You looked so unhappy when you mentioned your wife. I wondered…'

'Wondered what?' He lay down, finally, next to her, though he kept his arms rigidly at his side.

'Well, *why* you looked so unhappy. You pulled a sort of face.'

'Pulled a face? I *never* pull faces.'

'Well, you did. And it wasn't the sort of expression a widower makes who loved his wife and misses her. It looked as though…'

He made a low growling kind of noise, as though warning her not to proceed any further. She ignored it.

'And anyway, now you have as good as admitted that you weren't happy. What went wrong?'

He sighed. 'I never speak of my wife,' he grunted. 'She and I… We…'

Somewhere close by an owl hooted.

Gregory folded his arms across his chest.

She rolled onto her side and curled up a bit. Just until her knee touched his leg.

Which was warm. And solid.

'There was never any *we*,' he said, with evident irritation. 'The match was arranged by our families. I thought she was happy with it. She seemed happy with it. And I was…content to go along with the arrangement. She was pretty. *Very* pretty, if you must know. Which I thought was better than being saddled with a woman I would struggle to bed.'

Somehow it seemed rather brazen to be snuggling up to him, hoping he might snuggle up to her, while he was talking about having marital relations. She stealthily straightened her leg so that her knee was no longer nudging his thigh.

But she hadn't been stealthy enough.

'If you didn't want the sordid details,' he snapped, 'you shouldn't have pressed me for the confession.'

She hadn't pressed. Not really. But perhaps it was the strangeness of the day, the enforced intimacy they'd shared and were still sharing, that made him feel compelled to tell her all about it. Or the fact that they were lying in the dark, in a barn, feeling extremely awkward, and it was better to talk of something completely unrelated to themselves.

Besides, if he truly hadn't spoken of his miserable marriage ever, to anyone, he probably needed to unburden himself. He'd obviously never felt close enough, or safe enough, with anyone to do so.

She reached out until she found his hand in the dark, and clasped her fingers round it.

'I didn't mean to pry,' she said. 'But if you want to talk about it…'

He gripped her hand hard.

'She didn't like me touching her in bed,' he grated. 'She would never have curled into me the way you have just done, or held my hand, or smoothed my brow when I frowned. Or hugged me because she was pleased to see me.'

The poor man. She ran the fingers of her other hand over his. Squeezed it. The poor, lonely man. No wonder his face had settled into a permanently severe expression. No wonder he glowered at people in such a way that they kept their distance. He must find it easier to keep people away than let them get close enough to hurt him. As his wife had done.

'I was only seventeen when I married her. Not very experienced. And she, of course, was a virgin. It wasn't… The consummation wasn't entirely a pleasant experience for her. When she was reluctant to allow me to return to her bed I tried to be understanding. I thought I ought to give her time to become accustomed.' He gave a bitter laugh. 'And then she confessed she was with child.'

It sounded as though he was grinding his teeth.

'My father congratulated me for ensuring the succession so swiftly. It was about the only time he ever seemed pleased with me. But the irony was that it wasn't mine. The baby she was carrying. It couldn't possibly have been mine. And I was furious. All those months, while I'd been trying to be considerate, she'd been…'

'Oh.' It sounded such a feeble thing to say. But, really, what could she say to a confession like that?

'When she died I struggled to feel anything apart

from relief. You think that was wicked, don't you? That I was relieved I wasn't going to have to bring up some other man's get as my own? Or to face mockery by admitting she'd cuckolded me within six months of marriage?'

'She… Oh, no. The baby died as well?'

'The pregnancy killed her. That's what the doctor said. Something to do with her heart. I wasn't exactly in a frame of mind to take it in. My father had not long since died as well, you see. I'd just…stepped into his shoes.'

She heard him swallow.

'Later, I did feel sorry about the baby. And that was when the guilt started to creep in. I kept remembering standing by her graveside, feeling as though a huge burden had rolled off my shoulders. How all the problems I'd thought I had were being buried with her. How could I regard a child as a burden? As a problem? That wasn't right. It wouldn't have been the child's fault. You, of all people, must know it isn't right to inflict upon a child the feelings you have for its parents.'

'No,' she whispered. 'It isn't. But you wouldn't have done. I *know* you wouldn't.'

'You can't possibly know that,' he grated. 'Hell, I certainly couldn't.'

'I *do* know,' she said, raising his clenched fist to her mouth and kissing the grazed knuckles. 'You might have struggled to be kind to the child, but you would have tried. Otherwise you wouldn't have experienced any guilt over the way you felt when it died. You would have just shrugged your shoulders and walked away. You are a *good* man,' she said. 'And you deserved to have a wife who appreciated just how good and kind you are. A wife who would have at least tried to make you happy. A wife who wanted you to touch her. Give her children. None of what happened was your fault.'

He shifted in the hay beside her and gave a sort of disgruntled huff. Then he rolled onto his side, so that he was facing away from her. She might have thought he was putting an end to their conversation and establishing some distance between them if it hadn't been for the fact that he kept tight hold of her hand, so that as he rolled the movement tugged her up against his back. Just as though he wanted to drape her over himself like a human blanket.

She snuggled closer. For he'd made it clear he hadn't been rejecting her. It had been pride that had made him turn away, she was sure. Men didn't like appearing weak, and he probably regretted spilling all those secrets he'd kept hidden for years. He'd made himself vulnerable to her. Because he trusted her. Or thought she'd understand what rejection of that sort felt like after the way her own aunt had betrayed her.

Yes, if any two people knew what betrayal felt like it was them.

She hugged his waist, wishing there was something she could do to ease his pain. To let him know that she didn't think any less of him for struggling the way he had in the coldness of his arranged marriage, and with his feelings about the way it had ended.

And suddenly it occurred to her that there was one obvious way to do both.

'Do you know what?' she said. 'You *still* deserve a wife who wants to make you happy. Who appreciates how good and kind you are. Who wants you to touch her and give her children. And, what's more, I rather think *I'd* like to be that woman.'

She raised herself up on one elbow so that she could look down into his face. Not that she could see it clearly, in their gloomy corner of the barn. But she certainly felt his entire body tense.

'Are you saying,' he said repressively, 'that you have fallen in love with me? After just one day?'

'Oh, no,' she admitted. 'But I think I very easily could. I've resisted the thought of marriage before, because I couldn't see the point of exchanging one sort of prison for another. I just kept thinking I'd only have to put up with living in Aunt Charity's house for a limited time and then I'd be free. But I don't think marriage to you would feel like a prison at all. You don't seem to want to change me into someone else. You quite like me as I am, don't you?'

She hurried on, because now she'd started she might as well get it all out into the open.

'And I wouldn't even mind handing my fortune into your keeping, if we ever get our hands on it. I'd feel as if you'd earned the right to it. I'm sure you would put it to good use. Could you not do with an injection of capital into whatever business you are in? If you don't mind me saying so, you don't seem to be all that plump in the pocket, or you wouldn't have fallen into such difficulties today, would you?'

'You…you don't know what you are saying,' he hissed, rolling over onto his back so he could look up at her. And then, probably because he couldn't, he reached up to touch her face.

Then snatched it back.

She smiled to herself in the dark.

'I've already told you I wouldn't mind you touching me,' she said gently. 'The way a man touches his wife. In fact,' she admitted daringly, 'I think I would like it very much.'

'And I repeat: you don't know what you are saying.'

'Not…not entirely, no. But I do know that I couldn't lie next to any other man, the way I am lying here with you, and feel like this.'

There was a beat of silence before he said, in a voice that was scarce more than a whisper, 'Like what?'

'All sort of tingly and warm. As…as if something very wonderful is about to happen. Something to do with your lips. And your chest.' She reached between them and laid her hand on his chest, where she could feel his heart beating a rapid tattoo. 'And your legs.' She ran her bare foot up and down his calf. 'I have the strangest urge to wrap myself all around you like a vine.'

'It's the enforced intimacy—that's what it is,' he grated. 'We've been thrown together in unusual circumstances and you're feeling…grateful to me. Attracted, too, I don't doubt. Just as I'm attracted to you. Extremely so.'

Her heart leapt.

'Though I feel I should warn you that it might well be due to some after-effect of the drug they gave us.'

Her heart plummeted.

'And once this is over…'

No, no, it wasn't just because she'd unwittingly swallowed a sleeping draught. The only reason their enforced intimacy had made her admire him so was because all the tests they'd faced had proved what he was really like, beneath the harsh exterior.

'I will still feel like this tomorrow—I'm sure I will.'

'Prudence, Prudence…' He did reach up to cup her face then. 'God, whoever gave you such an inappropriate name? Practically begging a man to make love to you is the least prudent thing an innocent girl like you could do.'

'I haven't begged you to make love to me,' she protested, her pride stung. 'I was speaking in a hypothetical way, about marriage. *You* were the one who leap-frogged over the practicalities and went straight to the wedding night.'

'How can I help thinking about the wedding night when you're lying here half-naked and talking of wrapping yourself around me like a vine?' He pulled her down so that she was sprawled half over his body. Then, just to make sure she knew what he was talking about, he shifted slightly, so that his pelvis made contact with her hip. 'Can you not feel what you do to me?'

Oh, yes, she could feel it. She'd spent her early childhood following the drum. She'd learned a whole lot more about what went on between men and women than sheltered girls her age would have known.

'So you *do* want me, then? It isn't just me feeling like this?'

'Of course I want you,' he growled. 'I've wanted you ever since the moment you sat up in bed this morning and gave me an eyeful of your breasts!'

'But…you threw me out of your room.'

'I thought you were trying to entrap me. I thought…' He groaned. 'I don't know what I thought.' He ran his hands up and down her back. 'But I…' He hauled her close and breathed in raggedly. Clasped the back of her head to his throat.

He was trembling.

'Prudence, I beg of you, don't tempt me any more. You have placed your trust in me. Told me you think I am an upright, honest man. And it's true that all my life I have prided myself on doing the right thing. Even when I knew my wife had committed adultery I refused to sink to her level. But right now I am so close to behaving like the worst kind of scoundrel. It's bad enough that people will be accusing me of taking your innocence. If I do so in fact I will have become the very villain they sought to make of me.'

'No, you won't,' she protested. 'But I understand what you're saying. And you're right.' She sighed. 'If we sin together tonight we would *have* to marry.'

She didn't want it to come to that. She didn't want him to regard her as an obligation. She didn't want him to wake up in the morning feeling that he had no choice but to marry her because he'd ruined her reputation.

She supposed it would have to be enough to know that he wanted her. Wanted her enough to tremble and spear his fingers into her hair, to run his hand to the upper curve of her bottom before snatching it back. To know that the fierce attraction wasn't one-sided.

She snuggled into his embrace. 'We should just go to sleep, then.'

He made a strange kind of strangled sound. 'Sleep? How do you expect me to sleep *now*?'

'I don't know,' she said, yawning sleepily. 'But I don't think I'm going to be able to keep my eyes open for much longer. I'm exhausted. Aren't you?'

He muttered something under his breath that she didn't quite catch. By the tone of his voice, it wasn't anything particularly pleasant. So she didn't ask him what it was. She just closed her eyes and surrendered to the bliss of being held in his arms.

Chapter Ten

Technically, this was the second night he'd slept with a woman—but since last night he hadn't known anything about it, it felt like the first.

It was the first time he'd been aware of her generous curves pressing into his side. The first time he'd breathed in the scent of her hair and rubbed his cheek against the soft profusion of her curls. The first time she'd tucked her poor little ice-cold feet between his legs, seeking warmth—and inadvertently creating it in his own loins.

He ground his teeth at the effort it took to keep completely still, when what he wanted was to roll over and flatten her beneath him.

No—no, he didn't! To do anything of the sort would be worse than anything that had befallen her thus far. She trusted him. Had told him she would even trust him with her fortune, her future, before curling up at his side and trusting him with her very virtue.

He bit back a groan. She'd told him she thought he was upright, when the truth was that the only upright part of him was the very part that wanted to betray her.

Not that he *would* betray her. Whatever it cost him in terms of comfort, tonight he wouldn't do that.

He wasn't an idiot. Later, when she learned the truth about him, he needed to be able to remind her that he *had* been true to her—in this if in nothing else.

Someone up there, he mused, looking at the stars peeping through a gap in the roof, must be laughing at him. Because the first time he'd ever strayed from the narrow confines of his life—from the straight and narrow, if you wanted to put it like that—was the first and only time a woman had placed such faith in him. The first time that he had even cared about a woman's opinion of him, come to that.

Heaven help him, now she was sliding her cold little hand round his waist. It was just as he'd predicted. The temperature had plummeted once the sun had gone down. The fact that he could see all those stars through the barn roof meant that the sky had stayed as clear as it had been all day. There might even be a touch of ground frost by morning. He'd think about frost. Or snow. Or ice. Anything cold. To take his mind off the way she was squirming closer to him in her sleep, seeking the warmth of his body.

It probably didn't help that he'd slept so deeply the night before. It meant that now he didn't feel in the least drowsy. Right, then… Since he was wide awake, he might as well turn the sleepless hours to good account. He would consider Prudence's future, rather than what he wanted to do with her now. The satisfaction he'd gain from bringing down the pair of villains who'd cheated her and dragged him into their plot.

There. That was better. Considering the cold, relentless march of justice was a much more sensible way to spend the night than revelling in the way all her trusting softness felt in his arms. Or savouring the scent of her body mingled with the scent of warmed hay.

Damn. That had only worked for—what?—less than ten seconds?

It was going to be a very long night.

But at some point he must have drifted off. Because the next thing he knew he was being woken, for the second day in a row, by a voice raised in anger.

This time when he opened his eyes it was to see a ruddy-faced man pointing a gun in his face, rather than merely a woman threatening him with a bony finger.

'Do you realise,' he said coldly, 'how dangerous it is to point a gun at someone?'

At his side, Prudence gasped, and stiffened in his hold.

'Don't be frightened,' he said, remembering that it was the second time in as many days that she'd been shocked awake, too. 'He won't shoot us.'

'Oh, won't I?' said the man with the gun.

'No. There are laws preventing such things.'

'I can do what I like on my own land,' said the man with the gun, belligerently. 'Since you got no right to be 'ere.'

'No, perhaps not,' admitted Gregory, for he had very little patience with people who trespassed on his own land.

'Ain't no perhaps about it! I don't hold with vagrants making free with decent folk's property.'

'Oh, but we're not vagrants,' said Prudence, sitting up and pushing her wildly tousled hair out of her eyes.

The farmer—for he had to assume that was this man's status, since he'd claimed they were trespassing on his land—glowered at her. 'Thieves, then. On the run from the law I 'spect.'

'We are no such thing,' said Gregory, sitting up and putting his arm round Prudence's shoulders. It said something about how frightened she was that she shrank into his side and clutched at his shirt front. 'In fact the very opposite. We have been robbed.'

'Oh-ar?' The farmer sneered at them.

'Yes. You see, this young lady's guardians formed a plot to rob her of her inheritance. They drugged us both and abandoned her in my bed, then made off with all her belongings. And then,' he said, rubbing his hand over his head in what was probably a vain attempt to remove all traces of hay. 'Then I was robbed, too—of my purse. And I had to leave my horse and gig at an inn as surety. Which is why we are cutting across country on foot to...'

He floundered to a halt. It probably wasn't a good idea to name the property to which they were heading, or give any hint that it belonged to him, or the man might guess who he was. And then the tale of what had befallen him this past few days would be all over the county in no time.

He'd be a laughing stock.

'A likely tale,' the farmer said. 'Do you take me for an idiot? Come on—up you get,' he said, jerking the gun in an up and down motion. 'We'll see what Jeffers has to say about this.'

Jeffers? Oh, no. He couldn't risk being hauled up before the local magistrate. He'd had the wretched man over to dine once or twice when he'd been staying down here before.

'Oh, no, please—there is no need for that,' said Prudence plaintively. Then she elbowed him in the ribs. 'I don't know why you needed to make up such a silly story, darling.'

Darling? He turned to stare at her.

'The truth is…' She clasped her hands at her chest and gazed up at the man with the gun earnestly. 'We are runaway lovers.'

'Well, I dunno if that ain't as bad,' said the farmer. Although he did lower his gun just a touch.

'I know—you must think we are wicked. But we are so very much in love. And my guardians are so strict. And, yes, it is rather shocking of us to defy them all, but we haven't broken a single law. Except perhaps for trespassing on your land. And if only we could pay for spending the night in your barn we would. But, you see, we *did* get robbed. That part of Gregory's story is true. So we haven't a penny between us. However, we are perfectly happy to work for you for an hour or so to repay you for spending the night here. Aren't we, darling?'

She turned and gave him a look loaded with meaning.

'Work?' The farmer tucked his gun under his arm and gave them a speculative look.

'Well,' said Prudence. 'I'm sure you are a very busy man. Farms don't run themselves, do they? And wouldn't it be better to make us pay for our stay here than waste time running to fetch the local constable?'

'Ar…' said the farmer, scratching his chin. 'There is that. And I can tell from yer voice that yer a lady. No beggarwoman I ever knew of spoke like you. Even though you *are* dressed like that.' His eyes flicked over her rumpled dress, down to her bare feet. And narrowed.

'You ain't used to walking nowheres, either, are yer?'

Was Gregory imagining it, or did the farmer look as though he was starting to feel sorry for her?

'No,' she said plaintively, shaking her head.

He was. The farmer was definitely looking sorry for her. But then the state of her feet was enough to melt the hardest of hearts.

'You'd best get up to the house, then, miss,' said the farmer, albeit rather gruffly, 'and get them feet seen to.'

'Oh, that's very kind of you, but—'

'This 'ere chap of yourn can do some chores to pay for flattening what's left of my hay.'

'Oh, but—'

'He's right, P... *darling.*' He glared at her warningly, hoping she'd get his hint not to reveal their names. Though she'd already called him Gregory, hadn't she?

Thank goodness she didn't know any of his other names, or they might all have come tumbling out.

'Let me do some work while you get your blisters seen to. They robbed us in the night, you see,' he informed the farmer. 'At the last inn. Took all our luggage. My poor love has no stockings to wear and—'

'I don't want to hear about that sort of thing,' said the farmer, taking a shocked step back at the mention of Prudence's undergarments. 'What I do want to know is what kind of work you can do. Don't want you blundering about causing damage as I'll have to clear up after.'

'I have done a bit of work about the stables,' he admitted, after only the briefest of pauses while he searched frantically for some skill he possessed which might be of use to a farmer.

The farmer glowered at him. Then at Prudence. 'Run off with yer groom, have yer?' He clucked his tongue. 'Well, ain't none of my business, I s'pose. Too late to

do anything about it now, anyhow.' He glanced mean-
ingfully at the crushed hay, at the way Gregory's arm
stayed protectively round Prudence's shoulder, and the
way she leaned into him, one hand resting trustingly
against his chest.

'Come on, you,' he said, pointing a stubby, gnarled
finger at Gregory. 'Let's see what yer made of.'

The farmer's voice was loaded with contempt. He
might have some sympathy for Prudence, but he'd obviously cast Gregory in the role of evil seducer. For the
second time in as many days he was being accused of
the one thing he *hadn't* done.

The only difference this morning was that he now
heartily wished he had.

Prudence wiped round her eggy plate with a crust
of bread, fresh from the oven, and sighed with con-
tentment.

''Tis good to see you have a hearty appetite,' said
the farmer's wife, whose name was Madge. She had
taken one look at Prudence's feet, thrown her hands up
in horror, and then gone all motherly.

'Well, this is such good food,' said Prudence, with
a sigh. Madge had heaped her plate with bacon, fried
eggs and mushrooms. 'We hardly ate a thing yesterday.'

And she wasn't sure when she might be eating anything again. Gregory—for she couldn't help thinking
of him by his first name after spending the night in his
arms—had said they weren't far from his aunt's place
and was assuming they would be welcome. But she
wasn't banking on it. Aunts, she had discovered, could
be extremely unpredictable.

'Now, you must let me help with the dishes,' she said. 'Or something.'

''Tain't fitting for a fine lady such as yerself to ruin her hands with dishes,' said Madge.

'I'm not a fine lady. I'm just…' She didn't know exactly how to describe herself. 'When I was a girl…' She decided to explain as much as she could. 'We travelled all over the place. Papa was a soldier, you see. So Mama and I had to learn how to do all sorts of chores. I can kill a chicken, and milk a goat, and bake bread.'

'Ain't no call for you to go killing none of our chickens,' Madge protested.

'No, of course not, I just—'

'Very well, m'dear. You can do the dishes.' She frowned. ''Twill make it look as though I kept you busy, anyhow, won't it? If Peter comes back in sudden-like.'

'Thank you,' said Prudence meekly.

She was more than willing to let Madge think she was grateful to be spared the prospect of falling foul of her bad-tempered husband if that was what it took to help her overcome her scruples at having a guest do menial work.

The moment Prudence finished the dishes Madge urged her back to the kitchen table.

'Here, you eat a bit of this,' she said, spooning jam onto another thick slice of bread and butter. 'That varmint had no business dragging a lady such as you out into the wilds with no more'n the clothes on your back, and starving you besides.'

'It wasn't his fault—really it wasn't,' she protested, before taking a bite of bread and jam.

But she knew she'd made Madge think it was, by being tight-lipped in response to all her very natural questions. Madge must think she was having second thoughts, or was ashamed of having been so impetuous, or something.

She was just wondering if she could come up with a story that would clear Gregory's reputation, when the flavour of the jam exploded into her mouth.

'Oh, goodness,' she moaned. 'But this jam is good.'

'Last year's strawberries,' said Madge proudly.

'I dreamed about strawberries last night,' she admitted.

'Well, you can take a pot of this jam, then.'

'Oh, no, she can't!'

Prudence saw that the doorway, in which the door had been standing open, was now full of the farmer and Gregory. A distinctly grimy, damp, dishevelled and irritated Gregory.

'She's nobbut a hussy, running off with her groom. Should have put her to work—not filled her with jam what's meant for the market next week.'

''Tweren't meant for no market. That was from a jar I'd already opened!'

As the farmer and his wife launched into a heated argument Gregory jerked his head at her, indicating that she should get up and leave. Which she was only too glad to do.

'Thank you so much for seeing to my feet,' she said, edging past Madge just as she was taking a breath in preparation for slinging another pithy remark at her husband. 'One day you must give me the receipt for that ointment.'

Gregory shot her a look of disbelief, as though he couldn't imagine ever coming anywhere near this farm again.

The farmer, who'd glanced at Prudence's feet when she spoke of them, was now glaring at Madge in a very similar fashion.

'Where'd she get those stockings?'

'From me, of course, you cloth-head,' said Madge.

'Ain't it enough I caught the pair of them trespassing on our land but you must give 'em the food from our table and the very clothes off our back?'

Prudence had just reached the doorway, and Gregory's side, when Madge darted up to her.

'Here,' she said, pressing the remains of the loaf and the opened jar of jam into her hands in defiance of her husband, who was positively swelling with indignation.

'My kitchen,' said Madge, whirling back to him. 'My jam. I made it. And you swore I could do what I wanted with the money I make from it.'

'Ar, but I didn't mean for you to—'

They didn't wait to hear what the farmer hadn't meant for Madge to do with her jam, but took off as fast as they could go.

'What a charming scene of rustic marital bliss,' said Gregory with heavy sarcasm as they made for the barn. 'No wonder he came out here in a mood to shoot something.'

'Here,' said Prudence, thrusting the loaf and the crock of jam at him. 'You are clearly one of those men who wake in a bad mood and need something to eat before you are fit company.'

'It is no longer first thing in the morning,' he replied, taking the bread and ripping off a hunk. 'And it is all very well for you to complain of my mood when you have clearly been treated like a queen in that farmhouse kitchen while *I*,' he said, dipping the bread into the open jam pot, 'have been mucking out the cow byre.'

She wrinkled her nose. 'I thought I could smell something.'

He glowered at her.

'I hope you washed your hands.'

His glower deepened. 'I washed not only my hands but my boots, my breeches and my hair,' he said with his mouth full. 'Under the pump.'

'Oh.' Well, that explained why his hair was wet. 'I did the breakfast dishes,' she put in, hoping to placate him.

'Mrs Grumpy Farmer was clearly a decent sort of woman. Mr Grumpy Farmer did nothing but complain and berate me every time he came to check on my progress. And as for the disgusting state of that byre...' He shuddered expressively. 'No wonder he didn't want to clean it out himself.'

'Oh, dear. Well, I'm very sorry. Perhaps I shouldn't have volunteered our services to Mr Grumpy Farmer with the Gun. I just thought it would be better than having to explain ourselves to the local law. When you started telling him what had happened to us it all sounded so implausible that I could see exactly why he wasn't believing a word of it. Indeed, had I not lived through it I wouldn't have believed a word of it myself.'

'Hmmph,' he said, spraying crumbs down the front of his waistcoat as he stomped across the barn to the mound of hay they'd slept on the previous night.

'Um...' she said, shifting from one foot to the other. 'I can see how much you want your breakfast, but I really don't want to linger here any longer than we have to. Do you?'

'Your point?' He raised one eyebrow at her in a way that expressed many things at once. All of them negative.

'Well, you're clearly going to need both your hands to deal with your bread and jam. So you won't have one free to carry your valise. I was going to suggest I carry it, so we can make a start.' She bent to pick it up. 'It's not very heavy,' she said with some relief.

'And it does have some of your things in it,' he said, with a funny sort of glint in his eye.

'Does it? What—?' She suddenly had a vivid recollection of tossing her stays aside as she'd fled from his room. There were stockings, too. She hadn't stopped to pull them on. And he'd put at least one of them in his pocket. But—why? It wasn't as if they could be of any use to him. And he'd already proved that having only one stocking was of absolutely no use to her, either.

Sometimes men were a complete mystery.

'Come on, then,' he said, turning and heading out of the barn, leaving her to trot behind him with his luggage.

She supposed he was getting his own back on her for getting a decent breakfast while he'd been mucking out a cow byre. Because it certainly wasn't like him to behave in such an ungentlemanly fashion.

Not that she could complain, though, could she? She'd offered to carry it, after all. And even if he'd argued that it was his job, as a big strong man, to do so, she would only have pointed out that she was perfectly capable of carrying a small bag for a short while. In a way he was paying her a compliment by taking her at her word and letting her do as she'd suggested.

Or so he would say if she dared say anything derogatory about the way he was striding ahead, enjoying the bread and jam, while she trotted behind him with the luggage.

They walked along in simmering silence past various farm buildings, heading for the track she could see winding across the fields, while he demolished the bread. When the last crust was gone he frowned into the jam pot, then stuck his finger in and swirled it round to get at the very last traces. When his finger was sufficiently loaded, he raised it to his mouth and sucked it clean.

Prudence promptly forgot why she'd been irritated with him as she watched him half close his eyes in bliss. When he set about doing something he did it with total concentration. To the exclusion of everything else.

As if to prove her right, the moment he'd wiped the jar completely clean he set it aside on the top bar of the stile they'd just reached and turned to her with a smile.

'I'll carry that now,' he said, holding out his hand for the valise.

She handed it over without a word of protest. What would be the point? And, judging by the twinkle in his eye, he knew exactly what arguments had been going through her head while he'd been breaking his fast.

He tossed the valise over the stile, then stepped up onto the first rung and swung one leg over the top. When he was safely on the other side he leaned back and reached for her hand to help her over. Since she'd just mounted the lower step his movement brought their faces to within inches of each other. And she couldn't help noticing he had a smear of jam on his lower lip.

'You have…um…' she began, reaching out one finger to wipe the jam from his mouth.

He moved really swiftly, catching her hand and stilling it. And looked at her in a considering sort of way, as though wondering what to make of her. Why didn't he want her touching his face? Well, then, she wouldn't do so. But when she went to pull her hand back his hold on it tightened. And the look in his eyes went sort of slumberous. And then he pulled her hand right up to his mouth, dipped his head, and sucked her forefinger inside.

He swirled his tongue round her finger and her knees went weak. She pitched forward, bracing herself against the top of the stile with her free hand.

He released her finger from his mouth and looked at her. In a steady sort of way that seemed to dare her to do what she wanted. So she did. She leaned forward and pressed her lips to his. He tasted of jam. And fresh bread. And outdoors. And man.

She reached for him and clung as hard as she could with the stile between them. And they kissed and kissed and kissed.

When they finished her legs were shaking so much that the stile might as well have been a sheer brick wall. There was no way she was going to be able to get over it.

As though he knew how she felt, Gregory got onto the lower step, leaned over and grasped her round the waist, then lifted her right over as though she weighed next to nothing.

She landed on his side of the stile, breathless and shaky, flush with the solid mass of his body. And yearning for another kiss.

He steadied her, and gently but firmly pushed her away. 'We need to keep going.' Then he turned to pick up his valise. 'Come on,' he said, holding out his hand to her.

Which filled her with relief. He might have pushed her away, but at least he was prepared to hold her hand. It was like last night. The way he'd turned over, yet kept hold of her hand to let her know he wasn't rejecting her. So she put her hand in his. And noticed, for the first time, that Mr Grumpy Farmer lived on the prettiest farm she'd ever seen. There were primroses on the banks. Little white clouds scudding across the blue sky. Madge's stockings were of thick, serviceable cotton which cushioned her feet from her shoes so that they no longer caused her agony with every step. And the scent of green growing things was almost managing to overpower the rather unpleasant odour emanating from Gregory's general vicinity.

All in all, she didn't think she'd ever felt quite so happy.

Until, that was, she darted a look up at Gregory's face. For *he* didn't look as though he was wallowing in the memory of strawberry kisses over the stile, or indeed enjoying walking through the countryside in any way at all. He certainly didn't look as though he was thanking his lucky stars he'd fallen in with a wealthy girl who'd proposed marriage to him the night before.

On the contrary. Gregory looked the way a man might look if he was on his way to the scaffold.

A cold hand squeezed at her stomach.

She'd thought that last night in the barn, when he'd told her about his marriage, it had meant that they were becoming close. Which was why she'd blurted out the suggestion that they should marry. But he hadn't agreed, had he? Just because he'd kissed her, that didn't mean he wanted to go as far as marrying her, did it? She'd gone and jumped in with both feet again, as Aunt Charity would say, the way she always did. The way her mother always had.

A man like him couldn't possibly want a girl like her for a wife, could he? How could she have forgotten that she'd made an exhibition of herself by singing in the market place? Or that she'd very nearly killed him by throwing that bit of rock? Men didn't generally marry women whose behaviour they couldn't predict. Let alone women who might accidentally kill them if there were any loose rocks to hand.

'You don't want to marry me at all, do you?'

Her stomach cramped again. She'd made a total fool of herself. Here she'd been, assuming he must be dreaming about how he could invest her money to expand his business, whatever it was, but the truth was he hadn't actually said yes. And now she'd gone and kissed him, assuming he was as keen on the idea as she was.

'Last night, when you told me about your marriage, I thought… Oh, how silly of me.' It was all much clearer this morning. 'You were trying to explain why you didn't wish to marry again, weren't you? And I…'

'Hmm? What?' He turned and stared at her as though he'd completely forgotten she was there.

She wrenched her hand from his. 'I am sure we can come up with some other way out of our predicament.'

Even though she had kissed him. What was a kiss, after all? Men were always trying to snatch kisses—especially from girls who practically threw themselves into their arms. Even if they appeared to enjoy the kiss it didn't mean they actually wanted to *marry* the girl they'd been kissing. Men with less honour than him would make the most of the opportunity to have carnal relations with a girl if she was silly enough to indicate she was willing before he put a ring on her finger.

'You don't need to go to the lengths of marrying me,' she said.

What was the matter with her? he wondered. Why had she suddenly changed her mind about marrying him?

He grabbed her hand back and held it tightly. 'There *is* no other way out of our "predicament", as you put it, apart from marriage. No way at all.'

He'd gone over it time and time again. Although Prudence was so far removed from him socially that everyone would describe it as a *mésalliance*, he was going to have to marry her. Oh, not to avoid scandal. But because after that kiss there was no way he was going to let her go. And because he was almost certain she'd never agree to be his mistress.

If he offered her carte blanche, even though it was something he'd never offered any other woman, he couldn't see Prudence taking it as a compliment. In fact she was more likely to take such a proposition as an insult. She might even feel so insulted she'd never forgive him. And he couldn't risk that. She was going to be upset enough as it was once they reached Bramley Park, where he would no longer be able to hide his true identity from her.

But he wanted Prudence.

And he was going to have Prudence.

That was all there was to it.

Chapter Eleven

Prudence's fingers were going numb. Once or twice she'd been on the verge of complaining about the way he was crushing them, but she'd been afraid he might let go altogether. And at least while he was holding her hand she had *some* connection with him.

He hadn't spoken a word since telling her that there was no way out of their predicament but marriage. He'd never been what you'd call a chatty sort of man, but since then he'd become downright distant.

He was also walking slower and slower, dragging his feet, as though he was trying to put off reaching their destination for as long as possible. The only conclusion she could draw was that he was having serious second thoughts about marrying her. It was one thing admitting he wanted to bed her. But in the cold light of day perhaps he was starting to wonder if marrying her to get what he wanted was going a step too far.

Which was perfectly understandable, given the grief his last marriage had brought him. Especially since he hadn't known her long enough to be sure she would take her marriage vows seriously.

'There,' he said grimly as they crested a rise. 'That's Bramley Park.'

He came to a complete standstill, gazing down at a substantial park spread out on the slopes of the next valley. A high stone wall divided the neatly landscaped grounds from the rougher grazing land on which they stood. There was so much parkland she couldn't even see the house it surrounded.

'That is where your aunt lives?'

He nodded.

'She must be a wealthy woman.' Only wealthy people had houses stuck in the middle of so much land, with high stone walls to keep ordinary people out.

'Not really.'

'Oh? But—'

'Come on,' he said impatiently, veering to the left and tugging her after him down the slope towards the wall which bisected the lower part of the valley.

At length, they came to a section where a couple of gnarled trees grew close to the wall, their branches arching over the top.

'I should have asked,' he said, turning to her with a wary expression. 'Are you any good at climbing trees?'

'Actually,' she replied with a proud toss of her head, 'I am *very* good at climbing trees.' At least she had been as a girl. You couldn't grow up on the fringes of the army without learning all sorts of things that decently brought up girls really shouldn't. Or so Aunt Charity had frequently complained.

'Is there *anything* you cannot do?'

He'd said it with a smile. A rather fond sort of smile, she thought. Or was she just looking for signs that he liked her well enough to think that marrying her wouldn't be a total disaster? He might just as well be the kind of man to cover his doubts and fears by putting on a brave face.

'I believe,' she said, pushing back the waves of insecurity that had been surging over her ever since she'd kissed him, and he hadn't been willing to kiss her again, 'in rising to any challenge. Or at least that is what Mama used to say. Whenever things were hard, she'd say we mustn't look upon them as stumbling blocks in our way, but as stepping stones across troubled waters.'

'And what would she have said about walls that block our paths? That we should climb them?'

She was about to say yes, when something stopped her. 'I don't know about that. I mean, that wall was put there to keep people out, wasn't it? And I'm starting to get a horrid feeling that we may be…um…breaking in.'

He'd already admitted he didn't scruple to break into places when it suited him. He was one of those men who thought the end justified the means. Not that he was a bad man. Just a bit of a rogue, as Papa had been.

'We've already had a farmer threatening us with his gun this morning. What if some gamekeeper mistakes us for poachers? It is just the sort of thing that would happen, the way my luck has been running recently.'

'I can promise you faithfully that we won't be mistaken for poachers once we get over that wall,' he replied, drawing back his arm and tossing the valise over it. 'And, what's more, one cannot break into property that one owns oneself.'

'You are trying to tell me that the estate that lies beyond that wall belongs to *you*?' She eyed his clothing, then his black eye and his grazed knuckles dubiously. 'I thought you said it was your aunt's?'

'I said my aunt lives there,' he replied, planting his fists on his hips. 'Prudence, never say you've been judging me by my appearance?'

He ran his eyes pointedly from the crown of her tousled head to the soles of her shoes, via the jacket she'd borrowed from him, which came almost to her knees, and the stockings she'd borrowed from the farmer's wife, which were sagging round her ankles. Then he flicked his eyes back to her face. Which felt sticky with jam and was probably grimy.

'That's a fair point,' she admitted. 'To look at me nobody would ever suspect I was an heiress, would they? But just explain one thing, if you wouldn't mind? If this is your property, then why are we about to climb over the wall when there must be a perfectly good front gate?'

'Because it would take us the best part of an hour to walk all the way round to the main gate. And your feet have suffered enough abuse already.'

'You want to spare my feet? Oh.' She felt mean now, for suspecting his behaviour to be shifty. 'Then, thank you.'

'Don't thank me just yet,' he said, eyeing the tree, the height of the wall, and then her again. 'I really should have taken into consideration how hard it will be for you to climb up that tree in skirts.'

The very last thing she would do was admit that she hadn't climbed any trees for a considerable time.

'I will go first,' he said. 'And help you up.'

He strode up to the tree. Put his fists on his hips and frowned. Which puzzled her, for a moment, since there was a gnarly knot at a perfect height from which to commence his climb. But then she worked out that he must be considering it from *her* perspective.

'I am sure I will be able to manage,' she assured him. 'This tree has lots of handholds and footholds,'

'Footholds?' He looked from her to the tree, then back to her again, his expression rather blank.

'Yes,' she said, pointing to the stubby projection left behind from where a branch had snapped off years before.

'Ah, yes. Indeed.' He rubbed his hands together. Stayed exactly where he was.

'What is the problem?' What had he seen that she hadn't considered?

'The problem… Well,' he said, 'it is merely that I have never climbed this tree before.'

Oh, how sweet of him to warn her that he wasn't going to be able to point out the best route up it.

'There's no need to worry. Although I haven't climbed a tree since I was a girl, this one looks remarkably easy. Even hampered as I am by skirts.'

'Well, that's good. Yes. Very good.'

A determined look came over his face. He stepped up to the tree. Set one foot on the knot she'd just pointed out. Looked further up the trunk. As though he had no idea what to do next.

'Do you know?' she said with a touch of amusement. 'If I didn't know better, I'd think you've never climbed *any* tree before—never mind that one.'

His shoulders stiffened. Oh, dear, she shouldn't have teased him. Some men could take it, and some men couldn't. Funny, but she'd thought he was the type who could. He'd been remarkably forgiving so far, about all sorts of things she'd done to him.

Without a word he reached up for the most obvious handhold, then scrambled very clumsily up to the first branch thick enough to bear his weight. With only the minimum of cursing he pulled himself up and onto it, swinging one leg over so that he sat astride.

Then he turned and grinned down at her. 'Nothing to it!'

She gasped. 'I was only joking before, but it's true, isn't it? You never *have* climbed a tree, have you?'

He gave an insouciant shrug. 'Well, no. But I always suspected that if other boys could do it I could.'

'What kind of boy never climbed trees?'

'One whose parents were terrified of some harm befalling him and had him watched over night and day,' he replied.

'Oh. That sounds—' Very restricting. And a total contrast to her own childhood. Compared with her life in Stoketown, it had taken on a rosy hue in her memory. But, if she looked at it honestly, it must have been a very precarious sort of existence.

'I suppose,' she said thoughtfully, 'that is what parents do. Even mine—I mean, since they couldn't protect me from actual danger, they did what they could to stop me from being afraid by making light of all the upheavals and privations of army life. Treating it all—in front of me, at least—as though it was all some grand adventure.'

'Which is why nothing scares you now?'

'Well, I wouldn't say that,' she countered. Right this minute she was, if not exactly scared, certainly very wary of climbing up to join him. Because she'd suddenly become very aware that learning to climb trees was not the kind of activity that should have formed part of her education, if there were even some boys, like Gregory, who hadn't been allowed to do it. And also, more to the point, that when she'd been a girl she hadn't cared about showing off her legs.

'Come on,' he said, leaning down and holding out his hand to her. 'Up you get.'

'Wait a minute,' she said. 'I need to take some precautionary measures.'

She hitched up her gown and her petticoat as high as she dared, then reached between her legs and pulled the bunched material from behind through to the front, forming a sort of shortened, baggy set of breeches. It was the best she could do. She only hoped nobody came up over the rise and saw her display of legs bare to the thigh. With one hand clutching her skirts, and her face on fire, she set her foot on the knot she'd shown him earlier, took his hand, and let him haul her up onto the branch next to him.

'What a pity it is that ladies' fashions demand they cover their legs so completely,' he said, running his eyes over hers.

'Impractical, too,' she said with a nonchalant toss of her head, since it was impossible to blush any hotter. 'When a lady decides she needs to climb a tree, breeches would make it far easier.'

He grinned at her again, then shuffled along the branch to the top of the wall, slid across it, and dropped down into the shrubbery that grew right up to the base of the wall on the other side. He turned to her and held out his arms.

'All you need to do is slide to the edge and drop down. I'll catch you,' he said.

All she had to do? In a gown that was hitched almost to her waist?

'It's all very well for you. You *are* wearing breeches.'

Which protected his vulnerable parts. It was no joke, shuffling over a crumbling brick wall when shielded only by a cotton chemise and a bit of kerseymere, since his jacket was trailing uselessly behind her.

But at last she was right at the edge of the wall, her legs dangling down into the park. With Gregory standing below, a wide grin on his face.

'Enjoying the view?' she asked tartly.

'Immensely,' he said without a trace of shame. 'You have very beautiful legs. Even those hideous stockings cannot disguise how very shapely they are.'

'You really shouldn't be staring,' she scolded.

'I would be mad not to.'

'I should slap your face.'

'You will have to come down here first to reach it.'

So she jumped.

And he caught her. And steadied her. And then held on to her elbows for far longer than was necessary. And what with all the talk of legs, and the heated look in his eyes, somehow she didn't wish to slap his face any longer.

'Prudence…' he breathed. 'Prudence, about us getting married…'

Her heart sank. She'd already worked out that he didn't really want to marry her. That he was probably thinking of ways to let her down gently.

'I've already told you—you don't have to,' she said, nobly letting him off the hook. If he didn't want to marry her she wasn't going to force his hand. 'It was just a silly idea I had. I could—'

'No. You couldn't. I won't let you go—do you hear me?'

And then, to her complete surprise, he hauled her

all the way into his arms and kissed her. Savagely. The way she'd always suspected a man with a face as harsh as his could kiss.

Yes! Yes, yes, yes, yes, *yes*. It was heavenly. No question this time about who had initiated the kiss. Though of course she kissed him back for all she was worth.

'Oh, Gregory...' She sighed when he broke away. 'That was lovely.'

He reared back, an expression of astonishment on his face. 'Yes, it was.'

All the pleasurable feelings humming through her dropped through the soles of her feet.

'Didn't you expect to like it? After our last kiss I thought— Oh! Did I do something wrong? Was that it?' She tried to pull away from him.

But he held on to her tightly, refusing to release her from the circle of his arms.

'How could you have done anything wrong?' He shook his head in a sort of daze. 'You kissed me back.'

'Well, then, what was wrong with it?'

'Nothing was wrong with it. That was what was so surprising. Prudence...' He shifted from one foot to another. Took a deep breath. 'I never really saw the point to kissing—that's all. There are more...interesting parts of a woman I've always wanted to pay attention to, you see. But your mouth...'

He looked at her lips again. In the way he'd done before. The way that made them tingle, and part, and wait expectantly for the touch of his lips.

'Your mouth is worth...' He cocked his head to one side. 'Savouring—yes, that is the word. I would never feel as though I was wasting my time, no matter how long you wanted to kiss me.'

He cradled her face with one hand, then bent his head slowly, as if they had all the time in the world. This time he kissed her in a far less savage manner, as though—yes, that was just what it felt like—as though he was *savouring* her.

And she savoured him right back. Pressed herself as close to him as she could. Slid her hands inside his coat and wound her arms round his slender, hard waist. Raised one foot and ran it up and down the back of his booted calf. Feeling all the while as though her body was bursting into song.

'Oh, Gregory,' she moaned into his mouth when he paused to take a breath. 'Oh, please don't stop.'

'I must,' he growled against her lips. 'I thought I could kiss you for ever, but the truth is that I'm starting to find it hard not to throw you down behind the bushes and ravish you.'

'I don't think I'd care,' she admitted. 'I know I should, but somehow—'

'No. Don't say it. Don't tempt me.' He closed his eyes as though in anguish and rested his forehead against hers.

'Oh, very well,' she grumbled. 'I suppose you are right.' After all, she didn't really want her first time to take place out of doors, on the ground, did she?

'Come on, then,' he said with a sort of gentle determination. He took her hand. 'Let's get you into the house, while we can both still walk, and set things in train to make our union respectable.'

He picked up the valise and headed for a gap in the rather overgrown shrubbery.

'Gregory,' she said, when he let go of her hand for a moment to raise the branch of an overhanging beech sapling so that she could pass. 'Can I ask you something?'

He blinked. Visibly braced himself. 'You may ask me anything,' he said.

'Well, I'm sorry if you think I'm prying, but I simply cannot understand how it is your wife went with someone else. If you kissed her the way you just kissed me…' She blushed, suddenly realising that this was one of those topics properly brought up girls didn't mention.

'I told you—my wife hated intimacy of any sort. With me, that is. I never managed more than a peck on the cheek.'

Good grief. The woman must have been a complete imbecile. If only she'd let him kiss her, thoroughly, he would have made her feel gloriously wonderful. Although he'd only been a stripling when he'd been married. Perhaps he hadn't yet learned how to kiss like that.

How had he learned to kiss like that?

'You kissed other women, then, didn't you?' she blurted, after turning over the thought for a while. 'I mean, you have been a widower for a very long time. I suppose you've had a few…er…liaisons?'

He froze in his tracks. Turned and glanced over his shoulder at her. 'I've had more than a few "liaisons", Prudence, and you may as well hear about them now. But understand this.' He turned and looked her straight in the eye. 'I was angry. Bitter. I'd stayed true to my marriage vows while she…' His mouth twisted. 'Can you imagine how it felt to know I'd been faithful to a faithless wife?' He seized her hand. 'Just think how you felt the moment you knew that your aunt and uncle— the people you relied on to guard your welfare—had conspired to rob and humiliate you.'

'Yes, I think I see.'

'Do you? Then you will understand my burning need to make up for lost time. Why I bedded as many women as I could. Why I never risked feeling anything approaching affection for any of them. Why I made sure they knew exactly what their purpose was. Which was why I never kissed them the way I just kissed you. I may have kissed their hands in flirtation, or used my mouth or my tongue on sensitive parts of their bodies to arouse and inflame them…or—' He broke off, looking exasperated. 'Good God, Prudence, how do you manage to get me to tell you things like this?'

'I only asked you about kissing,' she pointed out. 'I didn't force you to tell me anything about your… liaisons.' Even though what he'd said had helped her understand him better. 'You could have just told me to mind my own business.'

'For some reason I don't seem to be able to tell you any such thing,' he growled, before turning his back on her and stalking off through the undergrowth.

She had to break into a trot to keep up with him. But neither the fact that he was walking so quickly nor the grumpy way he'd spoken to her could cast her down very much. For one thing, the confidence with which he was striding through the undergrowth proved that he was very familiar with the layout of the grounds. Which laid to rest her fear that they might be trespassing. For another, she couldn't help being pleased that he couldn't keep things from her. Last night's confidences might have been due to some after-effect of the drug. But there was no trace of it left in either of them today. If he couldn't keep anything from her, then it was because somehow she'd got under his guard.

She smiled. He was the kind of man who wasn't used to sharing confidences with anyone, but he couldn't hold back from her—not with his thoughts, or his kisses. After only knowing her for just over a day. Which made her feel very powerful, in a uniquely feminine way.

She was still smiling when they emerged, blinking, onto a massive swathe of lawn on which sheep were grazing. On its far side sat a very neat little box of a house, in the Palladian style, two storeys high. Or perhaps not so little. She counted seven windows across the top floor.

She turned to look at Gregory, who'd come to a complete standstill. He caught her enquiring look and glowered at her.

'This is it,' he said. 'God help me.'

'Whatever do you mean? Gregory, what *is* the matter?'

A muscle in his jaw clenched, as though he was biting back some unpalatable truth. Whatever could there be inside that house which had the power to make him look so reluctant to enter it? The dragon of an aunt? Surely she couldn't have too much influence over him, since he claimed to own the house? Unless he'd fallen on hard times and the woman held some financial power over him? Well, that wouldn't matter once they were married—unless she was the kind of old harpy who would make him feel bad about marrying an heiress.

'You'll soon find out,' he said grimly. Then seized her hand in his and set off for the house once more.

'Please don't worry,' she panted, for he was walking so fast now he'd clearly made up his mind to beard the dragon in her den that she was having to trot to keep up with him. 'Whatever is worrying you, I know you can deal with it. You can deal with anything.'

'I hope to God you're right,' he muttered.

He took a deep breath, like a man about to dive from a high cliff into murky water, then strode up the front steps and rapped on the door.

'Prudence,' he said, turning to her, a tortured expression on his face. 'Perhaps I should have warned you before we got here that—' He broke off at the distinct sound of footsteps approaching from the other side of the door. 'Too late,' he said, shutting his mouth with a snap on whatever it was he'd wanted to warn her of.

Never mind. Whatever it was, she could weather it. If she'd managed to survive this past two nightmarish days, she could weather anything.

But then, as the door swung open, something very strange happened to Gregory. He sort of…closed up. It was as though he had deliberately wiped all expression from his face, turning into a hard, distant, cold man she couldn't imagine ever climbing trees with a grin. He looked just like the man she'd first seen in The Bull— the man from whom everyone had kept their distance. And, even though she was still holding his hand, she got the feeling he'd gone somewhere very far away inside.

A soberly dressed man opened the door and goggled at the sight of them. Which was hardly surprising. Not many people looking as scruffy as they did would have the effrontery to knock on the front door of a house like this. But Gregory didn't bat an eyelid.

'Good morning, Perkins,' he said. 'Something amiss?'

'No, Your Grace,' said the flabbergasted butler.

Your Grace? Why was the butler addressing Gregory as 'Your Grace'?

'Of course not, Your Grace. It is just—' The butler pulled himself together, opened the door wider and stepped aside. 'We were not expecting you for another day or so.'

Gregory raised one eyebrow in a way that had the butler shrinking in stature.

'Your rooms are in readiness, of course,' he said.

'And for my guest?'

The butler's eyes slid briefly across Prudence. 'I am sure it will take Mrs Hoskins but a moment to have something suitable prepared for the young person.'

Gregory inclined his head in an almost regal manner. Then walked into the house in a way she'd never seen him walk before. As though he owned the place. Well, he'd told her he did. It was just that until this very second she hadn't really, truly believed it.

And there was something else she was finding hard to believe as well.

'Why,' she whispered as he tugged her into the spacious hall, 'is the butler calling you Your Grace?'

'Because, Miss Carstairs,' he said, in what sounded to her like an apologetic manner. 'I am afraid that I am a duke.'

Chapter Twelve

'A *duke*?'

No. It would be easier to believe he was a highwayman and that this house was a den filled to bursting with his criminal associates than that.

But then why else would the butler have addressed him as 'Your Grace'?

'This is Miss Carstairs, Perkins,' said Gregory—or whoever he was—to the butler, handing him his valise. 'My fiancée.'

'Your—?' The butler's face paled. His lips moved soundlessly, his jaw wagging up and down as though words failed him.

She knew how he felt, having just sustained as great a shock herself. Which made her realise her own mouth had sagged open on her hearing Gregory claim to be a duke.

She shut it with a snap.

'Fiancée,' Gregory repeated slowly, as though addressing an imbecile.

'If you say so, Your Grace,' said the butler, looking distinctly unimpressed. 'I mean…' he added swiftly, when Gregory raised one eyebrow in that way he had—a way, she now saw, that was due to his being a duke. A duke who wasn't used to having butlers, let alone stray females, dare to express a view that ran counter to his own. 'Congratulations, Your Grace,' said the butler, inclining his head in the slightest of bows whilst refraining from looking in her direction.

'Miss Carstairs and I fell among thieves on the road,' said Gregory. Or whatever she was now supposed to call him.

'Hence our rather dishevelled appearance.' He waved his hand in a vague gesture encompassing them both.

'I shall send for Dr Crabbe at once, Your Grace,' said the butler, his eyes fixed on the cuts and bruises on his employer's face.

Marks that she'd come to regard as an integral part of him. But which were not, to judge by the butler's expression of horror, by any means typical.

'Oh, no need for that. I am sure Mrs Hoskins can supply a poultice, or some soothing ointment of some sort that will suffice. And, while we are on the subject of ointment, Miss Carstairs will need some for her feet.'

'Her feet?' The butler, reduced to repeating his master's words in a strained manner, glanced down at her feet, and then to the staircase, from the direction of which came the sound of a slamming door.

A slender youth, in very natty dress, appeared on the landing and began to jog down the stairs, whistling cheerfully.

Until he caught sight of the three of them standing by the open front door. Which had him coming to an abrupt halt, mid-whistle.

'Halstead!'

Since the youth was staring at Gregory, Prudence

could only suppose that Halstead must be his real name. Or his title. Aristocrats always had a handful of each.

'The devil!'

'Language, Hugo,' said Gregory—or Halstead—or whoever he was. Though at least she could surmise that this youth was the Hugo with whom Gregory had suspected she'd done some sort of deal when they'd first met.

'Language be damned,' said Hugo, reaching for the banister rail to steady himself. 'You didn't last the full week. I've won.'

Won? Won what?

'Extenuating circumstances,' said Gregory, waving a languid hand in her direction. He spoke in a bored drawl. As though he was completely unmoved by the shock afflicting everyone else in the hallway, which he'd caused by strolling through the front door and announcing both his rank and his betrothal.

'No such thing,' said the youth, folding his arms across his chest. 'Ain't you always telling me that there's never any excuse for outrunning the constable? That if you only have a little backbone, or willpower, or a modicum of intelligence...'

'Not here,' muttered Gregory—she had to think of him by some name, and that was the one she'd grown used to. And if he hadn't wanted her to use it he should jolly well not have let her do so! 'We will repair to the morning room,' he said, taking her elbow firmly to steer her across the hall. 'While we await refreshments.' He gave the butler a pointed look.

The butler flinched. 'Her Ladyship is in the morning room, taking tea,' he said, glancing at Prudence, then back at Gregory, in ill-concealed horror.

'Ah,' said Gregory, coming to a full stop.

'No point in trying to keep anything from Lady Mixby,' said Hugo cheerfully, jogging down the rest of the stairs. 'Since the person she is currently entertaining to tea is a most interesting cove who claims you sent him here. By the name of Bodkin.'

Bodkin? Wasn't that the name of the man with whom he'd told her he'd broken into a mill? Making it sound as if he was some sort of...Robin Hood, or something. Going about righting wrongs. Now this Hugo person was making it sound as though it was a great jest. Coupled with his first remark, about not lasting a week and not winning, it sounded suspiciously as though Gregory had gone to the factory in the course of trying to win some kind of wager.

Now all those things he'd said about what she had been doing in his bed made perfect sense. He'd thought that Hugo was doing all in his power to make him lose whatever wager they had agreed upon.

'This way,' said Gregory, steering her across the hall with the grip he still had on her elbow.

She put up no resistance. She didn't have the strength. It had all seeped out through what felt like a great crack, somewhere deep inside her, where once her trust in Gregory had resided. She hadn't even felt this stunned when she'd discovered that Aunt Charity, who'd appeared to be a pillar of society, had turned into a criminal overnight. Into a person she didn't really know at all.

Because she'd never actually *liked* Aunt Charity, try as hard as she might.

But she'd started to look upon this man who was ushering her across the hall as a bit of a hero.

Now it turned out he was someone else—some*thing*

else—entirely. A duke. A duke who'd been so bored with his dull existence that he'd put on rough clothes and changed his name in order to win a bet.

The butler leaped ahead of them to open the door to a room that was flooded with sunshine. Three people were sitting there.

A young man, wearing clothes that were so plain and so coarse that he just had to be Mr Bodkin, was perched on the very edge of a hard-backed chair, his hands braced on his knees as though ready to take flight at the slightest alarm. There was also a bracket-faced woman at a table under the window, tucking into a plate of cakes and sandwiches, a teacup at her elbow. And on one of the sofas placed on either side of fire sat a plump little woman wearing lavender satin and a frivolous lace cap of white.

The plump woman uttered a piercing shriek when she saw them, and clapped her hand to her ample bosom.

Mr Bodkin started to his feet, took half a pace in their direction, then halted, saying, 'Mr Willingale...?'

The bracket-faced lady froze, a sandwich halfway to her mouth.

'Mr Willingale!' said the plainly dressed young man again, this time with more certainty. 'It *is* you. Thank heaven. I was that worrit when I got here and you hadn't arrived. I was sure summat bad must have happened to you.'

'I told you there was no need to worry,' said Hugo, sauntering into the room and closing the door firmly behind him. 'I told you we weren't expecting Halstead until the end of the week.'

'Halstead?' Mr Bodkin frowned. 'Who's Halstead?'

'I am,' said Gregory.

'But you told me you was Mr Willingale,' said Mr Bodkin, looking as bewildered as Prudence felt.

'Well, he ain't,' said Hugo firmly. 'He's Halstead. Duke of.'

So she wasn't the only person he'd lied to about his identity. It should have been of some consolation. Why wasn't it?

The youth in homespun glowered at Hugo. 'Beggin' Yer Lordship's pardon, but I know what he said.'

Hugo was a *lordship*? Well, naturally! If Gregory was a duke all his relatives were bound to be lords and ladies, too.

'Never mind that for now,' said Gregory firmly, as the two younger men squared up to each other. 'Miss Carstairs is in dire need of tea and a seat by the fire. Miss Carstairs,' he said, addressing the plump lady on the sofa, 'is my fiancée, Lady Mixby.'

The lady in lavender uttered another little shriek, though this time she clapped both hands together instead of clasping her chest as though she'd suffered a severe shock.

'Oh, how wonderful! You are going to marry again. At last! Come here, dear,' she said to Prudence. 'And tell me all about yourself.'

Gregory held up his hand repressively. 'You are not to pelter her with questions. None of you. Miss Carstairs has been through a terrible ordeal.'

And it wasn't over yet. This had all the hallmarks of being a continuation of the nightmare that had started when she'd woken stark naked in bed with a stranger. Since then nothing and nobody had been what they seemed.

'Oh, my dear, how selfish of me,' said Lady Mixby.

'You do look somewhat…*distrait*,' she said, kindly choosing the most tactful way to describe her dirty, dishevelled appearance. 'Come and sit here on the sofa,' she said patting the cushion beside her. 'Benderby!' She waved at the bracket-faced lady. 'Ring for more hot water and cake.'

Benderby put down her sandwich, went to the bell-pull and tugged on it. Prudence collapsed onto the sofa opposite the one occupied by Lady Mixby. Gregory sat down beside her. And took her hand.

What with being in a room full of titled people—not to mention Mr Bodkin—all of whom were already shocked by her appearance, she didn't have the nerve to create a scene by tugging it free. The only way to express her confusion and resentment was to let it lie limp and unresponsive in his.

Bodkin stomped across the room until he was standing right in front of the sofa, glaring down at them. 'Why does he keep saying you're a duke?'

'Because,' said Gregory calmly, 'that is what I am. The Duke of Halstead.'

'You're not!'

'I am afraid,' he said, apologising for his rank for the second time that day, 'that I am.' He gave her hand a slight squeeze, as though including her in the apology.

She didn't return the pressure.

'I am the Duke of Halstead,' said Gregory. 'The owner of Wragley's. To whom you wrote.'

'But you *can't* be! I mean we—' Bodkin clenched his fists, which were grazed about the knuckles, just like Gregory's. As if he'd thought the same thing as her, he glanced down at them.

'Yes, I do recall the incident,' said Gregory. 'Though

why you think that precludes me from being the Duke of Halstead, I fail to comprehend.' He leaned back and crossed one leg over the other.

'Well, because dukes don't go visiting mills and getting into fist fights with the foreman, that's why.'

'Is that so?'

Gregory drawled the words, looking down his nose at the poor man. Even though Bodkin was standing over them. But then he'd managed to look down his nose at *her* when she'd been kneeling over him in the lane, hadn't he? And now she knew how he'd managed it. He'd clearly spent his entire life looking down from a lofty height on the rest of the human race.

'Bodkin has been keeping us vastly entertained with his tales of how you and he broke into your own factory at dead of night and had to fight your way out,' said Hugo with glee. 'Lord, but I'd have given a monkey to have seen it!'

His *own* factory? Of course it was his own factory. He didn't work for anyone as any sort of investigator.

He was a duke.

'You would first have had to be in possession of a monkey,' said Gregory scathingly.

'I don't see why you need to bring monkeys into it,' Lady Mixby complained. 'As well as talk of brawling with common persons. No offence, Mr Bodkin. I am sure you are a very worthy person in your way, and I have found your company most refreshing, but for Halstead to declare he means to have a new duchess is far more interesting!' She waved one dimpled hand in Prudence's direction. 'For him to perform such a volte-face will rock society to its very foundations.'

It certainly would if they knew where she'd come from and how they'd met.

'We were not speaking of real monkeys, Lady Mixby,' said Gregory witheringly, 'but a sum of money. Vulgar persons describe it that way.'

'Halstead, I know I owe you a great deal,' said Lady Mixby, her face flushing. 'But I must really protest at *anyone* using vulgarity in my drawing room.'

'Bravely said, Aunt,' he said icily. 'I beg your pardon, Aunt, Miss Benderby, Miss Carstairs.'

'Never mind begging everyone's pardon,' said Hugo, going to stand behind Lady Mixby's sofa and placing his hands on its back. 'We're *all* of us dying of curiosity. Oh, and I had to let Lady Mixby in on the nature of our wager once Bodkin turned up, so you don't need to go into why you went haring off to Manchester under an alias, without your valet or groom.'

Well, that was what *he* thought. Prudence most definitely wanted to know the *exact* terms of the wager.

'No,' continued Hugo, 'what *we* want to know is how you came to acquire a fiancée who looks like a gypsy when everyone knows you'd rather cut off your right arm than ever marry again.'

So that was why Lady Mixby had said society was going to be rocked to its foundations. Well, she'd known about his reluctance to marry again. Because he'd confided in her. But she'd never suspected it was common knowledge. That put a different complexion on things entirely.

Gregory gave him a look that should have frozen the blood in his veins. 'I'll thank you to keep a civil tongue in your head,' he growled.

She supposed she should be grateful that he was trying to defend her but, really, who could blame Hugo for speaking of her this way when it was obvious they'd never have crossed paths if he hadn't been engaged in trying to win some sort of wager?

At that moment there was a knock at the door and the butler came in with a tea tray.

'Better bring a decanter of something stronger,' suggested Hugo as the butler deposited the tray on a table beside Prudence's sofa. 'Tea may suffice for this wench, but my poor old cousin looks decidedly in need of something more restorative.'

So did she.

'Ale,' said Gregory to the butler. 'If this young scapegrace must start drinking at such an early hour I would rather keep him away from anything too strong. Since I have good reason to know he does not have the head for it.'

'That was uncalled for,' said Hugo sulkily once the butler had gone off on his errand. 'Raking me down in front of the servants.'

'Would you kindly pour the tea, Lady Mixby?' said Gregory, ignoring Hugo. He'd been studiously ignoring her, too. He must know she was shocked, and felt betrayed and insecure. But he was explaining himself to the others. His family. As if he suspected them of thinking she was some terrible catastrophe that had befallen him and he needed to reassure them that he hadn't lost his mind.

Though if he gave her an opportunity to express any opinion at all she'd prove that she was, and he had.

'I feel sure we would all benefit from a cup.'

'I know I certainly would,' Lady Mixby muttered as

she lifted the lid to examine the state of the brew in the teapot. 'Milk and sugar?'

Lady Mixby plunged into the ritual of the tea tray with such determination that Prudence could only follow her lead. Though she felt rather like a marionette having her strings pulled as she responded mechanically to the familiar routine.

The one good thing to come out of it was that as Lady Mixby held out the cup of tea she'd poured, milked and sugared for her, it gave her the perfect excuse for wresting her hand from Gregory's. Though her hand was trembling so much that the cup rattled in its saucer with a sound like chattering teeth.

'Miss Carstairs,' said Gregory, reaching out to take the cup and saucer from her trembling fingers. 'I fear this has all been rather too much for you. I think you should go to a guest room and have a lie-down. A bath. A change of clothes. And something to eat and drink in peace.'

'Oh, what a good idea,' said Lady Mixby, leaping to her feet.

That did it. He might have said all the right things, but deep down he was ashamed of her. Just as Aunt Charity had felt shamed by having to house her, the product of a runaway match. Aunt Charity had spent years failing to make her acceptable to her congregation and the community of Stoketown. And in the end had just kept her out of sight as much as possible.

And this was how it had started. By sending Prudence to her room whenever there was company she wanted to impress.

'If you think for one moment,' said Prudence, snatching the teaspoon from the saucer as he took it away, so she could use it to emphasise her point, 'that I am going to let you shuffle me out of the way so that you can explain your behaviour over the last two days to everyone else and leave me in the dark, then you have another think coming!'

Gregory reached out and confiscated the teaspoon, then tossed it to the tea tray, where it landed with a tinkle amongst the china.

'You are overwrought,' he said repressively.

'Is that so surprising? I *trusted* you! I thought you were a decent, hard-working man. A man who'd set out to right wrongs and defend the helpless. Instead you are the kind of man who makes the kind of wagers that result in fist fights and falling into bed with strange women! I trusted you with my virtue, and with my money—'

Lady Mixby gasped and fell back to the sofa, her hands clasped to her bosom.

But Prudence was beyond caring. She'd sat there listening to him account for himself with growing resentment. She couldn't hold it in any longer.

'And now I find out that I don't even know your name!'

'Well, that at least is easily rectified. My name is Charles Gregory Jamison Willingale, Seventh Duke of Halstead. I think we can gloss over the lesser titles for now.'

'Oh, you do, do you?'

How could he sit there and calmly reel off a list of names whilst completely sidestepping the real issue? Which was that he'd deceived her. *Deliberately* deceived her.

'And as for explaining myself to everyone else…' He

glanced from Hugo to Bodkin with a sort of chilling
hauteur that made him look even more like a stranger
than ever. 'I have no intention of doing any such thing.'

'Oh, I say—that is dashed unfair!'

Gregory held up his hand to silence the outburst from
his indignant young cousin. 'No,' he said. 'What would
be unfair would be to divulge anything to anyone before
I have done so to my fiancée. She, of course, must take
precedence over anything you feel I owe you, Hugo. Or
indeed you, Lady Mixby.'

'Of course, of course,' said Lady Mixby, nodding her
head whilst clasping and unclasping her hands.

'We will all adjourn until dinner.' He got to his feet.
'Which will give Miss Carstairs and I a chance to bathe
and change and generally refresh ourselves.'

Hugo wrinkled his nose. 'Come to mention it, you
do smell rather ripe.'

When she made no move from the sofa, His Grace
the Seventh Duke of Wherever-it-was extended his hand
to urge her to her feet. But she had finally reached the
stage where, had she been a bottle of ginger beer, her
top would have popped off under the pressure building
up inside from constant shaking.

'Will you *stop*,' said Prudence, batting away his
hand, 'calling me Miss Carstairs? And telling everyone I am your fiancée. When obviously I can never be
anything of the sort!'

Dukes didn't marry nobodies. Especially not nobodies they'd only known five minutes.

He didn't even have the grace to flinch. Clearly all
the grace he had was in his inherited title.

'Overwrought,' said the man who had first appeared
to be a villain, had then for a few magical hours looked

to her like the answer to all her prayers, but who now turned out to be a duke. 'I can understand that the discovery you are about to become a duchess has come as a shock. But once you have had a lie-down and composed yourself you will see that—'

'Don't talk to me in that beastly manner. And *don't*—' she swatted his hand away again '—order me about.'

She was just taking a breath to unburden herself in regard to her sense of injustice when there came another knock at the door. This time it was a plain, practical-looking woman dressed all in black who came in.

'Excellent timing, Mrs Hoskins,' said Gregory smoothly, taking Prudence's elbow in a vice-like grip and lifting her to her feet. 'Miss Carstairs, as you can see, is in dire need of a change of clothes and a bath. As am I,' he said with a grimace of distaste. 'Miss Carstairs,' he said, giving her a level look. 'I will speak with you again at dinner.'

'*Dinner!* You intend to leave me in this state until dinner?'

'We keep country hours at Bramley Park,' he said. 'You will only have to wait until four of the clock. It will take you at least that long to bathe and change and,' he said, in the same steely tone he'd used on Hugo, 'to calm down.'

Calm down? *Calm down!* She'd give him 'calm down'. How dared he talk to her in that insufferably arrogant way? As though she was in need of a set-down?

'You can take your hands off me,' she hissed, wrenching her arm out of his grip. 'And think yourself lucky I am too well-bred to slap your face for your… impertinence!'

Lady Mixby gasped. Pressed both hands to her flushed face this time.

Prudence stuck her nose in the air and stalked from the room.

Chapter Thirteen

Prudence was well on her way up the stairs before realising she had no idea where she was going. She would have to slow down and wait for Mrs Hoskins, or she'd risk looking like an idiot.

As well as feeling like one.

For what kind of idiot proposed to a man she'd only known for two days? A man she'd met, moreover, in bed? And stark naked at that.

Her feet stumbled and slowed of their own accord, which gave Mrs Hoskins a chance to catch up with her.

'It's just along this way, miss,' she panted, indicating the left branch of the upper landing. 'I hope it's to your liking.'

Prudence hoped she'd made an appropriate response, because it certainly wouldn't be this woman's fault if it wasn't. But in the event, when she saw the room, it was almost enough to make her burst into tears. Because it was simply magnificent. The most beautifully decorated, perfectly proportioned room she'd ever had for her sole use.

To start with, everything matched. There were velvet

curtains in various shades of green all over the place, chairs with spindly gilt legs upholstered in toning shades of satin, and a mostly green carpet that looked as soft as moss. Clearly each item of furniture, each square yard of velvet and satin, had been purchased specifically to enhance the beauty of this one room.

It cast her own little room in her aunt's house in Stoketown completely in the shade. And *that* room had totally intimidated her when she'd first seen it. It had made all the rough-and-ready billets in which her parents had lived seem like hovels.

'Is something amiss? Would you prefer to have a room at the back of the house? It will not have such a fine view, but it would get less sunlight,' said Mrs Hoskins.

The housekeeper looked so concerned Prudence made a determined effort to pull herself together. She *could* step into this room. They wouldn't have had the carpet put on the floor if they weren't prepared to let people walk on it. True, they couldn't have imagined anyone with such mucky shoes ever setting foot up here, but she could remove them. She was at least wearing stockings today, even if they were borrowed and rather too large. So her feet wouldn't leave a trail of bloodstains behind.

'Oh, no—no need to prepare another room. Thank you,' she said, toeing off her shoes.

The chances were that all the rooms in this house were equally grand. Apart from perhaps the servants' quarters. And it would look extremely odd if she asked to have a look at *them*.

'This room is lovely. It is just a bit…' Her lower lip quivered. The truth was, the way Gregory had ordered her up here had reminded her far too much of the way Aunt Charity had always sent her to her room. When she'd 'answered back'. When she'd been supposed to 'think about what she'd done'. When her aunt had wanted some peace and quiet. When visitors had come. He'd told her to calm down and tidy herself up, as though he didn't think she was fit to stay in the same room as a duke's family. Not that she was going to admit that to Mrs Hoskins.

'I mean, after all that has happened this last few days, I...' Her breath hitched in her throat. It was as if her self-esteem was being crushed by a velvet brocade fist. How could a girl like her have had the temerity to propose marriage to a duke? Even the curtains were sneering.

A *duke*!

She wrapped her arms round her middle, where a peculiar swirling sensation had started up. Not only had she proposed to him, but she'd thrown a rock at him. Knocked him right down and made him bleed.

That had to be against the law—assaulting a duke. Might it even count as treason?

Her hand stole to her throat as she thought of the punishment meted out for treason. Which she deserved, didn't she? Since she'd been so adamant that her aunt and uncle should be brought to justice for merely drugging him!

'Oh, you poor lass,' said Mrs Hoskins, slipping a firm hand under her elbow. 'You look nigh to fainting away. What a terrible time you've had, to be sure. And you such a fine lady, I'll be bound—else His Grace would never be making you his duchess.'

Fine lady? She wasn't *any* kind of lady. She was an

army brat. That was what Aunt Charity had called her. The disgraceful result of a runaway match. And if she wasn't good enough for Aunt Charity how could she be good enough for a duke?

'You'll feel better for a warm bath and a nice lie-down,' said the housekeeper as she drew her into the terrifyingly opulent room. 'Milly and Sam will be bringing up the bath and some hot water, and then Milly will stay to help you bathe,' she said, steering Prudence towards the bed.

'No!' Prudence recoiled from the smooth satin coverlet and the starched white lacy pillows in horror. 'I mean, I don't think I should sit on the bed to wait, do you?' She indicated her clothes. 'I slept in a barn last night. I shouldn't want to dirty the coverlets.'

'A barn, was it?' Mrs Hoskins's eyebrows shot up her forehead and almost disappeared under the rim of her cap.

Oh, no. Now it would be all over the servants' hall that their duke had spent the night in a barn. He'd be livid with her. If he wasn't already. It was hard to tell now he'd taken to wearing that wooden mask instead of his normal face.

'Well, then, how about you come along over to the window seat and rest yourself there while your bath is made ready? The covers wash well if so be that you do make a mark on them,' she said soothingly. 'Not that I think it is at all likely,' she added.

'Yes, very well,' said Prudence, feeling like the worst sort of impostor as Mrs Hoskins led her across the room.

No wonder he'd been so angry to find her next to him in bed that first night. No wonder he'd raved about plots and schemes and kept on asking if Hugo had put her up to it. She sank down shakily onto the seat and buried her face in her hands. *That* was why he'd taken her up in his gig. He'd been trying to find out whether Hugo was cheating.

She knew the lengths to which men would go in order to win wagers. Over the most ridiculous stakes, too. It made no difference whether they'd staked the services of a beautiful mistress or a tin whistle—it was proving that they were 'better', in some ridiculous manner, than the man with whom they'd made the wager, and that was what counted. That was why he'd asked all those questions. It hadn't been chivalry. It hadn't been concern for her at all. No, it had been indignation at what he had perceived as an attempt to make him lose.

If they hadn't lost his purse he would no doubt have dropped her off somewhere once he'd satisfied himself that she really didn't know either who he was or anything at all about Hugo. Only he *had* lost his purse. And his horse and gig.

And then, to cap it all, she'd asked him to marry her.

A bustle in the room made her drop her hands and look up. A male servant had deposited a hip bath on a towel before the fireplace, and a maid was pouring water into it from a can of steaming water.

'Now, Milly,' Mrs Hoskins was saying sternly. 'You are not to pepper His Grace's intended with a lot of impertinent questions. She's been through a terrible ordeal, as anyone can see.'

Both Milly and Sam darted a glance to where she was sitting, trembling and probably ashen-faced because she'd realised what she'd done, and adopted similarly sympathetic expressions.

Which made her cringe. If they only knew how outrageously she'd behaved they'd be sorely tempted to eject her from the property. As swiftly as possible. Which made her wish she wasn't sitting quite so close to the convenient mode of exit a window might afford a brace of scandalised servants.

'I'll leave you with Milly now,' said Mrs Hoskins. 'She's not what you're used to, I'm sure, but she's a good girl.' Mrs Hoskins shot the blushing maid a stern, meaningful look before bustling out of the room, taking the male servant with her.

Milly dropped a curtsey. 'Sam will be bringing up some more hot water shortly,' she said. 'But don't you worry he'll come in here a-gawping at you, for I shan't let him. He'll leave it at the door. So if you want to get started…?'

She must look dreadful for everyone to be so insistent on getting her into a bath. And she probably smelled dreadful, too, since she'd not had an opportunity to bathe or change her clothes for a couple of days.

'I would like to get out of this dress and get clean,' she admitted. Though no amount of bathing and tidying was going to change who she was underneath. 'But I don't have anything to change into.'

'Oh, Mrs Hoskins explained about your luggage getting stolen. It must have been that frightening!' Milly's eyes were round, in a mix of horror and fascination. 'Thank goodness His Grace was at hand to rescue you and bring you here.'

Was *that* the story circulating around the servants' hall? Typical! Men would do anything to save face. He'd rather let people think he'd been doing something akin to rescuing a damsel in distress than for anyone to suspect that what he'd really been doing was…was…going to any lengths to win some stupid wager.

'Mrs Hoskins will be bringing you my Sunday best, miss,' said Milly as she unlaced Prudence's gown and helped her out of her chemise.

The girl said nothing about her lack of corset, or the coarse weave of her stockings, though she couldn't help wrinkling her nose as she rolled the whole lot into a bundle and took it over to the door, where she dropped it on the one patch of board that wasn't covered by expensive carpet. She wouldn't be a bit surprised to learn they were going straight to the bonfire, rather than the laundry.

Prudence stepped into the bath and sat down, hugging her knees to her chest.

'I do hope you like the gown,' said Milly. 'I know it won't be what you're used to, but Mrs Hoskins insisted, since I'm nearer to you in size than anyone else here.'

Prudence had a short but horrible vision of trying to make do with one of Lady Mixby's gowns.

'I'm very grateful to you for lending it to me,' said Prudence with complete honesty. Even a servant's Sunday best was far better than what she'd been wearing.

'Oh, I ain't lending it! His Grace is going to buy it off me. For five guineas—can you imagine? Why, I'll be able to get three new gowns, a bonnet and gloves for that. I mean,' she added, going red in the face, 'I beg pardon, my lady. I forgot I'm not supposed to gabble on. Mrs Hoskins said as how you're used to having a properly trained ladies' maid, and how I was to mind my tongue, but as usual it's run away with me. There I go again!'

Why was it that everyone kept talking about what

she was 'used to'? How did they *know* what she was used to? Nobody had asked. They just kept assuming she must be a fine lady, because only a fine lady would be entitled to marry a duke.

And she'd done nothing to correct their assumptions, had she? Because she didn't want anyone thinking she was a designing hussy who'd got her claws into their duke while he was travelling about the country under the name of Willingale, dressed like some kind of tradesman.

'His Grace is going to have Mrs Bennet—that's our village dressmaker—come and bring you some fresh things in the morning, and measure you up for whatever else you may need,' said Milly, vigorously soaping a washcloth. 'Shall I do your back first, my lady? Or your hair?'

'Oh, my hair,' she said. If she could make her hair look tidy she might feel more able to go downstairs when it was time to face all those titled people again. Aunt Charity had always said it made her look as wild and immodest as her mother had actually been. She'd always made her braid it and cover it under caps and bonnets. 'I can manage the rest myself, but my hair has always been a bit wild,' she said as Milly handed over the washcloth. 'Do you have a really strong comb you can lend me? Or perhaps we should just cut out the worst of the tangles.'

'If we do then you need not worry that it will show. I might be a bit of a gabster, but I'm good with hair. Done all my sisters' in my time, I have.'

'Well, that's good to know.'

And it was good to have the help of a maid again, too. A maid who didn't seem to mind being a maid, at that. Milly was taking her time massaging her scalp, and it felt absolutely wonderful.

So wonderful that she actually closed her eyes and started to relax. And as she did so her spirit began to revive. Just as it always had whenever she'd been sent to her room to 'think about what she'd done'. She'd never managed to stay cowed and guilty for long after one of her aunt's rebukes. Because as she'd thought about whatever it was that was supposed to be unforgivably immodest, or vulgar, or sinful, she'd remembered how often her mother or father had done or said the very same thing. And she had refused to betray them by being ashamed of behaviour they would consider perfectly normal.

She didn't fit in with Aunt Charity and her circle—that was what it amounted to. Any more than she'd fit in with a duke and *his* circle.

So there was no point in allowing herself to be intimidated by the luxurious surroundings, or the titles his family bore. Any more than she'd allowed herself to be beaten down by Aunt Charity's pious homilies. She'd soon learned that no matter how hard she tried to fit in, she'd never measure up. Because of who her parents were. And so she'd stopped trying.

And she wasn't going to start tying herself up in knots trying to fit in here, either. She was done with being intimidated. Gregory had no right to make her feel foolish, or guilty, or out of her depth. If dukes didn't want people to assume they were ordinary men, then they had no business going around under false identities.

They had no right making out they were heroes, either. Why, if there had been any rescuing going on, she'd

done her fair share. Who'd had the idea of singing for
food money so that he hadn't needed to pawn his watch,
which was probably a priceless family heirloom? And
whose quick thinking had saved him from being hauled
up before the local magistrate by Mr Grumpy Farmer?

The moment Milly finished rinsing her hair she
surged out of the tub on a wave of indignation. She
hadn't been able to rebel very successfully against Aunt
Charity because she'd only been a girl. But she was a
woman now. And over the last couple of days she'd discovered that she was well able to overcome whatever
fate threw in her path.

And that included deceitful dukes!

'Hand me that towel,' she said imperiously to Milly.
'And bring me those clothes.'

She was not going to let him hide her away up here
as though she was something to be ashamed of.

'Where are you going?' cried Milly when she walked
to the door and flung it open the moment she was
dressed.

'I need to have a few words with G…His Grace,'
she said, since she had no wish to offend the servants
by referring to their lord and master by the name he'd
given her. After all, her quarrel was with *him*, not them.

'Oh, no, my lady, you cannot disturb His Grace just
now,' said Milly in horror. 'He will be in his bath. He
had Sam and me fetch the water for yours first, so he's
bound to be a few minutes behind. And what with Sam
having no experience as a valet, even if His Grace is
out of his bath I shouldn't think he'll be ready to receive anyone.'

'I don't care,' she said, clenching her fists. After all,
it wasn't as if she hadn't seen it all before, was it?

Though admittedly not wet.

A rather scandalous vision popped into her head of all those rippling muscles with soapsuds sliding slowly over them.

'Oh, please, my lady,' wailed Milly, bursting the vision, and with it all the soapsuds. 'Don't go out yet!'

Prudence whirled round to see Milly wringing her hands.

'I don't want no one to see you with your hair like that.'

As Milly pointed to her head Prudence realised she still had a towel wrapped round her wet hair.

'They'll all say I can't get you presentable,' Milly continued. 'Let alone I haven't treated your blisters yet. They'll say I ain't up to the job. And then I won't be your maid no more. And I did so long to be your maid. And go to London and dress you for balls and such.'

Prudence wasn't ever going to go to London—not as the Duchess of Halstead anyway. The very idea was preposterous. She'd thought she was going to be marrying the rather hard-up and ordinary Mr Willingale—a man who made his living somehow by righting wrongs and sticking up for the underdog. Not a duke who went about the countryside in disguise as a means to alleviate his boredom. For he'd admitted he'd been leading a dull life, hadn't he?

But she did thank heaven that Milly had had the courage to speak her mind. If she'd gone barging into the Duke's room while she was so angry with him that she'd forgotten she had her hair wrapped in a towel she would have definitely embarrassed herself. Oh, yes, she could just see him lounging back in his tub, looking down his imperious nose at her, while she stood over him screeching her complaints.

'That's a good point, Milly,' she acknowledged. 'Thank you.' And she meant it. It was going to be much better to marshal her arguments so that she could break off their betrothal in a dignified manner. 'You had better dry and style my hair so that I shall look my best when I next speak to *His Grace*.'

'I shall run and fetch a comb and some scissors,' said Milly with evident relief. 'I won't be but a twinkling.'

'I will put some ointment on my feet while I'm waiting,' said Prudence, going to the dressing table on which Mrs Hoskins had placed the pot.

The minute she'd gone Prudence plonked herself down and plunged her fingers into the pot of greenish salve. Right, then. She'd use the time until Milly had made her presentable enough to appear in public to prepare a speech in which she'd explain that she couldn't marry Gregory, not now she knew who and what he really was.

But she hadn't come up with anything much before Milly returned with the scissors. And also a maid with a tea tray. And Lady Mixby.

'I hope you don't think of this as an intrusion,' said Lady Mixby. 'I just thought I would check that you have everything you need. Particularly that cup of tea you didn't drink downstairs. And just one or two little sandwiches and cakes, since you looked close to fainting. There is nothing worse, I find, than a hot bath if one is already a touch light-headed.'

There was nothing Prudence could do but say thank you.

Lady Mixby beamed at her. Then went across to the

little table on which the maid had set down the tea tray. 'I shall just pour you a cup and bring it to the dressing table while Milly makes a start on your hair. And then you can sip it and nibble at these few dainties while she works. Oh,' she said, setting the cup on the dressing table. 'I see Mrs Hoskins has found you a gown. I hope you don't mind that it appears to be dreadfully behind the fashion.'

Milly pulled her lips together and carried on doggedly combing out Prudence's tangles.

'Oh, no, I am very grateful for the dress. It is lovely to be in something clean and respectable again.'

Which was the absolute truth. Milly's Sunday best had turned out to be a rather lovely gown of mossy green wool, with a demure neckline and long sleeves. Since it was exactly the sort of thing she was used to wearing, it made her feel much more like herself instead of some kind of impostor creeping in where she had no right to be and pretending to be something she wasn't.

Milly flashed her a grateful look in the mirror as Lady Mixby went to the window seat.

'I am sure it must be,' said Lady Mixby, hitching herself up onto the cushions. 'I cannot tell you how shocked I was to see you and Halstead standing on the threshold of my drawing room looking like a pair of gypsies. Oh, but only for a moment. For then, you see, I recalled the Hilliard portrait of the First Duke. And saw that Halstead wanted only a pearl earring and a lace ruff and he would have passed for an Elizabethan privateer.'

He would, at that.

'Though I hear he has shaved now,' Lady Mixby continued, 'which is a great pity. He looked dangerously attractive with that hint of a beard.' She sighed.

'Milly, are you sure you should be using the scissors quite so freely? Poor Miss Carstairs will not have any hair left at this rate.'

'I have given Milly leave to do what is necessary,' Prudence explained when Milly's nimble fingers stilled for a second. 'It is much kinder for her to cut out the worst of the knots than attempt to remove them with the comb.'

'Well, if you are sure…'

'Oh, yes. It has been several days since I've had use of a comb, you see, and my hair has always been difficult to manage, even with regular brushing.'

Prudence had only refused to have it cut before out of a perverse determination to thwart Aunt Charity. She wouldn't mind having it all cut off now, while Milly was at it. Only just as she opened her mouth to make the suggestion she recalled the look in Gregory's eyes as he'd wound one curl round his finger. One curl of what he had called 'russet glory'.

'Several days! How perfectly frightful,' Lady Mixby was saying. 'And what kind of thief would steal a lady's comb? My goodness—what wickedness there is in the world. You must have a macaroon,' she said, hopping to her feet, going to the tea table and putting one on a plate. And then adding a couple more dainties and bringing them across.

'There. Three cakes. I was just saying to Benderby this morning how things go in threes. First Hugo came to visit, which he only does when he is quite rolled up. And then that strange Mr Bodkin person arrived, in possession of Halstead's ring. His very own signet ring, which was handed down from the First Duke—the one

I told you he resembles so nearly. Or would if he would only keep the beard and get himself a pearl earring.'

She sighed wistfully, giving Prudence the impression she had a rather romantic notion of pirates. Or Elizabethans. Or possibly both.

'That set us all in a bustle, as you can imagine. If dear Hugo hadn't been here I should have been quite terrified,' she said, absentmindedly popping the macaroon she'd fetched for Prudence into her own mouth. 'But he took charge in the most masterful way, considering his age, taking Mr Bodkin aside and getting the whole story from him before explaining it to me. At least, he explained *some* things, which all sounded highly improbable—but then when gentlemen go off in pursuit of some wager they often get tangled up with the most extraordinary company.'

Prudence was about to agree, since she'd had pretty much the same thought earlier, but Lady Mixby hadn't even paused to take breath.

'Why, you only have to think of cock pits and boxing saloons and places of that nature. Not that I have ever been in one. Nor would I wish to. They sound perfectly frightful.'

While Lady Mixby was giving a delicate little shudder at the thought of what might go on in a boxing saloon, Prudence took the opportunity to inject a word or two of her own.

'So Hugo told you all about the wager, did he?' She said it as though she knew all about it, hoping that Lady Mixby would enlighten her without her having to admit she was almost completely in the dark.

'Incredible, isn't it?' Lady Mixby's eyes widened. She leaned forward in a conspiratorial fashion. 'I would never have believed it of Halstead, had he not arrived here today without his valet and groom, looking so very unlike himself. Though, come to think of it, now I've seen his resemblance to the First Duke—who was little more than a pirate, really—I can believe him to be getting up to any amount of mischief. Not that I am implying he has done anything that is not fitting to his station in life.'

She looked at Prudence guiltily.

'*Has* he? Oh,' she added, before Prudence had a chance to draw breath. 'Not that I would blame you if you had done something you ought not... The way he looked just now, I can see exactly how it might be that you couldn't resist him. Though I would not have thought anything of the sort had you not said that about trusting him with your virtue. Oh, dear—how I do rattle on. I have ever been thus. It is why I never *took*, as a girl—why I never married. No rational man could have put up with me—that is what my father always said.'

'I'm sure that is not true,' said Prudence faintly, in the pause that came while Lady Mixby was popping a second fancy cake into her mouth.

'Dear girl,' she said, flicking crumbs from her skirt onto the expensive carpet. 'It is such a sweet thing of you to say, but the truth is we were all as poor as church mice in spite of our name. Such is the way of the world. Girls with plain faces only get proposals if they have a dowry large enough to make up for it. Whereas the veriest drabs will have oodles of men paying them court if they have money to back them,' she said with a shrug.

She was in blithe ignorance of the way she'd just plunged a knife into Prudence's already sensitised heart. Because she *did* have money, didn't she? Could that be why Gregory had tacitly accepted her proposal, in spite of the discrepancy in their rank? After all, the men in Aunt Charity's congregation had suddenly started looking at her differently once it had become common knowledge that she was heiress to the Biddlestone fortune.

Was Gregory really as mercenary as the men of Stoketown?

'But let us not dwell on the past,' said Lady Mixby, sighing and clasping her pudgy hands together. 'I am so looking forward to hearing all about how you met Halstead and how you came to fall in love. I know—you don't need to remind me,' she said, raising her hand in the air as though in surrender. 'Not a word about any of it until we are all together after dinner. Speaking of which,' she said, getting to her feet, 'I should really go and get changed. Or should I?' she said, just as she reached the door. 'Would it be terribly tactless of me to dress up when you have nothing decent to wear? Halstead himself is borrowing the Sunday clothes of the under-gardener, who is the only one of the male staff with broad enough shoulders to have a shirt that would fit. I shall ask Benderby. Such a treasure, you know. I can always rely on her to come up with a practical solution.'

The room seemed very, very quiet once Lady Mixby had left. Prudence had never come across anyone with the ability to speak continuously without pausing for breath before. Or with the tendency to flit from one subject to another like a butterfly.

How on earth could Gregory have led her to believe for one minute that Lady Mixby was a dragon? She was the very opposite. It almost seemed wrong to describe her as an aunt at all. In fact she'd been so welcoming that she'd completely dispelled the slightly oppressive atmosphere of the room. It no longer felt as though the furnishings had been expressly designed to depress the pretensions of impostors, but rather to enfold any weary guest in a sumptuous sort of embrace.

The only trouble was that now Lady Mixby had told her that one of Gregory's ancestors had been an Elizabethan pirate she couldn't help picturing him with a pearl earring and a rapier in his hand. So instead of arming herself with a quiver full of clever remarks with which to confound him, she now spent the time before dinner imagining him engaged in various nefarious pursuits. The most frequent of which imaginings involved him mounted on a black horse, holding up a stagecoach at midnight. Though the one of him lounging back in his bathtub, naked apart from some strategically placed soapsuds, came a close second.

By the time she was ready, physically, to go downstairs, she was no more prepared to cross swords with His Grace the Duke of Halstead than poor betwattled Lady Mixby would ever be.

Chapter Fourteen

'Miss Carstairs, how very much better you look,' said Gregory when she entered the dining room.

Prudence couldn't help raising one hand to her hair and flushing self-consciously. Did he really like the way she looked in this gown, with her hair neatly brushed, braided, and coiled on the top of her head?

His eyes followed the movement of her hand. He must have seen she was blushing, but his expression remained completely impassive. How different he was now from the man he'd been in that barn, when he'd described her hair as russet glory and trembled with the force of the desire he said he'd felt for her. This Gregory was a complete enigma. It was as if, the moment they'd set foot in Bramley Park, he'd deliberately snuffed out the man she'd come to know.

So how could she care so much about what he might be thinking? How could she long for him to find her as attractive as she found him, seeing him for the first time closely shaved and in a full set of clean clothes—even if they did belong to a humble gardener?

Bother Lady Mixby for putting that vision of him

with a pearl earring into her mind. Though, to be fair, she'd come up with that vision of soapsuds slithering over his naked masculine musculature all by herself.

Well, it was no use having visions of that sort. Because they were weakening her resolve to put an end to a betrothal which should never have begun.

She drew on every ounce of pride she possessed, and said, 'Thank you,' in as calm a voice as she could muster. 'The maid you sent was very proficient. It is entirely due to her,' she couldn't resist adding, 'that I no longer look as though I've been dragged through a hedge backwards.'

'You have never looked as though you had been dragged through a hedge backwards,' he said, in a manner that must have looked to everyone else like gallantry. 'Not even after you spent the night sleeping in hay.'

'Sleeping in hay?' Hugo, who'd leapt to his feet, was grinning. 'I heard a rumour that you spent last night in a barn, Halstead. And now you have confirmed it.' He rubbed his hands together in glee. 'I can't wait to hear how all this came about.'

'Come, let me place you at my right hand, Miss Carstairs,' said the Duke, ignoring Hugo as he led her to the rather small square table standing in the very centre of the room.

Hugo took the chair at his left without being asked.

'As you can see,' said Gregory witheringly. 'We are dining informally tonight.'

'I thought it for the best,' said Lady Mixby. 'All things considered.'

'Yes, but *some* of us have managed not to forget our manners,' he replied, as Mr Bodkin held out a chair for Benderby.

Hugo shot Gregory a look loaded with resentment, but didn't get to his feet. Really, he was a very badly behaved boy. He put her in mind of one of the subalterns once under her father's command, who'd come from a good family and had resented taking orders from men he regarded as his social inferiors. It had been insecurity, she'd overheard her father explain to her mother, that had made the lad so spiky and awkward, not any deep-seated malice. And once he'd proved his worth in battle his manners had greatly improved. What a pity there was no battle that Hugo could fight—that would knock some sense into him.

Benderby gave the butler a slight nod once they were all seated more or less where they wished, and he in turn marshalled Sam, his footman, into action.

'I do hope the meal will meet with your approval,' said Lady Mixby anxiously.

'I am sure it will,' said Gregory. 'Since Mrs Hoskins was not expecting us today, we can hardly expect her to have prepared anything fancy, can we?'

The housekeeper would have had a jolly good try, though. Having the Duke turn up out of the blue must have created a state bordering on panic below stairs.

'The cook here is excellent,' put in Hugo. 'I can vouch for that.'

'No doubt,' said the Duke. 'Since you have been availing yourself of his services for the past se'ennight.'

'Only five nights, in point of fact,' said Hugo smugly.

'Thank you, Hugo,' said Gregory repressively. 'There is no need to dwell on that just now. Is the soup to your liking, Miss Carstairs?' he asked, turning to her.

'The soup? You want to talk about the *soup*?'

He gave her a look that was almost as quelling as the

one he'd directed at Hugo. It made her want to seize the tureen and upend it over his head. But she wasn't going to allow him to goad her into that kind of behaviour.

'The soup is delicious,' she said, satisfying herself with imagining it dripping down his clothes.

The Duke of Halstead—for now that he was speaking in that odiously pompous manner she couldn't think of him as anything less—turned to Mr Bodkin.

'And you, Mr Bodkin? Everything is to your satisfaction, I trust?'

Mr Bodkin mumbled something indistinguishable, his face glowing an even deeper shade of red than it had been when Gregory had commended his manners while criticising Hugo's.

The poor man. As well as feeling out of place, he must now feel out of his depth, with all the undercurrents swirling between the diners seated at this table.

Lady Mixby tried to lighten the atmosphere by launching into typical dinner table conversation. But since it was mostly about people Prudence had never heard of, and events she'd never considered before, it only had the effect of making her feel a strong kinship with Mr Bodkin. And although she knew that they couldn't possibly talk about anything very confidential or meaningful in front of the servants, every time a new dish came to the table she grew more and more tempted to empty the contents over the Duke's head. Which in turn reinforced her earlier fears that she didn't belong here. Because what kind of woman would empty the soup tureen over the head of a duke?

But at length the servants stopped scurrying to and fro, ceased depositing fresh courses on the table and whisking away the old ones. Sam deftly removed the cloth and Perkins brought in a decanter of port on a silver salver. Lady Mixby stood up, signalling that it was time for the ladies to withdraw to…wherever it was that ladies went in this house. Prudence would just have to follow Lady Mixby and Benderby, who'd also risen from her place.

As she got to her feet Mr Bodkin shot her a look bordering on panic. She could heartily sympathise with his reluctance to be left to the tender mercies of Gregory and Hugo. At least while she'd been at table he hadn't been the only one feeling like a fish out of water.

Hugo had been wriggling in his seat like a schoolboy waiting to be let out of lessons for some time. He was evidently itching to have Gregory to himself so they could settle up over their wager.

As the men rose to their feet, she wondered whether she could breach protocol by inviting Mr Bodkin to join the ladies. She was just about to suggest it when Gregory picked up the decanter and made for the door which Perkins was holding open.

'Hi, where are you going with that?' Hugo objected.

'The morning room,' said Gregory. 'We shall all be more comfortable there.'

'*I* shan't,' said Hugo.

'Hugo,' Gregory growled. 'I told you I was not going to discuss…anything with you before I had explained it all to Miss Carstairs.'

'Yes, but—'

'The sooner we get it all out into the open the better,' said Gregory implacably. 'Lady Mixby, you will forgive us if just this once we break with tradition and accompany you to the morning room, won't you?'

'Of course,' she said at once. 'I am positively agog

with curiosity.' She flushed. 'Not that I... I mean of course I'm sure it is none of my business, but... Oh, do come along, Hugo!' She turned a beseeching look in his direction. 'Nothing so exciting has happened in this family for an age. I, for one, cannot wait to hear Halstead's account of how he met Miss Carstairs, and if he says he wishes to give it in the morning room then I see no reason why we shouldn't all go there at once.'

'Miss Carstairs?'

He was actually deigning to ask her opinion?

'It is well past time you explained yourself,' she said. Her patience had been stretched thinner and thinner the longer the meal had dragged on, and it wasn't going to take much for it to snap altogether. 'And if you call me Miss Carstairs once more, in that odiously pompous way, it won't be *tradition* that will be broken!'

'I say, Miss Carstairs,' said Hugo. 'I think I am beginning to like you.'

It was all she could do to resist the urge to poke out her tongue at him. He was the kind of boy who dragged everyone down to his level.

Fortunately Lady Mixby took her arm before she could poke out her tongue, or hurl any dishes, or slap anyone's face.

'I know you recall the way to the morning room, but let me get you settled into a comfortable chair—not too close to the fire, but out of any draught,' she said, leading her across the hall and into the reception room she'd been in earlier that day.

It was no longer flooded with light. The sun had moved round to shine through the windows in a different part of the house, leaving the whole room rather gloomy, in spite of the fire crackling in the grate. She wondered that the ladies chose to withdraw to *this* room in the evenings, and why they called it the morning room if it was used at other times of the day.

'Rather than have you all bombarding me with questions,' said Gregory, once they'd all taken seats in various parts of the room that Prudence thought ought more properly to be called the…the sitting room. Or the ladies' parlour. Or something that actually described the fact that ladies used it at many times of the day. 'I have decided it would be better for me to relate my story in my own words.'

Typical. *Everything* had to be his own way.

'But before I begin it occurs to me that it would be rather ungentlemanly of us to sit here drinking our port while you ladies go without refreshment. So I wonder if you would care to join us. Just this once? While we are dispensing with tradition?'

'Oh!' Lady Mixby's face lit up. 'How novel. Yes, I should *love* to try a glass of port.'

'Miss Benderby?'

'I'll not refuse, Your Grace.'

He opened his mouth, as though to ask Prudence if she'd like a glass of port, and then paused. Was he recalling her objection to him calling her Miss Carstairs in that odious manner? Was it too much to hope he was actually considering her feelings?

She turned to Lady Mixby. 'I have never tried it, either, Lady Mixby,' she said, 'and I'm not sure if I should.'

'I am sure it cannot be wrong, since His Grace has suggested it,' said Lady Mixby, making Prudence grind her teeth.

'You can have tea, if you would prefer it,' said *His*

Grace. 'I shall have to ring for more glasses anyway.
I can easily ask them to bring a pot and cups while
they're at it.'

'I will light the candles while we're waiting,' said
Benderby, getting to her feet. 'Then the servants will
have no excuse to come knocking on the door without
us sending for them.'

'Oh, what a good idea,' said Lady Mixby. 'This room
is always so gloomy in the afternoons. It will look so
much more cheerful with some light.'

So why do you sit here, then? Prudence wanted to
ask, but didn't. It would only show her up as someone
who didn't understand the way the upper classes lived
and made use of their houses.

As Benderby went round lighting the candles and
drawing the curtains Prudence succumbed to the temptation to try a glass of port. She had a feeling that a cup
of tea wasn't going to be enough to sustain her through
the rest of the evening. She was going to have to sit and
listen to Gregory explaining away the reasons he'd allowed an impertinent nobody to inveigle him into a
betrothal. Oh, why hadn't she asked to speak to him in
private earlier? They could now be explaining that it
had all been a mistake. That she'd had no idea who he
was when she'd proposed. That she was doing her best
to put things right.

Perkins arrived, and Gregory ordered him to bring
three more glasses.

'And will that be all, Your Grace?' Perkins glanced
round the room, his eyes resting briefly on the lit candles, the drawn curtains, and the full coal scuttle sitting on the hearth by the blazing fire.

'We shall ring if we require anything else,' said Gregory firmly.

Which left Perkins in no doubt that he had better not return to this room without that summons.

'I shall begin by explaining,' said Gregory to Prudence as he brought her a glass and poured just half an inch of the rich blood-red liquid into it from his decanter, 'why I told you my name is Willingale and not about my title.' He paused, his lips tightening for a second. 'I suspect that by now you have worked out that some of what I have been doing over this past week is on account of a wager I made with Hugo.'

Prudence nodded. Her feelings were so turbulent she couldn't have formed a sensible response even had she wanted to.

'Hugo is not only my nearest male relative, but my heir,' he said, sauntering across to where Hugo was lounging on an armchair and pouring a generous measure into the glass Hugo was holding out ready. 'Therefore I make him a quarterly allowance. Which he considers insufficient.'

Hugo snorted and pulled a face.

'We were having one of our regular discussions, during the course of which Hugo accused me of being miserly...'

Lady Mixby gasped. 'Oh, Hugo, how could you? Halstead is the most generous of men. You know very well he gave me a home here, saying it was so that I could look after the property which would otherwise remain empty and neglected. And he gives me a simply huge allowance. It is supposed to be for the household bills, which everyone knows his man of business settles in full because I haven't the ability to look after a…a cushion! I'm that scatterbrained. I'd only get into a scrape if I was obliged to balance the accounts, if ever I was given any to balance—which I must own I haven't.'

She paused with a frown as her speech became too tangled even for her to follow herself.

'Yes, yes, he's always been very generous to *you*,' said Hugo, as Gregory took her glass and gave her twice the amount he'd poured for Prudence. 'But he don't understand what it's like being on the Town these days. If he'd only increase my allowance I wouldn't have to keep going to him to bail me out.'

'And I repeat,' Gregory said wearily, arriving at the chair upon which Benderby was sitting and filling her glass to the brim. 'Until you learn a little sense, and stop allowing yourself to be gulled by a lot of Captain Sharps, raising your allowance will only serve to line their pockets.'

'And *I* repeat,' said Hugo, as Gregory went to the sideboard to fetch another glass. '*Anyone* can be gulled when first on the Town. It has happened to lots of my friends. So I said to him,' he said, turning to Prudence, 'that I'd like to see him exist on what he allows me out in the real world, without an army of servants at his bidding to smooth his way.'

'And I replied that not only could I exist,' said Gregory, taking the port to where the mill worker was perched on the edge of an upright chair by the window, 'I could also make myself useful—which is something Hugo has never even attempted to be.'

'Well, you can see how it was,' said Hugo to Prudence. 'He sat there behind his desk, looking down his nose at me, when he has never had any notion of what it's like to manage on a limited income, let alone have dealings with ordinary people on equal terms. So I challenged him to do it. To live for just *one week* like an ordinary man, on what he'd expect me to live on, without being obliged either to pawn something or ending up in the roundhouse.'

So *that* was why he'd been so reluctant to pawn his watch. And had been prepared to muck out a cow byre rather than risk being taken to the local magistrate. It would have meant losing the wager.

Prudence felt as if she'd been hit in the stomach by an icy fist. She'd made a fool of herself. Had sung in public and been molested by drunks because she'd thought he looked upset at the prospect of having to pawn that watch. How *could* he have let her do that?

'In my arrogance,' he said, 'I accepted. Not only to survive for one week on Hugo's terms but to achieve something useful, which I'd already stated I could do. The letter from *you*, Mr Bodkin, was lying on my desk. I had already decided to investigate your complaint. But with Hugo's challenge ringing in my ears I vowed to go in person to Wragley's and put right what was wrong, rather than just sending an agent.'

'What?' Mr Bodkin got to his feet, sloshing port over the back of his hand. 'You came up to Wragley's, pretending to be someone you're not, and goaded me into getting into a fight with my foreman, so's I lost my job and my home, because of some stupid wager?'

'Not exactly,' said Gregory. 'I *had* come to investigate the claims you'd made, and I was never pretending to be someone I'm not. My family name *is* Willingale. I just omitted to inform you of the titles I possess.'

'Aye, but—'

'I know, I know…' Gregory raised his hands in a placatory gesture. 'The foreman turned you out of your job and your home. But I did tell you, did I not, that if that happened you should come here and the Duke himself would make it all right? That if you handed the ring I gave you as a token to the lady who lived here she would take you in and house you until such time as the Duke could reinstate you?'

'Aye, but—' He rubbed the back of his hand with his other cuff.

'And I shall not only reinstate you, but will promote you to foreman, since I have excellent reason to know I can trust you to fulfil the role with complete integrity.'

Bodkin sat down abruptly. 'I never thought to... I mean, thank you, Mr Will... I mean, Your Grace,' he stammered, attempting to get to his feet again. And then sinking straight back down again under the weight of his sudden, unexpected elevation to factory foreman.

'I have already sent a letter of dismissal to Bigstone,' said Gregory. 'Though that is a mere formality.'

'Hold on a minute,' said Prudence. 'A formality? Don't you have to give a reason for dismissing one of your workers?'

There was a rustle of clothing as everyone turned to look at her as though wondering who'd spoken. Yes, they'd all forgotten she was there, so interested had they been in hearing about Gregory's determination to win his stupid wager with Hugo.

'Isn't it a gross abuse of your rank simply to turn a man off on a whim?'

'But it isn't a whim,' said Gregory, looking thoroughly perplexed. 'I have just told you—we found proof that he had not only been cheating me, but had abused his own power over the workers under him.'

'So you write one letter, explaining nothing, and—
poof! He's out on his ear. Is that how you normally op-
erate? Trampling over lesser beings as though they are
of no consequence?'

'She has a point, Halstead,' said Hugo. 'You do tend
to snap your fingers and expect everything to fall into
place.'

'It comes of being descended from a pirate, I expect,'
put in Lady Mixby.

Benderby glanced at Lady Mixby's empty port glass
with a shake of her head, while Hugo barked out a laugh.

'Yes, there have been times when you have looked as
though you'd have loved to tell me to walk the plank,'
said Hugo.

'I beg your pardon?' Gregory turned to Hugo and
raised one eyebrow in a way that somehow expressed
a sort of disdainful astonishment.

Hugo wasn't a bit cowed. 'Oh, don't bother to deny
it,' he said. 'You've wished you could be rid of me many
a time. You've told me to my face I'm just a drain on
your resources...'

Prudence remembered Gregory confessing something of the sort to her. And her reaction then: that he
wasn't really bad enough to do anything of the sort.

'And if it wasn't for the fact that my existence has
spared you from having to marry again,' Hugo continued, 'you'd wash your hands of me...'

That jolted her right back to her own dilemma.
Which was how to extricate themselves from a betrothal
she was becoming increasingly convinced he couldn't
possibly want.

'No, I would not,' said Gregory. 'I may find you extremely tiresome, but I would *never* wish any harm to

come to you.' He glanced at Prudence, as though recall-ing the very same conversation. 'Hugo…' He sighed. 'I have only ever wanted you to learn habits of economy because of the immense responsibilities you will have to carry. Hundreds of people's welfare will be in your hands. You will not wish to let them down.'

Hugo winced. 'I'm sick of hearing about duty and responsibility and not letting the family down. Espe-cially since, as Lady Mixby has just pointed out, our an-cestors got away with being pirates. Or leading armies into mad battles. Or offering up their womenfolk to the King for a mistress. All of which would be considered scandalous these days, apart from going into battle— but, since as an only son I'm too precious to risk having my blood spilled on foreign soil, apparently I cannot even make my mark that way.' He sat back and folded his arms across his chest.

Gregory blinked. 'So that accounts for your freakish starts, does it? The notoriety of our ancestors? Com-bined with the frustration of being constricted and robbed of any real challenge?' He paused, seeming to gather himself together. 'Much as I hate to admit it, I think I can see what you mean. For something of the sort went through my mind when you issued your wager. How, I wondered, would I have fared on a battle-field, like the Fifth Duke? Or on a voyage of discovery, like the First? When, as you had so recently pointed out, I had never been permitted out of doors without a retinue of servants to smooth my path.'

Something jogged Prudence's memory, too. Gregory confiding that he'd never climbed a tree as a boy. And then his clumsy attempt to do so. And then the look of utter triumph blazing from his face when he not only scaled it, but helped her up and over the wall, too.

She took a sip of her port as she mulled this over. She could see, she supposed, why he'd felt he had to prove himself, if he'd been so coddled and cosseted all his life. She could see how tempting it must have been to take up Hugo's wager. She only had to think of the way he'd reacted to her own challenge to think of other ways to deal with the loss of their transport. He'd not only taken her up on it, but raised the stakes—the way he'd done with Hugo.

It was simply part of his nature to rise to any challenge. And master it.

It was part of what made her admire him so much.

Not that it excused him for allowing her to believe he was the kind of man she could marry, when he clearly wasn't. Girls with an upbringing like hers didn't marry dukes. She didn't know how to move in the elevated circles to which he belonged. Why, she couldn't even join in the kind of conversations he held over a dinner table. Let alone penetrate the mystery of why a room was called a morning room when people used it in the evenings.

Prudence must have made some kind of sound, expressing her turmoil, because he turned to look at her, a question in his eyes. She was just lifting her chin to stare him down when Lady Mixby startled everyone.

'And of course you were already in low spirits,' she observed. 'With it being the anniversary of Millicent's death.'

He whirled on her, a look of complete shock on his face. Quickly concealed. So quickly that Prudence was probably the only person in the room who noticed.

'I recall it being close to Easter, you see...' Lady Mixby was carrying on, blithely unaware of having provoked such a strong reaction in a man who was trying so hard not to show any. 'I was bitterly disappointed at having to go into black gloves just when I was hoping to start enjoying all the pleasures of the season. I dare say that every time Easter comes round your mind gets jogged by little things that throw you right back to that terrible time. The daffodils coming into bloom, for instance. I can never see daffodils bobbing in the breeze but I think of that churchyard, and how sunny and cheerful it all looked in spite of the terrible tragedy you'd just suffered. To lose your wife so suddenly, and she so young... Well, you both were...'

She ground to a halt, finally noticing the grim way Gregory was staring at her.

'Oh, dear me. I do beg your pardon. How tactless of me...'

'Not at all,' he said through clenched teeth. 'Your remark was most perceptive. And your memory is perfectly correct. It was at Easter-tide when Millicent passed. The very date that Hugo came to me. A day I always wonder whether—'

The Duke of Halstead—Prudence *must* get used to calling him that, since she could never allow him to be anything more to her—stalked away from them all. Twitched the curtains aside and stared out of the window for a moment. Lowered his head. Raised it, took a deep breath, and turned round.

'And so I decided,' he said, raising his chin with a touch of defiance. 'To find out, once and for all, whether I was worthy of the name Willingale, or whether I was merely a shadow of a man. An apparition created by the brilliance of my title blazing over a great mound of wealth. Hugo had offered me the perfect way to find out. Because, as he's already pointed out, I could never seriously consider joining a regiment and fighting in a battle, nor sailing away to India on a merchantman—not with all the obligations I have. But I thought that perhaps my estates could do very well without me for just one week.'

Prudence recalled the things he'd told her about his wife and how she'd made him feel. And then she thought of Hugo blundering in, in the completely insensitive way that young men do, and challenging him when he had already been questioning himself.

Her heart went out to him. Beneath the pompous exterior he'd adopted since coming here and taking up his role as Duke was a man who was painfully aware of his own faults and failings. Even the way he had just spoken made him sound more like the Gregory she'd known before they'd come to Bramley Park and he'd turned into the self-contained Duke of Halstead.

She still felt hurt by his deception, but she could see why he'd set out on what had been far more than just a silly wager between two bored, titled gentlemen. He'd wanted to prove himself.

'Well, now you know,' said Hugo with a smile of triumph. 'Because you *couldn't* last a week on your own with only the resources available to me. So I've won.'

'On the contrary,' Gregory drawled quietly. 'I could very easily have stayed out the full week if I'd thought fulfilling the terms of the wager I had with you was the most important consideration. But by that time it wasn't.'

'It's all very well saying that *now*—' said Hugo.

Prudence's heart began to flutter. Because Gregory had turned to her and was looking at her in exactly the same way he'd looked at her when he'd kissed her, that second time, in the shrubbery.

'You can say whatever you like, Hugo,' said Gregory, without taking his eyes from her. 'I have nothing to prove to myself or anyone else any longer.'

Chapter Fifteen

Her heart plummeted. She'd so hoped he'd been going to say he'd decided she was more important than winning the wager. Instead he'd more or less said that nobody's feelings mattered but his own.

'I have learned a lot of things during the course of this week,' he said, turning to Hugo. 'That I am every bit as resilient and inventive as any of my ancestors. I got myself to Wragley's in disguise, located the false ledgers, and subsequently fought my way out. And then I extricated Miss Carstairs from the clutches of a pair of villains, survived the consequences of a robbery which left us penniless, and faced down a farmer with a gun.'

'I say, it does sound as though you've had an adventure,' said Hugo, with what looked like a touch of jealousy. 'You should be thanking me.'

'Yes,' he replied, looking a little taken aback. 'I suppose I should.'

'That wasn't what you said before,' Prudence pointed out. 'You practically accused me of being in league with Hugo to make you lose the wager,' she said bitterly.

'What?' Hugo sat up straight. 'You thought I'd stoop to cheating?'

'Well, you did procure that vile creature I hesitate to describe as a horse, and the most broken-down vehicle it has ever been my misfortune to drive. Can you wonder that I thought you were attempting to prevent me from even reaching Wragley's in the first place?'

'Oh, that,' said Hugo with a dismissive wave of his hand. 'That was just in the nature of a jest. You are never seen out on the road except in a spanking rig with the most magnificent horseflesh between the shafts. I thought it would be fun to see you brought down a peg.'

'Hence the clothes, too?'

Hugo grinned, completely unabashed. 'That's it. Though you have to admit the disguise I provided did the job, didn't it? Neither Bodkin nor Miss Carstairs suspected for one minute that you're actually a duke, did they? And you should have seen how inventive I was with reasons for your disappearance from London. Just as the Season was getting started, too. *Everyone* wanted to know where you were.'

'The only person who might have been really worried by my absence,' said Gregory repressively, 'and might have had the gall to demand answers, would have been Jenkins. And I'd already sent him to Ely to make sure I'd have a change of horses at all the posting houses en route. But never mind all that now,' he said, turning to Prudence. 'I admit when we first met I was so fuddled that I couldn't believe anyone but Hugo could be responsible for what was happening to us. And, yes, I was still obsessed with winning at that point. But the moment I knew you really had been the victim of a crime I decided to bring you straight here. Which meant forfeiting the wager.'

Oh. Now he came to mention it, she *did* recall the rather determined look that had flashed across his face when he'd said he was going to bring her here *straight away*.

'Surely you can tell that by the time we reached that barn none of that mattered any more?'

She recalled the way he'd held her all night. He had not only kept her warm, but had made her feel safe. Cherished.

He seized hold of her hands. 'What matters now is the future we can make together.'

A maelstrom of conflicting emotions surged through her—hope, longing, suspicion, fear. They brought tears to her eyes.

'We cannot make a future together.'

It wasn't what he really wanted. Why, Hugo had said he'd rather cut off his arm than marry again.

'What? What are you saying?'

'That I cannot marry you.' She reached inside herself for the little speech she'd prepared. 'We only met because of the sordid, money-grubbing plot hatched by my aunt and that vile man she married—'

'Which I can easily thwart. They cannot very well accuse you of having loose morals once you have married a duke. They wouldn't dare risk the notoriety and expense of challenging your grandfather's bequest with me at your back, either.'

'But I am not,' she said grimly, 'going to marry you.'

'Nonsense—of course you are,' said Gregory.

'There is no "of course" about it,' she snapped.

'Then why on earth did you propose to me?'

There was a gasp from Lady Mixby. And Hugo, who'd been in the act of taking a sip of port, sprayed ruby-red droplets in all directions. But Gregory didn't appear to notice.

'And why do you think I accepted?' he continued, in the teeth of her determination to set him free and the muted sounds of shock emanating from every other person in the room.

Damn Prudence for getting him so worked up that his usual mastery over his emotions, over his actions and speech, had totally deserted him. How could he be standing here with his cousin, his aunt, her companion, and a virtual stranger watching while he blurted out things he'd vowed nobody should ever know?

'But you didn't,' said Prudence, to his complete astonishment, relegating what anyone else in the room might think to a very minor position.

'Yes, I did!'

He cast his mind back. Came up blank.

'That is, I may not have said in plain speech, *Thank you, Prudence, yes, of course I will marry you*, but you knew I'd accepted. I spoke of our marriage the next day as a *fait accompli*. Subsequently I introduced you to everyone in this house as my fiancée. The wedding will follow as a matter of course.'

'It doesn't need to, though.'

She gazed at him in the way she did when she'd made up her mind about something.

'Yes, it does need to,' he said, scrambling for a reason that would reach her. 'I have…er…tarnished your reputation. You admitted as much in front of Lady Mixby.'

'Tarnished—fiddlesticks! Now that I know you are a

duke I'm certain you could dispose of me in some other way than by marrying me.'

'Perhaps I do not wish to dispose of you.'

'Of course you do. You cannot seriously wish to marry a mere Miss Carstairs, from Stoketown. What will everyone say?'

'I do not care what anyone will say. In fact I care so little that I have already sent the notice of our betrothal to the *Gazette*.'

'Well, you will just have to *un*send it, then!' She stamped her foot. 'I mean, send another letter telling them it was a mistake. I'm sure it will catch up with the first before it gets into print. You cannot marry me just because I've admitted, to *one* person, that we spent a night together.'

'And to the other people present. Besides,' he put in swiftly, 'this is not just about restoring your reputation, Prudence. It is about justice. Can't you see what would come of letting people like your guardians think they can go around abusing their position of trust? Or what it would mean if it ever got out that they'd tricked a duke, and that duke had let them get off scot-free?'

He simply could not permit anyone to cross him, or wound those he loved.

'Justice?' She looked pensive. 'Well, I suppose…'

'Obviously,' he plunged in, seizing upon what looked like a weak spot in her defences, 'not only must they return the money they thought to steal from you, but they must also be suitably punished.'

'Punished?' She looked at him rather reproachfully. 'Is that really necessary? Wouldn't depriving them of my money be punishment enough?' She pulled her hands from his. 'If you persist in hounding my aunt

she could end up in prison. Which would destroy her.
And I'd never forgive myself. Because she isn't a bad
person—not really. Until she married Mr Murgatroyd
she tried to do her duty by me, even though she found
it so hard. And who could blame her? My grandfather
left me the money she considered hers.'

'Did he not also leave her a similar sum?'

A frown flickered across her face. 'Well, yes,' she
said. 'I suppose he must have done. She was certainly
considered well-to-do.'

'But instead of being satisfied with her own inheritance she decided to rob you of yours, too?'

'No... I don't think she did. I think it was Mr Murgatroyd who put the notion in her head.'

'Nevertheless, she went along with it.'

'Isn't a wife supposed to obey her husband?' she
shot back.

'In theory. From experience, however, I can testify
that it is rarely the case.'

'Well, I'm sure it was in this case. Because Mr Murgatroyd isn't the sort of man a woman *can* disobey.'

'And yet she married him. Even though she was well-
to-do. She didn't have to do any such thing. And don't
forget I was on the receiving end of her diatribe that
morning in The Bull. She put on a performance worthy
of Drury Lane. Flung herself into the role of aggrieved
guardian of an ungrateful, unruly ward with a gusto
that had nothing to do with coercion.'

'Do you *have* to rub it in?' she complained, rubbing
at her arms. 'Don't you understand how much it hurts
already to know that they could do such a thing to me?'

Of course he understood. Didn't she see that was
exactly why he'd spent that sleepless night in the barn,

working out ways and means to see the pair of them destroyed? *Utterly* destroyed!

He tried to take her hand again. She hid it behind her back as though she couldn't bear to let him touch her.

'Well anyway,' she said firmly, 'there isn't any point in arguing about something that won't happen. For we will not be getting married.'

'Why do you persist in saying that?' He was starting to feel as if he was standing on quicksand. No matter what argument he put forth to smooth away the obstacles in their path, she persisted in trying to avoid walking down it with him.

'Because we cannot possibly marry.'

'I don't see why.' He'd never gone to such lengths for a woman in his life. He'd forfeited the wager, and he was now sacrificing his pride by standing here arguing with her about what should be a private matter in front of his family. What did she want from him? What more could he do?

'For heaven's sake, I didn't know who you were when I proposed!'

The way he saw it, she knew him better than anyone else ever had. It was only his title he'd hidden from her. Not who he really was.

'I don't know why you are being so stubborn about this,' she complained. 'You told me how much you hated women trying to trap you into marriage.'

'What? When did I say any such thing?'

'Practically the whole of that first day we were together. You accused me of being in league with Aunt Charity to do so.'

'Not in so many words,' he replied uncomfortably, aware that he *might* actually have planted the seeds of doubt in her mind that were bearing such bitter fruit today.

'But it was what you believed.'

'Not for very long,' he pointed out. 'I soon worked out that the plot was against you, not me. And that I was dragged into it purely by chance.'

'Yes, but it infuriated you, nonetheless. Now that I know you are a duke I can see why. And also why you cannot allow this foolish betrothal to stand.'

Foolish? His feelings might sound foolish to her, perhaps. But there were other reasons for the marriage which she must surely appreciate. Since they were all of a practical nature. And she was the most practical female he'd ever met.

'Then may I just remind you of the advantages of letting this betrothal stand? Once we are married I will be able to restore your inheritance—'

'Oh,' she gasped. 'So that is what this is all about. My inheritance!' Her face went white, but her eyes blazed with indignation. 'Yes, you… I remember now…you only started looking on me with interest once I told you about it. You—' She sat down hastily, one hand pressed to her mouth. As though she felt sick.

Not that she could possibly feel as sick as he did.

How could she accuse him of only wanting to marry her to get his hands on her money? How could she ignore everything he'd done for her, everything they'd been through together?

If that was what she thought of him, *really* thought of him, then they didn't have any future, did they?

He stalked to the window and stared out into the blackness. The same blackness that was swirling within him.

'Miss Carstairs, I beg your pardon,' he said, turning to face them all again. His face had turned hard. And his eyes were so cold they might have been chiselled from ice. 'It appears I have been labouring under a misapprehension. Naturally, if you have changed your mind about wishing to marry me, then you have the right to cry off. It is perfectly acceptable since it is an established fact,' he said, with a cynical twist to his mouth, 'that women change their minds as swiftly and unpredictably as the weather changes in spring.'

It felt as though he'd just plunged a dagger into her stomach. For a while there, when they'd been arguing, he'd begun to seem like the Gregory she'd thought she knew.

Now he'd turned back into the Duke of Halstead.

'You need only say the word, Miss Carstairs, to end this farcical betrothal.'

Farcical? Was that how he saw it?

Well, of course he did. She was a nobody. She still couldn't really understand why he'd kept on insisting they had to get married. Everyone knew he never wanted to marry anyone ever again—let alone her. And it was farcical for two people who'd only known each other for such a short time to get married. Especially two people from such different social spheres.

'I shall, of course, ensure you have the means to live comfortably until your own money is restored. After all, if you refuse to go through with the ordeal of marrying me then there is no reason for me to pay heed to your ridiculous plea for clemency for your aunt, is there? Until such time as she releases it, however, you may stay here. Or at one of my other properties, if you prefer.'

What had she done? Insulted him to a point past

bearing—that was what. Because marrying him *wouldn't* have been an ordeal. Not if he hadn't been a duke anyway.

How could she have been such an idiot? Gregory had never given her cause to suspect him of double-dealing. He'd been chivalrous to the point of…of saintliness! Any ordinary man would have washed his hands of her after she'd thrown that rock at him, but what had *he* done? Lent her his coat and bought her breakfast.

Even after she'd insulted him in the worst possible way just now, by accusing him of avarice, he was still going to do all that was necessary to get justice for her, to get her money back and ensure she had somewhere to stay while he was doing it.

But she'd had years of being an obligation already. She couldn't face forcing him to stick by a betrothal he'd considered farcical from the very first.

She opened her mouth to say the words that would end a betrothal that should never have begun.

And hesitated.

There was no consolation at all in telling herself she was about to do the right thing.

But she loved him too much to let him put his head in what he considered to be a noose.

She bowed her head and squeezed her eyes shut. Loved him? How could she have fallen in love in such a short space of time? Why, because she was her mother's daughter, that was why. Her mother—who'd fallen in love with a handsome young officer at the assembly and run away with him before a week was out.

Oh, Lord, but Aunt Charity was right about her. She was the amalgam of all the worst traits of her parents. Not only did she have her mother's impulsiveness, she had inherited a hefty dollop of her father's stubborn pride, too. That was what had made it so hard for her to swallow the discovery that Gregory was a duke. She'd had no qualms about proposing marriage when she'd believed she had the upper hand. When she'd felt as if she was graciously bestowing her hand upon a penniless but worthy suitor. But when he'd turned the tables on her...

She hated having nothing to bring to this union. Becoming a burden again. An obligation. And she'd rather retain at least a sliver of pride than face a lifetime of such humiliation.

She lifted her head and regarded him bleakly.

'Very well,' she said. 'I release you.'

And, just to prove how sensible she could be, she ran from the room.

She ran all the way up the stairs, so that she reached her room out of breath. There she was immediately challenged by the luxurious carpet, which lay, just like his title, directly in her path. She pulled off her worn-down shoes, wishing she could as easily discard her grubby background, then dropped them by the door, wishing it was as simple a matter to dispose of the way they'd met. Or the things she'd said to him just now. Things that had hurt and alienated him.

She ran across the sumptuous carpet and threw herself face-down on the bed. But even there the pristine eiderdown wouldn't give her leave simply to burst into tears. Not until she'd squirmed her way up the bed and got her face into a pillow out of which salt stains would wash could she really let go.

Chapter Sixteen

It was the most selfless and also the most stupid thing she'd ever done.

She could have been his wife. *His wife!*

And now her life stretched out before her as a long, grey, barren vista. Because he wouldn't be a part of it. He was too proud to remain friends with her. Even if he never managed to extract her money from Aunt Charity—because there was every chance Mr Murgatroyd had somehow lost it all anyway—and she became his pensioner, he'd take good care to avoid her. His pride would demand it.

She didn't know how she would bear it.

She'd been alone before. During those long, dreary years with Aunt Charity she'd felt terribly alone. But it would be as nothing compared to the misery of being without him.

She was just reaching for a handkerchief to blot up the tears when the door burst open so forcefully it banged against the wall and bounced back onto the man who stood there, breathing hard and looking as if he was about to commit murder.

'Gregory!' She sat up and swiped at the tears streaming down her face. 'What are you doing in here?'

He stalked across to the bed.

'Firstly, I want to know how much, exactly, you stood to inherit from your grandfather. Since you accused me of wishing to marry you so that I could get my hands on it.'

'I was very wrong to think that,' she said. 'I know now you wouldn't have done anything so underhand. It isn't *you*.'

'How much, Prudence?' He planted his hands on his hips and glowered down at her.

She supposed it didn't matter now. 'It was ten thousand pounds.'

He raised one eyebrow. 'Per year?'

'No. Ten thousand pounds total. In trust.'

He gave a bark of bitter laughter. 'I could drop that amount in one session at White's and not turn a hair. Haven't you taken a good look at this house? Don't you realise it's only one of my smaller properties? So far from London or any of the race courses that I chose it only as a rendezvous for settling up with Hugo? And you heard what Lady Mixby said about me letting her run tame here. What kind of man can afford a profligate widgeon like her for a pensioner, do you suppose?'

She swallowed. It had been bad enough to learn of the discrepancy in their rank. But now...

'My main seat is in Sussex,' he continued. 'It is one of the largest houses in the country. I employ hundreds of servants in my houses, and untold numbers in my factories, mines and farms.'

A cold hollowness opened up inside her. He was *that*

rich? So rich that her ten thousand pounds was like a drop in an ocean? Oh, to think she'd accused him of wanting to gain control of her money. What had seemed like a fortune to a girl born into an army family, then brought up amongst the middle classes, turned out to be small change in the world Gregory inhabited.

So why had he been so determined to stick to a betrothal *she'd* instigated when she couldn't even bring what he'd think of as wealth to the union?

Why, precisely for the reasons he'd given. Because he'd wanted to restore her damaged reputation. And to be in a strong position to bring her guardians to justice. And get her money back *for her*.

All very fine, honourable motives. None of which would have been of any benefit to him.

And she'd flung it all back in his face.

No wonder he'd looked at her with such coldness. No wonder he'd stalked away and turned his back on her. She couldn't have offered him a worse insult if she'd been trying.

'So that's that point dealt with,' he said. 'Secondly, let us discuss your attitude to the wager I had with Hugo. I saw your face when he said one of the conditions was that I was not supposed to pawn anything. What do you suspect me of there?'

She sighed. He was determined to make her eat her words. Even the ones she'd only thought.

'I felt like an idiot for not understanding why you'd been so reluctant to pawn your watch. I thought at the time that it was because it had some sentimental value to you, but now I can see that it meant you losing the wager.'

'I concede,' he said, 'that I was smarting over having to sink to the depths of visiting a pawn shop. But I told you later, didn't I, that I regretted not doing all in my power to bring you here safely? You must know by now that your welfare had become more important than winning a wager that I'd agreed to in a fit of…of temporary insanity?'

She recalled his horror when he'd seen the state of her feet. His words of contrition.

'I know you were sorry you'd let me walk all day with no stockings on,' she conceded, 'once you saw my blisters. But I can't help wondering if you agreed to my suggestion to leave the horse where it was because you were still trying to delay meeting up with Hugo until the agreed time.'

'It was not a deliberate delaying tactic,' he said, coming to stand over her. 'And you know how much I detested that horse. I was downright glad at the prospect of never having to set eyes on it again.'

She didn't like the way he was towering over her.

'You let me sing in the market square,' she pointed out, surging to her feet so she wouldn't feel quite so far beneath him. 'I was accosted by those drunken fops…'

'I didn't *let* you sing in the market square. I couldn't stop you. You even stole my hat to collect the takings.'

They were standing toe to toe now, just the way they had stood when they'd been arguing at the foot of the market cross.

'And don't forget,' he said, pointing his finger at her, 'that this morning I climbed the wall of my own property so you wouldn't have to walk all the way round to the front gate. Is that the act of a man who is trying to delay his return?'

'I suppose not,' she admitted grudgingly. 'But—'

'But nothing. You have no reason to break our betrothal. So I am not going to permit you to do anything so foolish—do you hear me?'

She gaped at him.

'But *why*? I mean, you cannot *possibly* want to marry me.'

'I want to know why you persist in saying that, Prudence. When I have given no indication that that is the case.'

'But… Well…' She twisted the handkerchief between her fingers. '*I* asked *you* to marry me. And you were thinking about it, I do believe, because you wanted to…to bed me,' she finished in a rush, her cheeks heating. 'And then in the morning, when the farmer found us and I sort of embellished our relationship so he wouldn't haul us off for trespass, I can see that you had to go along with it. And then, when we got here, I suppose you felt honour-bound to introduce me as your fiancée since you hadn't found the words to let me down gently.'

'What utter nonsense! If I hadn't wanted to marry you I would have introduced you to my family as a lady under my protection. I am a selfish man, Prudence. Nobody can make me do anything I don't want.'

'What are you saying?' She rubbed her forehead, where a vein was starting to throb.

He strolled to the foot of the bed and propped one shoulder up against the post.

'You do realise,' he said coldly, 'that after this episode you will be completely ruined?'

'Wh…what? Why?'

Was he threatening her? Saying that since she'd refused to marry him he wouldn't help her get her money back? No, no, that couldn't be it. He wouldn't do something so despicable.

Would he?

'Most women would kill to have been in your shoes,' he said. 'Betrothed to me, that is. No matter how the betrothal had come about. Nobody is ever going to believe you cried off. They will say that I jilted you—do you realise that? They will speak of you as my leavings. Is that what you really want?'

'No, of course I don't!' She gasped, sickened by the picture he'd painted of a future of shame. 'But surely you can see it will be even worse for you if we were to marry? I *had* to let you off the hook—can't you understand? If I made you stick to a vow you gave under duress I'd feel as if I was no better than…than…' She shook her head, at a total loss to think of anyone she could imagine doing anything worse than forcing a man into a marriage he didn't really want.

'So you maintain you broke the betrothal for *my* benefit?'

'Yes. You deserve better.'

'Isn't that for me to decide?'

'Well anyway, it's too late now.'

'No, it isn't,' he said. Then he strode back to her side of the bed and dropped down on one knee. 'I can see that I have made you think I am a touch reluctant to enter into the matrimonial state for a second time. So this time round *I* am asking *you*. So you can have no doubt it is what I want. Prudence…' He took hold of her hands. 'Would you do me the very great honour of becoming my wife?'

All the breath whooshed from her lungs, leaving her head spinning.

'You cannot mean that—'

'Why not?'

'Because you said…and Hugo said you'd rather cut off your arm than marry again—that everyone knows it.'

'You are surely not going to base your entire future on what Hugo says?'

'No, but he—'

'Prudence, listen to me,' he said sternly. 'You told me once—do you recall?—that you were reluctant to marry because you wanted to be free. Yet you changed your mind and proposed to me. Why can you not believe that meeting you has changed my view of matrimony, too?'

'But you—'

'Yes, I stood over Millicent's grave and vowed that no woman would have a hold over me ever again. I admit it. And I have never let another woman close. And I *did* gain a reputation in society, which I freely confessed to you, for keeping my numerous *affaires* on a purely physical level. I was determined that no woman would ever reduce me to the state she did.'

'Exactly! Which is why I cannot bear to back you into a corner now. You got all tangled up in my troubles, and now you—'

'Hush.'

He reached up to place one finger against her lips. It was all she could do not to purse them and kiss it.

'Look at me now. I am on my knees, asking you to marry me. I don't *have* to. Last time I *had* to marry a woman chosen for me by my parents. This time I am asking you to marry me because I *want* to.'

Her heart lurched. She wanted to say yes. Oh, how

she wanted to say yes. But all the obstacles that made their union impossible still existed.

'But I'm a nobody!' she wailed. She had a vision of a flock of outraged society matrons pointing their fingers at her and wagging their heads in disapproval if ever she appeared in public on his arm. Then going into a huddle and whispering about how she'd snared poor Gregory. Which would make her look scheming, and him like a pigeon for plucking. 'Worse, I'm the product of a runaway match. I grew up following the drum, for heaven's sake!'

'Yes, I've been thinking about that,' he said, 'and talking to Lady Mixby, who remembers all the old scandals. Your father wouldn't happen to be the same Edmund Carstairs who ran off with a girl he met at an assembly in some out-of-the-way place in the north where he was stationed while he was in the militia, would he?'

'Well, yes…' she admitted.

'Then you are from a good family.'

'Not directly. I mean, yes, my *father* was well-born, but once he married my mother he was entirely cut off from them all. And they never acknowledged me. Not even once both my parents had died. It was the Biddlestones who took me in when I became an orphan.'

Even though they'd done so grudgingly. And ended up betraying her.

'That will not be an obstacle to your social success. Everyone knows what a clutch-fisted man your grandpapa Carstairs is. People will be only too ready to believe he didn't want the expense of bringing you out, if we start rumours to that effect.'

'Why would we do any such thing?'

'To smooth your path, of course. Not that it will need all that much smoothing. For heaven's sake, your Carstairs grandfather is an earl, didn't you know that? The Earl of Sterndale. Which makes you perfectly eligible. The granddaughter of an earl may go anywhere, and marry as high as she pleases.'

'I don't think of myself that way. Not after the way he repudiated me when Papa sent me to him—'

'Yes, but since then your father has died a hero, hasn't he? And even I remember rumours about how your grandfather shut himself away for a week and was as surly as a bear when he came out. I shouldn't be a bit surprised to learn that he will acknowledge you now joyfully. Particularly if you are presented to him as my duchess,' he finished with a cynical twist to his lips. 'So that acknowledging you won't cost him a penny.'

She sucked in a deep, painful breath. Then forced herself to say what had to be said.

'In other words you are going to have to spend the rest of your life making excuses. Explaining me away. I had enough of that with Aunt Charity. And I couldn't bear it if you...' She turned her hands over in his and gripped his. 'I don't want you always to be ashamed of me.'

'Ashamed of you?' His eyes widened in surprise. 'Why should you think I could ever be ashamed of you?'

'Because you already are.'

'No, I'm not.'

'You are. From the very first moment we got here, and your butler practically had an apoplexy at the sight of me, you have been obliged to make all sorts of excuses to explain me away.'

'Perkins is far too good at his job to have anything like an apoplexy,' countered Gregory. 'And anyway, I don't care what servants think.'

'But *I* do. I don't want people whispering about me wheedling my way into your life. Or you being made to feel as though you need to hide anything about my past—which you've just admitted you would have to.'

Gregory's brows drew down. 'For heaven's sake, woman, the only reason I have come up with ways to smooth your path into society is because *you* are making an issue of your past. Nobody else cares or they wouldn't be so keen to see us wed.'

'They…your family…are keen to see us wed?'

'Admittedly Hugo is thinking primarily of himself. Once I start producing my own heirs he thinks he will be free to live as he pleases, instead of having to train to be a duke. And even as I stormed from the room, vowing I'd make you change your mind, Lady Mixby was wittering on about how romantic it was and how she was going to look forward to introducing you to society by means of a grand ball.'

She looked at him then. Really looked at him. With a growing surge of hope swelling in her heart. Because all she could see in his eyes was determination.

'So long as you aren't ashamed of me…'

'Never!'

She wished she could believe him. But actions spoke louder than words. 'Then why did you send me to my room the moment we got here?'

'Need I remind you that you were *trembling*? Which you'd never done before. Not even when you were woken by a farmer with a gun. At first I couldn't think why you were so overset. But then I reasoned that if even *I* felt self-conscious, because I smelled of the cow byre and looked like a vagrant, then it must be ten times as bad for you. I was at least among my own family—you were facing a set of strangers. Hugo was being abominably rude, and Lady Mixby was being…' He compressed his lips for a second. 'Lady Mixby. I thought you'd feel better able to deal with them all in a…er…complete set of clean clothes. And naturally you were upset with me, too, for not being completely honest about my identity. I hoped that if you had a chance to calm down you'd be able to see things weren't as black as they seemed. Besides, you needed to get your feet treated,' he finished on a shrug.

Once more she'd misjudged his motives. She'd been so angry, so hurt, when he'd hustled her upstairs, because it had put her in mind of the way she'd been treated by her aunt. She'd assumed he wanted her out of the way, too. Because she had already felt betrayed on discovering he'd been hiding so much from her when she'd thought they'd been so close.

But Gregory had been thinking of her all along. Not only that, but he'd pretty accurately judged how she'd been feeling during that first awkward meeting with his family. Even down to his oblique reference to her lack of decent underwear.

'Oh, you dear, dear man,' she said, reaching out her hand to caress his cheek.

He grabbed at it. 'Shall I take that as a yes?'

Chapter Seventeen

'Oh, Gregory…' She sighed. 'I wish I could say yes—I really do…'

He surged to his feet. 'You cannot possibly still be harbouring any doubts, surely?'

'I cannot help having a few,' she protested. 'I mean, when I suggested marriage I thought I had many practical reasons for doing so. Only when we got here they all turned out to be nonsense.'

'What do you mean, nonsense?'

'I have no title, nor even a fortune—not by your standards. I suddenly felt as if I had nothing to bring to our marriage except disgrace. So I couldn't understand why you seemed content to go along with it unless it was because you didn't want to go back on your word, once given. And anyway, had I known at the time you were a duke of course I'd never have been so…so…*forward* as to dare propose in the first place.'

'Which is one of the reasons I didn't tell you,' he said grimly. 'Don't you have any idea what it did for me when you whispered that shy proposal in that barn? To know you were willing to trust your fortune to me, thinking I had nothing? Prudence, nobody has ever thought I was of any account.'

'Of course they have,' she said, frowning. 'You're a *duke*.'

'No,' he groaned. 'You don't understand. Me.' He beat his chest with the flat of his free hand. 'This. The man. You heard Hugo. He said what everyone else thinks. That I am nothing without the title, and the wealth, and the body of servants whose only function is to maintain my dignity. Even my wife—' He stopped, his face contorting with remembered pain. 'You are the only person who has ever seen *me*. Wanted me. Gregory. Just Gregory.'

'But you are not just Gregory, though, are you? Can you not understand why I have felt as though I can't marry you?' She cupped his lean jaw with one hand. 'I wouldn't know how to begin to be a duchess. I'm so ordinary.'

'Not to me, you aren't! You are the only woman I have ever spent an entire day with. The only one I have ever held in my arms all night. The only one I could imagine ever wanting to do either with.'

'Are you sure,' she asked, searching his earnest face, 'that it isn't all because of the extraordinary adventure we've had? That once you get back to your real life you will wake up and realise you were carried away on a tide of…of recklessness, or something? I mean, when I proposed to you, you said I'd have changed my mind by the morning, once it was clear of that drug.'

'My mind is completely clear now,' he said earnestly. 'And I swear I will never grow tired of you, Prudence. Because you have seen *me*. The man I am inside. You looked right past the title—'

'Which was only because I didn't know it was there,' she pointed out.

'Even now you know I have it you would rather I didn't, which is completely astonishing. Do you think I could lightly let such a rare treasure slip through my fingers? A woman who sees me and not the title?'

'But you almost did, though, didn't you? You practically *invited* me to break off the betrothal. Just now.'

'I felt as though you'd ripped my guts out when you did it.'

'I felt as though I'd ripped out my own, too. Especially as you went all cold and hard and didn't seem to care. My only consolation was thinking that if you really didn't care then I'd done the right thing by you.'

'You little fool,' he grated, gripping her shoulders. 'Couldn't you tell it was pride that made me let you go? Pride that made me vow you wouldn't reduce me to grovelling, the way Millicent made me grovel? Not in front of my family anyway. It took me about two minutes to work out that if I could get you alone all I would have to do was kiss you and you would do anything I wanted.' He shook his head, as though in disbelief. 'But the moment I saw you lying there, weeping, I knew that kissing you into submission wasn't the answer. That I needed to break down all the barriers you'd thrown up between us, no matter how much I hurt you in the process.'

'You were a bit ruthless,' she admitted.

'Because I was fighting for *us*,' he said.

And not grovelling. He would never do anything that smacked of grovelling. But then, nor would she.

'And I'm about to be more ruthless still,' he said grimly. 'Because I cannot help thinking that if I'd made you mine in that barn you wouldn't have put me through all this tonight. You wouldn't have dreamed of breaking off the betrothal, no matter how many doubts you might have had about my motives, or my status, or any other damn thing about me. The one time in my life when I have an attack of conscience where a woman is concerned,' he said, shaking his head as though in disbelief, 'and it all blows up in my face!'

And then he swooped, hauling her into his arms and kissing her hungrily.

Oh, if only he'd acted like this, spoken like this, before, she would never have dreamed of breaking off the betrothal. She flung her arms about his neck and kissed him back as well as she was able, given her inexperience.

It appeared to be enough for him, for he plunged his tongue into her mouth and took her experience of kissing to a whole new level. It was as if he wanted to devour her. It was so breathtaking she was going dizzy with it. It felt as though she was falling.

And then she realised she *was* falling—backwards onto the bed.

'I'm done with being a gentleman, Prudence,' he snarled.

'Good…' She sighed as he rained kisses over her face.

'I cannot stand the thought of any other man touching you,' he moaned into her neck. 'I saw it happen, in my mind's eye, the minute you broke our betrothal. Men swarming round you like bees round a honeypot. You're so beautiful,' he said, rearing up and looking down at her as though he'd never really seen a woman before.

He cupped her cheek. His hand was trembling.

'I know I said I would get your inheritance back for you, but I'm not sure I could have done it if you weren't going to be my wife. It would have tempted even more men to court you. And you might have fallen for one of them.'

'I wouldn't. I couldn't. There is nobody for me but you, Gregory.'

His jaw hardened. 'I intend to make sure of that. To-night will be like a branding. No other man will ever have you after this. You are mine.'

'Yes,' she purred.

But he didn't seem to hear her acquiescence. For he had seized her wrists and pinned her hands high above her head, stretching her out beneath him like a sacrifice.

Her heart was beating so wildly it felt as though it was going to burst through her ribcage. He was going to take her here, now, with all his family downstairs, wondering what was going on. It felt so decadent. So thrilling.

'You do want me, don't you, Prudence? You wouldn't have proposed in the first place if that wasn't so. You wouldn't kiss me back with such enthusiasm if you didn't want me.'

Was that a hint of uncertainty she saw in his eyes? Had Millicent wounded him so deeply that even now he couldn't quite believe that a woman could truly want him?

'Yes, I want you,' she said. Hoping that all the love she felt for him was blazing from her eyes. 'You know I do.'

His hold on her wrists slackened. 'Even though we're not yet married?'

That question made her love him all the more. For

even though he was desperate to brand her he would still stop, right now, if he thought for one second that she had any reluctance at all.

'Even though you're a duke,' she replied.

'You're trembling again,' he said.

'It's excitement,' she panted. 'I know I ought to feel outraged or terrified by your threats to…to ravish me. But I don't want to protest, or struggle. The weight of your body, pinning me down like this, is…'

And then her words ran out. She didn't have enough experience to be able to describe what he was making her feel. But her body told him, arching up to make the contact with his powerful hips even stronger.

There was no longer any uncertainty on his face. It had been replaced by a knowing smile.

'What you are feeling now,' he drawled, 'is nothing to what I'm going to make you feel soon.' He nuzzled at her ear then, nipped at the lobe, then let go of one of her wrists so he could run his hand down her body, as though tracing her shape. It made her hips, her breasts, hunger to experience a similar caress.

She whimpered and writhed beneath him.

He nipped at her lower lip. Flicked his tongue into her mouth, making her open it to grant him access. Ran his hand back down her side and round to her hips. When she wiggled in response, he slid his hand round to her bottom and kneaded it.

He teased and tormented her with skilful caresses and kisses, rousing her to such a pitch that all she could think of was ripping his clothes off. Or hers. Oh, Lord, she needed… Oh, she needed…

She pulled his face to hers so she could kiss him. And

he let go of her other hand so that she could put both arms round his neck and plunge her fingers into his hair.

'Mine,' he breathed into her ear, before capturing her chin, turning her head and plundering her mouth yet again.

'Yes.' She sighed when he paused for breath. 'I think I can really believe it now. Only...'

'Only what?' He tensed. 'What now?'

'Nothing, really. It's just that if you *had* made me yours, that night in the barn, I would have felt as though I was bestowing some great gift upon you. Whereas now...' She glanced round the room. At the velvet hangings, the moulded cornices, the marble mantel, all of which shrieked of his wealth. And made her dreadfully conscious of how little she was worth.

'The reason I didn't make you mine that night is because I didn't want you to have no choice in the matter once you had discovered all there is to know about me. I knew you'd be shocked when you found out I'm a duke. I feared you might think I'd deceived you for some nefarious reason. I wanted you to be able to remember that I'd behaved honourably, in that one way at least, and then you might be able to forgive the rest.'

'Oh, Gregory.' What a selfless thing to have done for her. 'What a pity we cannot return to that night and do it right this time, knowing all there is to know about each other.'

'That,' he said, rolling off her and standing up, 'is an excellent idea. Come on,' he said, grabbing her hand and hauling her to her feet.

'What are you doing?'

'I think you can see perfectly well what I'm doing. I'm taking the quilt off the bed.'

'Why? What for?'

'Because we would both rather our first time together had been out in that barn.'

'Well, yes,' she admitted.

'Well, then, don't just stand there,' he said as he rolled the quilt and slung it over one shoulder. 'Get some blankets,' he said as he grabbed a couple of pillows. 'As many as you can carry.'

'What? But we cannot go all the way back to the barn. Not at this hour of the night.' She considered it. 'Can we?'

'No need,' he said with a wicked grin. 'I have somewhere much better in mind.'

She was so relieved he wasn't going to put off making love to her properly—or should that be *im*properly?— that she asked no more questions. She just set to, stripping down the bed as swiftly as she could.

They stumbled down the main staircase with bundles of bedding in their arms and crossed the hall to a door at the rear as quickly and quietly as they could. Gregory looked totally nonchalant, but Prudence was rather nervous of anyone seeing them and correctly guessing what they were up to. Not half an hour ago she'd broken their betrothal and stormed off upstairs. And then he'd stormed up after her. If he'd…subdued her in private she might have given the excuse that she hadn't had any choice in the matter. But here she was, carrying her fair share of blankets, proving she was as eager as he to behave with a scandalous lack of propriety.

By the time they went out through a door at the back of the house her cheeks—nay, her entire body was flushed with nervous excitement, and her heart was pounding. She was sneaking off into the night to make love to a duke, without being married to him.

She was then going to marry that duke.

She couldn't really believe either. It was like something out of a dream. The fact that it was another clear, moonlit night added to the surreal quality of what she was doing as they crossed a smooth, silvered lawn to a path which plunged them into the darkness of a shrubbery.

This path was wide enough that the branches didn't snag at her hair or her clothes, the way they'd done when he'd led her to the house. Though she was still in almost as much turmoil. That time she'd been worried someone might catch them and accuse them of trespassing. *Again.* This time she just felt…downright naughty. As well as slightly stunned that she was actually doing this. She wasn't the kind of girl who sneaked out into the night to have assignations with men. Not even men she was going to marry. Not that there had been any others. Because she'd always sworn she wouldn't marry anyone. Or at least that was the way she had been thinking ever since Aunt Charity had started trying to matchmake for her.

She shook her head as her thoughts got into a tangle as dense as the shrubbery through which Gregory was leading her.

But it wasn't long before the shrubbery gave way to another lawn, in the centre of which stood a low brick building with a thatched roof. It looked like a tiny one-roomed cottage.

'The summer house,' said Gregory, setting his hand to the door latch.

'A very substantial summer house,' she observed, eyeing the casement windows and the solid oak door.

'Well, it needs to protect the ladies who wish to take the air in summer from the weather we typically get in these parts,' he said, putting his shoulder to the door when it refused to budge. 'Ah…' He sighed in relief as it gave inward, scraping across the somewhat unevenly flagged floor.

She peered inside as he pushed the door wider. There was enough moonlight filtering in for her to be able to pick out a couple of upholstered chairs set under one of the windows, and a table with some straight-backed chairs under another. But what really caught her eye was a little brick arched fireplace, in a nook directly opposite the door.

They were certainly not going to be cold in here overnight. Not once she'd lit the fire, which would only take a minute or two. She found a tinderbox and candles on the mantel shelf, dry kindling in the grate, and plenty of logs in a box on the hearth.

'You see, Prudence?' Gregory came up behind her as she set one of the candlesticks back on the mantel after touching the flame to the kindling, and put his arms round her waist. 'I couldn't manage without you. Not even so far as to the summer house in my own grounds.'

'You have servants to light your fires,' she said, pulling his hands away so she could kneel down on the quilt which he'd spread out on the hearthrug.

'Nobody lights my fires the way you do,' he growled, dropping to his knees beside her.

He draped one arm round her shoulder. It slid to her waist as she leaned forward to peer into the grate and check the kindling. She tried to ignore the way he was stroking her bottom. But it wasn't easy. The flames that licked over the twigs when the paper caught fire were no less greedy than the sensations his hands were stoking in her body. Soon she could no longer be bothered with what was going on in the grate and she knelt back on her heels, turned to him, and lifted her face hopefully.

'Am I allowed to kiss you now, then?' he asked. 'Not too busy with more practical matters?'

He didn't wait for her answer but began to nuzzle at the sensitive spot just below her ear. It sent a shiver right down her spine. A delicious shiver of longing.

'Now, where were we…?' he murmured, placing a kiss on her jaw.

Chapter Eighteen

'Right about here…' She sighed, sliding her arms round his neck and kissing him back. He caught her hard into his chest. Then they surged together, kissing and running their hands over each other as though neither could quite believe this was really happening at last.

And soon that wasn't enough. She just had to tear his shirt from his breeches so she could get at bare skin. Which was all the encouragement he needed to start plucking at the ties at the back of her gown. He undid them with a dexterity clearly gained from frequent practice.

But she didn't care.

'Oh, yes,' she panted when he tumbled her down onto the quilt. 'Oh, God…oh, Gregory,' she moaned as he pulled the front of her bodice down. 'Oh, yes, push that out of the way.' She gasped. And gasped again as he closed his mouth over her breast. She plunged her fingers into his hair once more as he sucked, and licked, and nipped at her.

'I cannot live without you,' he bit out briefly, before

swirling his tongue round one painfully sensitised nipple. 'Don't make me do without you, my sweet love.'

His sweet love? Was she really his sweet love?

'Oh, Gregory,' she sobbed, as tears welled in her eyes.

Something arced between them and then they were kissing frantically. She clawed at his back as he pushed up her skirts. Wrapped one leg round his hips as he ran his hand up the outside of her thigh and kissed her neck again. Her face. The cleft between her breasts.

She was on fire. Burning up with the need that only he could create within her. That only he could assuage.

He raised himself slightly. Slid away so that he could bring his hand between her legs.

'Oh, yes,' she moaned as he delved, and stroked, and pleasured her. 'Yes. Please. Oh…'

Something like a shower of fireworks went off inside her, scattering her in a blaze of sparks across the heavens, before gently drifting her back down to the hearth. Where she discovered he was holding her close, his fingers buried in her hair, his chest heaving as though he'd just been running.

He dropped a kiss on her brow. 'Wait right there,' he said as he got to his feet.

She watched drowsily from between heavy lids as he gathered pillows and blankets, then came back and dropped to his knees beside her.

'Lift your head,' he said, passing her a pillow. She did as she was told without demur, seeing as he was only ministering to her comfort.

'Raise your arms,' he ordered next.

When she did so, he pulled the sleeves down her

arms and off. She raised her hips so that he could remove the gown altogether.

'Now for the stays,' he said. Then checked himself. 'Good God—your other stays are still in my valise. If anyone unpacks for me...'

She tried, and failed, to stifle a giggle.

'Are you laughing at me?'

'I'm sorry. I couldn't help it.'

'You will pay for that, you minx,' he growled.

And deftly removed every last stitch of her clothing with ruthless efficiency. Then he knelt back. And stared at her. For so long that she began to start wondering if she should be worried. Or if she ought to feel shy. A modest, virtuous woman would surely wish to cover herself? In at least a couple of strategic places.

All Prudence wanted to do was preen. Because the way he was drinking in the sight of her, lying naked and ready for him, made her feel like a goddess being worshipped by an acolyte.

'You look so lovely, lying there with the firelight flickering over your body, I cannot decide where to start,' he said at last. 'Should I start at your poor abused toes and work my way up?' He ran one hand along the length of her leg, round and over her hip, up and over one breast, ending by cupping her cheek.

'Or at your hair? Your glorious hair?' He leaned forward and started plucking out the pins.

'Wait, Gregory,' she said, as a thought suddenly struck her. 'I know where you should start.'

'Where? Where do you wish me to begin making love to you?'

She smiled up at him. 'I thought you already had. But, please, my dear, won't you put a couple of logs on the fire before you do anything else? I don't want the fire to go out at a crucial moment and for you to have to stop to get it going again.'

'I can promise you the fire won't go out all night,' he growled.

She didn't think he was talking about the one just getting going in the hearth.

'My practical little wife-to-be,' he said, tending to the fire. 'Always thinking one step ahead. You will be a formidable duchess, you know.'

She didn't really believe him, but she felt far too lazy, too replete in the aftermath of all those fireworks going off inside her, to be bothered to argue.

And she was glad she hadn't when he knelt over her with an intent expression on his face and shrugged out of his jacket. Then his waistcoat. Then his shirt. His chest was as magnificent as she remembered. Only now she had the right to run her hands over it. To follow the dips and hollows, experience the difference in texture between smooth skin and hairy, hard muscles and the soft skin of his nipples. To sit up and kiss the bruises marring his ribs.

He shuddered. Gripped her shoulders and pushed her away. 'Don't,' he grated. 'Not yet. Or I won't be able to keep my promise.'

'But I want to *feel* you,' she complained. 'Taste you.'

'*I* will make *you* feel,' he said, taking hold of her wrists and pinning them above her head.

Again.

'It will be like nothing you have ever felt before,' he vowed, before stopping her mouth with a kiss.

The feel of him on top of her, bare chest to bare breasts, was indeed like nothing she'd ever felt before.

She couldn't help rubbing herself up against him, to increase the wondrous pleasure of it.

He lifted himself off her, keeping her wrists clasped firmly in his hands as he kissed each breast, then her stomach, and then...

If he hadn't been holding her hands so firmly she would have tried to grasp his head and stop him. It wasn't easy to cast off all the morals her aunt had tried to din into her over the past dozen years. And for him to put his mouth *there* simply couldn't be right.

But it felt so good. The way he kissed, then nibbled, then licked...

'Gregory!' she gasped. 'Gregory, that is...' And then her ability to breathe and speak at the same time ceased. All she could do was writhe, and pant, and moan. Those fireworks were going to go off again. She could feel them building, fizzing inside her.

Then Gregory let go of her hands, shifted slightly to one side, and pushed one finger inside her.

She screamed. And went off like a rocket. One single, immense rocket that blotted out every single star twinkling feebly in her night sky.

'Gregory,' she moaned, as she slowly came back together.

'Shh...' He was next to her now, holding her in his arms, stroking her hair, dropping kisses on her brow.

'I don't think,' she panted, 'I can keep on doing this all night.'

He chuckled. 'A short while ago you were claiming you didn't want me to let the fire go out—not even for an instant.'

'I didn't know what I was talking about,' she complained.

To her immense relief he let go of her and sat up. Though she felt perversely disappointed when he then stood up.

Until she saw him undoing his breeches and shucking them off. She held out her arms as he came back to her, clasping them round his back as he lay fully on top of her. At which point a wave of shockingly fierce response had her pressing up against him. It was as though her hips had developed a mind of their own. And her legs, which parted in welcome.

'There, you see,' he said. 'You are still smouldering. You can blaze again. And again.'

Incredibly, it was true. For the feel of him there, hard against her softness, probing insistently every time he flexed his hips against hers, was making the explosive excitement start to grow all over again.

He kissed her, stroked her, licked and nibbled at her throat, her breasts, while his hands kneaded at her bottom. And then he shifted slightly so that he could reach for himself, where he lay between her legs, and rub himself along her wetness. Then he held himself poised, where she was melting and aching for him. And pushed, just a little, so that he was stretching and penetrating her.

She arched up to him—and felt a sting from which she instinctively recoiled.

He followed her down, allowing her no quarter.

Pushed again.

This time there was a searing pain which tore her out of the sensual haze in which she'd been floating.

He stilled. Kissed her cheek when she turned it away from the fire, away from the sight of him looming over her. Kissed her neck. Stroked her damp hair back from her forehead. Then reached between them and began to gently caress the point where they merged.

Unbelievably, the slow burn started up all over again.

She turned her face to look up at him. 'I can't, Gregory. Please, I...'

'You can,' he said. 'You only have to let go.'

Let go? What was she to let go *of*, precisely? He was the one pinning her to the floor. Moving inside her now. Pushing even deeper. Withdrawing. And circling his fingers over a place that seemed to be screaming for him to do it harder.

Harder?

Yes, she wanted more of him. More sensation.

The next time he pushed in she pushed up, against him, to increase the sensation.

'That's it,' he murmured. And kept on murmuring words of encouragement, and praise, and approval as he kept up a gentle, rhythmic thrusting.

Until she didn't want him to be gentle any more. Until she was gripping his buttocks and twisting her hips, clamouring to reach that place he'd already taken her to twice before.

And then she got there. Only this time it was even better because he was there with her. She could feel him pulsing deep inside her as he groaned into her ear. And it was better feeling him drift back down to earth with her, too. Feeling his heart pound against her chest. His breath coming in great, ragged gasps.

For a while they just lay there, getting their breath back, and in Prudence's case watching the firelight sending shadows flickering across the beamed ceiling.

Until he reared up, looked down at her with a smug smile, and said, 'There. You will *have* to marry me now.'

* * *

They slept wrapped in each other's arms until dawn. At which time the light crept in through the curtainless windows and roused Gregory. His breath billowed out like a cloud when he yawned. He reached over to the log box, extracted the last log and tossed it onto the fire.

From somewhere deep beneath the covers Prudence lifted her head and squinted up at him crossly.

'Lie down,' she complained. 'You're making a draught.'

'I'm taking care of you, you ingrate,' he countered happily.

She shifted against him, snuggling closer. 'You are,' she conceded. 'You got up some time in the night to fetch extra blankets, didn't you?'

'All on my own,' he jested. 'Without any help from a servant.'

He felt her smile against his chest.

'I suppose we ought to get back to the house before anyone notices we are missing,' said Prudence.

He snorted. 'Didn't you see the curtains twitching last night? They all know exactly where we went. So...' he rolled on top of her '...you will have to marry me now.'

'You said that last night.'

'I still mean it.'

'So do I,' she said, wrapping her arms round his waist and hugging him hard.

In this position, he approved of hugs. In fact there was a great deal to be said for hugs at any time of day. So long as it was Prudence doing the hugging.

'So you are still of a mind to marry me, in spite of my being a duke?'

'I think I shall have to,' she said. 'Not because of what we did last night. But because I could not bear the thought of life without you. Although,' she said, wriggling rather deliciously before swatting his bottom, 'I am still cross with you for not telling me the truth about your station before we got here. You might have warned me, and then I wouldn't have felt like such a prize idiot.'

'I was too worried about how you might react to broach the subject,' he admitted. Now that he was sure of her, it felt safe to confess many things. 'I'd been trying to think of ways to tell you about my being a duke long before we got here. But... Well, for one thing I wasn't sure you'd believe me. I had visions of you saying that you must have hit me really hard with that rock for me to suddenly start getting delusions of grandeur. Or of you becoming afraid that I was a dangerous lunatic, escaped from some asylum, and trying to run away from me again.

'I couldn't let you go,' he said, dropping a kiss on her brow. 'I needed to keep you near. Actually,' he admitted, with a burn of something that felt like guilt heating his cheeks, 'I'd even considered claiming to get lost and not finding Bramley Park at all just to prolong our time together without the dratted title coming between us.'

'You would really have rather stayed out on the road, facing farmers with guns and eating stale bread that I'd earned by singing, than come back to all this?'

'Without question.'

'But you didn't,' she pointed out, pragmatic as ever.

'I couldn't, in the end.' He sighed. 'On account of your feet. You were in pain, Prudence. And you needed a decent meal and clean clothes. It would have been monstrous to keep you in that state just to preserve the illusion that I was an ordinary man. Besides which, if I'd succumbed to the temptation to put off the moment when you discovered what I really am you might have thought it was because I was still trying to win that wager. And I couldn't have you ever thinking that I'd put something so trivial before your welfare. Whichever path I chose, I risked losing you. I was…' he shuddered '…caught on the horns of a horrible dilemma.'

'Oh…'

She gazed up at him with eyes full of what looked like understanding—at least he hoped it looked like understanding. And appreciation. And love.

'You really are the most darling of men,' she said at last.

'Event though I'm a duke?'

'Yes. Although…'

'What?'

'Well, it's just that I don't want you to ever regret marrying me,' she said.

'I couldn't.'

'Are you sure? When you were so set against marrying? Even more than I was, by the sound of it…'

'That was only because I hadn't met *you*,' he countered, seeing the real anxiety in her lovely brown eyes.

'No, be serious,' she said, swatting his bottom again.

Which he was starting to like.

'I want to be the best wife I can be for you,' she said. 'Only I don't understand how I can do that. I'm certain to let you down…'

'You couldn't! Because you love me. The reason I was so unhappy in my first marriage was because of… Well, you know the way Millicent behaved.'

'Yes, you explained a little of that. It sounded perfectly horrid.'

'It was. And they said *she'd* be the perfect duchess.' He couldn't help grimacing at memories of the pain and humiliation he'd experienced as a young man. 'She couldn't *ever* have been the perfect duchess. For all that she was born with a title and came from a noble family. And she had money—yes, all the things you say you don't have. But she didn't love me. Nor have any of the other women who have made an attempt to lure me into their clutches loved me. They've merely coveted the title. You are the only woman who has loved the man and rejected the title. That *is* what you've done, isn't it?'

He looked at her keenly, wondering even now if she was going to recoil from the duties and status that went with marrying him.

'Well, not *rejected* the title, exactly. It's just that it… it scares me a bit. Well, a lot. I don't know how to be a duchess, Gregory. And you ought to have a wife who can do you proud.'

'I ought to have a wife who can *love* me,' he came back swiftly. 'That's all it will take, Prudence, for you to be my perfect duchess. For you to love me.'

'It's lovely of you to say so, but surely it will mean more than that?'

'Prudence Carstairs,' he said, pretending shock. 'Are you admitting to being afraid of something? You who faced down a farmer with a gun?'

She blushed. And wriggled. Which almost made him abandon their conversation and simply give in to the physical appetite she was arousing. It took a serious effort of will for him to concentrate on what she was saying. But he made himself do so. Because this was important. To her, and therefore to him.

'Physical danger is something I'm used to,' she said dismissively. 'Running the gauntlet of indignant society matrons, all pointing their fingers at me and whispering behind their fans, is quite another matter.'

He took hold of her chin. 'If anyone dares to whisper behind their fan about you, you will simply look down your nose at them the way you did at me when I had the effrontery to try and stop you from singing in public. Remember that? I thought at the time you could have outdone any of the patronesses of Almack's for haughtiness. Even dressed in rags and singing your heart out at the market cross, you looked like a duchess to me.'

'Oh, Gregory...' She sighed, shaking her head. 'You aren't looking at me the way everyone else will. They'll say I'm an upstart. That I smell of the shop.'

'So what if they do? Why should you care about what anyone thinks or says but me? And don't forget,' he murmured into her ear, swirling his tongue round the shell-like whorls for good measure, 'if anyone dares to criticise you, and I find out about it, I will make them rue the day.'

'Would you? Yes, I suppose you would.' She bent her head to give him better access to her ear, and in doing so her neck. 'I shouldn't think anyone would dare do anything much, would they?'

'Of course not. I'm not a man to cross, Prudence. You can trust me to keep you safe...' he paused to apply his mouth to her throat '...and happy.'

'Yes...' she breathed as he reached the spot he'd been seeking and sucked. 'After all, I trusted you with my fortune and my future when I thought you had nothing at all, didn't I? I don't know why I thought you were suddenly someone else the minute I discovered you had a title.'

'I am not anyone else, Prudence. I'm just the man who loves you.'

'And I love you.'

'Thank God,' he breathed. 'I thought you were never going to admit it.'

'But—you knew. Didn't you?'

'No,' he growled. 'You kept me guessing.'

'But you knew.'

'No, I bloody well didn't.' He reared up onto his elbows and glared down at her. 'You have kept me on my toes ever since you ran from that ostler and climbed into my cart. From that moment on I've always been half afraid you would run off and I'd never see you again.'

'Well, I won't, my darling.' She reached up and stroked his cheek. 'My love, I will marry you, and stick to you like a burr for the rest of my days.'

'Thank God,' he breathed again. And lowered himself back down.

Chapter Nineteen

The sun was high in the sky and the fire was nothing more than a pile of embers when they finally emerged from the summer house.

Gregory didn't think he'd ever witnessed a more lovely morning. There had been a heavy dewfall in the night, which made even the dank shrubbery sparkle as though it was bedecked with jewels. The gloss didn't even fade as he caught sight of Hugo, pacing up and down the terrace. Nor even when, upon catching sight of them, he came jogging down the steps and headed across the lawn to intercept them.

'Good morning, Halstead,' said his cousin. 'Miss Carstairs.'

Gregory didn't have to look at Prudence to know she was blushing at being caught outside. Everyone must know they'd spent the night together in the summer house. Especially since she had the quilt wrapped round her shoulders, across which he'd draped his own arm. And with that glorious abundance of hair rioting all down her back she looked thoroughly loved this morning.

'Need a word,' said Hugo, completely unabashed.

What a pity he didn't have the tact to consider sparing her blushes.

'Last night, what with all the...er...fireworks between you two,' he said with a grin, 'we never did get round to settling up.'

'You need to confront me about that *now*? Is the case that urgent?'

Hugo's face fell. 'You must know it is—or I would never have lashed out at you the way I did. Fact is, I was jolly glad to have the excuse to get out of Town and hide away up here.'

'If you had only explained I would have bailed you out, you young idiot. And I shall, of course, settle all your debts—as agreed in the terms of our wager.'

'You'd have bailed me out anyway?' Hugo planted his fists on his hips. 'I wish I'd known that. I would have wagered on something worth having.'

'Such as?'

'A commission with a good regiment. In fact it would probably be to your advantage to get me into one which is serving overseas anyway. Then I won't be able to do your reputation any damage by letting the cat out of the bag about all this.' He waved his arm in a way that encompassed the pair of unmarried lovers and, by implication, the way they'd met. 'Inadvertently, of course,' he said, going slightly pink. 'When I'm in my cups, say.'

Gregory narrowed his eyes and hardened his jaw. 'You have first a more pressing duty to perform.'

'Oh?'

'Yes. I need you to go and procure a licence, so that Miss Carstairs and I can be married as soon as possible. And then to stand as my groomsman.'

'Of course,' said Hugo, standing a bit straighter.

'Only then will I purchase your commission. Not because I fear anything you might inadvertently do to my reputation,' he pointed out, 'but because this past week has taught me that every man deserves a chance to find out what he's made of.'

Hugo whooped with glee, darted forward and kissed Prudence's cheek.

'What was that for?' She tried to clap her hand to the spot where Hugo had kissed her, but he grabbed it and pumped it up and down.

'To thank you for agreeing to marry him. For putting him in such a mellow mood. Welcome to the family, Miss Carstairs,' he said, and then, with another whoop of delight, went haring off back across the lawn in the direction of the stables.

'You don't think badly of me?' he said, after they'd walked a little further across the dew-spangled lawn. 'For agreeing to purchase him a commission? You understand why I did so?'

'Of course.' She smiled up at him. 'In fact I was thinking only last night that it would be the making of him.'

'There—you see.' He smiled down at her. 'We are of one mind already. How can our marriage fail to prosper?'

Prudence could still think of plenty of ways their marriage might fail to prosper. If, for example, she ever decided to find his dictatorial manner objectionable. For he had decided they would get married within two days at the local parish church, had set Lady Mixby to arranging their wedding breakfast, Mrs Bennet the local dressmaker to furnish her with suitable clothing,

and Benderby to organise their subsequent departure
for London.

All without asking her opinion once.

But since he had made it clear that he needed her at
his side every moment of the day, and she had no wish
to stir from that position, it was hardly worth mentioning. And anyway, did she really care where they married so long as it was soon? And wasn't a quiet country
church preferable to a grand society wedding where a
lot of strangers would come to gawp at her?

He was going to have to return to London and take
up his responsibilities one day. The longer they put it
off, the more nervous she was likely to get about taking her place at his side. Besides, Lady Mixby and the
redoubtable Benderby were coming, too. Both of them
were in high spirits over the prospect of overseeing her
presentation, her first ball as Duchess of Halstead, and
the many and varied delights of the subsequent season
in London.

It wasn't that she was letting everyone ride rough-
shod over her. She wasn't. She was just so blissfully
happy that she didn't want to do anything to spoil it.
And, really, what would be the point of throwing what
might amount to a tantrum because her husband was anticipating her every need before she could even voice it?

She would be wise to choose her battles carefully—
not rip up at him over every little thing. Or the combination of his autocratic nature and her independent spirit
would result in them spending their whole life fighting.

They had been in London for a week before she finally had no choice but to take a stand.

'There—what did I tell you?' he murmured as yet

another doyenne of society bowed to them as their carriages passed in the park. 'Nobody has shown you anything but the greatest respect. Not even your grandfather.'

They'd gone to visit the Earl of Sterndale privately only the day before. And, just as Gregory had predicted, the old man had welcomed her with open arms.

'You have a look of my boy,' he'd said, with the suspicion of a tear in his eye. When she'd bristled with indignation that *his boy* had died without ever having been forgiven, the old man had said, 'Ah, yes, just that look.'

'It must be very gratifying to be always right,' she said now to Gregory. And then, because he'd raised one eyebrow at her, she hastily added, 'Even about your driving. You are managing *these* horses very competently.'

'Baggage,' he responded, though at least the brow had gone down. 'I would defy anyone to make the creature Hugo foisted on me go in a straight line.'

'It may be less cantankerous after having that week's rest at the inn, eating its head off,' she replied, paraphrasing the landlord.

'We will soon find out,' he replied with an evil smile. 'I'm making Hugo a present of it.'

'I wouldn't be a bit surprised if it doesn't make a very good sort of horse for a cavalry officer,' she said. 'It will need very little encouragement to lash out with its hooves, or bite persons who dare to attempt to get near its master.'

'Providing Hugo can persuade it that he *is* its master.'

They both laughed at the vision of Hugo attempting to train the horse, and harmony was restored.

'Good afternoon, Your Grace,' said the butler of the house in Grosvenor Square of which Prudence was now mistress, when they returned later that afternoon. 'Wrothers has informed me that the person you have been expecting from Liverpool is waiting in your study.'

From the way he'd said *'person'*, Bispham clearly did not think much of Gregory's visitor.

She half expected Gregory to tell the butler to dismiss them, as he'd dismissed so many people since their arrival in London. Gregory's secretary appeared to do nothing but turn away people who wished to have an interview with her husband.

Instead, Gregory turned to her with an abstracted air after tossing his gloves into his hat and handing them over.

'You will go to the morning room and take tea with Lady Mixby,' he said sternly. 'I will deal with this.'

He then strode off, leaving her standing in the hall staring after him.

Fuming.

She was not his servant to order about.

'Who is this person, Bishpham?' she asked as she shrugged her furs into his waiting hands.

'I really couldn't say, Your Grace,' he replied. 'But His Grace frequently has to have dealings with all sorts of odd people in the performance of his duties to the Crown.'

'Yes, I suppose so…' she began. Then went rigid as she heard a voice raised in anger. A female voice. An all too recognisable female voice.

All thought of meekly going upstairs to drink tea, as she'd been told, went flying out of the window. She stormed past the butler, across the hall, through the room over which Wrothers presided, and straight through into her husband's inner sanctum.

And she saw that she had not been mistaken.

'Aunt Charity!'

Her aunt was sitting on a hard-backed chair to one side of her husband's desk. He was standing over her, looking particularly intractable. Wrothers was standing in a corner, his arms folded across his chest.

'I told you to let *me* deal with this,' said Gregory upon seeing her.

'Deal with this? *Deal with this?* This is not a "this"— it is a her. I mean, it is my aunt.'

'Oh, Prudence, Prudence... I never meant it,' her aunt wailed.

'Didn't you?' Her heart was thudding uncomfortably high in her throat. As though she was going to be sick.

Gregory came round the table and to her side. 'I told you to let me deal with this,' he repeated, murmuring into her ear. 'This is likely to be an unpleasant interview.'

'I don't understand. Where did you find her? *How* did you find her?'

'Liverpool. And I had people search for her.'

Oh, yes, the moment Bispham had mentioned Liverpool, Gregory's relaxed demeanour had completely disappeared. He had known at that moment exactly who was waiting for him in here.

'Liverpool? What on earth was she doing there, of all places? And why did you have people searching for her?'

'I will explain it all later,' he said, ushering her inexorably towards the door. 'Go and have some tea and—'

'No. Absolutely not. I need to know what is going

on. What she thought she was doing. How she could have done it.'

'Prudence, will you just do as you are told?'

'No. Not this time.'

He gritted his teeth. 'And here was I, thinking you were becoming more malleable.'

'Malleable!' She rounded on him with real anger. 'I lost my virginity in that summer house—not my mind. The only reason I haven't objected to you giving me orders since then is because you haven't asked me to do anything I didn't want to.'

'And there was I also thinking I had turned my tigress into a purring kitten with my prowess in bed,' he said ruefully.

'Well, you thought wrong.'

'Clearly,' he said. And then tipped his head to one side. He nodded. 'Very well,' he said. 'You may stay.'

May stay? She was just about to protest at his choice of words when she caught a glimmer in his eye. And a twitch to his lips.

He was trying not to laugh.

And then she recalled that he had never minded her standing up to him. Out on the road they'd gone at it like hammer and tongs on more than one occasion and he'd never held it against her. In fact she wouldn't be a bit surprised to discover that it was one of the things that had made him fall in love with her.

Lifting her chin, she flounced over to another chair and sat down on it.

Her aunt, who had been watching the murmured and yet heated interchange warily, now burst into noisy sobs.

Gregory motioned for Wrothers to leave the room.

He did so, looking mightily relieved. It was Gregory himself who went to the sideboard and poured a glass of brandy. And then strode to her aunt and offered her the glass.

'Oh, Aunt Charity doesn't drink...'

Her aunt was a Methodist. Though not, apparently, a very consistent one. For she snatched at the glass as though at a lifeline and downed half the contents in one go.

Prudence waited in vain for her to cough and splutter. She simply gave a little shiver, then downed the rest like a seasoned toper.

When Prudence looked to Gregory he gave a wry smile, then made a gesture towards Aunt Charity as though to indicate that the lady was all hers.

She could ask whatever questions she liked. Though all she could think for a moment was, *How could you?*

'Perhaps you would like to begin with ascertaining what your aunt was doing in Liverpool?' Gregory suggested.

'You know very well what we were doing in Liverpool,' said Aunt Charity crossly. 'We were fleeing the country. It was all Mr Murgatroyd's idea,' she said, turning the empty glass round and round between stiff fingers. 'He said it was the only way to escape the gossip. To start a new life in the New World. He made it sound so...' She shook her head and shut her eyes briefly in what looked like a spasm of pain.

'He had lost all the money in Prudence's trust, I take it?'

Aunt Charity's shoulders slumped. 'He said he was going to triple it. That we would be so wealthy nobody would think it odd for us to leave Stoketown and set up in a nice, fashionable resort somewhere.'

'Why should you want to leave Stoketown?' asked Prudence.

Aunt Charity had been such a committed member of her congregation. So active in all the good works performed in the community.

'Because I couldn't ever hold my head up there. Not after Alfred.'

Alfred? Gregory mouthed at Prudence.

'Her first husband,' said Prudence. 'The one who drank.' She eyed her aunt's empty glass again, wondering if her aunt had been spotless during that period of her past.

'I thought if I married a really, really moral man that it would counteract the shame of having been dragged down by an habitual drunkard.'

So that explained why she'd married Mr Murgatroyd— one of the most moralising, narrow-minded men in the whole congregation.

'Because no matter how many good works I did,' Aunt Charity continued, 'people were never going to forget the...the *degradation*...of my marrying a man who turned out to be the very opposite of what I thought...and now I've done it twice!'

She burst into tears again.

Gregory calmly walked over, took the glass from her hand, replenished it and handed it back. The contents went the same way as the first.

'Mr Murgatroyd promised me he would take me away from it all. That if he could only have some capital he would make us so rich that we could shake the dust of Stoketown from our feet and live like kings. I should have known better than to trust in a handsome face and lying lips,' she finished bitterly.

'What happened to the money?'

'He invested it in a canal. A canal that never got dug. No chance of getting any sort of refund. And with you getting so near to coming of age, and not being the sort we could trust to be discreet about our shame, we had to do something. You wouldn't marry any of the men we knew would have covered it up. So he came up with a new plan.'

'To discredit me? And abandon me?'

'No!' She hunched her shoulders. 'Not at first,' she continued, looking a touch shamefaced. 'We were going to emigrate. All of us. We lied about taking you to Bath, it is true. Our destination was Liverpool all along. We intended to tell you the truth when we got there. But then we stopped at that funny little inn and saw… him…' She gestured to Gregory with her empty glass. 'Mr Murgatroyd said as how he wished to spare me an embarrassing scene at the dockside when we broke the news to you. And asked wouldn't it be better to leave you behind and start our new life without any reminders of the past? Because he was sure if we took you with us you would be bound to do nothing but complain and ruin our fresh start. And now I know I shouldn't have listened, but it was so tempting,' she wailed. 'He could always make me believe anything he said. Oh, what a fool I've been.'

'You left me at that inn because you thought I'd ruin your fresh start? How…how *could* you?'

'Well, it wasn't as if you were going to come to any harm, was it? Mr Murgatroyd made sure *he*—' she waved her empty glass at Gregory again '—was completely insensible before he carried you into the room, and I undressed you. I sat there all night. And the moment he began to stir I made all that commotion and brought crowds of people in before anything untoward could happen. You were never in any danger.'

Aunt Charity had sat there all night? It put a slightly different complexion on things, but still…

'But you just left me there. You abandoned me. What did you think would happen to me?'

Aunt Charity blinked. 'Well, we assumed you would go straight back to Stoketown, of course.'

'And how was I supposed to get there?'

Aunt Charity looked confused. 'Somebody would have told you how to get a seat on the mail.'

'The mail coach?'

'I don't see why not. We left enough money for you to travel swiftly and to tide you over for a good few months until you got on your feet again. Though I see we needn't have bothered,' she ended with a sniff, looking round the study and then at Gregory. 'It's just typical for you to end up with a duke.'

'You left Prudence money?' Gregory was frowning, looking from one woman to the other.

'Yes. Twenty pounds. As you very well know,' she said indignantly. 'It would have come in very handy in our new lives, let me tell you. Quite a sacrifice it was, parting with that amount. But I insisted.'

Prudence pressed one hand to her forehead. She supposed it might be true. That her aunt had left her some money. Aunt Charity would have seen her tuck her reticule under her pillow when she'd brought her that hot milk. She might have put some money in there.

'And all my things? What did you do with those?'

'Your things? Why, I packed them all up neatly and had them sent back to Stoketown by carrier as soon as we arrived in Liverpool. In fact it was while I was doing that that *he* gave me the slip,' she added bitterly. 'He said he was going to see about our berth on the ship, but when I got back to the hotel from the carriers it was to find all his luggage gone.'

Tears streamed down her face unchecked.

'I was afraid to go down to the docks at first, because he'd told me it was a rough, horrid place and that he'd handle things. By the time I'd plucked up the courage, the ship had sailed. And I was left there alone, with no means of paying the bill, since he hadn't left me with *anything*! And I know you sent that young man—' she gestured to the door through which Wrothers had gone '—to hunt me down and bring me to justice, but I have never been so glad to see anyone in my life.'

'It appears,' said Gregory with scorn, 'that rather than own up at once that she had no means to pay her shot your aunt stayed at the inn, racking up a substantial debt.'

'I spent most of my stay there on my knees,' said the tearful older woman. 'Praying for inspiration. Or a miracle. I know it will be hard for you to forgive me, Prudence, for the part I played in all this, but at least you have the satisfaction of knowing that I have already been punished by a higher authority.'

Gregory made a sort of snarling sound. He was looking at Aunt Charity as though he couldn't believe his ears.

'That's true,' Prudence pointed out. 'All the things she did to me have now been done to her. She has been robbed and abandoned. By a man she loved, at that.

So you could say her punishment is greater, since I found *you*.'

She got up and went to him, hands outstretched.

'You are going to ask me to let her off, aren't you?'

She nodded. 'We learned something about giving people a second chance, didn't we? In that barn? The farmer forgave us for literal trespass and spared us both a horrible time trying to explain everything away to the law. Could we not now forgive Aunt Charity for her trespass against us?'

He was still glowering.

'You have already forgiven her, haven't you?'

She nodded. 'Because if it hadn't been for her giving way to Mr Murgatroyd's persuasion we would never have met. Besides, she took me in when nobody else would.'

'Grudgingly, you said.'

'Nevertheless…' She spread her hands wide.

He stepped forward and took them. 'You are the most generous-hearted, lovely creature on God's whole earth. No wonder I love you so much.'

'Then you won't have her prosecuted?'

'How can I when to do so would offend you?'

As he drew her into his arms Aunt Charity collapsed into a fresh spurt of sobbing. Though now, Prudence suspected, they were tears of relief.

'Thankfully,' he said dryly, 'I have no end of properties in which I can stow indigent aunts. Some of them even further from London than Bramley Park.'

'So there are *some* benefits to marrying a duke, after all,' she said with a smile.

'Baggage,' he murmured, pinching her chin. 'You know very well that you adore being married to a duke.'

'Only because I happen to adore the Duke in question,' she countered.

'Long may that continue,' he said.

'Oh, it will,' she vowed, reaching up to kiss his cheek. 'It will.'

* * * * *

A MISTRESS FOR
MAJOR BARTLETT

To Louise Allen and Sarah Mallory

Chapter One

Sunday, 18th June—1815

'Limber up, fast as you can!' Colonel Randall rode up to Major Bartlett and pointed to a spot to the rear. 'We are heading to the ridge up yonder. You will recall we came in that way yesterday, past a place—what was it called?—Hougoumont. The French are massing their heavy cavalry between the château and the Charleroi road. Take up your position between the two infantry squares up there. And be quick about it!'

Major Bartlett kept his face impassive as he saluted. Quick? That was going to be a relative term given the sodden state of the ground.

'Right, lads,' he said, turning to his men. 'You heard the Colonel. *At* the double!'

The speed at which they turned the gun carriages and started ploughing their way across the field had much more to do with the shells exploding all around them, spraying them with mud, than willingness to obey their commanding officer. The sooner they got to higher ground, the sooner they could start inflicting some dam-

age on the Frenchmen currently trying to blow them to
kingdom come. Not that Major Bartlett had any complaints. He had a rather elastic attitude to obeying orders
himself. In any other unit his tendency to interpret orders to suit himself would have got him up on a charge—
indeed, had done so on several occasions. Only Colonel
Randall had appreciated that his ability to think on his
feet, rather than dumbly obeying orders, could be an
advantage, taking him into his unit and giving him promotion.

Still, when he glanced across the ridge, and saw that
his team had beaten Major Flint's to reach their desig-
nated position, he felt a twinge of pride in his men. They'd
worked with a swiftness and efficiency *he'd* drilled into
them, even if, at this moment, they'd worked the way
they had because their hides depended on it.

Flint's guns were ready to fire mere seconds after his
own. Even Rawlins, who'd only been promoted a matter
of days before, had his guns in position not long after.
And just as well. The French cavalry were approaching
at the trot.

The first salvo his men fired mowed down the lead-
ers. But they kept coming. Big bastards. On big horses.

'Dear lord, they'll charge right over us!'

Major Bartlett whirled round. Had one of his own
men dared say that?

'Not Randall's Rogues, they won't,' he snarled. 'Remember our motto—always victorious!' By any means.
Particularly when sent behind enemy lines, where his,
and his men's, talents for causing mayhem had so often
been given free rein.

'Aye,' roared Randall, drawing his sword and holding it aloft. '*Semper Laurifer!* Ready, Rogues… Fire!'

The guns roared again. Horses and men fell. Smoke swirled round the scene, blotting out the sight of the dead and dying, though Bartlett could still hear their screams and groans.

And then he heard cheering. From the infantry squares behind him. The cavalry charge was over. This one, anyway. He cast a quick, appraising glance over his men. All of them steadily reloading, preparing for the next attack, not wasting their time cheering, or capering about and having to be pushed back into position.

At this point, between cavalry charges, their orders had been to retreat into the infantry squares for cover. But his men, seasoned veterans, knew as well as he did that if they didn't stay right where they were, the squares would break and scatter. They'd seen it happen elsewhere already today. The infantry—with little or no experience—were watching the way the Rogues calmly went about their business as though those huge French horses were no more than skittles to knock down. Their staunch disregard of danger was probably the only thing giving them any hope.

Hope—hah! It was the one thing neither he, nor his men, had felt for a very long time. They were the damned. Doomed to death, one way or another. They just preferred to take as many of the murdering French to hell with them as they could. At least they could die like men, if they did so in defence of their country, instead of dancing on the end of a rope.

'Here they come again, lads,' he heard Randall shout.

And then came the thunder of hooves. The roar of the guns. The smoke, and the screams, and the mud, and the carnage.

And his men reloaded and fired. And loaded and fired.

And still there was no end to the French.

The next morning

Lady Sarah Latymor rubbed her eyes and peered up at the manger above her head. Could she really make out wisps of straw sticking through the grating, or was it just wishful thinking?

In the stall next to hers, she could hear Castor shuffling about, lipping at whatever provender Pieter had placed in his own manger. She reached out her hand and laid the palm against the partition. Being able to hear her horse, Gideon's last gift to her, moving about in his stall during the night, had been all that had kept her flayed nerves from giving way altogether. But it looked as though the worst day of her life was over now. She could, at last, make out the pale rectangle of her hand against the planking. Dawn was definitely breaking. And Brussels was quiet. Though Madame le Brun had warned her that French troops might overrun the city during the night, they'd never come. Which meant the Allies must have won. She could come out of hiding.

And continue her quest.

To find out what had really happened to Gideon.

He *couldn't* be dead. He was her twin. If his soul had really departed this earth, she would feel it, wouldn't she? Her stomach twisted and dropped, just as it had when her brother-in-law Lord Blanchards had broken the news. While her sister Gussie had broken down and wept, Sarah had stood there, shaking her head. Grown more and more angry at the way they both just accepted it.

Blanchards had brushed aside her refusal to believe that the hastily scrawled note he held in his hand could possibly be delivering news of that magnitude. He'd practically ordered her to her room, where he no doubt expected her to weep decorously, out of sight, so that he could concentrate on comforting and supporting his wife.

Well, she hadn't wept. She'd been too angry to weep. That anger had simmered all night and driven her, on Sunday morning, all the way to Brussels, the only place where she was likely to be able to find out what had really happened to Gideon. Had driven her about half a mile along the road to the Forest of Soignes before she'd been beaten back by a troop of Hussars, claiming the French had won the battle, and were right on their heels.

Hussars, she snorted, sitting up and pushing a hank of hair off her face. What did they know?

As if in agreement, Ben, the dog she'd teamed up with in the wake of the Hussars' cowardly scramble to safety, sat up, stretched and yawned.

'Did you have a lovely sleep, Ben?' she asked as the dog came to swipe his tongue over her face in morning greeting. 'Yes, you did. You marvellous, fierce creature,' she added, ruffling his ears. 'I could feel you lying at my feet all night long and knew that if any Frenchman dared to set one toe inside this stable, you'd bite him with those great big teeth of yours.' She'd felt safer with him to guard her than she would have done had she had a loaded pistol in her hand.

'Woof,' Ben agreed, settling back to give his ear a vigorous scratch with one hind paw.

'Well, I may not have had a wink of sleep,' she informed him as she flung her blanket aside, 'but at least I didn't waste all those sleepless hours. I have,' she said, reaching for the jacket of her riding habit, which she'd rolled up and used for a pillow, 'come up with a plan. We're going to find Justin.'

She frowned at the jacket. Pale blue velvet was not the ideal material for rolling up and pillowing a lady's head. Especially not a lady who'd taken refuge in a stable. She shook it, brushed off the straw and slid her arms into the sleeves.

Ben stopped scratching, and gave her a hard stare.

'It's no use telling me that now the battle is over, I should go to the authorities and ask them for details,' she informed him testily. 'They would simply order me to go home, like a good girl, and wait for official notification. Which would get sent to Blanchards. Well,' she huffed as she went to rummage in her saddlebag—which she'd draped over the stall door in case she needed it in a hurry—and came up with a comb, 'they *did* send notification to Blanchards, didn't they? And much good it did me.'

She raised a hand to her head, discovered that most of her braids were still more or less intact and promptly thought better of attempting anything much in the way of grooming.

'And anyway,' she said, shoving the comb back into the saddlebag, 'if I walked into headquarters, unescorted, they'd want to know what I was doing in Brussels on my own. And don't say how would they know I'd come here on my own, Ben, it's obvious. If Blanchards had come to Brussels with me, *he* would be the one at headquarters asking the questions. See?'

Ben shuffled forward a little and licked his lips hopefully.

'Yes, I do have more sausage in here,' she told him, dipping her hand once more into the saddlebag. 'You may as well have it,' she said, breaking off a piece and tossing it to the straw at his feet. Her stomach was still coiled into the hard knot that had made eating virtually impossible since the moment Blanchards had told her Gideon was dead. Though she'd still packed plenty of provisions when she'd run away from Antwerp, thinking it might take her a day or so to locate Gideon, or his commanding officer, Colonel Bennington Ffog.

She wrinkled her nose as Ben disposed of the sausage in a few gulps. Why she'd thought, however briefly, that Bennington Ffog might be of any use, she couldn't imagine. It would be far better to find her oldest brother, Justin.

'Now, Justin might be cross with me,' she said as she pushed open the stall door and ventured into the aisle, 'but he won't send me back to Antwerp without telling me what I need to know first. He might be the stuffiest, most arrogant, obnoxious man,' she said, peering out into the stable yard to make sure nobody was about. 'He may give me a thundering scold for leaving the safety of Antwerp, against his explicit orders, but he does at least understand what Gideon means to me.'

With Ben trotting at her heels, Sarah made her way to the pump, where she quickly rinsed her face and hands. Ben took the opportunity to relieve himself and have a good sniff round.

When she made for the stable again, though, he was right beside her.

'Good boy,' she said, pausing to pat his head, before reaching for her riding hat, which she'd set on one of the doorposts.

'The only problem is,' she said, holding her hat in place with one hand, while thrusting as much of her hair as she could under it, 'I'm not entirely sure where to find him. However,' she added, deftly securing everything in place with a hatpin, 'Mary Endacott will.'

Ben dropped down on to his haunches, tilting his head to one side.

'Yes, I know. She doesn't like me. And I don't blame her. But you have to admit, since she's lived in Brussels for years, and knows everyone, she's bound to know who we can ask for his direction if she doesn't already have it. And what's more,' she added, when he didn't look convinced, 'she's the one person who is likely to want to know it just as much as I do, since the poor girl is in love with him.'

She lowered her head to fumble the buttons of her jacket closed as her mind dwelt on the last time she'd seen Mary, when Justin had been ordering her to leave Brussels, too. If she'd done as he'd told her...

No. Mary wouldn't have left, not even had they still been betrothed. The school she ran was her livelihood. And Justin had forfeited any authority he might have thought he had over her the minute he broke off their re-lationship in such a brutal fashion.

Besides, she wasn't the sort of woman to give up hope and sit about weeping, any more than Sarah was. Even after Justin had said all those horrid things, Mary would want to make sure he'd survived the battle, even if he didn't want to have anything more to do with her.

She lifted her head, squared her shoulders and strode out of the stall on her way back to the water pump. This time she saw Pieter shambling across the yard, rubbing his eyes sleepily.

'Be so good as to saddle my horse,' she said.

He hesitated for a moment, only tugging at his cap and

making for the stable once he saw Ben come trotting out and joining Lady Sarah at the pump, where she was now filling her water bottle.

'I'm so glad I found you yesterday,' she said, bending down to stroke Ben's head as he lapped up the water splashing to the cobbles. 'At first I just thought stumbling across the regimental mascot was a sign I was in exactly the right place, at the right time. But today I'm thankful that having you with me means I won't have to face Mary alone.' It wasn't going to be easy. Mary had no reason to greet her warmly. Yet what was the worst Mary could do? Show her the door? Or not even let her inside? What was that, compared to what had already happened? If Gideon really *was* dead.

Which she *wasn't* going to believe until somebody gave her some solid *proof.*

She mounted Castor and, with Ben trotting at her side, that determination carried her as far as the Rue Haute, where Mary's school stood. But then doubts started assailing her from all sides. If Mary wouldn't speak to her, then who else could she turn to?

'At least I won't have to knock on the front door and beg for permission to speak to her,' she observed, drawing Castor to a halt. For Mary was standing outside alongside a horse, talking to a group of bedraggled-looking men who stood with their mounts.

But even though this meant she'd overcome the first hurdle she'd imagined, Sarah's spirits sank. For Mary was, as always, looking neat as a pin.

Whereas she must look exactly as though—well, as though she was still wearing the same gown in which she'd spent a whole day on horseback, fighting her way against a tide of refugees fleeing the very place she wanted to reach more than anywhere on earth. And crawled through the mud to rescue Ben, and ended by sleeping in a stable because the landlady, upon whose compassion she'd relied, refused point blank to permit a muddy, fierce dog inside her house.

No, you couldn't feel your best in a gown you'd been wearing for two days, especially when you'd put it through all that. Besides which, women like Mary, petite, pretty women with pert little noses, always did make her feel like a gangly, beaky beanpole.

It was Ben who came to her rescue, for at least the second time in as many days, by letting out a series of joyful barks and bounding right into the group of men milling about on the front path. Because she'd been staring at Mary and wondering how on earth she was to persuade her to help, she hadn't been paying the men much heed. But now she noticed, as they bent to ruffle Ben's shaggy head rather than scattering in terror, that they were wearing the distinctive blue jackets of artillerymen. The blue jackets of her brother's unit, their facings and insignia only just recognisable under a coating of dirt of all kinds.

Randall's Rogues. Here? What could that mean?

Forgetting her own qualms about how Mary might treat her, Sarah urged Castor forward.

'What is it? What has happened?' A chill foreboding ran a finger down her spine. 'Is it Justin?' Mary's lips thinned as she glanced up and saw Sarah. But after only a moment she appeared to relent.

'We don't really know. Nobody can find him. They think…they think…' She gave an impatient little shake of her head. 'Can you believe they came here to look for him?'

Only too well. Because none of these men had been

at the Duchess of Richmond's ball and therefore couldn't know their Colonel had broken things off. To them, Mary's school must seem the obvious place to look.

'So, we decided we had better go and search the battlefield for him, in case...'

She could tell, from the way she seemed to brace herself, that Mary feared the worst. Sarah couldn't bear to think of Mary giving up on her brother. Not in that way.

Besides, she *refused* to believe she could have lost two brothers in the space of as many days.

'He isn't dead,' said Sarah firmly. 'He's indestructible.' At least, he would have been, had he been carrying his grandfather's lucky sword. The one that protected its wearer during battle. The one he'd accused Mary of stealing because he couldn't find it.

An icy hand seemed to clutch at the back of her neck.

'You cannot possibly know that,' said the ever-practical Mary.

'Yes, I can,' she insisted, even though she knew she was being totally irrational. Even though he might not be carrying the Latymor Luck, after all.

'Why else would fate have led me to Ben? And why else would we have arrived just as you are setting off to search for Justin?'

Mary's expression turned from one of barely repressed despair to barely concealed contempt.

But the men all perked up.

'She's got a point,' said one of them. 'Dog has a good nose. Best chance of finding Colonel Randall, since he's not where we all thought he was.'

'Aye, for the colonel's own sister to turn up here, right now...it must mean his luck is still holding,' said another.

Mary only shook her head, closing her eyes for a moment as if summoning patience.

'I think you would be better returning to Antwerp,' Mary said to her. 'You are in no fit state to come with us.'

'I have been looking for Gideon and I will not, cannot, give up my search,' Sarah replied, struggling to control her emotions now. 'I cannot go back until I know what has happened to my brothers.'

Mary sighed, clearly reluctant. 'Oh, very well, I suppose you had better come with us, then. But try not,' she snapped as she mounted up, 'to get in the way.'

Get in the way? How dare she assume…?

But then, of course, Mary only saw what everyone else did when they looked at Sarah: a spoiled, empty-headed society miss. For which she had only herself to blame. She'd taken such pains to appear to be the model of decorum, always doing exactly as her parents or guardians told her without demur and observing every rule of etiquette. She'd even overheard Lord Blanchards remark that he couldn't understand how a woman with Gussie's strength of mind could possibly be related to such an insipid girl.

'Here,' said Mary, producing a large, scented handkerchief from her pocket. Then gave her a little lecture about why she might need it.

'Thank you,' Sarah replied, pasting on a polite social smile to disguise her true feelings. Mary might say Sarah would need to hold a scented hanky to her nose for her own sake. But was she also hinting that everyone could tell Sarah hadn't stopped to bathe that morning? She'd thought the odour of dog and horse were disguising her own stale sweat pretty well, but perhaps that dainty little nose was more efficient than it looked.

It was some consolation that Ben, who'd been so delighted to see the men at first, didn't stay with them when they mounted up, but came back to her and loped along beside her own horse.

Of course, that probably had more to do with the scent of sausage still lingering round her saddlebags, but at least he *appeared* to prefer her to the others.

Even though it was early in the morning, the road from the Namur gate was already crowded with wounded men struggling back to Brussels for treatment. And little groups, like hers, going searching for loved ones.

The closer they got to the scene of the previous day's battle, the more gruesome the sights became.

Not to mention the smells. Some of it was gunpowder. But underlying it was something far worse. Something which made her jolly grateful Mary *had* thought to drench a couple of handkerchiefs in scent and share one with her. Though at the same time, Mary's foresight only made her even more aware of her own shortcomings.

'Steady, there,' she crooned, over and over again, patting Castor's neck when she needed to urge him past a pile of what she'd identified, from the briefest of glances, as bodies, both horse and human. Although the words were almost as much for herself, as her horse.

She tried not to let her eyes linger on what lay beside the roads. It put her in mind of a butcher's shop. So many men, reduced to so many cuts of meat…

A dog ran across the road in front of their little party, a long trail of what looked like sausages dangling from its jaws.

She clenched her teeth against a sudden surge of nausea. Sweat prickled across her top lip. Ben, who'd been darting from one side of the road to the other, in an agitated manner, lifted his head and watched the other dog as it ran down a fork in the road ahead.

Sarah closed her eyes, just for a minute, breathing deeply to try to clear her head which had started spinning alarmingly.

I must not faint. I must not faint.

'Are you all right, miss?' One of the Rogues had noticed her lag behind. Sarah forced her eyes open, to see that the rest of the party had reached the fork in the road. Oh, lord, she hoped they weren't going to have to go past the place where the scavenger dog had taken its obscene booty. Thank goodness she hadn't taken any breakfast, or she would be bringing it straight back up.

She couldn't go that way. She *wouldn't* go that way!

'No, not that way!' She raised her arm and pointed to the other fork in the road. 'We must go that way,' she said, in as steady a voice as she could muster, considering her whole body was shaking.

'Begging yer pardon, miss, but down along there is where Colonel Randall ought to be, if he's anywhere,' said the soldier, pointing the other way.

Mary had turned in her saddle and wore the look she'd seen on so many faces during her life. The look that told her she was an exasperating ninnyhammer.

'You said yourself,' Sarah replied haughtily, 'that you've already looked where you thought he ought to be and couldn't find him.'

At that moment Ben, who'd been running back and forth with his nose to the ground, suddenly let out a bark and ran a few paces down the road she'd just indicated. Then turned and looked over his shoulder as if to ask why they weren't following him.

'Even Ben thinks we ought to go that way,' she insisted.

And though they hadn't wanted to listen to her, they all seemed to have complete faith in Ben's instincts. To a man, they turned and followed him.

Leaving Mary no choice but to do so, too.

Sarah's stomach lurched again. Only this time it was from guilt. What if she was leading them in the wrong direction, simply because there didn't seem to be so many gruesome sights this way?

Mary was right to despise her. She wasn't strong and brave. Or even sensible. She should have just admitted that the sights and smells were proving too much for her. Except that, to admit to such weakness, in front of Mary and those men...

She didn't just have the Latymor nose. She had the wretched Latymor pride, too. That made her go to any lengths rather than admit she might have made a mistake.

Not that it had done her much good. For things were no better on this road, than they had looked on the one the scavenging dog had taken. The bright colours of uniforms lay stacked in heaps where the men who wore them had fallen, smeared now with mud and blood, and worse.

And there were pieces of uniforms, too, containing severed limbs. And bodies without heads. And horses screaming. And men groaning.

And Sarah's head was spinning.

And her heart was growing heavier and heavier.

Because she was finally seeing what war really meant. Men didn't die from neat little bullet wounds. Their bodies were smashed to pulp, torn asunder.

Oh, lord—if this had been what happened to Gideon, no wonder they hadn't sent his body to Antwerp. Justin might be overbearing, but it was always in a protective way. He wouldn't have wanted her, or Gussie, who was in such a delicate condition, to be subjected to the sight of Gideon, reduced to…to…*that*.

Just as it finally hit her that it might be true, that Gideon might really be dead, one of the men gave out a great cry.

She looked up, to see Ben go bounding across a field to a sort of tumbledown building, round which even more bodies were stacked than by the side of the road.

'He's found him! The blessed dog's only gone and found him,' cried one of the men. And they all went charging up to the ruin.

Chapter Two

She heard somebody say *charnel house*.

Sarah's stomach lurched. She drew Castor to a halt as Ben scrabbled at the door of the barn until he found his way in.

'Justin is in there,' she cried in an agony of certainty. In the charnel house. Which meant he was dead. 'I know he is.'

'We shall see,' said Mary calmly, dismounting.

Sarah slid from her own horse, her legs shaking so much she had to cling to the pommel to stay upright.

'Here,' said Mary, thrusting her reins into her hands. 'You stay here and…and guard the horses while I go and see.'

Then, in a rather kinder tone, added, 'It might not even be him.'

But Sarah knew it was. Ben had scented…something. He'd ignored heaps and heaps of dead bodies. The dog wouldn't have barked so excitedly for no good reason.

And the Rogues hadn't come out yet, either.

It was her brother in there. In there, where Mary was going, her face composed, her demeanour determined and brave.

While the prospect of seeing Justin, her strong, force-ful brother, lying lifeless—perhaps even torn to bits like so many of the poor wretches she'd seen scattered in heaps along the roads...

And then any pretence she was guarding the horses fled as blackness swirled round the edges of her vision. Eddied up from the depths of her, too, as the extent of her useless-ness hit her. What point had there been in snatching up that bag of medical supplies when she'd fled Antwerp? Bridget, her old nursemaid, had told her she would need it. And Bridget had a way of *seeing* things. So yesterday, she'd imagined she was riding to Gideon's rescue, armed with the very herbs that he needed. But the truth was that Gideon was beyond anyone's help. And that she was so overset by the thought of seeing any of her brothers chopped and hacked about that she would have been no more use to Gideon than a...than a...

Actually, she would have been of no help to Gideon at all. Just as she wasn't being of any help to Justin.

They were right about her—those people who wrote her off as a weak, empty-headed nuisance. All she'd done by coming here was create problems for everyone else. Gussie and Blanchards would be worried sick about her, and even though she'd promised Mary she wouldn't get in the way— Sarah groaned. She was growing more and more certain that she was either going to faint dead away, or cast up her accounts.

Well, she wasn't going to do it in front of Justin's men. Only a couple had stayed in the barn with Mary. The rest had come outside again, probably, she suspected, to keep an eye on their rather suspiciously magnificent horses.

There was a half-collapsed wall to her left, which would shield her from view if she was going to be sick.

Which would conceal the evidence from the stalwart Mary, too, when she eventually came out.

If her legs would carry her that far…

They did. But only just. The effort of clambering over the lowest, most broken-down portion of the wall proved too much for both Lady Sarah's legs, and her stomach, which both gave way at the same time. She hadn't even gained the privacy she'd sought, either, because there was a group of peasant women busily ferreting amongst the rubble so they could rob the men who'd been partially buried under it.

They paused for a moment, but only a moment. With mocking, hard eyes, they dismissed her as being no threat as she retched fruitlessly, then calmly went back to stripping the corpse they'd just exhumed.

Or what had appeared to be a corpse. For suddenly, as the women turned him to ease the removal of his shirt, the man let out a great bellow, which both startled and scattered them.

Sarah gasped as he uttered a string of profanities. Not because of the words themselves, but because they were in English. His jacket, the one they'd just torn from his back, was blue, so she'd assumed he was French. But not only was he English, but his voice was cultured, his swearing fluent.

He was an officer.

And he was trying to get to his feet, though his face and shoulders were cloaked in blood.

Instinctively, she got to her feet, too, though with what aim she wasn't sure.

Until she saw one of the peasant women hefting a knife.

'No!' Sarah's fist closed round one of the stones that

had once been part of the wall and, without thinking of the consequences, threw it as hard as she could at the woman who'd started to advance on the wounded man. She couldn't just stand there and let them rob him of his very life. It was unthinkable!

She'd been of no use to Gideon, but by God she wasn't going to stand back and let those women casually despatch another Englishman before her very eyes!

'Leave him alone,' she screamed, throwing another stone in their direction.

Rage and revulsion at what they were doing had her quivering with outrage now, instead of despair.

The women paused, eyeing her warily.

The man, too, turned his head when he heard her shout.

He stretched his hand towards her.

'Save me,' he groaned, then swayed and slowly toppled forward.

Oh, no! If he landed face down in the mud, that would finish him off as surely as the peasant woman's knife. Sarah flung herself in his path, arms outstretched as if to catch him. Though, of course, his weight proved too much for her. She landed with a wet thud on her bottom, the unconscious, half-naked officer half on top of her.

But at least he was still breathing.

For now. The peasant women were still hovering. And her legs were pinned in place by his dead weight.

Well, this was no time to hold her pride too dear. Throwing back her head, she screamed for help.

At once, there came a familiar, deep throaty bark.

The women ran for it as Ben came bounding over the wall, barking and baring his fangs, and looking gloriously, heart-warmingly ferocious.

Once he was satisfied the women weren't going to come back, Ben turned and licked her face just the once, then started nosing at the man who lay face down in her lap.

Because the women had managed to strip the officer of everything but his breeches and one boot before they fled, Sarah could clearly see that his back was a mass of bruises. His hair was matted to his scalp with blood, which was still oozing from a nasty gash. She didn't know how he was alive, but he was. He was.

And Ben seemed terribly excited by the fact. He kept nosing at the man, then prancing away, and barking, only to come back and nose at him, and lick him as though he knew him.

And it suddenly struck her that the Rogues uniform was blue. And that her brother was lying not ten yards away.

Was this another of his men? One of his officers, if the tone of his voice was anything to go by.

Oh, dear. Justin had refused to introduce any of his officers to her, when she'd tried to show a sisterly interest in his brigade, on the day of a mass review of all the Allied troops mustering around Brussels. He'd told her that they were decidedly not gentlemen and she was to have nothing to do with them. Gideon's commanding officer, Colonel Bennington Ffog, had gone so far as to describe them as the very dregs of humanity. They'd both be appalled if they could see her sprawled on the ground with his head in her lap.

Just as the thought occurred to her, she heard a scrabbling noise and looked up to see two of the Rogues who'd escorted her and Mary out here, pushing their way through the lowest bit of wall.

The first one to reach her knelt down and, without so much as a by-your-leave, turned the officer's face so he could peer at it closely.

'Strike me if it ain't the Major,' he said, confirming her suspicions.

'How'd 'e come to be out here?'

'Damned if I know,' said the First Rogue to reach her. 'Last I 'eard 'e'd come to and was going to make for the field hospital.'

'Well, 'e went the wrong way,' said the Second Rogue on the scene grimly. 'Looks like 'e 'ad a second go round with more Frenchies, too, else I don't see 'ow 'e come to get buried under that wall.'

'Lucky you come over this way, miss.' They'd been talking to each other, but now they both turned to her with what looked like gratitude. 'Else we'd never have guessed 'e was 'ere.'

'No.' She shook her head. 'No, I…really…' She'd only stumbled on him because of her appalling squeamishness. She didn't deserve their gratitude.

'Aye, but it was you as drove off them filthy bi-biddies, what would have finished off the Major,' said his companion, hunkering down beside her.

'It was Ben,' she said glumly. They hadn't been scared of *her* at all.

'You was the one that called him, though, wasn't you?'

Yes. Oh, very well, she had done one thing right today.

'And you stopped 'im from falling face down in the mud and like as not drowning in it.'

That was true, too. She felt a little better. Until she recalled that she hadn't been strong enough not to get knocked to the ground.

'Any way you look at it, you've saved Major Bartlett's life.'

'Major Bartlett?' She looked down at the motionless man whose head she cradled in her lap. This poor, broken, battered wretch was all that was left of Major Bartlett? He'd been so *handsome*. So full of…of, well, himself, actually. He'd been lounging against a tree, his jacket slung over one shoulder, watching her and Gideon ride past, on the day she'd learned who he was. She hadn't been able to help peering at him, her curiosity roused by Justin's vague warning.

And as if he'd known she was wondering what kind of things he'd done, to make Justin think she might be corrupted merely by talking to him, Major Bartlett had grinned at her.

And winked.

Oh, but he'd looked like a young lion, that day, basking in the sun, with his mane of golden curls tumbling over his broad brow.

So vitally *alive*.

Just like the last time she'd seen Gideon. Her twin had been laughing as he preened before her mirror, telling her what a fine sight he was going to make on the battlefield. How she wasn't to worry about Frenchman wanting to shoot him, because they'd all be too busy riding up to enquire who'd made his exquisitely cut uniform.

Had anyone, she wondered, her lower lip quivering, held Gideon in their arms as he was dying? Or had he been left face down in the mud, because the only woman anywhere near was too worried about her reputation to go to his aid?

Her eyes welled with tears.

The Second Rogue cleared his throat. 'No need for tears, miss. You done well, leading us 'ere.'

'Aye, saved both 'im and yer brother, I reckon,' hastily put in the other, as though equally appalled by the prospect of being landed with a weeping female.

'Saved? My brother?' She blinked rapidly a few times. They weren't talking about Gideon. They didn't know him. They meant Justin. 'Your Colonel…is he…?'

'Stopped a bullet, but Miss Mary, she reckons as how she knows someone what can patch him up.'

'Oh, thank God. Thank God for Mary, anyway.' *She'd* been worse than useless.

'Aye, she's doing a grand job with 'is lordship, in there,' he said, jerking his head towards the barn, 'by all accounts.'

'Can you stay 'ere and keep an eye on the Major while we go and sort out 'ow we're going to get 'im and the Colonel back to Brussels?'

Exactly where they thought she might go, when she was pinned to the ground by a heavy, unconscious male, she had no idea.

But they were still crouched there, watching her, as though waiting for a response.

Did they really think she would try to wriggle out from under their major and leave him lying in a pool of mud?

With a little shock, she realised that it was what most people who knew her would expect. And what Justin would demand.

But she wouldn't leave a dog in a state like this. In fact, she hadn't. Yesterday, when she'd seen Ben trapped underneath an overturned wagon, she'd thought nothing of crawling under it to untie him from the broken axle, after pacifying him with bits of sausage, because she'd recognised him as the regimental mascot. And Randall's Rogues never left one of their own behind. Not that she was one of them, except by virtue of being Lord Randall's sister, but if she couldn't turn her back on a dog, even a dog she feared might bite her, simply because he belonged to her brother's regiment, then she definitely couldn't do any less for one of his officers. It wouldn't even be as hard, in some ways. The dog had been so frantic with fear she was half-afraid he would bite her. This man could do nothing to her. He wasn't even conscious.

'Of course I can,' she snapped. 'I shall be fine.' Even though mud was steadily oozing up through the fabric of her riding habit, chilling her behind. Well, she wasn't going to take any harm from sitting in a puddle for a few minutes, was she? She was as healthy as a horse. Nor was it as if she was ever going to be able to wear this outfit again, after what she'd put it through the day before.

And at least she was shielding this poor wretch from one minor discomfort. Without her lap to lie on, he would have been frozen, never mind at risk from inhaling mud and drowning in it.

The two Rogues looked at each other and a message seemed to pass between them because, as one, they got to their feet.

'Dog will stay on guard,' said the Second Rogue. 'Dog. Stay.'

Ben promptly lay down, head on his paws, just as though he completely understood the command.

'We'll get some transport fit for you, don't you worry,' said the First Rogue gruffly, before vaulting over the wall with his comrade.

She wasn't the least bit worried about how she was

going to get back to Brussels. It was this poor man that needed all the help he could get. And her brother. Justin.

Oh, dear. Justin would be furious if he could see her now. Even Gideon had warned her to stay away from Major Bartlett. Although, Gideon being Gideon, he'd explained exactly why.

'For once I agree with Justin,' he'd said with a slight frown, when he'd caught the major winking at her. 'He's such an indiscriminate womaniser they call him Tom Cat Bartlett. The only reason he's out here in the Allée Verte this early in the morning is no doubt because he's slinking away from the bed of his latest conquest.'

On hearing that Bartlett was a rake, she'd put him out of her mind. She detested rakes. And she would never have willingly gone anywhere near him again. She sucked in a short, sharp, breath. For here she was, cradling his head in her lap, comparing him to her beloved brother Gideon, who'd warned her against him.

And yet, weren't they both soldiers, too? Wounded in the service of their country?

He certainly didn't *look* like a rake any more. If the men hadn't told her, she wouldn't have recognised him. The once-handsome face had become a grotesque, smoke-blackened, bloodied mask through which wild green eyes had stared at her.

Beseechingly.

Her heart jolted.

The poor man was in such a state that he'd thought she, who'd have just lost her breakfast beside the same wall that had buried him, if she'd been in any state to eat any, could help him.

He must be out of his mind.

'All right, miss?'

She looked up to see the two Rogues had returned, looking mighty pleased with themselves.

'We've got one of those French sick wagons,' one proclaimed. The other nudged him in the side, with a quick frown.

Oh…oh, dear. They'd obviously stolen it. Well, what could she expect, when robbery with violence was, according to Gideon, what Justin's men did best?

'Can't very well drape him over the back of an 'orse, miss. Jolting a man with a head wound would finish 'im off for sure.'

'Yes. Of course. I quite see that,' she said mildly, employing the vague smile that had stood her in good stead in so many awkward situations. It worked again. The men made no further attempt to justify their actions.

They just manoeuvred Major Bartlett off her lap and into the vehicle they'd parked on the other side of the wall—far more gently than she would have expected from men who acted and spoke so coarsely, and who'd just committed who knew what violence in order to ensure their officers had the best transport back to Brussels.

They'd no doubt go and fetch Mary now, so that she could oversee the journey and then their nursing. So Major Bartlett was off her hands.

She glanced down, then, and winced at the state of them. But there was a small stream not far away, she thought, where she could rinse them. Behind that thick border of rushes.

As she dabbled her bloodstained hands in the water, she wondered what she should do next. Gideon must be dead, she supposed, even though her whole being revolted against the notion. And Justin didn't need her to stay and nurse him. Mary would do a much better job.

Besides, seeing his sister, when he came to himself—*if*
he came to himself—would make him so furious it would
probably cause an immediate relapse. He hadn't wanted
her to come to Brussels at all. Had ordered her to leave,
more than once.

There was nothing for it but to go back to Antwerp
and explain herself. Her shoulders drooped as she pictured the scold Blanchards would give her for worrying
his poor wife at such a critical stage. Gussie had suffered
a couple of miscarriages early in her marriage and then,
for some inexplicable reason, failed to become pregnant
again for a worrying length of time. The Marquis of
Blanchards was naturally very protective now that it was
looking as though his wife might finally be about to present him with an heir. And his patience with Sarah had
been wearing thin even before she'd run away. He hadn't
minded taking her to Paris, when Gussie had suggested
the trip. No, it wasn't until Bonaparte had fled Elba, and
most of polite society had scurried back to England because France was no longer safe, that he'd begun to look
at her sideways. For Gussie wouldn't have been so determined to go to Brussels if Sarah's twin hadn't been
stationed there. Nothing, now, would prevent him from
packing her off to England, where he could return her
to Mama's care.

And he'd do so in such blistering terms that Mama
would marry her off to the very next person who ap-
plied for her hand, no matter what Sarah thought of him.

But what did it matter who they chose to take her off
their hands? Without Gideon, she was only going to be
able to live half a life, wherever she was. Whoever she
was with.

Her head bowed, she made her way laboriously up

the bank, picked her way though the mud and clambered over the wall.

'Ready, now, are you, miss?'

The First Rogue was standing at the rear of the wagon, his arms folded across his massive chest.

'If you will excuse me,' she said, lifting her chin and gesturing for him to step aside, 'I need to let Mary know that I am returning to Antwerp, so that she can inform Justin when he recovers.'

'Antwerp?' The man gave her a quick frown.

'Yes. If you wouldn't mind going to fetch my horse.'

The man gave her a dirty look and muttered something that sounded a bit unsavoury. She shrugged and went to look inside the wagon.

Only the Major was there.

'Just a moment,' she said. 'Before you go and fetch my horse—' which he'd shown no sign of doing as yet, anyway '—could you tell my why Justin isn't in here? And where is Miss Endacott?'

'Miss Endacott was adamant we wasn't to move the Colonel,' the Rogue growled. 'Not yet a while.'

'But the Major must have treatment. At once! Why, he's already been lying out all night, with an open wound. Somebody needs to clean him up and stitch him up.'

She'd been about to leave both men to Mary's care. But would Mary have the time to do anything for Major Bartlett if Justin was too poorly to even move? Besides, he'd begged her to save him. *Her.* Not pretty and practical Mary Endacott, but her.

Well, there was no question of riding off and leaving the Major behind, not now. She couldn't simply abandon him, hoping that somebody would do something for him. No matter what kind of man he was, he didn't deserve to be left untended. Perhaps to die of neglect. She wouldn't wish that fate on *any* man.

With half her mind troubled by the thought that might have been exactly what had happened to Gideon, she scrambled up into the back of the wagon.

'I will stay with the Major until we can get him to a hospital,' she informed the rather startled Rogue.

She'd seen makeshift hospitals springing up outside the Namur gate. Wounded men had been staggering, or been carried, towards those with medical expertise even while the battle had been raging.

'I'll go and fetch your horse then, miss,' said Rogue One. 'Wouldn't do to leave a fine animal like that out here. Someone's bound to try to steal him.'

The other Rogue, who'd been leaning nonchalantly against the side of the wagon, shook his head as Rogue One darted off.

'Terrible amount of thieving goes on after a battle,' he observed drily as they waited for Rogue One to fetch not only Castor, but also the two horses they'd ridden to the battlefield, and tether them to the sides of the wagon. 'You wouldn't credit it.'

'Oh, wouldn't I?'

They both glanced up at the tart tone of her voice, then grinned at each other.

'Now look, miss,' said the one she'd come to think of as the First Rogue. 'The road is mortal bad. No matter how careful we drive, won't be able to help jolting the Major. You must do what you can to cushion his head.'

'Need both of us up here, see,' said the Second Rogue, 'making sure nobody thinks they can swipe this cart off of us to carry their own wounded.'

Which was all too real a threat, since it was clearly what they'd just done.

'Heaven forbid,' she said, smiling her vague smile again, then going to the head of the stretcher, just as they'd suggested.

She watched out of the corner of her eye as the First Rogue climbed into the driver's seat and took the reins, while the Second Rogue got up beside him and draped his musket across his knee.

She'd half-hoped Ben would jump up into the wagon with her, but he chose to run alongside, snarling at anyone who got too close.

It didn't seem to take half as long returning to Brussels as it had coming out. Which was probably because concentrating on the Major's welfare kept her mind, and her eyes, off the sights and smells that had disturbed her so much before.

Not that trying to prevent an unconscious man's head from coming to further harm was without its own perils. Even though the wagon was well sprung, it couldn't compensate for the churned-up state of the road. Every time they went over a particularly deep rut, Major Bartlett's head would jolt no matter how firmly she thought she was holding it in her hands.

Pretty soon, she wondered if the only way to really protect him would be to kneel on the floor, wrap her arm about his neck and sort of cradle him to her bosom.

The thought of doing so made her blush all over. But then she chided herself for being so missish. He wasn't taking liberties, after all. The poor man had no idea where his nose would be pressed.

Just imagine if this had been Gideon, she told herself

sternly. Wouldn't she have cradled him to her bosom, to prevent further injury during the trip back to Brussels?

The sad fact was, she'd never know.

Her vision blurred for a second or two. But she resolutely blinked back the tears, sniffed and reminded herself that though Gideon was past helping, this man wasn't. By some miracle, he'd survived. So even though she hadn't found Gideon, her search for him *hadn't* been a total waste of time. She might not be good for much, but she could at least prevent the Major from coming to any further harm as the wagon bounced along over the bumpy road.

It was one small thing, one practical thing she could do to stem the tide of death that had swept Gideon from her. Gritting her teeth and consigning her gown to perdition, she wrapped her arms round Major Bartlett's neck and held his bloodied head as tight as she could.

Chapter Three

The scene that greeted her when they reached the make-shift hospital was one of chaos.

She clambered out of the wagon, and went to the driver's seat to speak to the Rogues.

'This is awful,' she said, indicating the men with terrible injuries who were lying groaning all over the ground, flies buzzing round open wounds.

'Aye, well it's like this, miss,' said the First Rogue. 'Surgeons are too busy hacking off the arms and legs of the poor b-blighters they think they can save to bother with the ones who lie still and quiet, like our Major. They put those to the back of the queue. And by the time they get round to them, well, mostly there's no need for them to try anything any more.'

'We can't leave the Major here,' she said, appalled. 'Do you know of some other hospital we can take him to? A proper, civilian hospital? Where he can get the treatment he needs?'

The First Rogue scratched his chin. 'Hospitals in town are all full as they can hold. Saw them laying the wounded out in the park and all along the sides of the streets, too. And that was before we come out 'ere. Gawd alone knows what it'll be like by now.'

'Well, what about taking him back to his lodgings, then? His man could help, couldn't he?' Justin's own body servant, Robbins, was always tending Justin when he was wounded. Gideon had told her so.

'His man's used up,' said the Second Rogue brusquely.

She'd heard Justin apply that term to the butcher's bill after a battle. He didn't speak of his troops dying, but of being used up.

'What are we to do with him, then?' It never occurred to her, not for one moment, to simply mount Castor, ride away and leave him. In some weird way, it felt that if she just left the Major's fate in the hands of providence, it would be tantamount to submitting to the horrid inevitability of death itself.

Which would somehow dishonour Gideon's memory.

'You've got all those medical supplies in yer bags,' said Rogue Two.

'How...how did you know?'

He shrugged. 'Had a look.'

He'd gone through her saddlebags, while she'd been climbing over the wall, and throwing stones at the looters? Or had it been later, when she was washing her hands in the stream?

'I didn't take nothing,' he protested.

'Look, it's plain as a pikestaff you've been sent here to save our Major,' said Rogue One. 'If you nurse him, there's a chance he'll pull through.'

'Me? But...' She thought of the wounds covering his body, not to mention the huge tear across his scalp.

Then she saw their faces harden. Take on a tinge of disappointment. Of disapproval.

Of course, they wouldn't believe she didn't feel *capable* of nursing their Major. They had no idea how inadequate she felt. They would just think she was too high and mighty to lower herself to their level.

'I suppose I could try,' she explained. 'I mean, the little I might be able to do is bound to be better than nothing, isn't it?'

'I took a gander when we put 'im in the wagon,' said Rogue Two. 'His skull ain't broke. A lady like you could stitch him up as nice as any doctor. And then it'll just be nursing he needs.'

'Plenty of drink,' said Rogue One. 'Get all his wounds clean.'

'We'll help you with that. Lifting him and turning him and such.'

They made it sound so simple.

They made it sound as though she was perfectly capable of taking charge of a severely wounded man.

Her heart started hammering in her chest.

Perhaps she really could do it. After all, they'd said they'd help her. And now she came to think of it, hadn't she already done much, much more than anyone would ever have thought possible? She'd reached Brussels unaccompanied when everyone else was fleeing the place. She'd rescued the snarling, snapping Ben from the teetering wreckage of a baggage cart. She'd ignored the Hussars and made her own judgement about whether the French were about to overrun Brussels, and been right. She'd even stood up to those women who'd been trying to murder poor Major Bartlett. And that after riding across a battlefield without totally fainting away.

And she *could* sew.

And even though she'd never nursed anyone in her

life, she had listened most attentively to every word of Bridget's advice, because she'd believed she *was* going to be nursing Gideon. Marigold was for cleansing wounds to stop them from putrefying. Comfrey was for healing cuts. And apparently she could make a sort of tea from the dried meadowsweet flowers, which was less bitter and nasty than willow bark and almost as effective at reducing fever.

Poor Gideon wouldn't need any of that, now. He was beyond anyone's help.

But this man had fallen, literally, into her lap.

Had begged her to save him.

And there was nobody else to do it. He had nobody.

Just as she had nobody.

Well, she thought, firming her lips, he might not know it, but he had *her*.

'Very well, then,' she said, clambering back into the wagon. 'I will do my best. We'll take him to my lodgings.'

She'd already begun to prove, at least to herself, that she wasn't that fragile girl whose only hope, so her entire family believed, was in finding some man to marry her and look after her.

This was her chance to prove to them, too, that she didn't need anyone to look after her. On the contrary!

With her head held high, she gave the Rogues her direction, then knelt down to cushion the Major's head against her breasts once more for the remainder of the journey.

Pretty soon they were drawing up outside a house on the Rue de Regence, unloading the Major by means of the stretcher with which the cart was equipped and banging on the door for entry.

'Oh, my lady,' cried Madame le Brun. 'You found him then? You found your brother?'

The men holding the stretcher glanced at her, then looked straight ahead, their faces wiped clean of expression.

Sarah blinked.

The night before, when she'd turned up frightened, and bedraggled, clutching Castor's reins for dear life, she'd told Madame le Brun how she'd run away from Antwerp to search for her twin, because she'd heard a rumour he'd been killed, but refused to believe it. She'd explained that she'd returned to her former lodgings because she hadn't known where else to spend the night, with the outcome of the battle currently raging still being so uncertain. The house where Lord Blanchards had rented rooms when Brussels had been the centre of a sort of cosmopolitan social whirl might not have been in the most fashionable quarter of town, but it was well kept and respectable. And Madame le Brun had been a very motherly sort of landlady.

It would be terrible to lie to her. Sarah hated people who told lies and she avoided telling them herself. Yet there was a difference, she'd always found, in letting people assume whatever they liked. Particularly if the absolute truth would cause too much awkwardness.

'He is very gravely wounded,' she therefore told Madame le Brun, neatly sidestepping the issue of his identity altogether.

'I shall be nursing him myself, so it will be best to put him in my room. The room I had when I was here before.'

She smiled vaguely in Madame's direction, but spoke to the men. 'Careful how you get him up the stairs.'

At that moment Ben provided a welcome diversion by attempting to follow them inside.

'Oh, no. This I cannot have,' shrieked Madame le Brun, making shooing motions at the dog, who'd acquired an extra layer of mud since the last time she'd seen him. 'The stables! The stables is the place for the animals.'

Ben took exception to anyone trying to get between him and the three members of his adopted pack who were already mounting the stairs. He bared his teeth at the landlady, and growled.

In the ensuing fracas, the Rogues manoeuvred the stretcher up the stairs and into Sarah's old room. And no more questions were asked about the wounded man's identity. By the time the landlady, the dog and Sarah caught up, in a welter of snapping teeth and loudly voiced recriminations, the Rogues had got their Major on to her bed.

'Madame,' said Sarah, 'we can settle the question of what to do with the dog, who as you can see is very devoted to his master, later, can we not? What we really need, right now, is plenty of fresh linen, and hot water, and towels.'

Even though she hadn't actually ever nursed anyone before, it was obvious that the first thing they needed to do was get the poor man cleaned up.

'Oh, *le pauvre*,' said Madame le Brun, crossing herself as she caught her first proper sight of the Major's battered and semi-clothed body. 'Fresh sheets, yes, and water and towels, too. Of course. Though the dog…'

'Yes, yes, I promise you I will deal with the dog, too. He won't be any bother. But please…' Sarah allowed her eyes to fill with tears as she indicated Major Bartlett's body.

'Very well, my lady. Though I cannot think it is right for an animal so dirty to be in the room with one so badly hurt...'

'The dog it was as found him,' put in the First Rogue.

'Yes, we owe Ben a great deal,' said Sarah.

Madame le Brun grumbled about the invasion of her property by such a large, fierce and dirty dog, but she did so on her way out the door.

Sarah could hardly believe she'd won that battle. Why, only the night before, she'd cowered in the stables because Madame wouldn't let the dog in the house, and Sarah had been afraid that someone trying to escape Brussels before the French forces arrived might try to steal her horse. She'd been too timid to do more than wheedle a blanket and some paper and ink from Madame. Today she'd got the dog *and* a wounded officer right into her very bedroom.

It was a heady feeling.

Which lasted only as long as it took for her to notice that the Rogues were intent on stripping the Major of his clothes. They'd already pulled off his one remaining boot. Ben pounced on it and bore it off to the hearthrug, from which vantage point he could keep an eye on proceedings while having a good chew.

'You'll be wanting to fetch those medical supplies, I shouldn't wonder,' the First Rogue suggested gruffly, pausing in the act of undoing the Major's breeches. 'While we start getting him cleaned up a bit.'

'Yes, yes, I shall do that,' she said in a voice that sounded rather high-pitched to her own ears. She turned away swiftly and scurried out of the room, thoroughly relieved the man had offered her a good excuse for making herself scarce.

She pressed her hands to her hot cheeks once she'd shut the bedroom door behind her. Her legs were shaking a bit, but she *wasn't* going to succumb to a fit of the vapours just because she'd almost seen a man have his breeches removed.

She forced her legs to carry her to the head of the stairs and made her rather wobbly way down. She was going to have to get used to a lot more than glimpses of a man's, well, manliness in the days to come, if she was going to be of any use.

In fact, she was going to have to breach practically every rule by which she'd lived. She'd always taken such pains to keep her reputation spotless that she'd never been without a chaperon, not even when visiting the ladies' retiring room at a ball. She could scarcely believe she'd just encouraged two hardened criminals to install the regiment's most notorious rake in her bedroom—nay, her very bed.

Where he was currently being stripped naked.

Oh, lord, what would people think? Actually, she knew very well what they would think. What they would say, if they found out.

Right, then. She squared her shoulders as she marched across the yard to the stables. She'd better think of some way of preventing anyone finding out what she was doing, or they'd all be up in arms.

At least all the gossipy society people she knew from London had fled Brussels. She'd seen many of the most inquisitive in Antwerp. Even if any of them had remained, Madame le Brun thought Major Bartlett was actually her brother, so she *couldn't* let anything slip.

And as for Justin... She chewed on the inside of her lower lip, as it occurred to her he might still be in that tumbledown barn, too gravely ill to move, let alone worry about what his flighty little sister was getting up to. Actually, he might have no idea she'd returned to Brussels, if he was still unconscious. Not that she wanted him to remain unconscious.

She bowed her head and uttered a silent, but heartfelt, prayer. And immediately felt a deep assurance that Justin couldn't be in more capable hands. Moreover, even when he began to recover, Mary wasn't likely to mention anything that might hamper his recovery.

She retrieved the medicine pouch, then made her way back to the house, feeling sorrier than ever for poor Major Bartlett. Having to rely on such as her. Nobody, not by the wildest stretch of imagination, would ever describe *her* as capable.

A crushing sense of inadequacy made her pause outside her bedroom door. For on the other side of it lay an immense set of challenges. All wrapped up in the naked, helpless body of a wounded soldier.

She pressed her forehead to the door. She'd already decided she wasn't going to be one of those people who thought propriety was more important than a man's very survival. But even so, it wasn't easy to calmly walk into a room that contained two rough soldiers and a naked man.

What if she tried to think of this as a sickroom, rather than her own bedroom, though? And of Major Bartlett as just a wounded soldier, rather than a naked and dangerous rake? Her patient, in fact. Yes—yes, that was better. She wasn't, primarily, a woman who'd been forbidden to so much as speak to him, but his *nurse*.

It made it possible for her to knock on the door, at any rate. And, when a gruff voice told her she could come in, Sarah found that she could look across at the Major with equanimity—well, *almost* with equanimity. Because he wasn't lying in *her* bed. He was in his sickbed. All she had to do was carry on in this vein and she'd soon be able to convince herself she wasn't a sheltered young lady who regarded all single men as potential predators, but a nurse, as well.

A nurse, moreover, who'd promised, when his men had begged for her help, that she would do her best.

In her absence, Madame had fetched water and towels. And the men had put them to good use, to judge from the mounds of bloodied cloths on the floor.

'He ain't so bad as he looked,' said the First Rogue. 'A lot of bruising and cuts to his back where the wall fell on him, but nothing broken, not even his head.'

'Really 'as got nine lives, 'as the Tom C—' The Second Rogue broke off mid-speech, but Sarah knew perfectly well what he'd been about to say.

Well, well. Perhaps he hadn't only gained that nickname because of his nocturnal habits. Perhaps a good deal of it was down to him having more than his fair share of luck, too.

'Sooner we can get it sewn up the better,' put in the First Rogue hastily, as though determined to fix her attention on the man's injuries, rather than his reputation. 'Cut right down to the bone, he is.'

They were looking at her expectantly.

Oh, yes. They'd said that she ought to do the sewing, hadn't they?

'I…' She pressed one hand to her chest. In spite of the lecture she'd given herself, about proving how capable she was, now that it came to it, her heart was fluttering in alarm. At this point, Mama would fully expect her to have a fit of the vapours, if she hadn't already done so because there was a naked man in her room.

'You can do it, miss,' said the Second Rogue. 'Far better than us clumsy b... Uh—' he floundered '—blighters.'

'I don't know how,' she admitted, though she was ashamed to sound so useless.

'We'll direct you. And hold the Major still, in case he comes round.'

Yes. Yes they would need to do that. The pain of having his head sewn back together might well rouse him from his stupor. After all, hadn't he roused once before, when the looters had been tearing off his shirt?

'I can't...'

'Yes, you can, miss.'

She smiled ruefully at the man. 'I was going to say I can't go on thinking of you as Rogue One and Rogue Two, like characters in a play. You must have names? I am Lady Sarah.' She held out her hand to Rogue One. 'How do you do?'

He took her proffered hand and shook it. 'Dawkins, Lady Sarah.'

'Cooper,' said the other with a nod, though rather than shaking her hand, he pressed a pair of scissors into it. 'You need to start by trimming his hair back as short as you can get it, round the sabre cut,' he said.

'S-sabre cut?'

'Cavalry sabre, I reckon,' said Cooper. 'Only thing that would knock him out and slice the scalp near clean off like that, all in one go.'

I will not be sick. I will not be sick.

'Do you think he would prefer it,' she said brightly,

in a desperate attempt to turn the conversation in a less grisly direction, 'if I cut it short all over? Only he will look so very odd, shorn in patches, when the bandages come off, won't he?'

'Time enough for that when he's better, miss.'

Yes, but keeping up a conversation was still a good idea. She was less likely to either faint, or be sick, if she could keep at least a part of her mind off the grisly task she was having to perform.

'Yes, of course,' she said, ruthlessly snipping away the matted curls. Lord, but it seemed like a crime to hack away at such lovely hair. Not that it looked lovely any more. She felt a pang at a sudden memory of how glorious it had looked, with the sunlight glinting on it, that day in the Allée Verte. She'd never imagined a day would come when she'd be running her fingers through it. Not for *any* reason.

'We can ask him how he wants it done when he's better, can't we? Perhaps get a barber in to do something that will disguise this hideous crop I'm giving him.'

She laughed a little hysterically. Then swallowed.

'It is amazing what a professional *coiffeuse* can do, you know.' *Snip.* 'Even with hair like mine.' *Snip, snip.* 'It is completely straight, normally. It takes hours of fussing, from a terribly expensive woman, with her special lotions and a hot iron, before Mama considers me fit to venture out of doors. And it takes such a long time to prepare me for a ball that I have gained the reputation for being dreadfully vain.'

She must sound it, too, prattling on about styling her hair, at a time like this. Except that with her mind full of hairdressers, and ballrooms, somehow it was easier to cope with the grim reality of what she was doing.

'Reckon that'll do now, miss,' said Cooper, gently removing the scissors from her fingers and handing her a needle and thread.

'Th-thank you.' She was sure her face must be white as milk. Her lips had gone numb. And her hands were trembling.

Could she actually puncture human flesh with this needle? She shut her eyes. If only she could keep them shut until it was over.

Or if only Harriet were here. For Harriet—who'd had the benefit of an expensive education—would simply snatch the needle from her hand with an impatient shake of her head and say *she'd* better take charge, since everyone knew Sarah was far too scatterbrained to nurse a sick man.

But Harriet wasn't here. And backing out of the task was unacceptable. She'd just be proving she was as weak and cowardly as everyone expected her to be.

Everyone except Gideon. *You show 'em*, she could almost hear him saying. *Show 'em all what you're made of.*

'Al...Always victorious,' she muttered, under her breath. 'That's our family motto,' she explained to the men, when she opened her eyes and saw them looking at her dubiously. She'd chanted it to herself all the way from Antwerp, the day before, to stop herself from turning back. Had whispered it, like a prayer, when she'd been cowering in the stable with her horse, to give herself heart.

'Motto of our unit, too,' grunted Cooper.

'Of course, of course it is,' she said, taking a deep breath and setting the first stitch. 'Justin—that is Lord Randall, your colonel—he took the words from our family coat of arms, didn't he? From the Latin, which is *Semper Laurifer.* Sounds like laurel, doesn't it? And we do have laurel leaves on our family coat of arms. I suppose whoever took that motto did so for the play on words. Laurel. Laurifer. After a long-ago battle. Because there have always been soldiers in our family. And I dare say plenty of earlier Latymor ladies have had to stitch up wounds. I can almost feel them looking over my shoulder now, encouraging me to keep up the family tradition.'

She was babbling. In a very high-pitched voice. But somehow, reciting family history, whilst imagining the coat of arms and all her doughty ancestors, helped to take her mind off the hideous mess into which her fingers were delving.

'G-Gideon told me that in the case of your unit, Justin, I mean Lord Randall, said you could use whatever means necessary to ensure you always won. Which sounds rather ruthless, even for him. I found it very hard to believe the things he said my stuffy, autocratic big brother got up to during the Peninsula campaign. But Gideon was so full of admiration for the sheer cheek of the way he went behind enemy lines, blowing things up, smashing things down and generally causing mayhem.'

'Confounding the French, the Colonel called it,' said Dawkins.

'And that's how you got the name of Randall's Rogues,' she said, glancing at the unconscious Major's face. He'd been with Justin, doing all those things that had made Gideon green with envy. *'I know it is far more fashionable to belong to a cavalry regiment like mine,'* he'd grumbled, *'but what I wouldn't give to have command of a troop like Justin's. That's the kind of officer I want to be. One who can take the refuse from half-a-dozen other regiments and forge them into something unique.'*

He might not have wanted this man to get anywhere near her, but Gideon had admired him, in a way. He was just the kind of officer Gideon had wished he could have been.

'Not much longer now, miss,' said Dawkins kindly, as her gaze lingered on the Major's face, reluctant to return to the ghastly wound she was supposed to be tending. 'You're doing a grand job.'

'Yes,' she said with a shudder. Then took a deep breath. 'I've decided,' she said, getting back to work, 'that if the men in my family can go about claiming they can do whatever they like to make sure they come out victorious, because of a couple of words engraved on the coat of arms, then so can I. From now on, I will be Always Victorious. In this case—' she swallowed as she set yet another stitch '—I will do my best for this poor wretch. If, for example, I am going to be sick, I will do so *after* I've finished patching his scalp back together.'

'That you will, miss,' Dawkins agreed.

Though miraculously, and to her immense relief, she wasn't sick at all. True, she did stagger away from the bed and sink weakly on to a chair while the men slathered a paste that smelled as if it consisted mostly of comfrey, on to the seam she'd just sewn.

She wished she had some brandy. Not that she'd ever drunk any, but people said it steadied the nerves. And she certainly needed it. Needed something…

'We'll go and fetch the Major's traps now, miss,' said Dawkins as soon as they'd finished covering her handiwork with bandages.

'What?' And leave her here, all alone, in sole charge of a man who looked as though he was at death's door?

'You won't be long, will you?'

'No, but—' They exchanged another of their speaking looks. Oh, lord, what news were they going to break to her this time?

'We'll be back with his things in no time at all, miss. But we can't stay after that. We have to report back.'

Her heart sank. When they said they'd help her, she'd thought they meant until he was fully recovered. But they had only spoken of lifting him and cleaning him up, hadn't they? And they weren't civilians who could come and go as they pleased. If they didn't report to someone in authority, they would run the risk of being treated as deserters.

'Yes. Of course you do.'

'Nothing to do for him now but nursing, anyhow. You can do that as well as anyone. Better, probably.'

She leapt to her feet. 'No. I mean…I have never nursed anyone. Ever. I am not trying to back out of it, it's just that I won't really know what to do,' she cried, twisting her hands together to hide the fact they were shaking. 'What must I do?'

'Whatever he needs to make him comfortable.'

'You've got meadowsweet to make a tea to help bring down the fever, if you can get him to drink it.'

'Fever?'

'He's been lying outside in the muck, with an open wound all night, miss. Course he's going to have a fever.'

Oh, dear heaven.

'Bathe him with warm water, if that don't work.'

'And if he starts shivering, cover him up again,' said Dawkins with a shrug, as though there was nothing to it.

For the first time in her life—she swallowed—she was going to have to cope, on her own, without the aid of a maid, or a footman, or anyone.

But hadn't she always complained that nobody trusted her do anything for herself? Now she had the chance to prove her worth, was she going to witter and wring her hands, and wail that she couldn't do it?

She was not. She was going to pull herself together and get on with it.

'Give him the medicine,' she repeated, albeit rather tremulously, 'bathe him if he gets too hot, cover him if he gets too cold. Anything else?'

'Landlady will have a man about the house to help when he needs to relieve himself, I dare say.'

Yes. Of course she would. There were a number of servants flitting about the place. She *wouldn't* be all alone.

'And we'll tell the company surgeon where the Major is, so he can come and have a look.'

'Oh.' That would be a relief.

'But don't think he'll do anything you couldn't do yourself, miss,' said Dawkins.

'And don't let him tell you the Major should be in a hospital,' said Cooper vehemently. 'They won't look after him proper there.'

Coming from Cooper, that was quite a compliment. He'd been eyeing her askance every time she felt faint. His hostility had actually braced her, once or twice, just as much as Dawkins's kindness and encouragement had. Because every time Cooper looked as though he expected her to fail, it made her more determined to prove she wouldn't.

And now, to hear him say he trusted her to give the

Major better care than he'd get in a hospital, made something in her swell and blossom.

'I won't let you down,' she vowed. 'I won't let him down.'

With a parting nod, the men left.

'Oh, goodness gracious,' she said, sinking on to the chair again. 'Whatever have I let myself in for?'

Chapter Four

The guns had ceased. The battle was over, then. Won or lost. Leaving the field to the dead and dying. And the crows.

Flocks of them. Tearing at his back. His head. They'd go for his eyes if they could get at them.

No! He flung his arm up to protect his eyes. And felt considerable surprise that he could move it. Hadn't been able to move at all before. They'd buried him. Tons of rock, tumbling down, crushing him so he could scarcely breathe, let alone fend off the crows.

Who had dug him out of his grave? He hadn't been able to save himself. He'd tried. Strained with all his might. He'd broken out into a sweat, that was all, and dragged blackness back round him in a smothering cloak.

But he'd be safer under the earth. Crows wouldn't be able to get their claws into him any more. Or their beaks.

'Put me back in the ground,' he begged.

'Don't be silly,' came a rather exasperated-sounding voice.

'But I'm dead.' Wasn't he? Above the ringing in his ears he'd heard the other damned souls all round him, begging for mercy. Begging for water.

Because it was so hot on the edge of the abyss.

Or was it powder caking his mouth, his nostrils, so that everything stank of sulphur?

'Is it crows, then, not demons?' He'd thought they were wraiths, sliding silently between the other corpses scattered round him. But he'd seen knives flashing, silencing the groans. Sometimes they'd looked just like battlefield looters, not Satan's minions.

But whoever, or whatever it had been before, they'd got their claws deep into what was left of him now.

'There are no crows in here,' came the voice again. 'No demons, either. Only me. And Ben.'

Something cool glided across his brow.

He reached up and grabbed hold of what turned out to be a hand. A human hand. Small, and soft, and trembling slightly.

'Don't let them take me. Deserve it. Hell. But please...' He didn't know why he was begging. Nobody could save him. He'd begged before, for mercy, just like all the others. Or would have done if he'd been able to make a sound. He'd understood then that he wasn't even going to be permitted one final appeal. He'd had to stay pinned there, reflecting on every sin he'd committed, remembering every man he'd killed, every act of wanton destruction he'd engineered.

'Nobody's going to take you. I won't let them.'

The voice had a face, this time. The face of an angel. Though—he knew her. She was...she was...

His head hurt too much to think. Only knew he'd seen her before.

That's right—for a moment, just one, the power of speech had returned. And he'd begged *her* to save him. It had something to do with the darkness ebbing and hearing the sound of birdsong, and working out that he couldn't be dead yet, because birds didn't sing in hell, and that if he wasn't dead, then there was still hope. And though there had been all those great black creatures clawing at him, tearing at his clothes, he'd found the strength to make one last, desperate stand.

And *she'd* been there. She'd driven them away. Told them to leave him be. And they'd gone, the whole flock of them. Flapping away on their great ugly wings. And he'd fallen into her arms...

Hazy, what came next. She'd carried him away, somehow, from the mud and the stench. Pillowed on cushions of velvet, soft as feathers.

Was she an angel, then? There seemed no other logical reason to account for it. Beautiful women didn't suddenly materialise on battlefields and carry dying men away. Which meant he'd been right in the first place.

He was dead.

'Did you fly?' How else could she have carried him here? Besides, she was an angel, wasn't she? Angels had wings. Only hers weren't black, like the crows. But blue. Palest blue, like sky after the rain had washed it clean.

'Oh, dear, oh, dear,' the angel sobbed.

'Why are you weeping? I'm not worth it.'

'I'm not weeping.' The angel sniffed.

'If I'm dead, why does it still hurt so much?' he groaned. 'Look, they know my soul belongs to their master. That's why they're clawing at me. Perhaps you should just let me go. No need to cry, then.'

'No! And it's not claws. It's your wounds. Here, try to drink some more of this. It will help with the pain.'

Her arm was under his neck, lifting his head. And she pressed a cup to his lips.

More? She'd given him a drink before?

Ah, yes. He did remember wishing someone would give him something to drink. The thirst had been worse than the pain, in that other place. He'd understood that bit in the bible, then, about the rich man begging Lazarus to dip even one finger in water and cool his tongue. And known, too, that like the rich man he deserved his torment. He'd earned his place in hell.

But his throat was no longer raw. His tongue wasn't stuck to the roof of his mouth. And he could speak.

So she must have given him water, before. Couldn't have been anyone else. Nobody else gave a damn.

'I was so thirsty.' And now he was tired. Too tired to drink any more. Or speak. Or even think.

It was the longest night of Sarah's life. He'd been lying there quietly enough until the Rogues left her on her own with him. But from the moment the door shut on them, it seemed to her, he hadn't given her a moment's peace.

Not that it was his fault, poor wretch. He couldn't help starting to come out of his deep swoon. Or being thirsty, or hot, or uncomfortable. Only it was such a tremendous responsibility, caring for someone as ill as that. It was almost impossible to get more than a sip or two of the meadowsweet tea between his lips. And sponging him down didn't seem to help for more than a minute or two. And then only at first. As the night wore on, his fever mounted and he started muttering all sorts of peculiar, disjointed things about hell, and demons, and thrashing about in the bed, as though trying to dig his way out from under some crushing weight.

And it was downright scary when he started speaking to her in that clear, lucid voice, in such a bizarrely confused manner.

The only thing that calmed him was to answer him as though he *was* making sense. To assure him that he wasn't already in hell, whether he deserved it or not. And to promise she wasn't going to let him die.

She would have promised him anything if only he would lie quietly and let her sleep. She was so *tired*. She'd hardly slept the night before, in the stable, she'd been so scared. Nor the night before that, she'd been in such a state over the report of Gideon's death.

Yet, when Madame le Brun came in to ask how *her brother* was getting on, and if she wanted to take a short break, she found she was unable to leave him for long.

She was glad to have a meal, for she hadn't eaten a thing all day. And she did feel better for a wash and a change of clothes. But once she'd seen to her immediate needs, she couldn't rest for worrying about the Major.

Not that she must think of him as the Major, she decided, as she went to take Madame le Brun's place at his bedside. If he really had been her brother, she would have thought of him as... What was his first name? They called him Tom Cat, so the chances were it was Tom. Well, that was what she must call him, for now. The truth would come out soon enough. The truth about his real identity. And his real name if it wasn't Tom. And it wasn't as if it would make any difference to him what she called him, the state he was in tonight.

His eyes flicked open, yet again.

'It's so hot. Are you sure...?'

'Quite sure. This isn't hell. It's Brussels,' she said, dipping the cloth in a basin of tepid water on the bedside table, then smoothing it over his face, his neck and his chest. Though it didn't seem to be doing much good. His skin felt hotter than ever.

'But you are my guardian angel, aren't you?' he said hopefully. Then groaned and shook his head.

'Can't be. Wretches like me don't deserve guardian angels.'

'Everyone has a guardian angel,' she put in hastily. 'Whether they deserve one or not.'

And if that were true, then she was exactly the sort of guardian angel someone as sinful as Tom probably would get. The sort who wasn't sure what she was doing. And who was terrified of the responsibility. The sort who simply didn't measure up. Second-best.

She was even wearing second-hand clothes. Madame le Brun had insisted she couldn't nurse Major Bartlett wearing her muddy riding habit and had lent her one of the *femme de chambre*'s gowns. Jeanne wasn't as tall as Sarah—well, very few women were. And Jeanne was a bit more stout. So that the gown both hung off her, yet was too small at the same time. It was a perfect example of all that was wrong with her situation.

If only she hadn't been in such a hurry when she'd left Antwerp. If only she'd stopped to pack at least a nightgown. Irritably, she dashed away the single tear that slid down her cheek. How could she be crying over the lack of a nightgown, or anything else of her own to change into come morning, when poor Major Bartlett—no, she had to think of him as Tom—was fighting for his very life?

It was everything that had happened over the last few days catching up with her, that was what it was, *not* the lack of decent clothing. Ever since the night of the Duchess of Richmond's ball she'd done nothing but dash from one place to another, in a state bordering on panic. Leaving a trail of personal possessions in her wake.

She could weep when she thought of the trunks and trunks stuffed full of clothes she'd bought during her brief stay in Paris, all stacked in her cramped little room in Antwerp.

If only she could write to Gussie and ask her to send her things here. But that simply wasn't possible. For one thing she didn't want Gussie to know exactly where she was, or what she was doing, because it would worry her. And anyway, Gussie wouldn't send what she needed. She'd send Blanchards instead, with strict instructions to bring her back to safety. Which would mean poor Major—poor Tom—would be left to the care of strangers. Well, technically she was a stranger, too, but he'd asked *her* to look after him. Not Madame le Brun. Or anyone else. Not even Mary Endacott.

And he was staring at her in a fixed, glazed way as though she was his only hope.

'Drink this,' she said, in as calm a voice as she could, holding a cup of meadowsweet tea to his lips. Meek as a lamb, he opened his mouth and swallowed.

Because he trusted her. He didn't care that she had no experience. Was too feverish to notice what she was wearing. Unlike that day in the park, when he'd run a connoisseur's eye over the riding habit she'd just obtained from Odette, the brilliant dressmaker they'd discovered in a little street off the Place de la Monnaie.

Oh, my goodness! She'd placed an order with Odette only last week—and Blanchards had been in such a hurry to get them on to the barge bound for Antwerp last Friday that he hadn't let her go to collect it. She placed Tom's empty cup on the bedside table, watching his eyelids

droop, though her mind was on all those gowns awaiting collection from the shop. She could very easily send
a message to the modiste, requesting immediate deliv-
ery of everything that was ready and include a list of all
the other items she needed, too. Stockings and stays and
petticoats and so forth. No doubt the bill for doing her
shopping would be steep, but then when had she ever had
to worry about money? Not even the management of it.
Justin, as head of the family, took care of all that side
of things, so that all she had to do was send her bills to
whomever he'd appointed to take care of her day-to-day
needs. At the moment, it was Blanchards.

That thought brought a grim sort of smile to her lips
as she went to the writing desk and turned up the lamp.
He'd already written, in response to the explanation she'd
scrawled as she'd been cowering in the stable, with Castor in the next stall and Ben at her feet. And his letter
had been so horrid and unfeeling she'd crumpled it up
and thrown it in the kitchen fire on her way back from
fetching the medicine pouch. He'd totally ignored her attempt to reassure Gussie she was safe. He'd accused her
of having no consideration for her sister's delicate condition, of *flitting off to Brussels on a wild goose chase,*
and ordered her to come back, without once acknowledging
it might be the depth of grief she felt over losing Gideon
that had sparked her rash behaviour.

He hadn't let Gussie know she wasn't in Antwerp at
all. Because of his over-protective nature, he'd simply told
his wife Sarah was *with friends* and would *return soon.*

Oh, but she could just see his face, when her bills
started turning up in Antwerp. He would be so vexed
with her for disobeying his order to return. Doubly vexed

at not being able to tell Gussie why he was annoyed, since he'd kept Sarah's whereabouts secret.

Well, she sniffed, that served him right for keeping secrets from his wife. No man should try to deceive his wife, not even if he thought it was for her own good. Indeed, she was teaching him a valuable lesson.

As well as proving that she could manage without him. That she could manage *fine* without him.

Tom blinked at the angel's fierce profile as she dipped her pen into the inkwell and wrote something down. Her golden hair glowed, the way he'd seen angels in churches glow when the sun shone through the stained-glass windows.

'You've even got a halo,' he said.

She looked up, startled, and dropped her pen.

'I'm disturbing your writing. Is it important?' But, of course, it must be important. Anything an angel wrote was bound to be important. 'Sorry.'

'You don't need to be sorry. It's just a list.'

'Of my sins?' Then he *would* be sorry. 'Have you got enough paper?'

She came close. Floated towards him on a violet-scented cloud.

'I have plenty of paper, thank you.'

She sat on a chair next to his bed. The wicker work creaked.

He was in a bed. She was on a chair. He frowned.

'This is a strange sort of hell.'

'That's because it isn't hell,' she said in that clipped, practical voice he was coming to recognise. 'It's Brussels.'

'Not hell? Why not?'

'Never you mind why not,' she said sternly. 'Come on, drink some of this.'

'Why?'

'It will make you feel better.'

'Just looking at you makes me feel better.'

'I wish that were true,' she said tartly. 'Then looking after you wouldn't be half so much work.'

'Why are you doing this, then?'

'Because…I…I…well, if you don't get well again I will never forgive myself.'

'Not your fault.'

'I will feel as if it is if you die on me,' she said glumly.

'You don't want me to die?'

'Of course I don't want you to die. How can you even ask?'

'Better dead. Nothing to live for really. Just got into the habit.'

'Well it's about the only habit of yours, from what I've heard of you, that I *don't* want you to break.'

'You're crying again. Didn't mean to make you cry.'

'Well, then stop talking about dying and concentrate on getting better.'

'And now you're angry.'

'Of course I'm angry. Hasn't there been enough death already? Stop it, Tom. Stop it right now.'

He reached out and found her hand.

'Sorry. Will try and do better.'

'Promise me?'

'If it means that much to you,' he said slowly, hardly able to credit that anyone could really care that much whether he lived or died, 'then, yes.'

After that, every time he felt the pit yawning at his back, he reached for the angel. She was always there.

Even when he was too exhausted to drag his eyes open and look for her, he could tell she was near. He only had to smell the faint fragrance of violets for a wave of profound relief to wash through him. For it was her scent. And it meant she hadn't left him.

He'd thought he would always be alone. But she hadn't left him to his fate. And had promised she wouldn't.

'Hush,' she whispered, smoothing that cool balm over his burning face and neck. 'Don't fret. You are going to be fine. I won't let anything happen to you.'

He doubted her only the once, very briefly. When he thought he saw the brigade surgeon hovering over him like a great vulture.

She couldn't have saved his life, only to turn him over to that ghoul, could she? The man liked nothing better than cutting up poor helpless victims, to see what made them tick. Oh, he said he was trying to cure them, but he spent far too much time writing up his findings in all those leather journals. The journals that were going to make his name some day. His findings, he called them.

Cold sweat broke out all over him at the prospect of falling into his hands. He'd cut him up, for sure. Lay his kidneys out in a tray.

'Lieutenant...' He had to screw up his face. 'What's the name?' Foster, that was it. 'Angel...' He thought he didn't care whether he lived or died, but the prospect of being dissected in the name of science?

'Don't let him cut me up.'

Lieutenant Foster straightened up, and gave Lady Sarah a hard stare.

'You can see how confused he is. Doesn't know his

own name. Seems to think he's a lieutenant. This is often the case with head wounds. Even though the skull itself is not fractured, injury to the brain can leave a patient with no memory, or impeded memory, or even physical impairment.'

'But he is going to get well, isn't he? I mean, he won't die, now?'

'There's no telling, with head wounds. Men can appear to be getting well, then suddenly collapse and die,' he said, looking more animated for a moment or two. 'Delicate organ, the brain. All you can do is keep him as quiet and as still as you can. Let nature take its course.'

The surgeon's eyes flicked round Sarah's room—no, the sickroom—lingering for a moment or two on the pile of material she'd been cutting up for bandages, the bedside table with the bowl of water and sponge, pausing with a perplexed frown at the potted geranium on the windowsill, that Madame le Brun had brought in *to cheer the place up.*

'There is nothing I can do for him that you can't do just as well here,' he finally declared, brusquely. And marched out of the room.

She hadn't expected an army surgeon to have the bedside manner of a family doctor, naturally, but couldn't he have spared just a moment or two to advise her? Encourage her? At least let her know she'd done an adequate job of stitching Tom's head? And congratulate her for getting his fever down?

No wonder Cooper had insisted she should nurse the Major herself and keep him out of hospital. She wouldn't trust a dog to that cold-eyed man's dubious care.

As if he could read her thoughts, Ben whined and nudged her hand with his nose.

'You are supposed to be in the stable,' she said with mock sternness, though she ruffled his ears at the same time. 'Guarding my horse.' Although Castor didn't need guarding so closely now. Since the news of Bonaparte's flight from the battlefield had circulated, the city had started to become almost civilised again, from what Madame le Brun reported. Which was both a good and a bad thing. Good in the sense that England and her allies had defeated Bonaparte's pretensions. But somewhat dangerous for her reputation, if any of her old crowd discovered she'd returned ahead of them and was holed up with a notorious rake.

'We both need to keep our heads down,' she said. 'Or we'll be in trouble. But I can't be cross with you, you clever dog, for bounding up here the minute that nasty doctor came calling. I felt so much better with you standing guard over both me and Tom. Even so, now he's gone I feel completely drained,' she told Ben, before sitting down by the bed and closing her eyes. The dog laid his head on her knee in what felt remarkably like a gesture of comfort. For a moment or two she just rested. Almost dozed. But then Ben whined and pawed at her knee.

'What is it?'

But as soon as the words left her mouth she saw why Ben had roused her. Tom was awake. He was lying there looking at her with a faint frown creasing his brow, as though he wasn't too sure who she was. Though for some reason, she felt his confusion was no longer due to fever. His eyes were clear and focused steadily on her. In fact, he looked like any man who'd just woken up in a strange place with no recollection of how he'd come to be there.

A pang of concern and self-doubt had her leaning forward to lay her hand on his forehead. But, no—the fever hadn't returned.

'He's gone?'

The Major's voice was hoarse, but for the first time, what he said actually made sense.

'The doctor? Yes.'

He reached up and seized her hand. 'You didn't let him take me. Thank you.' A little shiver went right through her at the look of adoration blazing from his clear green eyes. Oh, no wonder he had such a reputation with the ladies, if he looked at them all like that.

'Of course I didn't,' she said, a little perturbed by both the fear the company surgeon could inspire in potential patients, and the feelings Tom could provoke in her now he had his wits about him. It was a warning that she was going to have to sharpen her own.

'I promised I would look after you myself.'

The grip of his hand tightened. 'Do you always keep your promises?'

'Yes. Of course.'

His mouth tightened fractionally, as if there was no *of course* about promises. But then in his world there probably wasn't. A man of his type probably made dozens of promises he had no intention of keeping. And she'd do well to remember it.

'I am in your hands, then.'

'Yes.'

He sighed and closed his eyes. 'Thank God,' he mumbled. And promptly fell asleep, as though a great weight had rolled off his shoulders.

He trusted her.

Just as those Rogues had trusted her.

Before she had a chance to let it go to her head, she

reminded herself that anyone would be preferable to that doctor, who seemed to view the injured as interesting cases rather than people with feelings.

Though Tom was making her feel as if it were more than that, by the way he hadn't let go of her hand, even though he'd fallen asleep. As though he really, really needed her.

It would wear off, once he recovered, and got to know her better, of course. Though for now, why shouldn't she bask in his apparent need? It felt good. Since there was nobody here to tell her how she *ought* to behave, and think, and feel, she could make up her own mind.

She decided that even though he was a rake, whose mere glance could send heated shivers down a woman's spine, there was no harm in just sitting holding his hand while he was asleep. Besides, she was so tired. All she wanted to do was just sit and rest for a while.

So she sat there, her hand in his, half-drowsing, until a knock on the door heralding the arrival of Madame le Brun, with a tray of food, jolted her awake.

Sarah let go of his hand to stretch and yawn as Madame placed the tray none too gently on the bedside table.

'That smells good,' croaked Tom. 'What is it?'

Sarah glanced at the contents of the tray. 'Some broth and some bread. And wine.'

'Nectar.' He sighed.

'Ah! He is awake,' said Madame, 'and wanting his dinner.'

'That is a good sign, isn't it? It must mean he is getting well.'

'Yes. But he is a strong one, that one,' said Madame, casting her eye over his naked torso with what looked like feminine appreciation. And for the first time, Sarah looked, too. At least, for the first time since the battle, she permitted herself to look at him as a man, not just a patient.

She'd thought him handsome before. When she'd seen him in the park, fully clothed. But she'd never run her eyes over his torso, the way she was doing now. With appreciation of his muscled beauty.

She blushed at the inappropriate turn her mind was taking. She was his *nurse*. She was supposed to be convincing Madame le Brun that he was her *brother*. She had no business going all gooey-eyed because he had the kind of body artists would want to sculpt in marble.

'Will you help me to sit him up?' she asked Madame with what she hoped sounded like brisk efficiency. 'Then we can feed him some broth.'

'I can do it,' he grumbled.

But he couldn't. So between them, Sarah and Madame le Brun propped the Major up on a mound of pillows and fed him soup until his eyelids started to flutter closed.

'Weak as a kitten,' he muttered in disgust as they helped him lie down again.

'But now you are eating and the fever has gone, you will be up and going around in no time,' Madame chided him gently as he drifted back to sleep.

That was good news. Before much longer he wouldn't need Sarah any more. He would be up and going around, as Madame so quaintly put it. She wouldn't need to sit over him, alternately sponging his overheated body, or covering him when he shivered.

She would be able to leave, like as not, before anyone discovered she'd had anything to do with him at all. And her reputation would remain intact. She would be safe.

So why did she feel like crying again?

Chapter Five

Stupid, stupid thing to do. Sit crying over... Sarah shook her head. She wasn't too sure actually what she was crying about.

She was turning into a regular watering pot.

With a growl of self-disgust, she got up and went to the desk. Rather than moping, she would do better to reply to all the letters which were piling up.

Gussie first. She'd wronged Gussie. Wished she could put it right. But most of all, she didn't want Gussie to worry about her.

Dear Gussie, she wrote. Then paused, chewing on the end of the quill. She couldn't very well write, *I've brought a notorious rake home with me and have been living with him. He has such a dreadful reputation Justin wouldn't introduce him to me, even though he is an officer.*

She rested her head in her hands for a moment or two. There must be a way to allay her sister's concerns without telling an outright lie.

I am in Brussels, she wrote, with a defiant tilt to her chin. She didn't want to keep her totally in the dark, the way her husband was so determined to keep her in the dark. It simply wasn't right!

But neither could she tell the whole truth.

I think I went a little mad when Blanchards told me Gideon was dead. Of course, I know, really, that Blanchards wouldn't lie to me about something like that, but then, he might have been mistaken, mightn't he? The report might have been sent in error, or something. Anyway, I felt that I couldn't believe it, the way you both did, without proof. I ended up going as far as the battlefield to search for answers and stumbled across Justin instead. He is gravely ill and needs constant care.

That would give a good enough reason for her continued absence from Antwerp, without alerting Gussie to what was really going on. Justin needed constant care right enough, but it was Mary who was giving it. They'd managed to get Justin back to his lodgings, Mary had explained via a curt note, where she would now be staying so that she could nurse him without interruption from Sarah or anyone else.

Even if Blanchards suspected she was being economical with the truth, he wouldn't voice his suspicions. His first priority was to Gussie and his heir. *His* letter had revealed that he had already hidden the news of her absence from Antwerp. He would carry on doing what he could to shield Gussie from worry.

Which was just as well, because if anyone found out that she was living with a man to whom she was not related, with no proper chaperon in place, there would be an almighty scandal. Which would reach as far as London, never mind Antwerp.

Oh, dear. She really should have thought things through. She pressed her hand to her forehead as she went over everything she'd done since Blanchards had told them Gideon was dead.

Dead.

A shudder went through her. How could anyone *think things through* when they were given news like that? Of course she hadn't thought things through. She'd just reacted.

But at least she'd done what she could, since then, to mitigate some of the damage her behaviour might have caused. She'd gone to ground, as it were.

That doctor was the only person who might possibly start spreading gossip. She frowned. But he could only do so if he knew who she was. She thought back over his visit, wondering if he'd ever once called her by name. No, he hadn't. And with the amount of injured men he'd have to attend, given what she'd seen of the battlefield, he wouldn't have time to concern himself over something as minor as her reputation even if he did know who she was.

She hoped.

So all she had to do was warn Madame le Brun that she wasn't receiving visitors, if anybody by some remote chance did happen to discover she was back in Brussels, and her secret would be safe.

'Angel? Are you there?'

At the sound of his hoarse voice, Sarah leapt to her feet and went back to the bedside. She'd let him call her that while in the grip of fever, because there hadn't seemed any point in correcting him. But now it dawned on her that even he didn't know who she really was, either.

He'd forgotten he'd ever seen her. Because she'd made no lasting impression on him.

How depressing.

'I'm here. I was only writing some letters. '

He reached out and grabbed her hand as though his life depended on it.

'Couldn't see you. Thought you'd gone. Or that I imagined you perhaps.'

'No. You didn't imagine me. And I won't go anywhere. Not until you are well enough to do without me.'

'Then I hope I never get well,' he said vehemently. Because when he was well, her family would take great care to keep her well away from a man like him.

How did he know that?

Because an image swam into his mind, of a girl on horseback, blushing because he'd winked at her. And snatches of her companion's conversation drifting to his ears. *For once I agree with Justin...*

Hell's teeth, no wonder he'd had the feeling he knew this woman, even though he was sure he'd never spoken to her before. She was Colonel Randall's precious, virginal little sister. Lady Sarah Latymor.

'Oh, don't say that!'

Bless her, but Lady Sarah looked as though she really cared. Actually, he rather thought she *did* care, for some obscure reason. Else why would she be here, nursing him, when in the normal course of things, men like her brothers protected women like her from men like him?

With good reason.

'Why not? If it is true?'

'Because,' she said sternly, 'I want you to get well.'

Of course she did. As soon as he was well enough, she could walk out of his life again. For good. For some reason the prospect of never seeing her again was so distasteful he couldn't help grimacing.

'Oh. Do you have a pain? Do you want some more of this medicine the doctor left?'

He started to shake his head, only to wince. 'I hurt everywhere, but my head worst of all. It feels as if somebody's tried to slice the top off it.'

'They pretty much did. Let me fetch you that laudanum.'

'No. Not yet. It makes me sleepy. And I want...' He squeezed her fingers, absurdly grateful to discover that she hadn't pulled her hand away from his.

'Talk to me? Just for a while.'

'Very well,' she said, squeezing his hand back. And then cleared her throat. 'This may seem a funny question for me to ask. But, do you know your name?'

Only too well. And yet... 'Why do you ask?'

'The surgeon seemed to think you may have trouble remembering things.'

Perhaps there was a God, after all. He hated feeling this weak, but he'd never got anywhere near Lady Sarah when he'd been fit and active. Now here he was, holding hands with her, in a bedroom of all places.

The thing was, if he admitted he knew who he was, then he'd also have to admit that he knew she shouldn't be in this bedroom.

Not that she was doing anything wrong. No—it was one thing *her* flouting convention to nurse a wounded man. Quite another for that wounded man to permit her to do it, if he knew that just being seen talking with him, in a public street, would have been enough to stain her lily-white reputation. He'd be up on a charge. Cashiered out of the regiment. Or maybe just shot. Because Colonel Randall had made it plain that none of his officers was fit to kiss the hem of her gown.

He wasn't. But before she returned to the safety of her oh-so-respectable family, he promised himself, he'd do more than kiss the hem of her gown. He'd taste those fastidious lips of hers.

'Perhaps,' he purred, 'I would prefer to forget some things.'

'Does that mean you don't know who you are?' She looked appalled.

His conscience, an attribute he'd never thought he possessed, gave him an uncomfortable nudge in the ribs. It wasn't fair to repay Lady Sarah's kindness by putting on an act that worried her.

Though it wasn't as if he'd set his sights on *seducing* her. He never bothered seducing women, even the ones that very plainly weren't virgins. He just bedded them if they were willing, walked away from them if they were not.

She most definitely would not be willing. But he couldn't walk away from her. He couldn't walk anywhere. In fact, even if he'd woken up to find himself in the bed of a rapacious widow, he wouldn't be able to rise to the occasion.

Lady Sarah was safer than she knew.

He gave her a rueful sort of smile, hoping it made him look confused, as well as utterly innocent.

'For today, do I have to be anyone in particular? Couldn't you just call me...' His smile turned a touch mischievous. 'Just call me *Sir*.'

Just as he'd hoped, Sarah's concerned expression relaxed into something approaching amusement.

'Well, at least you remember you are an officer in the army.'

'Yes,' he admitted. 'And I suspect I enjoy giving orders.'

She pulled a face. 'So I suppose you'd like me to jump to attention and salute you, too, wouldn't you?'

'No,' he said, with complete honesty. The last thing he wanted was to have any woman behave in such a subservient manner. He liked his women to be with him because it was what they wanted. He liked them enthusiastic, and inventive, and...

His mouth went dry. Good lord, but it was dangerous, picturing *this* girl being enthusiastic and inventive.

'What I'd really like,' he said, lowering his eyelids into a practised smoulder, since, he reasoned, there wasn't any harm in testing the waters, 'is for you to kiss me. As my nurse, don't you think it is your duty to kiss me better?'

Her face flushed as her lips pursed up in disapproval.

'That does not form part of my duties.'

'Well, perhaps you'd like to do it for pleasure, then?'

To his surprise, she didn't automatically say no. She looked at him thoughtfully, her head tilted to one side.

His heart hammered in his chest, making his blood pound through his veins, just because she was thinking about kissing him. If she actually bent forward, and pressed her lips to his, the wounds in his head would probably burst, killing him on the spot.

But what a way to go.

'Kill me...' He shook his head. 'I mean, kiss me, Angel. And let me die a happy man.'

For a moment she looked as though she was still toying with the idea. She actually swayed forward in her seat. But then she shook her head and sat back.

'No. It won't do. You don't know who you are, nor who I am. You are confused and weak, and don't know what you are saying.'

Damn. He should have told her there was nothing wrong with his memory, in spite of what the doctor had said.

She snatched her hand away, then, as though she'd just become aware he was still holding it.

'Besides, you don't really mean it, do you? I'm not the kind of girl men want to kiss.'

'What? Why would you say that?' He wouldn't have been surprised if prim Lady Sarah had slapped his face for impertinence. But never would he have dreamed she'd think he was offering her false coin.

'Isn't it obvious? Or did the blow to your head knock all the sense out of it along with your memory?'

'Possibly,' he acknowledged slowly. One moment he'd decided he wasn't going to do any more than flirt with her, just a little, the next he was imagining her climbing on top of him and taking all sorts of liberties while he was helpless to resist. And then asking if she wouldn't mind kissing him, just to get things started. That wasn't the way to deal with a society princess. No wonder she looked so offended.

'But I do want to kiss you,' he admitted. Then, deciding to turn the conversation away from his murky motives, added, 'And to be honest, I don't understand why you think other men don't.'

'Well, just look at my face. The nose. It looks aristocratic and manly on my brothers. But on a female, well...'

She shrugged. 'Anyway, I don't want men to kiss me.' She shuddered in what looked like genuine revulsion.

Which made him feel a little better. At least it wasn't him, specifically, she didn't want to kiss.

She'd always had a sort of cool air about her, now he came to think of it. She hadn't appeared to favour any of the men who'd clustered round her.

Had a sort of untouchable quality to her that had made some of them, men like her twin brother's commanding officer, look upon her as a challenge to their masculinity.

At that moment, an immense black dog shambled up to the bed, got his front paws on to the mattress and gave his face a hearty, thorough licking.

'Good grief, it's Dog,' he exclaimed, temporarily forgetting he was supposed to have lost his memory. 'Where did you come from?' He ruffled the dog's velvety ears.

'Ben, get down,' said Lady Sarah sharply. 'Tom isn't well enough for that sort of play.'

So she knew his name was Tom. And she was calling the dog Ben, too, the way some of the men had started to do, the last few days.

'Well, at least someone wants to kiss me.' He laughed, as Dog's whole body wriggled in joyous greeting.

She pulled the dog off him. But he couldn't help noticing that for all her sharp manner, she'd glanced at his mouth—albeit briefly—with a sort of fascination. As though she wouldn't mind finding out what a kiss would be like.

Which was a start.

But if he was ever going to get that kiss, he'd have to find out why she'd shuddered with revulsion at the mere prospect. Which meant getting her to talk to him. Trust him.

But what did a man like him have in common with a girl like her? What could they talk about?

Well, there was always the dog.

'How on earth did you come to have Dog?'

'Oh,' she said, taking the hound's head between her hands and gazing into his eyes with a familiarity that caused Tom a pang of something that felt a lot like envy. 'We sort of rescued each other, on the road to the Forest of Soignes. He was tied to one of the baggage wagons, which got overturned when a band of cowardly Hussars came pell-mell along the road from the battlefield. And he was so scared. I couldn't leave him trapped like that, could I?'

Tom looked at her with new respect. He could just imagine how the dog would react, tethered and scared. It would have been all snapping teeth and frantic attempts to get free. He didn't think he knew any *men* who would have gone near Ben in that condition.

Not that he could say anything. He wasn't supposed to know who he was, let alone recall all the instances when he'd witnessed this dog in action.

Though, come to think of it, he'd already given himself away by admitting he recognised Dog. Not that Lady Sarah had taken any notice of his slip.

'And then,' she said, ruffling the dog's ears, 'he returned the favour by chasing off a nasty deserter who'd been trying to steal Castor—that's my horse—while I'd crawled under the wagon and wasn't paying attention. But you saw him off, didn't you?' she said, petting the dog's flanks. 'Yes, you did. You are a good boy.'

The thought of Lady Sarah facing such peril, with only the flea-bitten hound to look after her, made his blood run cold.

She'd crawled under a wagon to help just about the most intimidating dog he'd ever come across, then had to face a deserter attempting to steal her horse? And she was speaking of it just as though she was relating an outing to the shops. What would it take to ruffle her aristocratic sang-froid?

His imagination promptly supplied a whole slew of highly improper activities where she'd end up distinctly ruffled.

The dog's tongue lolled out in ecstasy as she patted and stroked him. He shut his own mouth firmly to make sure he wasn't doing anything similar.

'And we've been inseparable ever since. Haven't we, Ben?'

'Ever since?' He looked at the window and the sunlight streaming through it. And recalled the endless hours of confusion and fever. 'How long have I been here? What day is it, now?'

'It's Tuesday.'

'Tuesday?' She'd been nursing him for the best part of two days. Not that long for him to lie semi-conscious, after what his body had been through. Thirst and loss of blood would have weakened him to the point where he didn't know who he was, or where he was, even without the blow to the head. So he had some excuse for being right where he was.

But what was her excuse? What was she doing in Brussels at all? The civilians had all fled last Friday, from what he'd heard.

And why had nobody come looking for her?

He turned away from the window to look at her. And noted a slight flush staining her cheeks.

The hussy! She knew full well she shouldn't be here

with him. Not now he was awake. Yet she wasn't making any attempt to leave.

It wasn't because she'd developed a *tendre* for him, that was for sure. She shuddered at the mere idea of kissing.

So what was she doing with him?

If only he could simply ask her. But if he did that, they'd be dealing with truths he wasn't yet ready to face.

He lowered his eyelids and studied her awkward posture, the very self-conscious way she was petting the dog now, as an excuse to avoid looking back at him, he'd guess.

'You know,' he said with mock severity, 'since we have established that I am simply an officer in the army, with no past and no name, and therefore nothing I can tell you, it is up to you to sustain the conversation.'

Her eyes flew to his, a little spark of outrage flashing at his temerity in touching on her social obligations. Because she was the kind of girl who normally stuck rigidly to all the rules of etiquette.

Still, now he had her looking at him again. He'd made her forget her awkwardness at being here.

'And I do like the sound of your voice,' he admitted with complete sincerity. Even the hint of exasperation in it, when he'd been half out of his mind with fever, had been strangely comforting. Had sort of grounded him.

'Besides, I am too weak to strain myself with talk. I shall just lie here and listen to you while you entertain me.'

'You…you are a complete hand!'

He nodded solemnly. 'Yes, I rather suspect I am. But what are you, apart from my guardian angel? Do you have a name? No—' He pulled himself up. If she told him her real name, then he'd be obliged to acknowledge her relationship to his commanding officer. That was, if he owned up to not suffering from memory loss. Which he wasn't ready to do, not yet, even if he didn't want her to believe in it. Hell, but this was getting complicated enough to give him a headache, if he hadn't already got one.

'Just let me guess.' He studied her face as though trying to pick a suitable name. Which he was doing. If she wasn't a Sarah, what would he call her? After a bit, he came up with, 'Helen.'

'Do I look like a Helen?'

'Helen of Troy. The face that launched a thousand ships.'

'With a nose like this I suspect Paris would have had me carved into a figurehead on one of those ships,' she said waspishly. 'You do talk nonsense.'

'If not Helen, what, then?'

She thought for a minute, and then looked as though she'd come to a decision. 'Do you know, if I had a choice, I rather think I should like to be called Elizabeth.'

So. She wasn't any more keen to face up to the truth, either, or she would have told him, in that brisk, no-nonsense voice she'd used when he'd been rambling in his fever, who she really was.

'Lizzy,' he corrected her. 'Elizabeth is far too formal for the situation in which we find ourselves.'

'No,' she said firmly. 'Elizabeth. And you may as well know that I choose the name because she ruled the whole land without ever letting anyone force her into marriage.'

'The Virgin Queen,' he said thoughtfully. 'Yes. That does suit a girl who shudders at the prospect of a man's kiss. For no man is fit to so much as kiss the hem of your jewelled gown.' He certainly wasn't. That was what made this situation so piquant.

Catching the direction of his gaze, she ran her hands over the elegantly simple gown she wore.

'This gown is hardly practical for nursing a wounded soldier, is it? Though I didn't know I was going to be doing any such thing when I ordered it. Which was before we all fled to Antwerp...' She faltered to a halt, pleating a section of her skirt between her fingers. 'I suppose that sounds as if I think of nothing but clothes, but it was no joke, I can assure you, arriving here without a clean stitch to put on.'

'I am a soldier, your Majesty. Of course I know what it is like to lose baggage when I'm on the march.'

'Oh, but you haven't! That is, I mean, two of your men brought your things round. So you can have a clean shirt whenever you want one.'

Was she hinting she wanted him to cover himself up? He supposed he really ought to. Men didn't loll about, shirtless, when a woman was in the room, not unless that woman had no morals to speak of.

'I hated not having clean clothes of my own,' she said, as though it was a crime. 'People say I'm terribly vain, you know. And I do spend a lot of time shopping. But can I tell you something? You won't tell anyone else?'

'My Queen, I am your loyal subject. I shall regard your confidence as though it were a state secret,' he said, dipping his head in a mock bow. Then wincing at the hammer blow that rang through his skull.

'Idiot,' she said with a concerned frown. 'Lie still! And listen. My secret is when I dress well, I feel as though it takes attention away from how very plain I am.'

'Plain?' He studied her face. To him, at that moment, it looked like the most adorable face in the world. He supposed it must be because he felt he owed her his life or something, because, in all honesty, her nose *was* just a touch too prominent for a female. And her lips too prim. And her hair—it was a beautiful colour, but looked as though she'd stiffened it with some sort of lotion so that she could curl it. And those curls were now sort of fraying round the edges. But her eyes...

'You have the most remarkable eyes,' he told her. 'That blue, it's quite lovely.'

'They are my best feature,' she admitted. 'I do try to emphasise them. But—' she shrugged '—there's no getting past the nose.'

'That nose,' he said on a burst of inspiration, 'is the kind of nose born to rule. And you said you wanted to be a queen, did you not? Therefore, it suits you perfectly.'

'No wonder you're so popular with the ladies,' she said with a shake of her head.

'Am I?' A flash of shame made him look as confused as he was trying to convince her he felt. He had never once thought his reputation as a prolific lover would make him uncomfortable. What was it about Lady Sarah that made him wish he'd lived a more respectable life?

Instantly she looked contrite. 'Oh, I am sorry. I shouldn't remind you of...well, we'd agreed, hadn't we, that just for now, we can be whoever we want to be.'

His heart did a funny sort of skip in his chest. Because what she'd just said meant she wanted to be with him, just as much as he wanted to be with her.

Even though they both knew it couldn't last.

'So. You have chosen to be the Virgin Queen,' he said, settling himself more comfortably against the pillows.

Which was apt, given the fact she was a lady of unimpeachable virtue.

'Because, you say, you don't want to be forced into a marriage you cannot stomach. Is there any danger of that?'

She sighed. 'Mama has been very patient with what she calls my crotchets, so far. She hasn't put any pressure on me to accept any of the offers made for my hand. But she never gives up hope. She says she wants me to be happy in marriage. But—' another one of those frowns flitted across her forehead '—I don't see how she can even use the word *happy*, in the same sentence as *marriage*, without a blush. Not when her own has made her so utterly miserable. Papa was a rake, you see.'

She gave him a considering look. One which it took every ounce of his meagre strength to hold without hanging his head.

'Mama,' she said tartly, 'was expected to turn a blind eye to his many infidelities. Which took a great deal of resolution, given that Chalfont Magna's littered with his natural children. He took great pleasure, I think, in conducting his affairs right under her nose. In humiliating her.' Her lips flattened into a grim line. 'It wasn't even as if he needed to prove his virility, particularly, since he repeatedly got her with child, as well. She presented him with two sets of twins, and two girls as well as his heir, not counting the many miscarriages in between,' she ended speaking on a shudder. 'Can you blame me for hoping I never get married?'

Absolutely not. Not when she put it like that. 'You do make it sound unpleasant,' he admitted. 'But not all men are like that.'

'No?' She pursed her lips and gave him a rather withering look. 'No,' she said again, this time with more than a hint of resolution. 'I am not going to come to cuffs with you over this, not while you are so poorly.'

Then she startled him by giving him a rather mischievous smile.

'And actually, it is rather amusing to hear you saying exactly what Mama is always telling me.'

'No!' He widened his eyes in horror that wasn't altogether feigned. Well, what man wished to hear he'd started saying the same things as a matchmaking mama?

'My sisters, too. Since they have married men they declare are perfect paragons, they have redoubled their efforts to find me a man just like their husbands.'

'So, how have you foiled their plans?'

'Oh, very easily,' she said airily. 'I have become adept at it, over the years. I never argue. Never throw tantrums. With the result that nobody ever knows exactly what I'm thinking. So they assume I cannot think for myself at all. I have meekly gone through several Seasons without ever bringing myself to accept any of the *flattering* offers made for my hand. So many, you know,' she said, putting on a particularly vacuous expression, and fanning herself with her hand. 'How is a girl to choose?'

Tom's eyes lit with unholy amusement. 'I'm beginning to suspect you are an unprincipled baggage.'

She lifted her chin haughtily. 'How dare you speak thus to your queen, Sir Tom?'

'I most humbly beg your pardon, your Majesty. I, um, forgot myself.'

She giggled.

And then, abruptly, sobered.

'The dreadful thing is, I think you are right.' She shifted in her chair and looked him straight in the eye as though imploring him to understand. 'I had no scruples about encouraging Mama to send me to France, when she got the notion that she might stand a better chance of marrying me off if only she could introduce me to some new people. Because, you see, it was exactly where I wished to go. Because Gideon was stationed there. Gideon, my twin brother,' she explained, just as if he really might not know.

'It was *not* because everyone who was anyone was flocking to Paris, instead of London, for the Season,' she added a touch tartly.

'They actually thought I might be dazzled into marriage by some wealthy European princeling. As if becoming a princess would make marriage any more palatable!' She shook her head with scorn. 'But I shall never regret the trip to Paris, nor our subsequent removal to Brussels when Bonaparte went and invaded France, since it meant that I have managed to spend these last few months close to Gideon.'

A shadow passed across her features. But then she pinned a bright smile to her face. 'So. Now you know why I wish to be called Elizabeth. Why I admire her so much.'

The smile didn't reach her eyes. And he wished he could do something to help ease her sorrow. The sorrow neither of them could mention without destroying their truce.

'Your Majesty,' he said, taking her hand and kissing it with complete gratitude, 'you honour me with your confidence.'

Sarah could see exactly why Tom had gained such a reputation with the ladies. Even pale, covered in bruises and with his head bandaged, he was an utterly charming companion.

Of course, it was all nonsense, this declaring his devotion, as her courtier. A man like him was never going to be devoted to anyone for more than five minutes. But for the first time, she didn't really care.

There was no harm in playing along, just for an hour or so, at being whoever they wanted to be. Not when they both knew it was a game.

She'd certainly never liked the person her family had obliged her to be. And she wasn't looking forward to returning to the dull conformity of that life, either. Actually, it would all be far worse than it had been before she'd lost her head and run away. She would be in disgrace with them all. And there would be a shockingly empty, aching void in her life where Gideon had been.

So, on the whole, it was better to play the queen to Tom's courtier. To bask in his practised flattery. To laugh at his witty repartee.

Far better than the alternative. Reality, with all its pain.

Chapter Six

When Madame le Brun came in with another meal of her good wholesome broth, and fresh bread, he managed a whole bowlful before growing drowsy.

Sarah took it as a personal victory. The sense of achievement was like sunshine bursting out from behind storm clouds. He'd been so close to death when his men had brought him here. And she'd been so timid. So clueless. As she took the empty bowl and set it on the tray for removal later, she realised that, even though she would never be a queen, she most definitely wasn't the same person she'd been two days ago. Tom had changed her—or, rather, nursing him back to health had changed her. Had given her faith in herself. She wasn't the useless, empty-headed female everyone had kept telling her she was. No—she'd decided that death wouldn't have this man and she'd flung herself into the task of saving him.

Maybe that was what had made the difference—she'd never flung herself into anything before. For the most part she'd been content to just drift along, taking the path of least resistance.

She turned to him abruptly. 'Thank you,' she said, before she had a chance to change her mind.

His eyes widened. 'Thank me? Whatever for?'

'For making your own memory loss into a game. It has helped keep my own reality at bay.' Suddenly she saw, too, why she'd been so keen to play along, even though she'd suspected he wasn't as confused as all that. Little things, like the way he'd recognised Ben, then tried to cover his moment of spontaneity by turning the subject, had made her suspicious. But not suspicious enough to challenge him. For one thing, he wasn't well. For another—what would she do if she didn't have Tom to nurse? She couldn't go to Justin and ask about Gideon. Justin really was too ill to burden with her problems. Nor was she prepared to slink back to Antwerp with her tail between her legs and beg everyone's pardon for running away. So, on the whole, she was grateful to him for providing her with the excuse for staying right where she was, until she was ready to face the future.

'I don't know what I will do when this is all over, but, you know, pretending to be a queen to your courtier has been a sort of golden interlude in a time of darkness.'

'Has it? Been golden for you? I'm glad,' he said sleepily. 'I only wish I could give you many more such days.'

'Ah, but both of us have been pretending to be someone we are not today. That can't go on for ever, can it?'

He winced. She could tell that though he was in pain, he was fighting it. Trying to stay playful and flirtatious. And awake.

'I have one last command for you which, as my loyal subject, you must obey.'

He smiled and half-inclined his head.

'I shall obey without question,' he vowed, falling neatly into her trap.

'Then drink your medicine and sleep,' she said firmly.

'Unfair,' he protested.

'Not at all,' she replied sternly. 'You need to rest. Come on,' she said, measuring the drops into the glass, just the way the surgeon had shown her. 'Drink it all up like a good boy.'

'A good boy?'

She shrugged. 'That is how my nurse always used to talk to me and my brothers when we tried to wriggle out of taking our medicine. And then she'd say that we needed our sleep. Because sleep is the best medicine of all.'

'Yes, you are right. It's just that I...' He shot her one of those melting looks that made her toes curl, even though she knew it was only put on for effect. 'I don't want today to end. I will remember it all,' he vowed with so much sincerity she really wanted to believe him. 'Every moment. Every smile you have granted me. Like treasure.'

'That's a lovely thing to say,' she said as he drank the laudanum mixture.

'But you don't believe me?' He gave her an aggrieved frown, then shut his eyes and slipped almost at once into exhausted slumber.

'The danger is,' she murmured softly, 'that I *want* to believe you. Even knowing what kind of man you are.'

She sat down at his bedside, the discarded medicine glass in her hand, just staring at him, her head tilted to one side as she tried to work out how she could feel the way she did about such a notorious rake. And why it was that the sight of his naked torso now could give her thrilling little goosebumps, when it hadn't affected her in the slightest when she'd been sponging it down. Why hadn't she reacted to the magnificent way he was put together until he'd woken up and started talking to her? It was the same body, after all.

Because, she realised on a flash of inspiration, it wasn't his looks alone that made him so attractive. She'd thought him handsome when she'd first seen him, but hadn't wanted to linger in his vicinity any longer than she had to. It was him. The man he was inside. The things you couldn't know unless you talked to him.

No wonder Justin wouldn't let her speak to him. His charm was well-nigh lethal. What woman wouldn't like a man who looked like this and who could be so playful, willing to obey her every command just as though she was a queen and he her devoted slave?

Actually, come to think of it, it wasn't just his charm that tugged a positive reaction from her. The charm wouldn't have affected her at all had she not already seen him at his lowest—if she hadn't seen him battling his demons and then clinging to the sound of her voice, or the touch of her hand, as though she was his only anchor.

As though he was just as lonely as she was.

It was just as well she knew it was all make-believe, or she might be in real danger of falling for him. Fortunately she knew just how charming men could pretend to be, if they thought it would get them what they wanted. But deep down, they were all selfish, inconsiderate tyrants.

All men? Even Gideon?

Oh, it felt disloyal to think of him in those terms. But hadn't he always been as self-absorbed as any of the males in her family? True, he'd been more willing to spend time with her. To talk to her. But he'd never dreamed of putting her wishes first. She had always been the one supporting him. She'd been rescuing him from the consequences of his scrapes since they'd both been in the nursery and she'd unlocked windows to let him in when he'd sneaked out to steal apples. She'd even been distracting his company commander so that he could do whatever it was he'd been up to in Brussels before that last battle.

Even the plan to come to France—supposedly on the hunt for a husband—had come about because she'd sensed, from the letters he'd written, that he needed her. In between the descriptions of the social whirl in which his regiment was involved she could detect a sort of malaise. She'd wanted to help him. And so she'd fostered Gussie's and Mama's hopes, so that she could be at hand to help when whatever it was she could sense coming actually came.

Only she'd been too late. Or not in the right place at the right time. Or something. She'd failed him. He was dead, and she was left sitting here watching over...

As if he knew she was thinking of him, Tom moaned. His eyes flickered under his lids. He flung his arm out, throwing off the sheet.

She leaned over and felt his forehead. It wasn't unduly hot.

'Can't get out,' he muttered, fighting to get free of the sheet, which had become twisted round his legs. 'Mustn't let them get me.'

Poor Tom. He must just be having a nightmare.

'Angel!' He reached out blindly. For her.

She caught at his flailing hand, and held hard.

'Shhh. I'm here. You are safe.'

'Violets.' He sighed and settled down again.

She sat back, pushing a stray tendril of hair from her

forehead. She was bone weary and ready for bed herself. She glanced longingly at the pallet bed she'd had Madame le Brun bring in here, in case Tom's fever mounted again during the night and he needed help.

She smiled at the irony. Today he'd been addressing her as *your Majesty*, but his need of her meagre nursing skills meant she was going to have to sleep on a pallet like a chambermaid.

She'd just pulled all the pins from her hair and started attacking the snarls with a comb when Tom cried out for her again.

After settling him and going back to her preparations for bed, only to have him cry out for her again, and again, she finally gave up all thought of getting a decent night's sleep.

In fact, the only way she might snatch even a few moments would be to lie down next to him.

She chewed on her lower lip, a little shocked at herself for even considering such a thing. But then he cried out again and reached for her, and, instead of merely holding his hand and stroking his brow, she clambered on to the bed beside him and gathered him into her arms. After all, it was only like the time she'd held him close, in the French ambulance, to prevent him jolting his poor head. It wasn't an attempt at seduction. It might be unconventional, to get on to the bed and cuddle him like this, but it wasn't *really* improper.

When he sighed and stilled, as though finally he felt safe, she knew she'd done the right thing. Which brought a warm glow of satisfaction deep inside. It even helped to soothe her own bone-deep loneliness. Because nobody had ever needed her like this before. Not even Gideon.

She held Tom more tightly. Holding someone who

was clinging to her was very comforting, she discovered. She'd never just cuddled anyone, as far as she could recall. Or been cuddled, either. Once, she recalled Bridget cuddling Gideon, after he'd fallen and scraped his knee. The old nurse in charge of the nursery had reprimanded her. Said he wouldn't grow up to be a proper man if she mollycoddled him.

So no more cuddles. For either of them. For Mama only visited the nursery briefly, at nights, to see them safely tucked up in bed, and Papa not at all.

'What a pair we are,' she said, shifting so that she could lay her head on Tom's chest. 'Like two survivors of a shipwreck, clinging together in the wreckage.'

There were certainly no words that anyone could say that could bring her the slightest bit of comfort over losing Gideon. Nothing to compare with just being held like this, as though she was as necessary as breathing. So she wasn't going to worry about the propriety of it. Not when she was so tired.

Not when it felt so good.

Tom didn't want to wake up. There was a deliciously fragrant, warm woman in his arms.

Why, though? He never slept with women. Once he'd taken his pleasure, he got out of their beds as soon as decently possible.

Though to say she was in his arms wasn't strictly accurate. They had their arms round each other. She'd got one leg over him, too, keeping him warm with the flow of her skirts. Which was odd. He must be losing his touch if she was still clothed, while he was stark naked. She was cradling his head to her breasts, too—his head which hurt like the very devil.

He glanced up through the mass of golden curls pillowing his cheek and cursed under his breath. It was Lady Sarah Latymor in his arms. She had spent the night in bed with him!

Didn't she know the difference between sitting decorously at his side, mopping his brow and spooning liquid into his mouth to quench his raging thirst, and holding him in her arms?

Probably not. In her innocence, she'd sought to soothe him, that was all. She'd done so every single time he'd reached for her, when the nightmares had come rolling in, swamping him, smothering him. He'd got so he'd dreaded closing his eyes for fear of what would assault him next.

And, oh, it had felt good when she'd first clambered on to his bed and rocked him. It had taken him back to his childhood and the way he'd wished there'd been someone, anyone, to come and rock him to sleep as a child. Though there never had.

Looked like she'd rocked herself to sleep, too. Poor girl must be exhausted. He didn't think he'd been an easy patient to look after. But she'd never given up. Never left him to the nightmares, or the fever, nor even fled the impropriety of being alone with him once he'd come to.

He wished he could lie here like this for ever.

Actually, no, he didn't. He wanted to kiss her, not just lie here. Her lips were parted slightly. If he moved just a touch, if he raised his head, he could steal a kiss and she'd never know. If he was gentle enough, she wouldn't wake, she was sleeping so deeply.

He huffed out an irritated breath. She might not know, but he would. He'd feel as if he'd betrayed her. She hadn't climbed into his bed for *that*.

He was a bit disgusted with himself for being tempted

to steal from her what should be freely given. What kind of man even thought about repaying all her care of him by treating her with such disrespect? She deserved better.

Whereas he deserved the physical agony which clawed at just about every part of his body. The pain he suffered was just sentence.

Everything hurt. His head, particularly, pounded…

No, actually, the pounding was coming from the region of the door.

One of the household servants?

No. They wouldn't enter until given permission to do so. Whoever this was had flung open the door and come striding across the room.

'Bartlett? They tell me you're…'

Bartlett's instinct was to bury his nose deeper between Lady Sarah's breasts and close his eyes, to blot out the furious face that belonged to that voice. The face of Major Flint.

He stifled a groan. He couldn't have been discovered by anyone worse. Because Major Flint just happened to be this girl's half-brother. An illegitimate half-brother, but nevertheless he would still count her as family. Particularly since Flint owed his career to her legitimate brother. Colonel Randall, so rumour had it, had recognised the Latymor nose—the nose which was the bane of Sarah's life—and given Flint a field commission on the strength of it.

He was finished.

Flint's shocked cry roused Lady Sarah, who leapt guiltily from the bed, pausing only to fling a sheet over the lower half of his body. As if Flint hadn't seen a naked man before.

'What the hell,' said the clearly shocked Major Flint, 'are you doing here?'

Ah, well, it had been good while it lasted. Perhaps Flint would save him the bother of facing Colonel Randall by simply running him through where he lay. It wouldn't be a bad way to go. At least his last day on earth had been spent with her. Lady Sarah. In a kind of...what had she called it? A golden haze. Unreal. Too perfect for such as him. A day never to be repeated.

'You!' Lady Sarah sounded appalled. Had she really thought she could get away with this? Had she really thought that telling the landlady he was her brother would prevent the truth coming out, in the end?

'You're Adam Flint! Justin wouldn't introduce you to me at the review.'

Bartlett forced his eyes open, to take his last look at her. She sounded really distressed now. Apologetic.

Naturally. Something twisted inside him. It had been all very well caring for him when she'd thought she could keep it secret. But now her behaviour was about to be exposed. She'd crumble in the face of Flint's fury. Flint was a hard man. He'd grown up in the gutter, gone into the army like so many of his kind, but then risen through the ranks by his own merit—until the day his half-brother had started taking an interest in him. He was one of the few officers tough enough to be able to control such men who ended up in Randall's Rogues, probably because he was, really, one of them. He'd make mincemeat of a fine lady like Sarah.

'He wouldn't introduce *any* of the Rogues,' Flint snapped. 'And for good reason. None of us should be associating with you. Let alone him.' Flint stabbed an accusing finger in his direction.

Couldn't argue with that. Ramrod Randall knew his men were scum and the officers leading them fit only to lead scum. Naturally he wanted his precious little sister guarded from them all. He'd even tried to get her to leave Brussels altogether when she'd shown too much interest in the Rogues. It had only been because her twin, the one who was in a fashionable cavalry regiment, kept her busy with a far more acceptable set of people that he'd relented.

'I know the reason he wouldn't introduce me to *you*,' she said, self-consciously tidying her unbound hair into a hasty plait. 'You're my natural brother. I'm not supposed to know any of you exist, let alone associate with you.'

That's right, she'd told him there were dozens of them. She'd told him her mother was obliged to ignore them all.

And she hated it. She'd spoken of what her mother had suffered. Why hadn't he seen that she suffered, too? That she hated the hypocrisy of having to behave as though she was ignorant of her father's behaviour.

'And stop shouting. Poor Tom's head hurts.'

Poor Tom? That sounded as though she cared for him. And wasn't afraid to let Flint know it.

A great hollow opened up inside of him. Somewhere in the region of his heart. A hunger. Yearning.

'Poor Tom's head,' Flint growled, 'is going to be ripped from his shoulders. Now get your cloak and bonnet. I'm taking you home this minute. For you can't stay here.'

Farewell, Lady Sarah. It was a privilege to know you. Albeit briefly...

But far from meekly going to the peg on which her cloak hung, Lady Sarah stood her ground.

'I *am* home. This is *my* lodging.'

'Well, then, I'll take you to your brother.'

'You can't do that,' she said triumphantly. 'Mary End-acott says he's too ill to be disturbed.'

She was like a little terrier, standing up to the farmer's prize bull, he marvelled, as the battle raged over his bed. Dodging, and yipping, and nipping with her sharp little words. While Major Flint, more used to applying brute force to those under his command, bellowed and raged with increasing impotence, confused by her speed and nimbleness.

He felt like weeping. She was still defending him. The way she'd done from the first. Not just from strangers, and his injuries, but now from her very family. The ones who cared about her and her reputation.

Nobody had ever fought for him before. Defended him. They'd all been more inclined to condemn him without a shred of evidence. Any trouble in the vicinity? Bound to be Tom's fault. So he got the punishment whether he'd been involved or not.

'Bartlett!' Major Flint was bending over him, bellowing right into his face just as though he was a raw recruit who could be intimidated by such measures. He hadn't been intimidated by such tactics when he *had* been a raw recruit.

Out of habit, he adopted the same measure he'd done then. Widened his eyes as if bewildered as to why he was up on a charge. Though he couldn't resist taunting Flint just a bit, as well.

'Sir?'

'Don't *sir* me, Bartlett. We're the same rank, damn it.'

Yes, damn it, they were. Both of them had ended up as majors in Randall's rag-tag unit of misfits. And neither of them had been able to inherit the land, or title, or wealth that their noble fathers had enjoyed.

There was a vast gulf between them. She was on one side, a lady of unimpeachable virtue. And he was on the other. A rake and a rogue. They'd held hands across the gulf for a short while, but now it was time to let go.

The argument raged on above him, while he went under a wave of utter misery. He'd known he couldn't, in all conscience, stay here with her for long. Though why it mattered to him so much he couldn't say. He'd never even felt the merest twinge of regret when the time had come to part from any other woman.

'Leave him alone,' Lady Sarah insisted, snagging his attention once more. 'He has no idea who he is, what happened.'

What? Where had she got that notion? A dart of shame speared him. Yesterday. When he'd been trying to stave off reality, that's where. That puerile game he'd started, hoping to prolong his time with her. In the hopes of snatching a kiss or two.

'He doesn't know you.'

He took a breath to explain. Then thought better of it. He wasn't going to contradict Lady Sarah, not when she was doing her best to defend him. Major Flint might have been the closest thing Tom had ever had to a friend, but over the last couple of days, she'd earned his loyalty, too.

'He seems to think he's a lieutenant.'

He frowned. Now that was...no, actually he couldn't think where she'd got that notion from at all. He'd never said anything about his army rank. Had deliberately kept reality out of all their conversations.

Which meant...his heart took a great bound. She was

making it up. Lying. For him. She said he was too weak to move? He wouldn't move, then.

She said he couldn't remember who he was? He wouldn't make her look a fool by arguing. Besides, his memory *had* been a touch hazy, at least when he'd first come round.

'Perhaps in his mind he is back when he first joined the army,' she finished on what looked like a burst of inspiration.

When Flint's scowl turned in his direction, he therefore did his best to look confused. She'd put her reputation on the line for him. So he'd do whatever necessary to back her up.

'Have you seen the head wound?'

'Yes, of course,' she said, turning a bit pale. And stunned him still further by describing it in all its gory detail. Including an account of how she'd stitched it up.

To think of this sheltered young woman doing *that* for him.

'He is going to get better,' she was insisting now, with tears in her eyes. 'He *must*.'

Flint was looking at him with a thoughtful frown now. Was looking at Lady Sarah differently, too. She wasn't the woman they all thought she was, that was why. Her own brother seemed to think she couldn't cross the road without an escort, but in the last couple of days she'd come to Brussels alone, tamed a fearsome dog, seen off a deserter, scoured the battlefield for survivors, stitched him up and nursed him back from the brink of death.

Flint had just opened his mouth to say something, when the dog scratched at the door to be let in. Sarah ran to let him in with what looked like relief. She drew a lot of comfort from that dog, he'd noticed, though she went through the motions of chiding him whenever he came indoors—if the landlady was anywhere near.

For once, the dog didn't take a blind bit of notice of her. Instead, it flung itself joyously at Flint, who took great pleasure in making the animal sit at his feet.

Bartlett couldn't blame him. It was the first time, since setting foot in this room, he'd had the slightest bit of control over any of the occupants.

'How the devil did Dog get here?'

'His name's Ben,' she corrected him and gave a brief account of her adventures.

Major Flint straightened up from scratching Dog behind his ear. 'This animal,' he said sternly, 'is coming back with me now. And so are you,' he informed Lady Sarah. 'Pack a bag. I'm taking you to Randall's house.'

'I won't go.' She sat on the end of his bed, placing one hand possessively on his leg. 'You would have to carry me kicking and screaming all the way.'

Thwarted again, Flint changed tactic. 'Then I'll have *him* moved.'

'That could kill him!' Tears sprang to her eyes.

He stirred guiltily. He wasn't as ill as all that. And he should tell her he wasn't worth a single one of her tears. He should sit up, get dressed and go with Flint. And nip this—whatever it was that was happening between them—in the bud.

'How do you know,' she said, abruptly changing tack, 'that Gideon is dead?'

'Because I was there,' said Flint tersely.

'Are you certain?'

'Certain I was there, or certain he's dead? Yes to both. You don't get up after wounds like that.'

Bartlett's mouth firmed as he promptly changed his

mind about leaving her. He might have caused her to shed a tear or two, but he wouldn't let them run down her face, the way Flint was doing, had he a handkerchief to hand. Or the strength to wield it. How could the man speak of her twin's death in such a callous manner?

'Was he shot? Was it quick?'

For God's sake, tell her it was quick, Bartlett silently willed Flint. Whether it was the truth or not.

'Sabre wounds.'

Bartlett almost groaned. How could the idiot say that, when he knew full well that she knew exactly what sabre wounds looked like, having just treated his own?

She must have felt the same, because suddenly she was on her feet, pointing at the door.

'Get out,' she screamed, making the dog shrink into Flint's leg in surprise. 'Get out—and if you come back here again disturbing Tom then I'll use his pistols on you!'

His pistols had been stolen. But Flint didn't know that it was an empty threat. Not that it was all that much of a threat. Flint wasn't a man to quail at the prospect of having a slip of a girl waving a pistol at him. Not when he was accustomed to facing down whole columns of enemy infantry during a battle and packs of drunken deserters in the aftermath.

Nevertheless, Major Flint turned and stalked out, clicking his fingers so that the dog went trotting after him.

Sarah watched the dog leave as though it was betraying her. Tears were still rolling down her cheeks. And she was trembling.

'Ben went with him,' she said. And sat down abruptly on his bed as though her legs had no strength left in them.

He nearly had done, too. Thank goodness he hadn't. She shouldn't be alone, not when she was so upset.

'Ben is his dog,' he explained, reaching out to take the little, trembling hand she'd rested on his leg and giving it what he hoped she'd find a comforting sort of squeeze.

'No—' she shook her head '—Gideon told me he belonged to all the Rogues. That you'd adopted him when you found him on some farm where you stayed.'

He bowed his head. Swallowed. Her need to hear the truth was greater than his need to prolong his pretence of memory loss. 'It was Major Flint who took the trouble to tame him. And though the creature accepted the rest of us as part of Flint's pack, I suppose you would call it, he clearly feels he belongs to Flint.'

'Oh,' she said. 'Yes, I see. It was foolish of me to think…'

He held her hand a bit tighter.

'You were magnificent,' he stated resolutely.

'Me?' She gave a convulsive shiver. 'Look at me. I'm shaking like a leaf. It was horrible. Horrible. That was the first time I've ever stood up to someone like that. Face-to-face. I didn't know I could. And now I just feel sick.'

'It is always like that after a battle, for everyone. It's odd. You can do incredible, awful things while the battle rages, without turning a hair, but then after, well, tremble like aspens.'

'I wish I hadn't had to. That was the first time I've ever spoken to Major Flint and it was as though he was my enemy. And he's my—' she gave a little hiccup of a sob '—he's my b-brother. And he's taken Ben. I thought we were a team,' she said, gazing at the door through which they'd just gone. 'I don't care if he is Major F-Flint's d-dog…I…'

She bowed her head and gave in.

Normally, the sight of a woman in tears would have made him run a mile. But not when that woman was Lady Sarah. He knew there was nothing he could do to assuage the grief Major Flint had just inflicted, one way and another. But he could at least hold her while she wept.

The way she'd held him during his darkest hours.

Chapter Seven

Tom struggled to a sitting position, then scooted up until he could kneel behind her and put his arms round her. Though he'd half-feared she might flinch away, she actually turned and buried her face in his chest.

Though he was naked, battered and bruised and practically a stranger to her.

Pretty soon he was shaking with the effort of staying upright and keeping his arms round her, and half-bearing her weight. Heavens, but he was weak. His head was starting to spin by the time her sobs subsided.

'I'm so sorry—' she sniffed '—I'm not usually such a watering pot. And all over a man taking back his own dog, of all things.'

'It wasn't just that though, was it?' he said grimly. 'You'd only just heard your twin brother was cut to pieces by cavalry sabres.'

She flinched. Pulled out of his arms. Scrubbed at her eyes with a corner of the sheet.

He'd offended her. As well as blowing any chance he could carry on feigning ignorance of his identity and his past. Exhausted and depressed, he gave up the struggle to stay upright and lay back down against the pillows.

'Oh, Tom, I'm so sorry. Here I am weeping all over you when I'm supposed to be the one looking after you.' She leapt to her feet, tidying the sheet over him and generally fussing round the bed.

'No. *I'm* sorry. I thought I could be of help. I know I can't take the place Ben had in your affections, but I thought I could at least hold you. But I can't even do that.' He tried to lift his arm from the bed. 'I'm useless. Trembling like a whipped pup.'

'Don't ever let anyone tell you you're useless,' she flung at him angrily.

'Is that what they did to you? Is that why you fought Flint over me?' That made sense. In himself, he was nothing to her. But he had just worked out that her family had no idea what she was capable of. So perhaps he'd become a sort of symbol of her prowess.

She had the grace to look abashed.

'It doesn't matter.' He shrugged one shoulder. 'I've always known I'm not worth fighting for, myself.'

'Please, don't be disappointed in me. I didn't know you when I found you on the battlefield. And I was… Oh, you can't think what a difference it made when your men put their faith in me. When they believed I was capable of nursing you. When nobody has ever thought I'm capable of *anything*.'

'Yes. I think I can.' He gave her a rueful smile. 'Nobody's ever thought I was worth a damn. And in *my* case, they were right.'

'Oh, no. I'm sure that's not true. You're an officer in the army. Artillery, no less. Which shows you have intelligence. And to rise to the rank of major, you must be, um…'

He gave a snort. 'All it shows is that I've survived.'

'Oh, no! Far more than that. One thing I do know about the artillery is that you cannot buy promotion, or use influence to gain it. You must have earned every single promotion you've ever had.'

'Be that as it may, if Major Flint had found you nursing someone like Bennington Ffog…' His lip curled as he named the man who'd been her most prominent admirer. The fop who'd been in charge of her twin's regiment. And the man after whom his own men had named the Dog. Bennington Dog, they called him, shortening it to just Ben when the animal didn't respond to the mouthful of English. Which made them swear the name was all the more appropriate. Not only did the hound have fur the exact shade of the Colonel's luxuriant whiskers, the two of them had about the same level of intelligence. And having seen the man lolloping around after Lady Sarah with his tongue hanging out, the way Ben had done the day before, he couldn't disagree with them.

Not only that, but they were both hunting mad. He'd had a notion that if he'd thrown a bone and shouted 'fetch,' the Colonel would have yelled 'tally ho' and gone off in hot pursuit.

'Not even Flint would have suggested removing you from his bed and leaving *him* to rot. Or risk moving him, rather than have you tainted by the association. If Flint had found you in *his* arms, he'd have been talking about making it right by marrying him.'

'Oh. Yes. I hadn't thought of that.'

'Well, you should.' He seethed. Nobody thought Bennington Ffog was unsuitable—though he had less brains than his horse—because he had money and breeding. Whereas even Flint didn't want *him* anywhere near her. 'Your brothers would prefer to see me dead than married to you.'

She gave a bitter little smile. 'That's what you think. I think they'd prefer to see me married to *anyone* than being…being…oh, why are we talking about marriage? You don't want it, any more than I do.'

'It isn't a question of wanting it, or not. I haven't anything to offer a woman. Let alone a lady. I can't marry.'

Her eyes flicked down over his naked torso with a certain sort of gleam.

Good God! She seemed to think he *did* have something to offer a woman. His heart beat a little harder. His plan to get her to let him kiss her didn't seem so far-fetched, after all. She was attracted to him. How that could be when she'd seen him at his very weakest, when he could hardly sit up for five minutes, when he was covered with cuts and bruises, he couldn't think.

But she'd definitely given him a hungry little look. Even if she had swiftly wiped her face clean of expression and resumed her mask of polite, ladylike respectability.

She already looked on him as a kind of symbol of rebellion. How far, he wondered, could he get her to rebel? Against the narrow confinement of her life? Against the injustice of having to put up with men like Bennington Ffog slavering over her?

'I'm sorry I got cross. I don't want to fight with you, Tom. I just…' She rubbed wearily at her forehead.

She probably didn't want him slavering over her, either. She was only just beginning to change her mind about kissing him. He'd better not push his luck, after that one slim sign of encouragement, or she'd bolt like an unbroken filly. He'd have to persuade her to trust him, before making another move.

What? What was he thinking? He never bothered to *persuade* a woman to trust him, or attempted to woo her gently. But then no other woman was like Lady Sarah. Wasn't she worth making an effort for?

Besides, he wasn't going anywhere. And neither, to judge from her spirited resistance to Flint's orders, was she.

And his aim wasn't full congress. He knew he could never be with her, in that way. All he wanted was a kiss. Just one. Willingly given.

'You've worn yourself out looking after me,' he said, reaching up to soothe the little frown line pleating her brows. She didn't slap his hand away, but closed her eyes and sort of sank into his caress. The innocent little gesture of gratitude made his heart skip more than it would have done had another woman come in here and stripped naked.

'If I had any decency about me,' he growled, 'I'd offer to leave here and go to a hospital or something. That would be the honourable course to take. But I'm not going to.'

Her eyes flew open. She regarded him with frank curiosity. 'Because you aren't an honourable man?'

Hell, no. He wasn't in the slightest bit honourable. Or he wouldn't be planning ways to gain her trust so that he could take advantage.

'More to the point,' he said with what he hoped was a disarming grin, 'because you haven't *asked* me to leave. For some reason, which I suspect has nothing to do with me at all, you want me right where you've got me.'

She flushed. Moved away a little, so that her forehead was out of his reach. He let his hand fall back to his side.

'You're right.' She lifted her chin. 'I do want you to stay here with me. It may be terribly shallow of me, but while I'm looking after you, while you have to depend on me for everything, I feel as if my life has some purpose, for once.'

'Well, I'm happy to stay as sick as you like, for as long as you feel you need to nurse someone.'

'Oh, Tom, don't say that. I want you to get well. You *have* to get well. To show everyone that…and to myself that—' She broke off, shaking her head. 'It's terribly selfish of me, isn't it? To be nursing you just to prove a point?' She peeped up at him from under lowered lashes.

He reached out and took her hand.

'I'm sure you have perfectly good reasons for everything you do. I know, better than anyone, that people are apt to judge others on their actions, without pausing to consider what their motives might be.'

She gasped. Clasped his hand a little tighter. 'That's very generous of you.'

He gave a wry smile. 'Not really. But after the way Major Flint jumped to all the wrong conclusions about us, because of what he saw—me naked, you clasped in my arms—' he quirked one eyebrow suggestively '—he assumed guilt. People always assume the worst. Though how he could have thought the worst of you…' He scowled, not only because Flint had suggested it, but also because he minded that Flint thought it.

He'd never cared what anyone thought of any of his women before. Not that Lady Sarah was his woman.

Perhaps he felt protective towards her because no other

woman had ever gone to such lengths on his behalf before. Even if it was only to prove a point.

'Tom, you have got to stop thinking I'm some kind of angel. I'm not. I stumbled into looking after you for a whole series of stupid, selfish, reasons. Not one of them was the slightest bit angelic, I assure you.'

'Tell me, then. I should like to know how you came to stumble upon me. What someone like you was doing on a battlefield at all.'

She searched his face for evidence that he condemned her for being on the battlefield. She couldn't find it. He just looked interested. Curious.

When was the last time anyone had wanted to know why she'd done anything? Been interested in hearing her side of things, rather than just passing judgement on her?

'I went to the battlefield searching for Gideon,' she said. 'Or his body. Or some answers. That was what I told myself. But I suspect it was all lunacy, really. I just couldn't believe he was dead. They wouldn't tell me anything that would have convinced me. Not even when the funeral was to be, or where,' she said, hitching her knee up on to the side of the bed so that she could look him full in the face. And judge his reaction. She took a deep breath.

'And I was so sure that Gideon couldn't have died without me knowing it, in my heart. Our nurse always used to say we were one soul, living in two bodies, you see. And we were so close, so very close, that I thought… I thought…' She shook her head. 'How could I have been so wrong? So foolish?'

He gripped her hand tightly. 'You weren't foolish at all.'

'Oh, but I was. I realised it not long before those Hussars came charging along the road, scattering wreckage in their path. I felt just like Ben, who was howling with panic from under that broken wagon. Stuck there, with no idea where to go next. And then when that deserter tried to steal Castor—' She shuddered.

'You must have been terrified.'

'No! That was just it. Not of him, at any rate. Only of losing the horse. Not for any sensible reason, either. But because he was the last present Gideon had given me. My last tangible link to him. He had another grey, to match, and we used to go riding out together. Cutting a dash, don't you know? Golden-haired twins on matching horses. He even wanted me to have a riding habit made up in the same colour and style as his uniform, to heighten the effect. So that people would say we looked like the heavenly twins, Castor and Pollux.'

'I saw you,' he said.

'Yes, so you did,' she replied, remembering the day and him leaning up against the tree. 'You winked at me.'

He wriggled uncomfortably, opening his mouth as though reaching for something to say. But there wasn't anything she wanted to hear about that day. That time. The man he'd been then. So she plunged on hurriedly.

'Anyway, I couldn't bear losing Castor. So I went back to Brussels to find somewhere safe to hide him, in case the French really were about to overrun the town. I slept in the stable with him, because I was afraid to take my eyes off him. I'd only been under the wagon trying to untie Ben for a few moments, you see, and that was all it took for the deserter to get his reins in his hands. I never gave a thought to my own safety, or anything sensible.

It was all about keeping some link, any link, to Gideon.'
She hung her head.

'Even when I started to accept he really had…died…
my head was still full of nonsense. When you just fell
into my lap, I told myself *that* was the purpose for my
being there. It made me feel better, for a while, to think
that maybe some fate had directed me to you. That those
feelings I had, that I simply *had* to come back to Brussels, were some kind of intuition, or something. That's
how foolish I've been…'

'No. I won't hear you say bad things about yourself.'

'But I ran away from home. Worried my poor sister,
who is in a fragile state of health. Angered her husband.
Flouted Justin. All because I refused to accept the truth.
Oh, how could I have gone about spouting all that nonsense about not sensing his spirit leaving the world? Madame le Brun must have thought I was deranged, turning
up on her doorstep babbling the way I did.'

'Sometimes,' he said grimly, 'when something bad
happens and you don't want to believe it, you get this
shout inside. This great, overwhelming *No!* It drowns
out everything else. All common sense. Even when the
evidence is right before your eyes you won't see it. All
you can hear, or say, or feel is that *No.*'

She stared at him in amazement. She'd half-expected
him to roll his eyes, the way her older brother and sisters
did whenever she mentioned her belief about her link to
her twin. They always said she should have grown out
of the tales her 'ignorant, ill-educated and superstitious'
nurse had told her.

'I've never held all that much regard for common
sense,' she told him. 'Because,' she added hesitantly, 'nobody has ever been able to explain, for all their rational,

cynical cleverness, how it was that I always knew when Gideon was about to get into a scrape. How I could always sense when he was on his way home. Or how, when he was home, we only had to look at each other to understand what the other was thinking.'

'Really? That's astonishing.'

He meant it, too, she could tell. He wasn't humouring her, or even making fun of her, let alone trying to rob her of her beliefs.

'Thank you for saying that, Tom, about the *No*.' Even though everyone she knew insisted Tom was bad, what he'd just said had actually helped her untangle her muddled thoughts. Had helped her look upon her loss and confusion from a new perspective.

How was that possible, when he scarcely knew her?

'You speak as though you have felt just like I did when they told me Gideon was dead. Almost impossible to believe, it was so bad. Did something like that happen to you?'

'Yes,' he said gruffly. 'When my father died. I lost everything I thought I had. Everything I thought I was. And, even once the shout of *No* died down,' he said, giving her a very speaking look, 'I still didn't know who I was. There was no going back, yet it took me a long time to forge a new path for myself. But you will get there,' he assured her. 'You are strong.'

He thought she was strong? Then he was the only man…no, the only person ever to think so.

'And you are an adult. With a family to support you. Not a child who has no understanding of the way the world works.'

'A child?' He had lost everything when he'd been a child?

'What happened to you, Tom? How have you ended up the way you are?'

'The way I am?' He stretched his lips into a cynical smile.

'Yes, the way you are,' she retorted. 'Smiling like that as though…as though…well, it's a mask, isn't it? And don't bother arguing, I can see when someone is hiding behind smiles and attitudes, because I've done it myself, practically all my life. And because I've seen you without it—the mask. The fever tore it away. So stop talking all that rot about not being good enough and having nothing to offer. It's an excuse. You don't *want* to let anyone close. That's all there is to it.'

'Be careful, Lady Sarah,' he growled. 'Or I might start to think you'd changed your mind about staying single.'

'Don't change the subject,' she snapped. 'I can tell when someone is trying to distract me from answering the question. If you don't want to tell me, then don't. If it is some deep, dark terrible family secret, then just say so.'

He winced. 'Secret? It's no secret. My family has caused so much scandal there is no hushing it up.'

She knew exactly how that felt.

'And you have to live with it,' she said. 'Find a way to hold your head up in public, when you know full well people are whispering about the scandal behind their fans.'

'Yes, I have to live with it,' he breathed. 'I have to live with the fact my father hanged himself. After gambling away everything he'd ever owned.'

'Oh, my goodness!' Sarah clapped her hand to her mouth in horror. 'I thought my father was an utter disgrace, but even he never forgot what he owed to his name. Not entirely.'

'Exactly,' he said with a bitter smile. 'Most men, if they should get to the point where they feel there is only one way out, would make it look like a hunting accident. So that their children could still inherit. Well, actually, there were only debts left to inherit. My grandfather had already lost the title.'

'Lost the title?' Tom came from a noble family? 'How on earth did he manage to do that?'

'Spoke out in support of Charles Stuart's claim to the throne,' he said grimly. 'Then threw in his lot with the Jacobites. So there you have it, Lady Sarah. My grandfather was a traitor. My father, well, the best you could say of him was that he was unhinged. But after two generations of scandal, nobody has any doubt that I have tainted blood.'

'You really did lose everything,' she said in a hollow whisper. 'It makes what I've lived through, what I've thought I've had to endure...' She shook her head in shame.

'None of that,' he said sharply. 'What happened to me when I was a child doesn't make your own woes any less significant to you.'

'My woes are petty, though, aren't they? I've always had a secure home. And family. Even though I always thought that out of them all, only Gideon ever actually *liked* me.'

'From what you've told me so far, your father blighted your childhood in his own way.'

'Yes, but he was just a lecherous old goat who couldn't keep his hands off any pretty woman unfortunate enough to cross his path. And rather than having no sense of obligation to the title, he made absolutely sure,' she said with a bitter twist to her lips, 'that every single child my mother bore was his. He only left her alone when he was certain she was pregnant. By him.'

'My father's problem was the opposite of yours, then. He was totally infatuated with my mother. When she died—bringing me into the world, as it happens—he lost interest in everything else. Hanging himself was probably his way of ensuring I knew how much he disapproved of me surviving at the cost of the only woman he'd ever loved.'

'Our fathers were both as bad as each other,' she said, her lips tightening. 'How could yours abandon his child the way he abandoned you? Leaving you with nothing? Worse than nothing! He burdened you with the belief that somehow his failings were your fault. Ooh—' she clenched her fists '—I thought my father was a bad man, but to act the way yours did is downright unnatural.'

Tom had never really talked about this with anyone before. It was something everyone who knew him knew, anyway. He'd been taunted about it, frequently, but nobody had ever asked him how he felt about it. Let alone taken his part, the way Lady Sarah had just done.

She had such a generous heart, to get all indignant on behalf of a little orphaned boy, rather than react to the disgrace she'd just learned was his inheritance. In that, she was unique. Society ladies, in his experience, had always fallen into one of two camps. There were the ones who turned their noses up at him. Who even twitched their skirts aside to avoid getting accidentally contaminated.

And those who got sexually aroused by the aura of disrepute surrounding him.

Not one of them had appeared to understand exactly how he felt about it, or had even been that interested, come to that.

'What happened to you next? You were only six, you say?' Sarah curled up in the chair next to the bed and rested her cheek on her hand. 'Did you have to go into a foundling home?'

'No. Worse. My father's sister took me in.'

'How could that possibly have been worse?'

'Well, her husband looked upon me as the spawn of a weak, degenerate man, who was in his turn the spawn of a traitor. And felt it was his Christian duty to ensure I didn't follow in their footsteps. Which was his excuse for taking every chance he could to beat the evil out of me.'

'Did not your aunt try to stop him? After all, your bad blood ran in her veins, too.'

'Ah. Well, looking back, I can see she was too afraid of him to stand up to him. He was a vicious bully. But as a child, I didn't understand. I just thought she believed what he said and didn't think it worth the bother of looking for some evidence of good in me. Of course,' he said, his smile turning a little wicked, 'their attitude had a predictable effect. Since I soon learned that trying to be good didn't ameliorate their treatment, there didn't seem much point in trying. In fact, rather the opposite. If I was going to get a beating, I decided I may as well have done something worth getting the beating for.'

'Good for you.' She gave a determined nod. 'I hope you made their lives as miserable as they made yours.'

He gave a bark of laughter. 'Well, do you know, I rather think I did. I became a regular little hellion. They couldn't keep me in school. I much preferred being out of doors with the other village lads, of whom I was pretty soon the ringleader. Before long, if there was any trouble within fifteen miles of our village, they laid it at my door,' he finished with a glimmer of pride.

'My uncle said if he didn't put a stop to my criminal career I'd end up hanging, just like my father. And so he decided the best course was to let the army have me. Only then he faced a bit of a dilemma. As the son of a gentleman, he couldn't very well have me enlist like a common man. But neither did he want to go to all the expense of buying me a commission. So he sent me off to the Royal Military Academy at Woolwich, where they trained me to become both an officer and an engineer,' he finished with a grimace.

'There is nothing wrong with that,' she retorted. 'Justin himself chose to serve in the artillery, like our grandfather.'

'Yes, but it isn't the done thing, is it? Far more acceptable to go into the cavalry, or the Guards.'

'People don't just go into the cavalry to be acceptable,' she said, a little flash of annoyance in her eyes. 'Gideon wanted to… He would have…' She stopped and drew in a shuddery sort of breath. 'He idolised Justin, but he didn't want to ape him. So Mama bought him a commission in a cavalry regiment. She was the one who wanted him to be fashionable. Gideon never cared for any of that. He's like… I mean, he *was* like me. Never happier than when on horseback. Whenever he was home we used to pack our saddlebags and just take off. We'd stay out all day,' she said with a faraway look in her eye. 'It started when we were very little. We'd slip away from the schoolroom and hide somewhere on the estate. We'd dam streams and climb trees, and make dens in the woods. Even when they sent him away to school, he couldn't wait to come home so we could play together. And tell each other all the things we couldn't put in any of the letters we wrote. Once or twice he brought friends to stay, but they only spoiled things by asking why on earth he let a girl tag along. And he'd declare I wasn't a bit like most girls. That I could stay out all day and not get tired, or complain about mud, or brambles. And he never invited them again.'

She wasn't a bit like most girls. Most women. He could talk to her. As though she was a…a friend.

He wished he'd known her when he'd been a grubby, half-starved boy. He might not have grown up so certain the whole world was against him. He was just wondering whether to tell her so when Madame le Brun came in with a breakfast tray.

'Good morning. You are looking so much better,' she said, running her eyes over him assessingly.

'Down to your amazing cooking,' Tom replied, casting aside the temptation to confess things better left unsaid. He gave the landlady the benefit of his most flirtatious smile. 'And having my every whim catered to by two such beautiful women.' He leaned back and tucked both hands behind his head. 'You are making me feel like a sultan in a harem.'

To Sarah's amazement, the landlady, who must have been fifty if she was a day, blushed and laughed in a very girlish way, then shook her finger at him, in mock admonishment. She then spent rather longer than she needed, flitting about the room setting things to rights. When she left, Sarah shook her head at Tom.

'What?' He shrugged and widened his eyes in mock innocence. 'Flirting does no harm. She enjoys it.'

He'd got in the habit of flirting with women, he realised, as he took a spoonful of the eggs Madame had brought. All women, no matter what their age. Making them blush and simper gave him the upper hand. By making them react to what he was doing, rather than letting them get in first, he controlled them. Kept them in their place.

Flirting was the quickest way to discover whether they'd be willing to lift their skirts, too. If a woman was amenable, his next objective was normally to find out how quickly. If she wasn't, he always moved on to the next likely prospect without hesitation. It was a ruthless method. A foolproof method that got him bedded more frequently than any other officer in the Rogues. Or any other unit in which he'd served.

Maybe that was why he'd toned things down with Lady Sarah. He didn't want to try and control her, or keep her in her place. It felt more important to get to know her—right down to the very bones of her. And flirting too brazenly would only put her on her guard against him.

Oh, he still wanted to kiss her, make no mistake. More than that. Much, much more. Though he didn't want it to be like the crude encounters of his past, that satisfied a momentary itch. He wanted…he wanted…

All of a sudden the words of the marriage vows popped into his head. *With my body, I thee worship…*

A chill curled its fist round the back of his neck. He wasn't contemplating *marriage*. It was just that Sarah was the kind of girl who deserved marriage. Yes, that was it. She should have someone who loved and cherished her, and all the rest of it. Hadn't she already roused all sorts of similar responses from him? Feelings of protectiveness, and friendship, and loyalty. The chill receded. Now he knew where the sudden understanding of the marriage lines had come from, there was no need to panic. He wasn't in danger of doing anything stupid, like falling in love with her, and proposing marriage himself.

Men like him didn't fall in love.

Didn't know how.

Chapter Eight

Sarah took her dish of chocolate to the writing desk and gazed out of the window as she sipped at it. Another funeral procession was snaking along the street. Every day, more young men were dying of wounds inflicted in the battle that had taken Gideon from her. Her nose felt hot. Though she blinked rapidly, she couldn't prevent a single tear sliding down her cheek. Though why should she even try to hold it back? She'd lost Gideon, and to know so many more young men were dying was utterly tragic.

She *wasn't* upset by the fact that, though Tom was now well enough to flirt with the landlady, he'd started treating her more like a…like a sort of sister. Yes, a sister, that was it. They'd just spent the morning talking with each other exactly the way she and Gideon used to. Sharing thoughts openly. Trusting the other with cherished beliefs and the pains of their past.

She delved into the top drawer and pulled out a handkerchief. She blew her nose as quietly as she could, glancing at Tom in case he'd noticed her distress.

But he was lying back on the pillows, his face ashen, his breakfast tray tilting at a dangerous angle.

She got up quickly and saved it before it went crashing to the floor. Didn't pause to look back, but went with it to the door.

'I will leave you to sleep,' she said, keeping her face, and in particular the evidence of her tears, averted. 'You look exhausted.'

She would be a fool to sit about all day, waiting for this connoisseur of women to look at her *that* way. It wasn't going to happen. Men didn't find her attractive. Oh, plenty of them had shown an interest in marrying her, once they knew who she was, who she was related to and how much wealth she had at her back. But as a woman? No. She had less appeal, apparently, than a fifty-year-old Belgian landlady.

It was all very well Tom saying he was willing to stay sick for as long as she needed him. But he didn't mean it. As soon as he was strong enough to walk, he would reclaim his freedom. He'd told her he wasn't the marrying kind. Which meant, really, that he didn't want to be tied to one woman.

Particularly not a foolish, fey, plain one like her.

'I need to wash and change, and, well, heavens, but I have been neglecting Castor. Talking about how I used to spend all day riding about with Gideon has made me quite...' She bit down on her lower lip. It was one thing making excuses, another to embroider them to the point where they became outright lies.

'Of course,' he said with a tight smile. 'You should go out and get some fresh air. It will do you good. And in truth, I do want to sleep. There really is no point in you sitting here all day, is there?'

'None whatever,' she said with a toss of her head.

* * *

It was a relief to reach the stables, with its familiar smells and sounds.

'It's not as if I *want* him to flirt with me,' she informed Castor, giving his velvety nose a rub. 'Why would I? I detest rakes.' Though she didn't detest Tom.

'It's just as well I did want to come out for a ride, isn't it? Because the last thing I would ever do is sit about all day waiting for some man to admire me. Or pretend to, because that is what rakes generally do. Ooh,' she breathed, leaning into the reassuringly solid column of Castor's neck, 'I thought he looked full of himself, the first time I saw him. He may not have a title, apart from his army rank, but he's certainly become lord of that room. He's one of those men who are born bossy, just like my brothers. Both Justin and Major Flint expect everyone else to do what they say. In fact, they don't even always need to say anything. Just the way they walk shows they think they are lords of all they survey. Not that Tom can actually walk at the moment, but if he did, he'd be strutting about the place, turning heads. Female heads, that is.'

Castor blew heavily through his nostrils, as if in complete agreement.

'And the worst of it is, I don't really understand why I mind. I knew he was a habitual womaniser when I scooped him up out of the mud. It's more than likely that he'll have a go at getting Jeanne to kiss him while I'm out.'

Her stomach clenched into a cold knot. She half-wanted to run back upstairs, to prevent any such thing from happening.

Instead, she firmed her mouth and led Castor to the mounting block. 'If I find he's done any such thing,' she muttered between clenched teeth as they set off, 'I shall tip his next bowl of broth over his head.'

She hadn't gone more than a few yards before revising this punishment. But only because she remembered she was the one who'd have to change Tom's bandages if she did douse them in broth.

By the time she reached the end of the Allée Verte, she'd devised and discarded a dozen plans for punishing Tom. None of which would make her feel the slightest bit better. No, the only thing that would make her feel better would be making certain, somehow, that he wasn't kissing anyone else.

Even if it meant keeping him occupied with her own lips. It went against her principles, but it was the only course she could see that would satisfy her pride. Not that she'd ever kissed a man before, but how hard could it be? Anyway, Tom's vast experience would more than compensate for her own ignorance.

If she could get him to see her as kissable, that was.

Her determination to appear amenable to kisses took a nosedive the moment she set foot in his room, for in her absence he'd washed and shaved, and put on a shirt. In her imagination, during the ride home, it had been the piratically whiskered, half-naked Tom she'd approached and snuggled up to, and offered her mouth to.

This Tom, this clothed, clean, *proper* man, didn't look like her Tom at all. He made her feel shy and nervous, and aware of how improper her plan had been. Without the four days' growth of beard, he also looked very pale, which smote her conscience. He was her patient, for heaven's sake. He'd been grievously wounded. The last thing he needed was for some inquisitive spinster to fling herself on his chest and make demands he'd shown no sign of wanting to fulfil.

'What's the matter?' he said, with a quick frown. 'Has something happened?'

Nothing she could confess. Only stupid things that had gone on inside her own head, which she hung in shame.

And caught sight of the hat she was clutching in nervous fingers.

'I don't like this hat,' she said inanely, 'anywhere near as much as the one I lost that day I went searching the battlefield.' It was either that, or blurt out her confused, contradictory reactions to seeing him properly clothed, instead of all naked and tempting. 'I suppose it doesn't matter. The riding habit it matched had to be burned, anyway.'

'Never mind your hat. Or your gown. I know that isn't what is upsetting you.'

'No. You are right.' She went to the window and stood looking out for a moment or two, gathering the strength to turn round and face him again. The new Tom. Or was it the true Tom? She blinked away her confusion. Whichever it was, it was no longer *her* Tom, that was what was upsetting her.

'It is the terrible waste of it all,' she said, instead. 'So many men, young men at that, with nobody to care what becomes of them, from the looks of it. Oh, the citizens are doing what they can. Taking them food and drink. And some of the hotels are putting straw down for them to make them more comfortable. But I just…' She wound the stings of her hat round and round her fingers. 'I wish I could *do* something.'

'You are doing something. You are nursing me. You saved *me*, Lady Sarah.'

'Yes. Thank goodness your men brought you here. I've heard some officers, ones who went back to their own billets, died while waiting to get medical attention. So I know I saved you. But you are just one. And there are so many more of them out there.' She waved her hand towards the window. Her hat caught at the potted geranium, spraying the sill with blood-red petals. 'And I feel so helpless. I dare say,' she muttered darkly, 'Mary has turned her school into a regular hospital by now.'

'Mary?'

'Mary Endacott. The woman…' She'd been about to say, the woman who was going to marry Justin. But who knew how that was going to end?

'The woman who helped me make my way to the battlefield, to search for my brother. The one who is nursing him, now. She's so capable, so organised. I'm sure *she* won't be stretched to her limits nursing just one man.'

'Lady Sarah, don't disparage yourself this way. What you have done for me is nothing short of miraculous. I never thought—'

'No. And nor would anyone else think me able to cope with anything so real as stitching up wounds or nursing a sick man through a fever. A social butterfly, that's all I am.'

'No, Lady Sarah. You are so much more than that.'

'What?' She flung her poor abused riding hat across the room in vexation. 'What more to me is there than fashionable clothes and insipid conversation?'

'Loyalty,' he replied without a second's hesitation. 'To your brother. Not many society women would stir themselves out of their safe drawing rooms to go hunting for an injured brother. Nor take pity on anyone else, if she didn't find who she was looking for. Nor put themselves through such an ordeal. Most society women would have turned me over to the care of servants, rather than contaminate their fair little hands with my blood, my sweat.'

'No, I'm sure that's not true.'

'Oh, but it is. This Mary person may be more used to dealing with practical matters, if she's a schoolmistress. But don't compare your greatness of heart to her ability to cope with things as a matter of course.'

Heavens, no wonder she wanted her first kiss to come from his lips. He might not mean the half of what he said, kissing her might mean nothing to him, but oh, how she wanted to believe he admired her. He kept on making her feel as if there was something about her, apart from her title and wealth. As if he'd seen something in her that nobody else ever had.

She smiled at him sadly.

'You are so sweet, Tom, to say things like that. But—'

'I'm only saying it because I believe it. Lady Sarah, you may have led a sheltered life up till now, but these few days have shown what you really are, deep inside. And what you are is brave and compassionate, and kind. You haven't run from your fears, or hidden behind propriety. You just rolled your sleeves up and did what had to be done.'

Perhaps that was what she should do now. Roll up her sleeves, take his face between her hands and show him what she needed.

Her heart banging against her ribs, she went to the bed and sat down. Reached out her hand.

But what if he didn't really mean all those things he said? What if he didn't find her attractive?

Instead of leaning forward and kissing him, she just took the hand he held out to her and pressed it to her cheek.

'Oh, Tom.' No wonder he was so successful with women. He knew exactly what to say to make them feel good about themselves. To make their hearts melt with tenderness towards him. To want to press kisses all over his dear, battered face.

This was what made rakes so dangerous. This was exactly why she avoided them.

Fortunately, Madame le Brun came in just then, with another tray of soup and freshly baked bread, before she could summon up the courage to really make a fool of herself.

And after they'd eaten, she took care to keep the atmosphere light.

But as night drew on and the time for going to bed loomed ever closer, Sarah became more and more aware that tonight it was all going to be very different. The impropriety of sharing a room with Tom when he'd been crazed with fever hadn't bothered her very much at all. Besides, she'd remained fully dressed, since there hadn't been the time, or the opportunity, to change into her nightwear.

But tonight he was in his right mind. And even though she'd had Gaston install a screen between his bed and the pallet she was going to use, it still felt positively scandalous to come into his room in her nightgown, rather than her day clothes. Especially when she'd been thinking about kissing him, on and off, all afternoon.

Not that he'd shown any inclination to attempt anything improper, she sighed, flicking her braided hair over her shoulder. For all his talk about her being loyal and brave, and compassionate, he hadn't said anything about her being desirable.

Not that she wanted him to, she huffed as she lay down on the pallet and pulled the blankets up to her chin. Not now her fit of jealousy, or whatever it was, when she'd thought about him kissing someone else, had worn off. She *didn't* want *that* kind of attention from such a notorious rake. It would be terribly wearing, having to fend him off all the time.

And she would fend him off. Of course she would.

She turned on her side and thumped the pillow into shape. She mustn't forget that if he did attempt to seduce her, it would only be because it was his nature to try to bed the nearest available woman. She had too much pride to join the long line of women who'd fallen prostrate at his feet.

Even if he asked her to.

Which he hadn't. Wouldn't.

She turned over again, vainly trying to find a comfortable position. Which was impossible when she was so very aware of him lying there, not four feet away, clad only in a nightshirt, so far as she could tell.

But her eyelids soon grew too heavy to hold open. She hadn't slept in more than brief snatches for days. Had worked harder, and been through more than she ever had in her whole life.

And, according to Tom, had learned what she was really made of. She'd always known she didn't have what it took to be a brilliant social hostess like Gussie, she might not have any interest in all the worthy causes that so fired up her other sister Harriet, she might not be practical and clever like Mary, but for the first time in her life, none of that seemed to matter.

Loyal and brave, he'd said. *Compassionate and kind.* Those things were all much better than being clever, or accomplished, weren't they? At least, the way he'd said it sounded as though he thought so.

Which made her almost believe it, too.

How he wished he hadn't said he didn't need anything for the pain. It was all very well hating the way it clouded his mind. And he certainly didn't want to end up craving it, the way he'd seen so many men fall victim to laudanum once it got its hooks into them.

But nor did he relish lying here, wide-awake, feeling like one enormous bruise. Everything ached. Everything.

He slid one hand under the sheet, seeking to ease the place he ached most of all. The one ache he could do something about, for himself.

He must be on the mend, if *that* could be giving him so much trouble.

It had started to sit up and take notice the moment Lady Sarah had left the room to go and prepare for bed. There was a little room, a room that had been her maid's when she'd stayed here before, she'd told him, which she was now using as a dressing room. Which was right next door. Her washstand must be on the other side of the wall from the head of his bed, because he'd distinctly heard the sound of water being poured into a basin. And splashing. His imagination had supplied the rest. He'd imagined buttons unpopping. Clothing slithering to the floor. Porcelain-white skin, all wet and soapy. Water running down her body just where he wanted to run his hands. Then, of course, she'd rub herself dry with a towel. Her face first, and then her arms, her legs, her breasts…

His breath quickened. He whipped his hand away, clenching it into a fist. What was he doing? He couldn't sully her with his lustful imaginings, when she was lying there, unaware. It felt so wrong.

He stifled a groan as the ropes of her pallet creaked. She was turning over. Trying in vain to get comfortable, because he'd taken possession of her bed. And now she was throwing the blankets off. Because she was too hot. Well, it was a hot and sultry night.

He was certainly sweating. Was she?

His mouth watered at the thought of swiping his tongue over her neck, down, over her breasts, tasting the salt of her. The woman taste of her. He wanted to lick her all over, until she moaned with pleasure.

Right on cue, she did moan. Shifted on her bed, just as though she was responding to his unclean thoughts.

He pressed the heels of his hands over his ears. Reached over his head for his pillow. Pulled it over his face.

But it couldn't block out the sound of Sarah's sudden, strangled scream.

Tom flung the pillow aside. Of course she wasn't lying there dreaming of an earthy encounter with him. He sat up as she moaned again. No—by the sound of it, she was having a nightmare.

A pretty nasty one, if he was any judge. She was whimpering now. And from the way the screen suddenly rattled, she'd flung out her hand to ward off…something.

He got out of bed, planted his feet on the floor and waited a second or two for the room to stop spinning. Then tottered the few feet to the end of the screen, rounded it and stood looking down at her. His breath caught. God, but she was lovely, lying in the abandoned sprawl of sleep. She'd kicked off all her blankets, and rucked her nightgown up to her knees. A gentleman wouldn't let his eyes linger, but he couldn't help savouring the sight of her beautiful, shapely legs.

'Lady Sarah,' he murmured gently, dropping to his knees at her side. 'Wake up.'

She whimpered again. In the feeble light that made it to this darkened corner of the room from his bedside candle, he could see silvery trails of tears streaking her cheeks, which brought him to his senses. No longer did he want to run his hands over those invitingly bared legs. He wanted to scoop her up into his arms and comfort her.

'Lady Sarah,' he said again, a little louder. 'You are having a nightmare.'

He reached down and shook her shoulder gently. Her eyes flew open wide.

'Tom!' Before he had a chance to explain that he had a perfectly innocent explanation for kneeling over her as she slept, she'd flung her arms round his neck and buried her face against him.

'Oh, Tom, it was horrible. Horrible!'

'It's over now. It was just a nightmare.' He put his arms round her. Inhaled the fragrance of sleepy woman. The scent that was normally a prelude to becoming intimate.

He gritted his teeth. That wasn't what Sarah needed from him tonight. She wasn't an experienced woman looking for a good time, but a vulnerable young lady who'd only stumbled into his life by accident. And what she needed after a nightmare was to feel safe, secure.

Actually, tonight she probably would be perfectly safe from him, even if his conscience wasn't shouting at him like a regimental sergeant-major. He simply wasn't fit enough to do her any real mischief.

'No.' She shuddered. 'It wasn't just a nightmare. It was Gideon…and…'

She went still. Her eyes narrowed.

'What are you doing out of bed?'

'You were crying out. So...'

'I woke you? Oh, Tom, I'm so sorry.'

'Lord, Sarah, you've lost enough sleep sitting up with me through my nightmares this past couple of days.'

'That's not the same. You were wounded.'

'And you weren't?'

'I meant physically.'

'Yes, but you've been through a terrible ordeal.'

'I wasn't hacked at by French cavalry, then buried for hours under a pile of rubble,' she replied tartly. 'Come on, Tom, let's get you back to bed.'

He leaned back on his heels. 'You don't think I can make it there on my own?'

'Well, I don't know, do I? This is the first time you've been out of bed. And I don't want all my hard work undone by having you go off into a swoon, or something. Then we'd have to wake up Gaston to carry you back, because I certainly don't have the strength.'

He could hear the concern in her voice though she was covering it up by saying she was only being practical.

She'd just suffered a horrific nightmare, yet she was trying to put his needs first.

Although—he glanced at her as she got her shoulder under his and helped him to his feet—perhaps doing something for him was helping her to push the nightmare aside. After all, that's what she'd been doing with him for the past few days. Nursing him had been salving her own hurt at not being able to do anything for either of her brothers.

So he let her lead him back to bed, where he meekly lay down while she tucked a sheet round his chest. The exertion of walking to her bed and back had dealt a death-blow to his arousal, thank goodness, or he wouldn't have been able to look her in the face.

'There. Comfortable?'

Not entirely.

He nodded.

'Good. Well, I should go back to bed, now.' She glanced over at the screen and gave an almost imperceptible shudder.

'Don't want to shut your eyes again, just yet?' He reached for her hand, and she took it. Clung to it. Shook her head. Then sat down in the chair beside his bed, her back ramrod straight, her eyes huge in her chalk-white face.

'And the last thing you want is to talk about it, I dare say,' he said sympathetically. 'I don't think I could talk about the ones I've had, the last few nights. They were so hellish. Bits of things that had really happened, all mixed up with horrors I didn't know I was capable of imagining.'

'Yes—' she gasped '—it was just like that. The bodies.' She gripped his hand so tightly that it was only then he became aware that formerly it had been just about the only part of him that hadn't hurt. 'Bodies everywhere. All hacked to bits. Or lying in the street, begging me for water when I didn't have any to give them. B-but they all of them had Gideon's face.' Her voice sank to a hoarse whisper, her mouth quivering with repressed pain and tears.

Propriety be damned. She needed more than just a hand to hold. Uttering an oath, he tugged her down on to his chest and wrapped his arms round her. Rocked her.

'It wasn't him,' he grated. 'He didn't go through any of that.'

'How do you know? How can you know what he went through?'

'Well, I don't, that's true. But…' He shifted uncomfortably. He'd thought he'd never speak of the things that had leapt up and leered at him through his fevered dreams. But Sarah needed to hear that what she was experiencing happened to other people, too.

'One of the nightmares I had, over and over again, was about a woman. A pregnant woman we discovered after we'd driven the French out of a Portuguese village. It was about the worst thing I'd ever seen. But she's been dead for years now. So why did she leap out at me again last night? Right in the middle of all the things I was reliving from the battle that had just happened? It is as if the worst things, the things you won't allow yourself to think about while you're awake, jump out to taunt you when you're powerless to stop them.'

'Yes,' she breathed. 'I *had* been thinking about Gideon. That he might have lain there, alone and broken, like all the others I saw. And then, when I went to sleep, what I'd really seen got all jumbled up with the things I'd been fearing.'

She was shaking. Trembling all over, as though gripped by a fever.

His heart went out to her. He'd already established that she wasn't in any real danger from him tonight. Even if his conscience couldn't keep his lustful nature in check, in his weakened state, she'd have no trouble tipping him out of bed if he forgot himself. Besides, he wanted to comfort her, not seduce her. To repay her for all she'd done for him. Couldn't he, just once, give a woman something apart from an orgasm?

'Stay here with me for the rest of the night,' he breathed into her ear. 'Let me keep your nightmares at bay, the way you kept mine from me.'

'Did I? I didn't think so. They didn't seem to stop.'

'They didn't entirely. But somehow, the scent of you reached me even during the worst of them. The scent of violets will always remind me of you. Of the feeling of security that came from lying in your arms.' He breathed in deeply. 'For I knew the hellish landscape couldn't be real, because surely violets couldn't bloom in such a place. Even when I couldn't recall how I'd got there…' He shook his head.

'Oh, dear. The surgeon said you might never fully recover your memory.'

'I know I'd been in the thick of fighting all day. My ears were ringing. But to be honest, I can still only recall bits and pieces. The noise and the smoke. I know there was thunder, the night before we fought the battle in which I was injured. In my dreams, that thunderstorm got all jumbled up with the thunder of the guns. And the smell of the smoke became the flames from the pits of hell.'

'I'm not surprised you got dreams like that. We could hear the guns as far as Antwerp, on Friday. It did sound like a distant thunderstorm. I can't imagine what it must have been like to have actually been there.'

'You shouldn't have to,' he said fervently. A shiver went through him as her hand slid across his chest and came to rest, trustingly, over his heart.

'What else did you dream about?'

'I dreamed I was dead,' he said bleakly. 'And buried

in my grave. Of course, I was only pinned down by all the stones from the wall that fell on me. But in my half-conscious, confused state, the men roaming the field by night looking for plunder became demons, collecting the souls of the damned. I wasn't totally convinced I wasn't dead until morning, when birds started singing. I knew birds wouldn't sing in hell. But even they got muddled up in my nightmares. The singing birds, and the wraith-like looters, merged into great black crows. There are always crows after battles, pecking at the bodies. I felt as though every cut of mine, every bruise, was evidence that they'd been there, feasting on my flesh.'

'Oh, Tom!' She flung her arms round his waist, hugging him tight. 'All those odd things you said make perfect sense now. It must have been dreadful.'

'I'm sorry, I'm sorry. I'm such an idiot.' Heaven help him, he'd just planted a whole new set of images in her head. 'I shouldn't have spoken about all that. It can't have helped.'

'It did, actually,' she retorted, 'because you're a man. And a soldier. If even someone like you can have dreams like that, then it makes me feel that I'm not such a poor sort of creature, after all.'

'Everyone has nightmares after a battle,' he said grimly. 'Nobody knows how to stop them. And nobody speaks of them.' He gave a puzzled frown. 'Not usually, anyway.'

Without warning she pulled out of his arms, got up and disappeared behind the screen.

He sighed. Just when he thought he'd been making progress he went and said something that sent her running for cover. As though she didn't she trust him.

He snorted in derision. Of course she didn't trust him.

Which was just as well. Every chivalrous impulse he felt towards her was almost immediately countered by an appallingly lustful one.

To his amazement she reappeared with one of the blankets from her bed draped over one arm.

'Just for tonight,' she said, climbing on to his bed beside him, on top of the sheet that covered him, 'we'll hold each other. I will keep your nightmares away from you,' she said, snapping the blanket open and arranging it over her legs. 'And you will keep mine away from me.'

She snuggled down next to him, tucked her head in the crook of his arm and draped her own arm over his waist. 'What do you say to that?' She twisted her head to look up at him.

It sounded like heaven.

It sounded like hell. It had been bad enough when she'd been across the room, with a screen and four foot of empty space between them. Now she was in his arms, close enough to kiss if she moved her face just a fraction further.

'I say yes.' He groaned and moved his own face just the necessary fraction.

His lips brushed hers lightly. Surely, just once wouldn't be such a terrible crime, would it? A kiss goodnight.

She gasped, and for a moment he thought she really was going to tip him out of bed. But then, miraculously, she pressed her own lips against his. Clasped him more tightly and wriggled closer.

'Don't do that,' he gasped.

'Am I hurting you?'

'No. Yes. It's agony,' he growled, burying his face in her neck. He hadn't been so aroused since his first fumbling encounter with a willing chambermaid. But

this was no chambermaid. This was Sarah. An innocent. An angel.

He couldn't sully her. Not in his imagination and not
in reality, either. He might have crossed many lines during the course of his career, but debauching respectable
females hadn't been one of them.

'Go to sleep,' he bit out. 'Lie still and go to sleep.'

'But what about you?'

Yes, what about him? His aim had been to get a kiss
from her, nothing more. But now he had kissed her, it
wasn't enough. And if she didn't lie still and stop wriggling in that inviting way, he might forget what he owed
her and attempt to go further.

'I will lie here and hold you. It is my turn. Whenever
the bad things try to come back, you will feel my arms
round you and know it's not real.'

'But...'

'Hush. I will keep you safe. I won't...' He shifted
slightly, so that she wouldn't be able to feel his newly
awakened arousal pressing into her hip. 'I would never
harm you, Sarah. I couldn't.' His whole being revolted at
the thought of any harm coming to her, from *any* source.
'I'd rather die.'

She went very still. And very quiet. For a moment he
wondered if she knew the effect she'd had on him and
was trying to decide whether it was more dangerous to
stay in the bed with a randy soldier, or go back to her
own bed and risk the nightmares returning.

Eventually, she gave a little sigh and snuggled back
down. It seemed, for whatever reason, she'd decided to
stay right where she was.

She trusted him.

His eyes stung. When was the last time anyone had

trusted him? With so much as sixpence, let alone their very virtue?

Never. Nobody had ever had such faith in him. They'd all expected him to break his word. To behave badly. To let them down and cause mayhem.

His grip on her tightened as he swore to himself that he'd never do any of those things. He'd never break his word to her. Never let her down or cause her a moment's grief.

No matter what it cost him.

Chapter Nine

Lady Sarah woke with a smile on her face. Tom had been right. Whenever the dreams had threatened to turn troubling, she'd somehow sensed his arms round her. Known she wasn't alone, the way she'd been when she'd really gone to the battlefield. And though there were times when her dreams grew distressing, they never descended to the depths of horror she'd suffered before.

But even better had been his physical reaction. He'd stood to attention for her. She snuggled into his side, basking in the knowledge that he *could* feel desire for her, after all. She'd never been pretty, but these last few days, without a maid to help her, she hadn't even looked presentable. Her choice of outfits was limited to those few gowns sent to her by Odette, from that last order before they'd fled for Antwerp. Her hair was a complete mess. And her complexion must be blotchy, too, since she'd been crying on and off practically the whole time. She always looked particularly unappealing when she wept, which was one of the reasons she didn't do it often. Her nose, always her worst feature, glowed deep crimson, making it even more obvious and unattractive than ever.

And her eyes, which actually were the one feature that wasn't half-bad, got bloodshot, her eyelashes all clumpy, effectively destroying their appeal.

And yet he'd been aroused. Better than that, she hadn't had to risk her pride by trying to get him to kiss her. He'd done it without the slightest provocation. Well, not deliberate provocation, anyway. She hadn't been thinking about getting him to kiss her when she'd climbed into bed with him. Not at all.

She sighed happily. He'd promised she need not fear, that he would rather die than harm her. By which, she knew, he meant he wouldn't act on the desire that his masculine body had made all too obvious.

Which, now she came to think of it, was a very unrakish thing to do. Rakes didn't care about anyone but themselves. She should know. Her father really had been a rake. Whenever he'd wanted a woman he'd just taken her—whether she was willing or not.

How could people accuse Tom of being a rake? Tom was…Tom was…just a man, an unmarried man, who enjoyed life to the full. It wasn't as if he was doing anything so very different from what her brothers and other officers did. Only, by the sound of it, more regularly and with a greater variety of women than them.

'You are awake, aren't you?'

She wriggled round at the sound of his low, gruff voice, to look up into Tom's face, and couldn't help sighing. Overnight his beard had started growing in, which made him look much more like her very own Tom again. The rather desperate, powder-blackened warrior who'd fallen into her lap on the battlefield. Though that wasn't what made her sigh. Not entirely, anyway. It was the look in his sea-green eyes. *Such* a look. Even a sensible, practical woman would want to drown in it.

And she'd never been, either.

She sighed again. 'Thank you for last night.'

'Hmmph.' He shifted as though he was in pain. 'Lady Sarah, I am glad I could be of service, but right now…'

'Yes? What is it?' She sat up, searching his face intently. He looked as though he was in great discomfort. 'Are you in pain?'

He grimaced. 'I need…I need…' He closed his eyes, clenching his fists on top of the sheet that covered him. 'Could you send for Gaston, do you think? And then give me a few moments' privacy?'

He probably needed to use the chamber pot.

She blushed and got out of bed. 'Of course.' She went to the bell pull by the fireplace and tugged on it sharply. 'Now that you are a little better, you probably want to try to get out of bed for a short while today, too.'

'And shave,' he growled, rubbing his hand over his chin. 'It is amazing how much better I felt yesterday after Gaston gave me a wash and shave.'

It was the proper thing to do—have a manservant see to his most intimate needs. The sensible thing. Yet hearing him start to think of propriety and sense saddened her. She'd much rather he wanted to do something improper, and reckless, like a bit more kissing and cuddling.

Oh, well, there was no point in refining on what wasn't to be. She might as well go to the little dressing room next door to wash and dress herself, while Gaston saw to Tom.

The moment she'd poured out her water, though, she started to get cross with herself. Why had she just meekly walked away, when it hadn't been what she wanted? Why had she allowed him to dismiss her so easily?

Her irritation made her movements jerky and brisk, so that she was ready to ring for Jeanne to do up her day gown in no time at all. Funnily enough, it never did take her very long to prepare for the day now she no longer had a personal maid in constant attendance. Since returning to Brussels she'd dispensed with all the other nonsense, such as trying to get her hair to curl and then arranging it in a fashionable style. She simply combed it, braided it, coiled it up and pinned it out of the way. And since she only had the choice of two or three outfits, she didn't have to agonise for ages about which would be the most appropriate for the events she was scheduled to attend, either.

She tapped on Tom's door. *Tom's door.* She pulled herself up short. When had it become his room? And how had he managed to make her feel like a visitor?

She felt even more like a visitor when she saw that he'd rearranged the furniture. Or had Gaston do it, anyway.

'I can see out of the window from here, without having to get out of bed,' he said hastily, when her reaction must have flitted across her face.

'Of course. It must be very boring for you having nothing to look at all day.' Yet another sign he was recovering. He needed something to do. Something to look at. Other than her.

'It looks like a glorious day,' he said. 'You should make the most of it. Go out and get some air.'

She didn't wince. Nobody, looking at her face, would guess how much his attitude hurt. But then she'd had years of enduring brutal attacks from her father, more subtle campaigns waged by her mother, followed by the cut and thrust of society gossip. Letting anyone know what she was thinking would have been fatal, on so many occasions.

'Well, if you really don't need me,' she said brightly, 'I would love to go for a ride.' He wanted her to leave him in peace, did he? Very well, then. At least Castor would be genuinely pleased to see her. No blowing hot and cold with him.

No wonder she preferred horses to people. They didn't play games. Say one thing one minute, making you think...

Not that horses could talk. But if they did, they would be honest and open, and straightforward.

'Aside from my brief ride out yesterday I have been woefully neglecting Castor. And after he looked after me so splendidly, too.'

'Did he?' Tom didn't sound interested. He was gazing out of the window with a rather wild air, as though planning his escape. From the clutches of a respectable female, no doubt. Now that he'd started to respond to her, as a man, he clearly felt it was time to put some distance between them. Why, he'd told her he didn't want to get married. He'd couched it in terms of not having anything to offer a woman. But she knew what he'd really meant was that he didn't want to get tied to just one. She knew how men's minds worked. Unless they had a title and needed an heir, or a bride with a dowry to solve their financial problems, not one of them really wanted to get leg-shackled.

She'd seen it in her father's behaviour. She'd observed it in Justin's. But most important, she'd heard it from Gideon's own lips.

That kiss, and then spending the night in each other's arms had probably scared the life out of him. He probably thought she was going to get silly, romantic ideas now. Which was why he was acting all starchy and unapproachable.

In another day or so, he would be up and about, and, to judge from the way he was acting this morning, that would be the end of their strange friendship.

All of a sudden, some imp of mischief, some spirit of rebellion that had been fermenting over the past few days, came to a head.

She marched over to the bed, seized him round the back of the neck with one hand and planted a kiss full on his mouth.

He made a strange gasping, gurgling sound. The green part of his eyes got almost entirely swallowed by the rapid expansion of his pupils. He reached up to put his arms about her, too.

'No. That's quite enough of that for now, Tom,' she said, darting away. It would have been different if he'd started it, if he'd shown any inclination to take things further. She might have…well, actually she didn't know how she would have responded to a flirtatious, eager Tom this morning. She only knew that she wasn't going to let him think he could dictate how she should behave any longer.

Nor give him the idea that she was so desperate she was flinging herself at him. That wasn't what the kiss was about at all.

'I don't want to get you over-excited. Not in your delicate condition.'

'In my *delicate* condition?' He glared at her ferociously, as though to prove there was nothing the least bit delicate about him. Her last sight of him that morning was of him staring at her, with an expression on his face she was going to cherish for ever. As though he wished he had the strength to get up and chase after her. Although she wasn't totally sure what he would do to her, if he could catch her. Put her over his knee and spank her, as likely as kiss her, probably.

Either of which would, at least, be preferable to his indifference.

Although the day was fine and Castor had been keen to get out and gallop away the fidgets, there was too much evidence of the battle wherever she looked to be able to fully enjoy her ride.

By the time she returned, her pleasure in provoking Tom into a reaction had completely dissipated. And it wasn't just the sight of soldiers lying wounded all over the road, the broken gun carriages, splintered wagons, or the smoke rising from mounds of carcasses that had been made into great bonfires, that had done it.

It was the guilt. Guilt caused by realising that whenever she was with Tom, actually in his presence, Gideon always got pushed to the back of her mind.

So it was with a heavy heart that she finally stepped through the back door of the lodgings, later that morning.

'Ah, *ma petite*,' said Madame le Brun, bustling up towards her, wiping her hands on her apron. 'It is such sad news, is it not? To hear that your gallant officer, your beau, he has fallen in battle.'

'My...my beau?'

She hadn't had a beau.

'Who do you mean?'

'Why, that cavalry officer with all the moustaches. The colonel.'

'Oh. Colonel Bennington Ffog,' she responded dully. She'd experienced a jolt, it was true, when she'd read his name on the lists of the dead, but it was hardly more than she'd felt for any of the other names she recognised of men she'd talked to, and danced with, in the preceding weeks. Even though he had been her most frequent escort. After Gideon.

'Never mind,' said the landlady, placing her hand on the sleeve of Sarah's riding habit. 'The major, he is much more the man for you than that other one.'

Sarah felt her face flood with heat. 'The...the major? You mean you know that Tom isn't...isn't my...'

'Your brother?' The landlady gave her a knowing look. 'But no. No man looks at his sister the way that man looks at you. And I recall both your brothers. They have your nose. That one—' she jerked her thumb upwards '—he is much more handsome. And then it made me to wonder at the way you said you did not want visitors, when last time you were here, there was a constant stream of callers, and you and your sister and her husband the marquis, you were all so caught up in the going to parties and balls. It all became clear,' she said in a conspiratorial tone, 'when the other English officer came, the one with also your nose, the one with a voice loud enough to be heard over a salvo of cannon fire.'

Sarah's stomach hollowed out. She thought she'd been so discreet. She thought nobody would guess she was living in one room with a man to whom she was not married. And yet now this landlady knew. And Major Flint knew.

And how many others?

'You haven't told anyone, have you? That Major Bartlett and I... That the Major isn't...'

Madame le Brun pulled a face. 'As long as you pay your rent, what do I care what you get up to behind the closed doors?'

Was that a subtle threat? Was the woman going to increase her rent, in return for her silence?

'Besides—' she gave a wry smile '—to begin with, I wondered if perhaps he was French.'

'French?'

'Those men who carried him in, they wore the blue jackets. And they drove a French wagon. And so to begin with I did not tell anyone there was a wounded officer here at all.'

'I... Well...' Sarah recalled how the woman had fussed over her the night she'd turned up, on horseback, with only what she could cram into her saddlebags. How willing she'd been to hide her in the stables in case the French overran the city. How she'd even put up with Ben lolloping up and down the stairs, a law unto himself, once she'd seen how much comfort he brought Sarah during the long hours of watching over Tom.

And felt ashamed that for one terrible moment, she'd suspected Madame le Brun of attempted bribery.

'Thank you, Madame.'

'It is nothing,' she said with a careless shrug. 'But you—' she reached up and patted her cheek in a motherly fashion '—do not mourn too long for the other one. He was not a worthy suitor for one with such spirit as you.' She pulled a face. 'I have heard about the behaviour of your British cavalry during the battle. How all their brains belong to their horse. How they charge recklessly here and there.' She waved her arms wide. 'They do no damage to the enemy, they get themselves into bad positions and practically hand themselves and their poor horses to the other side for the butchery.'

'What?' Sarah's mind reeled. She had come to Brussels to learn the truth. But did she really want to hear exactly how Gideon had died? If it had been in that manner?

Oh, why hadn't she just stayed in Antwerp, in blissful ignorance? If only she'd never seen a battlefield, she could still picture Gideon falling down neatly, swiftly, feeling no pain and suffering for only a moment.

As it was...

'Excuse me, I must return to the Major. See how he is.' With a fixed, rather strained smile, she turned and strode along the corridor, and up the stairs.

It felt as though a cold hand was squeezing at her insides. Major Flint had said Gideon had been cut with sabres. Cavalry sabres, like the ones that had knocked Tom unconscious, while nearly slicing off the top of his head.

She most certainly didn't want to learn that her reckless, charming, rather wild twin had thrown his life away in some stupid, pointless charge such as Madame le Brun had described. And got himself butchered.

She came to a dead halt the moment she entered Tom's room and just stared at him, her arms wrapped round her middle.

He'd been reading a newspaper, by the looks of it. Pages were scattered all over the bed.

'What is it? What has happened?' He stretched out his hand to her, causing a flurry of newsprint to drift to the floor.

Sarah ran to him. Flung herself into his arms and buried her face in his shoulder.

He rocked her, stroked her hair, but didn't say a word. Didn't tell her it was going to be all right and she shouldn't get herself into a state. He just waited, patiently, until she felt ready to form words.

'Gideon,' she said, sitting up and pushing her hair off

her face. 'He was in the cavalry. And Madame le Brun said…about the cavalry… There have been stories about how they all charged about in disorder and got themselves cut to pieces without doing any good. And I can't bear it. I can't bear to think of him throwing his life away in such a stupid fashion.'

'He didn't. I'm sure he didn't.'

She pulled herself out of his arms, his words jarring deep. 'Tom…don't. Don't mouth stupid platitudes at me. Not you of all people!'

'Me of all people? What do you mean by that?'

Yes, what did she mean? Why had it hurt so much to have her fears dismissed as though they were nothing? 'I thought…I thought…' He'd kept saying she was an angel. Looking at her as though he almost worshipped her. But now he'd spoken to her just the way everyone else did.

Had it been an act, after all? The practised charm of a rake? 'I've been such a fool,' she gasped. 'I actually thought you *respected* me. That you would be honest with me if nothing else. That you wouldn't treat me as though I'm completely bird-witted!'

He took her shoulders firmly and looked straight into her eyes.

'I do respect you, Sarah. You have no idea how much. And I don't think you're in the least bit bird-witted. I think you're perfect.' He traced the line of her jaw with one finger.

She pulled back, only preventing herself from slapping his hand by an immense effort of will. This was absolutely not the time for him to finally start with the flirtatious gestures.

'And I would never lie to you, do you hear me?'

But he just had.

'I think we both know that I'm very far from perfect,' she began bitterly.

'Why can you not see what I see? Why can you not believe in yourself?'

'Because…' She shook her head irritably. 'Oh, there are too many reasons to go into them now. But if you really do mean to be honest with me, then what do you mean about being sure he didn't throw his life away?'

'Just think about it, Lady Sarah. Your brother died at Quatre Bras. It wasn't anything to do with a cavalry charge, so far as I know. No—from things I heard, he was with Colonel Randall at the time.'

'He was with Justin?' She stared at him in confusion. 'Why is this the first I've heard of it? Why didn't you tell me before?'

He let go of her. Looked down at his hands as he clasped them over his stomach. 'I'm sorry. I should have thought of it. Knowing that you only came to Brussels at all to find *him*. Your twin.' He sighed. Looked up at her, his eyes bleak. 'The surgeon was right. In part, at least. I…I don't remember all that much about the battle. Just impressions, really, of the hours immediately before I was injured. And then nothing, until I started coming round and couldn't move because I'd been buried under all that masonry.' He grimaced as if in remembered pain. 'That episode stuck in the forefront of my mind, to be honest. It was only when you talked about hearing the cannon fire on Friday, it came back to me. *That* was Quatre Bras. That was where he died, wasn't it?'

'Yes. That's right. I…' Her stomach gave a funny lurch. 'I just panicked, didn't I, when Madame le Brun started talking about the way so many of the cavalry officers died in the battle on Sunday.' She'd overreacted to him saying he didn't think Gideon had thrown his life away, too. Tom hadn't been dismissing her fears, the way others would. No, he'd really meant it. He had grounds for saying what he had. Only, it had hurt so much to think he might not be taking her seriously, after the way he'd made her think…

She shook her head. She wasn't going to waste time wondering what Tom thought of her, let alone what she thought of him. It was irrelevant! She'd come to Brussels to find out what had happened to Gideon. She shouldn't have let Tom sidetrack her so completely.

Although, it wasn't all his fault. She rubbed at her brow. 'You know, part of me still can't grasp the fact that he's dead. I came to Brussels convinced he couldn't be dead. It was only when I rode over the battlefield where I found you, and saw all the…' She shuddered. 'Saw how frail men's bodies really are.'

'Sarah.' He reached for her, took her into his arms and drew her head to his chest.

And it felt so good that she just nestled there. Listening to the strong beat of his heart under her cheek. Feeling the strength of his arms, holding her. Keeping the rest of the world at bay.

Keeping the reality of her bereavement at bay.

That was what she'd been doing, she saw. While she was busy, nursing Tom, she didn't have time to dwell on the truth. She'd been pushing it away for as long as she could. By any means.

She'd just decided to pull out of Tom's embrace and do something, when a knock came at the door. Giving Sarah the perfect excuse to untangle herself, sit on the chair by his bedside and run a hand over her hair to smooth it, before shouting out permission to enter.

It was Madame le Brun, with a troubled expression on her face.

'I know you said you do not want the visitors. But this man, he says he has come from Colonel Randall, your brother. And so I thought...' She spread her hands wide in one of those Gallic expressions that said so much.

Sarah's heart seemed to flip over in her chest. On the one hand, she did want to learn how Justin was faring. But on the other, if he was sending messages to her, here, then it meant he'd discovered where she was. And probably who she was with, too.

Which meant the fat would be in the fire.

Well, she'd survived all sorts of things so far this week. Done things she'd never imagined she could do.

Including kissing a rake. Deliberately. To shock him.

She wasn't that timid, diffident girl who would do anything to avoid confrontation. To say whatever people wanted to hear, if it meant they would leave her be.

She squared her shoulders.

'You did quite right, Madame. Send him up.'

Though as soon as Madame had shut the door on her way out, Sarah reached for Tom's hand. Somehow, nothing seemed so bad when she could hold his hand.

Not that she needed him to protect her from her own brother.

On the contrary. If Justin really did know she was here with a man they'd nicknamed Tom Cat, it was more likely *she'd* need to protect *him*.

'I won't leave you, Tom,' she vowed. 'No matter what he says. What threats he uses. Not while you need me.'

She'd got that look on her face again. The look of a lioness guarding her cub. Which made him feel much better. When she'd come in looking so bereft, after he'd just seen Bennington Ffog's name on the casualty list, he'd experienced such a bitter wave of jealousy he could still taste it. Even when she'd confessed that her heartbreak was for her beloved twin, rather than the man who'd spent the last weeks of his life practically turning cartwheels in order to gain her favour, from what he'd observed, the jealousy had scarcely abated one whit.

There just wasn't room in Sarah's heart for any man, not while it was still filled with Gideon Blasted Latymor.

Except, she had flung herself into his arms for comfort, hadn't she? Appeared hurt when she thought he didn't respect her.

Ah, but then when he'd explained himself, she'd let him take her in his arms and settled in as if she felt she belonged there.

And now she was bristling at the prospect of receiving a messenger from Colonel Randall.

He'd been half-joking when he'd said he would gladly stay ill for ever if it meant keeping her beside him. But there was no denying that whenever she thought he needed her to defend him, she forgot all about her dead twin and took up the cudgels on his behalf. And it was such a sweet feeling, having somebody thinking he was worth defending. Nobody had ever tried to defend him from anything.

No wonder he wished, so badly, that he belonged to her. With her.

The door opened then, and a short, squat man with iron-grey hair came in.

'It's Robbins, isn't it?' Sarah got to her feet and held out her hand to him, in a particularly regal fashion. With a smile Tom would describe as queenly.

Tom just about managed to bite back an appreciative grin. She'd fought Major Flint openly. But it seemed she was going to subdue Robbins with a combination of charm and hauteur.

'I have a letter here from Miss Endacott,' said Robbins, darting Tom a brief look from his shrewd grey eyes.

'Thank you,' said Sarah as she took it from him with a dazzlingly sweet smile. As though she was blithely ignorant of any impropriety in her situation.

It didn't have the effect on Robbins she'd probably intended. On the contrary, his eyes grew flinty.

'And how is my brother? The Colonel?'

'Mortal bad, miss,' said Robbins harshly. 'When Major Flint told him how you and Major Bartlett here are fixed, he got very upset. Took two of us to keep him from coming straight round here with a horsewhip.'

'Well, I'm very sorry he was upset,' said Sarah with a toss of her head. 'But would he rather I'd left one of his officers lying on the battlefield at death's door?'

'Couldn't rightly say, miss, but what I do know is that the upset made the bullet move. Miss Endacott had to call for a surgeon to dig it out. Getting on nicely he was, until then. But now *he's* the one at death's door.'

Sarah gasped as he turned on his heel and marched out.

'I never meant to cause any harm,' she said, turning pale. 'I thought I was helping.'

She looked down at the note in her hand, and tore it open feverishly.

'Oh. Oh. Mary says… Oh, it is just as Robbins said. I thought he might have been exaggerating. Trying to scare me, but…' She sat down in the chair by his bed as though someone had cut the legs from under her.

'I didn't even wonder why he hadn't sent a letter. I just assumed he couldn't know— That Mary would be shielding him from anything that might upset him. But I should have…' She shook her head, staring wildly, and Tom thought probably sightlessly, round the room. 'Not Justin, too. I can't lose both of them.'

Tom reached for her and pulled her on to the bed, right on to his lap. It was a measure of her distress that she didn't make the slightest attempt to stop him. And it was a measure of his character that he was glad of the opportunity his colonel's relapse had given him. Not that he wanted her distressed. Just that in moments like this, she turned to him. Sought comfort in his arms.

And that might be because he was the only person here.

But what did he care?

About anything—when she was in his arms.

Chapter Ten

'What am I to do?' she said. 'What *can* I do? It's all my fault. All my fault.'

'Now you stop that right now.' He cursed Robbins soundly and colourfully under his breath. 'If Colonel Randall was really as dangerously ill as Robbins implied, surely Miss Endacott would have written to inform you before? She knows how much you care about your brothers. She was with you when you found him near the battlefield, wasn't she?'

The wild, desperate look faded from Sarah's eyes.

'You really think so?' She looked at Tom in confusion. 'But then why…?'

'Robbins is extremely loyal to the Colonel. Your brother inspires that in the men. Gutter rats, who've never had anyone to look up to. Anyone they can trust. Until he showed them that a man in authority isn't necessarily going to stamp on them, just because he can.

'I wouldn't be a bit surprised if Robbins is trying to ease the Colonel's worries by making you feel guilty enough to run back to him and stay where he can keep an eye on you.'

Her eyes filled with tears.

'No! Surely he wouldn't?'

'Oh, I think he would.'

'Oh!' She sat up a little straighter. 'What a mean, dirty, low sort of trick to play on me.'

'That's the way the Rogues work, Sarah. And, to be fair to Robbins, he probably thinks he's doing you a favour, too. Getting you away from me.'

Her mouth firmed into a tight line.

'I wish everyone would stop trying to organise my life the way they think is best for me, without even asking me what I want.'

She wriggled off his lap, got back on to the chair, and looked down at Mary's note again.

'Do you know, I think you may be in the right of it. Mary doesn't say anything about it being my fault. Not at all. Which I'm sure she would if she thought it. She doesn't like me very much. With just cause, I may add. I—' She bit on her lower lip, then took a deep breath, lifted her chin and looked him straight in the eye.

'I tricked her into going with me to the Duchess of Richmond's ball, you see. Gussie was too poorly to take me and I was desperate to find Gideon. Because he'd been—' She broke off. 'Well, I knew I couldn't attend without a chaperon. And I couldn't think who else to ask. I thought she was the one person I might be able to persuade, because she was bound to want to see Justin one last time before they all went off to fight, just the way I wanted to see Gideon.

'Only Gideon wasn't there, so it was a waste. No—' she sighed and shook her head '—it was worse than that. Justin ripped up at her. Accused her of stealing his lucky sword and insinuating herself into my good graces so she could get her hands on his title… Oh, all of it was so unjust. And it was all my fault. If I hadn't made her take me, none of it would have happened. They would still be together. They'd be getting married.'

'You can't know that.'

'Yes, I can. She told me,' she said gloomily. 'Besides, he danced every dance with her. And looked at her the way I've never seen him look at anyone else. Ever. And she looked at him the same. They were in love, Tom. And I ruined it.'

'No. If they really loved each other, nothing you or anyone else could have done would have ruined it.'

'Oh, stop making excuses for me, Tom. I am the most selfish woman alive. And sly, to boot. Yes, sly! To think I congratulate myself on never telling an outright lie. I just hint, you see, then let people think whatever they want, particularly if it enables me to do exactly what I want. Take the ball, for example. I made Gussie think I was going with a respectable matron, rather than another single lady. And let Mary think Gussie knew I was going with *her*, when I hadn't actually spoken her name at all.'

'Well, that isn't so bad, is it? I mean, it wasn't as if you were sneaking out to meet a lover, or really misbehave, was it?'

'No. But that's just it, you see. I'm always making excuses for sliding out of confrontation, rather than standing up for myself and telling them what I really want. I even sneaked away from Antwerp, rather than telling Blanchards I needed to come here. Well, he wouldn't have let me come, you see, so rather than alert him, and have him take steps to stop me I…' She shook her head, closing her eyes briefly. 'It was Sunday morning. Gussie wasn't feeling well enough for church. So I asked him if he was going to stay with her. And let him assume I meant to go with friends. And went and changed into my riding habit, telling my maid that I planned to go for a ride, and she could take the morning off, which got rid of her. Because, you see, none of the staff Blanchards hired had ever seen me being anything but ridiculously proper, never venturing anywhere without a maid, or a groom, or some other respectable escort. They wouldn't have dreamed I could do anything so unladylike as saddle my own horse, let alone ride off on it without summoning my groom. But I didn't,' she said, lifting her chin defiantly, 'because he wouldn't have let me get anywhere near Brussels, either. And anyway, if he'd known of my plans and failed to stop me he would have lost his job.'

After a moment's pause, he ventured, 'You're not totally selfish. You took steps to protect that groom. And you did stand up to Major Flint.'

'Yes. Yes, I did, didn't I?' She took in a juddering breath. 'But it was the first time I've ever done anything like that. You must think I'm dreadful.'

'No. I could never think that.'

'Haven't you heard a word I've just said, Tom? I'm cowardly, and deceitful, and stubborn and wilful, and unfeminine.'

'Unfeminine? How can you say that? I watched you charming and flirting your way through Brussels society these past few weeks.'

'Oh, no, Tom, acquit me of that. I never flirt.'

'Nevertheless, you had no end of admirers.'

'I did nothing to encourage them, though,' she insisted. 'In fact, I made sure that the only ones whose escort I accepted were ones I was sure wouldn't look upon me with marriage in mind. It's a game I've become adept in playing. Keeping Mama happy. For if she sees me surrounded by admirers, she thinks I am at least *trying* to select a suitable husband.'

'But you aren't?'

'No. Even the trip to Paris was an attempt to persuade her I was doing my best to make a good match. Between us, Gussie and Gideon and I put notions of foreign princes into her head, until she started thinking it was all her own idea to send me to meet new and more exciting men than the ones I ran across Season after Season in London. And all the time—' her shoulders slumped '—it was just a ruse to get close to where Gideon was stationed.'

'But…Bennington Ffog…'

'Oh.' She shifted guiltily. 'Well, you see, he was Gideon's commanding officer. And Gideon had asked me to be kind to him. And it wasn't as if he was clever enough to outwit me by manoeuvring me into a situation where he could get an opportunity to propose. Besides…' she lifted her chin, 'I was pretty sure he didn't have marriage in mind. I always thought he just enjoyed being more successful with me than any other officer. It suited us both.'

She shuddered. 'Oh, heavens. I'm turning into my mother! For years, she used to get her own way only by scheming and cunning. And at the time, I didn't blame her, because Papa was such a brute that I'm sure it was the only way she could survive. But what excuse do I have?'

She put her hands to her cheeks in chagrin. Screwed her eyes shut for a moment. Then drew herself up, and faced Tom with new resolve on her face.

'I'm going to change, Tom. I'm going say what I believe, from now on. Like my sister Harriet. Yes, I shall be forthright, and honest, and *good*.'

'Really?' Tom's heart sank. If she really did turn over a new leaf, where did that leave him? Discarded, most like.

As if to confirm his fear, she said, 'I shall go straight round to visit Justin and tell him that he is not to worry about me.' She waved a hand between them. 'About us.'

'No. I mean, do you think that is wise?' His heart was hammering. The Colonel was bound to make her capitulate. Not only had she just admitted she hated confrontation, but Ramrod Randall wasn't the man to brook any opposition to his will. Not that he could say so. Not after she'd just informed him she was going to stand up for herself. She'd think he didn't have any faith in her.

With the skill of an experienced soldier, he reached for the one weapon he knew he could use against her without it blowing up in his face. He'd play on her nurturing nature.

'If he is really so ill he cannot even write a letter, but must have Miss Endacott do it for him—' and, come to think of it, he must be in bad case, or he'd have torn Sarah from his arms well before now '—then do you think he is really well enough to endure a confrontation?'

'Oh.' She looked deflated for a moment, then brightened up. 'Well, perhaps I won't go right this minute. Tomorrow will be soon enough, won't it? One more night together won't make much difference, will it? From the way Robbins looked at me, and Major Flint, too, my reputation was ruined from the moment I brought you up to my room. Are you really so bad,' she said, turning on him a look of naked curiosity, 'that just nursing you is enough to ruin a perfectly innocent woman?'

'Yes.' Though he burned with shame to admit it, he'd vowed never to lie to her.

'Why? What have you done?' She leaned her chin on her hand and gazed at him with fascination.

He felt a blush steal across his cheeks. Even his ears felt hot.

'I cannot speak of such things to you. I don't want to corrupt you.'

'Fustian! Talking about the sort of things men do in the pursuit of…adventure,' she said cheekily, 'cannot possibly corrupt me. Why, Gideon used to tell me *everything*.'

'I'm sure he didn't,' Tom retorted. 'A man doesn't fill his own sister's ears with tales of his…um, exploits of a…carnal nature.'

'Oh, he didn't go into detail,' she said airily. 'But I know he had his amorous adventures. And I know Justin has them, too. And now I come to think of it, when it comes to having a wild childhood, I don't think there are many things you can have done that my own brothers haven't done in their time. Fighting, stealing, plundering hapless farmers' crops, letting bulls out of their fields, burning hay ricks, setting their terriers on to the chickens.'

'Colonel Randall did all those things?'

'Oh, not *him,* no. And the other exploits were divided up between the other three. Gideon was always getting into scrapes. But my younger brothers, the twins who are now at Eton, are positive hellions. Do you know, I don't believe you are any worse than my own brothers. What I think is that people are painting you blacker than you are, because of what your father, and grandfather did. Which is grossly unfair.'

'There may be a nugget of truth in that. But I'm still not the kind of man Lord Randall would want you to associate with.'

She cocked her head to one side and examined him

thoughtfully. 'That is true. And you aren't what Mama or Gussie would call eligible, either. Not a bit. Because you don't have a title, or land, or money. Which isn't your fault. But none of that makes you a bad man.'

'I am the very last man *any* of your family would welcome as a husband for you.'

'True,' she said thoughtfully. 'But then I don't want a husband,' she added, brightening up.

'Do you know, it might turn out to be a jolly good thing to have lost my reputation. After this—' she waved her hand to encompass the cramped room and Tom's battered body lying in the bed '—even Mama might abandon her attempts to marry me off to someone respectable. I shouldn't think anyone respectable would want me, now, would they?'

'Not if they found out about it, no,' he admitted.

'I could go and live on one of the smaller estates, somewhere deep in the country,' she said dreamily. 'I wouldn't need many servants. In fact, the fewer the better, because one thing I've discovered over this last week is how much simpler life is without maids and dressers fussing round me all day long. As long as I can keep Castor, and go for plenty of rides, I won't want much else.'

Her face fell abruptly.

'Mama will be very upset, no doubt. She has such ambition for me. And Gussie will feel guilty because Mama entrusted me to her care. Which will so infuriate Blanchards that he will probably never forgive me. He will cut me out of their lives. I shall miss them,' she said sadly.

'But Harriet won't care for that. Funny, I'd always thought of Harriet as living a dreadfully dull existence with her rural dean, but one thing I will say for her—she isn't the slightest bit fettered by convention. With her radical views, I wouldn't be surprised if she didn't become a frequent visitor. Unless—' her face fell again '—she hears about my part in her friend Mary's disappointment.'

'Sarah.' Tom reached for her hand, his conscience flayed raw. She was sitting there reckoning up what her association with him would cost her, while all he'd been able to think of was ways of keeping her in his life for even one more night. Of perhaps beguiling her into letting him kiss her a few more times.

'Harry and Jack won't be allowed to have any contact with me, naturally. Until they come of age. When, with any luck, curiosity may well drive them to seek out their notorious older sister. So, it won't be the end of the world, will it? Being ruined, I mean. Only a bit unpleasant, at first, weathering all the scenes that are bound to lead up to my banishment.'

He couldn't let her do it. Couldn't let her throw her life away on his account.

'Sarah—' he began again.

'Hmm?' She turned and smiled at him. A smile of such sadness that it was like having salt flung on to an open wound.

'It isn't too late. For you. I'm certain that with Colonel Randall's influence, and his money, they could find someone to marry you and bury this incident.'

Her smile faded.

'I have no intention of letting them do any such thing,' she said indignantly. 'I haven't spent the last four Seasons deliberately avoiding matrimony to surrender now, just when freedom, total freedom, is finally within my grasp.'

'But…'

'And another thing. Since we are both agreed that my

reputation is damaged beyond repair, there doesn't seem any point in playing at propriety any longer, does there?'

His heart gave a heavy thud, then began to race as though it would burst through his ribcage.

'What are you saying?'

'I need you, Tom. I don't want to wait until I have a nightmare to give me the excuse to seek the comfort of your arms. And, well, not to put too fine a point on it,' she said, blushing, 'I want to spend tonight in your bed.'

Could he really be that lucky? Was Sarah really asking him what he thought she was asking him?

Randall would kill him when he found out.

Not that that would stop him. If Sarah wanted him, then…then…his head began to spin.

'There's no point in pulling out that truckle bed,' said Sarah, 'and having it made up when I fully intend to sleep with you, Tom. The way I look at it, if everyone thinks I'm ruined, I may as well enjoy some of the benefits, mayn't I?' she said cheerfully as she whisked out of the room to go and prepare for bed.

Even though he'd had his bed moved away from the wall, so that he could no longer hear those preparations, he could still picture what was happening next door.

He should ring for Gaston. Wash. Shave. He ran a rather shaky hand over his jaw. Let it drop to his side. If only he was a little stronger. Better equipped to make her first time memorable. The way he felt right now, she would be lucky if he could last long enough to make it even mildly pleasurable.

But then she was coming back into the room, clad in a sensible nightgown with a demure wrap over the top, a blanket draped over one arm.

A blanket? Why the blanket? What did she mean to do with that?

He got his answer when she lay on the *top* of his bedclothes and draped the extra blanket over her legs, just as she had done when she'd sought his comfort from her nightmares last night.

'There.' She sighed, snuggling down trustingly into the crook of his arm. 'That is comfortable, is it not?'

Not. He was painfully aroused. His heart was stuttering like a stammering schoolboy. And sweat was trickling down his spine.

He managed to form a noise that was a sort of pained grunt, that she might take for agreement.

'We can hold each other all night—' she sighed with a blissful purr that made her sound like a kitten '—and keep the nightmares at bay.'

He certainly wouldn't be having any nightmares tonight. Because he wouldn't be able to get a wink of sleep, with her breasts pressed against his ribs like that and the softness of her hair flowing over his throat.

'I won't let anything bad disturb you tonight,' he grated, dropping a kiss on the crown of her head. Most particularly not him. Dear God, how could he have imagined she'd been inviting him to deflower her? He should have known her request was a completely innocent one. For she was innocent. Pure.

And he couldn't betray her by letting her get so much as a whiff of his own base desires. He would just hold her, since that was all she wanted of him. Watch over her while she slept.

Preserve the innocence she'd entrusted to him.

'Tom?'

'Mmm?' He hoped to goodness she wasn't going to

expect him to carry on a lucid conversation. Not while nearly all the blood in his depleted system was raging south of his waistline.

'I still feel dreadfully guilty, you know, about Justin. I did try to take measures to prevent creating a scandal, so that nobody who cares about me would get upset. I wrote to Gussie as soon as I got here, trying to explain as much as I dared...'

'I saw you sitting at the desk, in a halo of light, writing something. You looked so fierce, and pure and bright, all at once. Just how I pictured a guardian angel should look.'

She looped one arm about his waist as she shifted into what was, for her, a more comfortable position. Lord, why had he been all noble last night and promised she need not fear him? Now he had to live up to her expectations.

He sucked in a deep, juddery breath. He'd been stupid enough to make her a promise and he couldn't break his word. Not to her. That was all there was to it.

'That only proves how very ill you were. Likening me to an angel, indeed.' She gave a very un-angel-like snort and began toying with the buttons on his nightshirt, driving him almost demented as he pictured those slender fingers sliding them undone, slipping inside, running over his chest.

Gliding lower...

'I know that now,' he said huskily. 'You are very much a woman.' A woman who was becoming increasingly more inquisitive and bold. If he wasn't shackled by that stupid promise, he'd have been trying to see just how bold she could be. She'd already shocked him by kissing him that morning, in a defiant sort of way, as though seeing how far she could go.

He twined one of her golden locks round his finger.

'But still, you shouldn't blame yourself for what happened to Colonel Randall.'

She stiffened. For a moment he thought he'd offended her. He braced himself for a haughty demand he stop playing with her hair.

'Do you know, I think you are right? I took the greatest care to guard my reputation— Oh, not that I give a fig for it, Tom, so don't worry on that score. No, but I do know that Justin wouldn't want people gossiping about me. Though heaven alone knows why he's so consumed with preserving the family name, when our father made it a byword for depravity when he held the title. Nevertheless—' she shrugged '—my presence in Brussels would have stayed secret had it not been for Major Flint.

'Not even Madame le Brun gossiped about the wounded officer I'd hidden in my bedroom, you know. She says she doesn't care about any scandals so long as I pay my bills.'

'Very practical,' he panted, wondering whether he should take hold of her hand and remove it from the vicinity of his buttons. The only problem with doing that was the temptation to guide it to where he wanted her to touch him the most. Giving her a subtle hint, then letting her explore a little wasn't the same as deliberately rousing her, was it? It wouldn't be breaking his promise if she was the one to take the lead.

Would it?

'Yes. So, if anyone is to blame for Justin having a relapse, it is him. Major Adam Flint,' she hissed, curling her fingers into his shirtfront like little claws, relieving him of the bother of doing anything about its innocently seductive exploration of his chest.

'He just marched in there, without a thought for the

damage he'd cause, and blurted it all out. And not even the truth, either, I dare say. But his own version. Painting you as black as he could, and making out that I've suddenly become a…a sort of…lightskirt, or something,' she finished indignantly. 'When you are so ill you can hardly get out of bed, never mind get up to the kind of mischief he was implying you'd wrought.'

That was probably true, he reflected gloomily. He'd gone dizzy just thinking about deflowering her. If he'd attempted anything even remotely strenuous, he'd probably have passed out like a light.

'He's just like Papa,' she went on. 'He may go by the name of Flint, but every inch of him is typical Latymor male. He throws his weight around. Barks out orders left, right and centre without a care for how anyone feels about anything. Or how it's going to affect them.'

'I don't think that's quite true. He just…didn't foresee what the outcome would be.'

'Don't you take his side, Tom! Men,' she huffed. 'You always stick together, in the end. I suppose,' she added morosely, 'it comes from you being brother officers. You have great respect for him, or something.'

'Well, I do, as it happens.' He released the lock of hair he'd wound round one finger and let it slither straight to flow over his knuckles. 'I haven't always respected all the officers I've served with, in the various regiments I've gone through. But Major Flint is competent. Good with the men. Fair. Brave.'

'Oh, don't go on about him,' she said sulkily. 'The more you praise him, the more I want to wring his neck.'

At that moment, they heard someone hammering on the street door. Since Madame le Brun had already locked up for the night, it came as a bit of a surprise when, a few moments later, they heard the sound of someone knocking on their bedroom door.

'Oh, no. What now?' Sarah got out of bed, went to the door and peered out on to the landing.

'Excuse me, but it is the other one,' panted Madame le Brun, as though she'd just run up the stairs. 'The major with the loud voice and the angry face. Demanding to see you. But, after what we said, what you told me, am I to let him in?'

'No! On no account.'

'That is what I thought, *mon chou*. Leave him to me,' she said, scurrying out of the room and down the stairs.

After a moment or two, they heard the sound of booted feet marching to take a position right under their window.

'Lady Sarah! Major Bartlett!'

'Well,' gasped Sarah, 'if that doesn't beat all! It's as if he deliberately wants to cause a scandal.'

She flew to the window. Threw up the sash, pushed the potted geranium to one side and leaned her head out.

'Haven't you done enough? Not content with upsetting Justin, you have to come here shouting our names out as though you want to make sure I'm ruined!'

'I wouldn't have to shout for you,' Tom heard the infuriated voice echo up from the pavement, 'if you'd let me in.'

'I'm in bed,' she retorted. 'Gentlemen don't come visiting ladies at this hour of the night. Come back in the morning at a respectable time.'

'You are behaving like some Billingsgate doxy,' Major Flint bellowed in the voice that had the power to make the hardened men under his command quake in their shoes. 'And I have just come from leaving your brother's coffin in the Chapel Royal.'

Sarah gasped. Went white. And then her hands, as

though seeking some way to express her rage and frustration, clenched round the potted geranium.

'You…' She inhaled sharply as she formed what was probably the worst word in her vocabulary. 'You bastard,' she flung at him, along with the poor unsuspecting geranium.

Tom heard the sound of pottery shattering on the paving flags. And he grinned. At least she wouldn't have a second head wound to tend because, knowing her, if she'd actually hit her target, she would have been mortified. Would have run down to her half-brother, dispensing tears and bandages in equal measure.

Fortunately for all concerned, Major Flint beat a hasty retreat. No doubt rueing the day he'd attempted to cross swords with his doughty little half-sister.

His grin faded when he caught sight of Sarah's face, though. She looked stricken as she gazed after the Major's retreating figure.

And then it hit him. Major Flint had brought her the intelligence she'd been seeking ever since coming to Brussels.

The location of her brother's body.

Which meant her quest was at an end.

Or very soon would be. Right now, she was too shattered by the skirmish with Major Flint to think about the future. But once she'd recovered from the initial shock, once she'd realised he wasn't ill enough to need constant nursing, there would be nothing to keep her here.

This could be the last night he spent with her.

Chapter Eleven

She cried herself to sleep.

But at least it was in his arms.

As he held her, watching her finally succumb to exhaustion, he resisted the pull of weariness. If this was to be his last night with her, he wasn't about to waste it sleeping. Not when he could savour the feeling of holding her in his arms. Not when he could watch her features, softly lit by candlelight. Even when the candle guttered and went out, he couldn't take his eyes off her. She looked even more ethereal by moonlight, the planes and hollows of her face stripped of colour. He loved the way expressions flitted across her face. The way she quieted when he smoothed her hair back from her forehead whenever a frown began to pleat it.

If only dawn would never come. For soon after daybreak, she would wake, and get up and leave him. Oh, perhaps not altogether, not yet. But now that she knew where Gideon was, now that she could finally lay him to rest, and he was recovering, she wouldn't have any reason to stay.

All too soon, so far as Tom was concerned, she stirred,

rubbed her eyes and stretched her arms over her head. Sat up.

One look at her face was enough to tell him she was already, in her mind, far, far away from him.

'You are going to the Chapel Royal?'

She nodded. Got out of bed. Folded the blanket over her arm. 'And then I will go to visit Justin. Straighten things out. Oh, don't worry, Tom,' she said when he must have made some movement that betrayed his despondency. 'No matter what Justin says, I won't leave you. After all, he has Mary nursing him, so why should he begrudge you your own nurse?' She lifted her chin in that defiant gesture which was becoming so familiar to him. 'It isn't as if you have anyone else to care for you.'

But it wasn't the same. He had no doubt that Mary was watching over the Colonel with such devotion because she was deeply in love with him. Whereas love wasn't even *on* the list of reasons Sarah had for taking her stand in this bedroom. She wanted to defy her family. She wanted to prove her own worth.

No wonder she could so easily withstand the physical attraction that she was occasionally starting to feel for him. The last thing she wanted was to be hampered by whatever might be starting between them, just when she was finally breaking free of the hold her family exerted over her.

She bent down and gave him a fierce hug.

He put his arms round her and hugged her right back.

So what if she was only using him, for any, or all, of the reasons he'd just come up with? He wasn't the man to look a gift horse in the mouth. He inhaled the faint air of violets that still clung to her. Savoured the feel of her breasts, pressed against his upper body.

Memorised it all.

'I shan't be long,' she said, straightening up.

'Take all the time you need with Major Latymor. To lay him to rest. I will have Gaston wash and shave me, and try sitting out of bed for a while. But I shouldn't be a bit surprised if I need a nap before long.'

'Oh, poor Tom,' she said, looking down at him ruefully. 'I keep forgetting how very ill you are. You really don't look at all well today. Is there anything I can get for you while I'm out?'

'No, thank you. I will need to replace the pistols that got stolen while I was unconscious. And get some new boots. I had a spare pair in the baggage the men brought here, but now they are my only pair. But all that can wait until I'm up to visiting the boot-maker myself.'

'Clothes,' she said, suddenly looking a little shocked. 'Oh, my goodness, I haven't done anything about mourning. And I'm going to pay my respects to Gideon. I have only the most frivolous blue bonnet and spencer. Getting some blacks would have been the very first thing Gussie would have done.'

'Yes, but you've been sitting over me night and day. So don't you go condemning yourself for thinking more about saving a life than what you should be wearing to do it!'

'You don't really mind what I look like, do you, Tom?' she said thoughtfully.

'You always look utterly beautiful to me,' he said staunchly.

She blushed. And lowered her eyes.

'Thank you,' she said quietly. And then stood completely still for a moment or two, as though contemplating adding something else.

But in the end, she simply shot him a brief smile, before darting out of the door.

* * *

It took next to no time to walk to the Chapel Royal. Sarah could scarcely believe that Gideon could have been so close to her and she'd not felt anything.

But he wasn't really here, was he? Not in that coffin. That was only his earthly remains. His soul was… Her breath stuck in her throat.

Somewhere else. Of course. That was why she could sense nothing of him here.

Only, when she reached further, with all her being, only a massive great nothing echoed back.

Nothing.

Her heart started beating so wildly she found it hard to breathe. She had to get outside. Out of this cold, empty chapel and into the sunshine.

She stumbled into the nearest shop and tried to concentrate on kitting herself out in black.

But it was all a blur. All that seemed real was her deep inner cry of *No*. *No*, Gideon couldn't be gone. *No*, she didn't want to be alone. So alone.

She'd been filling her days with activity, with purpose, all to silence that *No*.

She'd ridden to Brussels, spent the night curled up in a stable with Castor and Ben, braved Mary's hostility, even gone on to the very battlefield where she feared he had fallen and finally grabbed at the chance to save one poor wretch from the grinding jaws of death, in a vain attempt to silence that deep, instinctive denial.

But none of it had worked.

Except it wasn't exactly the same kind of *No*, any more. It wasn't a refusal to accept the truth.

It was a *No* of anger. Of protest.

All of a sudden she came to herself to find she was

standing outside the door to her lodgings in the Rue de Regence. She had no idea how she'd come here, when her plan had been to visit Justin.

But it was a foolish plan, she decided, going inside. She wasn't strong enough to face Justin. And she would have to be very strong indeed to stand up to him, particularly when he was so ill and she so filled with remorse for being a cause of it.

Right now, she just needed…she needed…

She ran up the stairs to their room. Tom. She needed Tom.

He was sitting on top of the bed, clad in breeches as well as a clean linen shirt and waistcoat. He took one look at her, and held out his arms.

She flew to him. Buried her face in his shoulder, and just sobbed. With grief. With some gratitude, too, because she hadn't had to say a word. One look at her face and Tom knew what she needed most.

'He wasn't th-there,' she hiccuped, when she eventually grew calm enough to be able to form words. 'Nothing of him at all. I couldn't…couldn't feel him any more. He's gone, Tom. Really gone.'

'Shhh.' He rubbed his hands up and down her back soothingly. 'From this world, perhaps, but he will always live in your heart.'

'Memories,' she said scornfully. 'I don't want them! I want *him*! I want my brother back. I need him. He was the only one who understood me. The only one who gave a damn…'

He tensed. 'That's not true any longer. I—' he took a deep breath '—*I* give a great deal more than a damn for you. In fact, I— Well, I've never said this to any woman before—never thought I would, either—but I think—

well, I don't know any other way to describe what I feel for you. So it must be love.'

'What?'

'I think,' said Tom gravely, 'that I love you, Sarah.'

She felt her jaw gape open.

'I suppose this wasn't the best time to make a declaration of that sort, was it? For a seasoned rake, I seem to have lost my touch. To have put a look like that on your face.' He ran one finger along her jaw, with a rueful smile. 'But I couldn't just sit here and listen to you say that nobody loves you any more, when it simply isn't true.'

'But you can't!'

'Why can't I?'

'Because I'm not pretty.'

'I told you that I don't care about that. And this morning, I thought you looked as though you believed it. To me, you are beautiful. And it has nothing to do with the way you look.'

'But you can't love me for anything else. For heaven's sake, Tom, I'm such a ninny! I haven't a sensible thought in my head. No mind for study, or books. Even the very few times I've tried to do a good deed,' she said, remembering her attempt to befriend and encourage Mary Endacott to become her sister-in-law, 'it turns into a disaster. You...' She smoothed her hand over his bruised brow. 'You seem to have got me mixed up in your head with some creature you've fashioned from your imagination. Your fevered dreams.'

'No. I liked the look of you before you rescued me from the battlefield and brought me to your bed. I used to watch you, riding about the place with Gideon, or a group of your admirers, and wish I was the kind of man who had the right to form part of your court.'

'Did you? Did you really? Oh, Tom.'

'And since we've been shut up together like this… talking to you, watching you move about the room, making it feel like home, when I've never had a home in my whole life. I've never talked to another person, the way I've talked with you, this week. Never wanted to. Never had anyone show the slightest interest, if you must know. Never known this sense of connection before. You only have to raise one eyebrow, just a fraction, and I know exactly what you're thinking.'

Yes, he did seem to understand her, without her going into lengthy explanations all the time. Even just now, when she'd said Gideon wasn't in the Chapel, he hadn't asked a lot of tiresome questions about where the coffin had gone, then, or if she'd gone to the wrong chapel, the way Gussie or Harriet would have done. Her sisters, with their very down-to-earth turns of mind, would have taken her literally.

But Tom just knew she meant she couldn't *sense* Gideon.

They were in tune, in a way she hadn't been with anyone.

Not even, if she was totally honest, with Gideon.

The world seemed to tilt crazily as she admitted it. Oh, *she'd* understood *him*, right enough. Had sensed what mood he'd been in when he'd written to her, even before she opened the letter and read its contents.

But had he ever really cared about her to the same extent? While he'd enjoyed talking to her, hadn't it always been about his adventures? His ambitions?

No! Her stomach cramped into a cold knot. He had listened to her. He had!

But she'd had to explain what she felt. What she thought. He'd never simply *known*.

Not the way Tom seemed to do, instinctively.

Now it was her heart that seemed to lurch.

'I haven't anything to give you, Tom,' she whispered, guilt-stricken. 'You know how I feel about marriage.'

'I'm not asking you to marry me, Sarah,' he said with that wry grin he always used, she suddenly realised, when he was pretending something didn't hurt him. She recognised it easily, since she was in the habit of employing meaningless, vague smiles herself.

'We've already established that I could never be acceptable to your family. I just wanted you to know, that's all.'

'Oh.' She sat back and looked at him. Really looked at him. If she wasn't so set against marriage, if she didn't think it would feel like a sort of prison, she could make a very good case, with her family, for exactly why he *would* make her an ideal husband.

'They aren't as high in the instep as some families are, you know,' she said. 'I know Mama was thrilled when Gussie married a marquis, but she was almost as happy when Harriet chose her scholarly clergyman. And even Justin doesn't care that much about popular opinion. Otherwise he wouldn't be so involved in the artillery, would he?

'It isn't that,' he said, gazing at her steadily. 'You don't have any idea of how cruel the world can be to people who have stepped outside the bounds of respectability. I've lived with the stigma of being the grandson of a traitor, and the son of a bankrupt who committed suicide, all my life. The village boys used to sing a song about me, you know. *Tom, Tom, the traitor's son, Stole a cake and away did run. The cake was eat, and Tom was beat, Like as not, he'll end in the Fleet.* Which pretty much summed up my childhood,' he said with that lopsided smile. 'I was so miserable in my aunt's house I would rather go into the village and steal food than go back for meals. And I was beaten regularly, as I've already told you. And everyone always predicted I'd come to a bad end.'

'Oh, Tom. How horrid for you.' She hitched one hip on to the bed and took his hand. 'Nobody should have treated you that way, just because of what your father had done. Or your grandfather.'

'I'm not telling you this because I want you to feel sorry for me,' he said fiercely. 'I want you to understand what it would be like. I don't want to inflict that kind of public mockery on any woman. Let alone one I truly care for.' He gripped her hand so hard it made her wince.

Then, seeing it, he drew her fingers to his lips and kissed them fervently.

'These days here with you, like this, I know they are all I can ever have. And I don't mind. It's more than I deserve.'

'That's utter rot!' She drew her hand away sharply, and tucked it in her lap. 'You hold the rank of major. You've fought bravely in battle. And apart from a bit of womanising—'

'A lot of womanising,' he corrected her, drily. 'Let us be accurate.'

'Very well, a lot of womanising,' she said, blushing. 'I've never heard anything bad about you.'

'Perhaps your family have kept it from you, have you thought of that?'

'Oh. Well, yes, they do tend to keep things from me.' Nobody but Gideon had ever answered any of her questions properly. It was always, *no need for you to worry your head about such things*. Or, *not a suitable topic for ladies*.

She lifted her chin and eyed him militantly. 'Very well, then, Tom. Tell me yourself. What have you done that is so bad you don't think you are fit to marry me? Apart from having the misfortune to have been sired by a man who was an utter disgrace. Which, let me tell you, makes us just about even as far as I'm concerned. What are your vices? Do you gamble?'

'No. Do you think I could follow the course of a man I hold in such contempt? I hate watching my fellow officers losing their possessions to one another on the roll of a dice or the turn of a card. As far as I'm concerned, if a man wants to take another man's property he ought to just steal it honestly.'

'Do you steal things, then? Habitually?'

'Not now I have the means to keep my belly full, no. Not unless I'm ordered to do so by a commanding officer to bring confusion to the enemy, at least.'

'So it's just the womanising, then.' She took a deep breath and, though her face went bright red, asked him the most important question of all. 'Are you in the habit of taking women against their will? Taking no account of whether they might be virgins?'

'No!' His shock and disgust were genuine, she could tell. 'I've enjoyed a lot of women. But I've always ensured they enjoyed the encounter every bit as much as I have. More.'

'That sounds a touch boastful.'

He glowered at her.

'No. It's just the way I happen to like it. Sex is a natural appetite. And like any appetite, men have preferences. Mine are for energetic, enthusiastic encounters. I need the… Hell, I shouldn't be talking like this with you.'

She gave a small, cat-like smile.

'Tom, what you have described is not the temperament of a rake. You are just a normal, healthy male, who needs…companionship every now and then.'

'Are you actually trying to persuade me to marry you? Is that what you want? Was all your talk about staying free just words?'

'No! I— You are twisting my words,' she finished hotly. 'I'm not talking about whether I want to marry you. Or anyone.' She got to her feet and paced across the room to the window. 'I'm saying that your reasons for not wanting to marry me, or for thinking you aren't good enough, are totally stupid. That's all.'

'Is it?'

There was a coldness in his voice that sent a shiver down her own spine.

'This—' he waved his hand between them '—whatever this is, it can't come to anything. It can't survive outside this room.'

'Does that matter?' She strode back to the bed and grabbed at the hand he'd been waving at her. 'Does it matter that there is no future for us? What we have now is precious.' Her voice faded to a whisper. She bowed her head over his hand, raised it to her lips and kissed his knuckles. One by one. 'I've never cared about any other man the way I've come to care for you, these past few days. I've never felt moved, when a man said he loved me, the way your declaration just now moved me. I never wanted any man to love me.' She looked up at him, confusion clouding her eyes. 'Tom, let's not talk about this any more. About feelings, or the future. Let's just…'

'Enjoy the moment?' There was a bleakness in his eyes, even as he gave that lopsided smile, and shrugged. 'Yes. Why not? It's what I'm best at. Seizing whatever opportunities come my way. Forget I said anything. I told you it was foolish. Ill timed. Shows how low this wound has laid me,' he said, touching the bandage over his head. 'In my right mind I'd never have done anything so crass as scare a lady away with such maudlin talk as I've been spouting these last few minutes. I don't suppose,' he said, drawing his hand from hers and looking towards the door, 'you could persuade Madame to bring me some brandy? And something to eat apart from the pap she's been ladling out?'

Sarah went to the door. 'I will go and ask,' she said, keeping her face averted, so he wouldn't see the tears that were stinging her eyes.

If he felt he was maladroit, what did that make her?

Touched in the upper works, Gideon would have said. It was the only thing to account for any of her behaviour, this last week.

The smells that assailed her nostrils, when she reached the kitchen, were so delicious they made Sarah's stomach rumble.

She paused in the doorway, watching Madame and her kitchen maid bustling about, wondering how she could feel hunger, could carry on having *any* feelings, when Gideon—who'd been her whole life—had none.

And yet there was no denying she wanted some of Madame's soup and a slice of her fresh, crusty bread.

And Tom.

'Tom has asked if he can have something a bit more, um…' She faltered, loathe to speak disparagingly of Madame's provision so far. 'Substantial.'

'Ah, that is good, no? It means he is getting stronger. Gaston said he thought so this morning, when he went up to give him the wash. But you, *ma petite*? How are you?'

Madame le Brun carried on doling out sympathy and good cheer along with the soup, and somehow had Sarah back upstairs and sitting down at the table with Tom to a meal which included some thickly sliced ham, coddled eggs and thinly sliced cucumber, as well as the soup, without once letting her give way to her grief.

It was only after she'd consumed about half a bowl of soup that Sarah's conscience reminded her she had no right to enjoy anything.

'What is it,' said Tom. 'Not hungry?'

She flung her spoon aside in disgust. 'I have no right to be. I had vowed to go and visit Justin this morning. But after the chapel, I…' She shook her head.

'You can still go. Later.'

'If I get there and find he's died, while I was wandering about the shops…I'm never going to forgive myself.'

'I shouldn't think it likely, now. And before you rip up at me about not taking you seriously, listen to me,' he said, laying his hand on the back of her wrist. 'Just listen. If he had died, or if there was any danger of him doing so, don't you think Miss Endacott would have urged you to go and sit at his bedside?'

'I don't know. I think she would rather keep me away, lest I aggravate his condition.'

'That may be the best course,' said Tom, with a particularly firm look on his face. 'You say you would never forgive yourself if he died before you saw him again, but how much worse would you feel if you went and he grew upset over us, and had a fatal relapse?'

'You are right,' she admitted shakily. The soup she'd

already eaten curdled in her stomach. 'Perhaps I should stay away until he's completely out of danger,' she said in a small voice.

'Look,' he said, rather more gently. 'The fact that she has let you know he's had an operation must mean she has more hope for him, don't you think? And this may sound rather brutal, but the fact that he's survived that operation at all is the critical thing. That was the most dangerous point, for him.'

'I just feel so...' She pursed her lips, and shook her head, searching for the words to explain. 'Useless. I've always been useless, I know that, but it hits particularly hard, knowing Justin is lying there, fighting for his life, and what did I do? I went shopping, Tom. Shopping!'

'You went to the chapel first, to pay your respects to your twin. You are grieving, Sarah, you can't expect to be in any fit state to do much. Don't be so hard on yourself. Why, you have done wonders for me.'

'Yes.' She turned her hand over to grasp hold of his. 'At least *you* didn't become one of those officers who died of their injuries while waiting for a proper doctor to see to them.'

'No. I owe you my life.'

'It wasn't just me,' she put in hastily. 'Your Rogues made sure I was going to be able to look after you. They even stole a French ambulance to get you back here in comfort.'

A wry grin twisted his beautiful mouth. 'One thing you have to say for the way your brother has set up his troop of Rogues—we never leave one of our own behind.'

She bit down on her lower lip. 'That was what Major Flint did, wasn't it? He took charge of Gideon's body, since Justin wasn't able to do it. Just as though Gideon was one of his own Rogues. Oh, dear…' She shut her eyes on yet another wave of guilt. 'I really shouldn't have thrown that flower pot at him, should I? Adam had only come to tell me where Gideon was. He hadn't come to interfere, or blacken my name. Not on purpose.'

'No, but he need not have called you those foul names,' said Tom hotly. 'I could run him through for thinking, for one moment, that you would…you would…' He ground his teeth.

'I don't think,' she said mildly, 'you are quite up to running him through, are you?'

'No, but I could shoot him,' he finished grimly.

'I beg your pardon, but didn't you tell me that your pistols had been stolen?'

'A minor inconvenience,' said Tom, making a dismissive gesture with his free hand. 'I can soon buy some more.'

'Well, I don't want you to shoot him,' she said tartly. 'If you two fought a duel over me, it would be bound to cause a dreadful scandal. Not that I care,' she added hastily, in case he thought she regretted any part of their few days together.

'Well, *I* care,' he grumbled. 'You shouldn't have to forfeit your position in society because of the selfless way you've looked after me, this week.'

'I don't give that for it,' she said, snapping her fingers. 'If you'd ever been a part of society, you'd know that mostly it is one long struggle for position. Everyone is trying to impress everyone else. Either by having more money, or more influence than anyone else. And most of them are trying to drag others down, so that they can clamber over their shredded reputations. It's brutal.' She shuddered.

'But you have been one of the leading ladies,' he said with a frown.

She pursed her lips. 'Only because of my family. I never really took part in any of the posturing and striving for position. I would gladly have stayed at Chalfont Magna all year round if only Mama would have permitted it. But she would have made such a fuss. It was easier to go along with Mama's plans—to pretend to go along with them, anyway, than openly defy her. I...' She shook her head ruefully. 'I went to all the balls, endured those London Seasons, even behaved like a pattern card of virtue at Chalfont Magna, because it all seemed so much *easier*. I didn't even speak out when Mama decided to hire a governess and keep me close under her eye, rather than risk sending me away to school. Harriet came home with her head stuffed full of radical ideas, you see. You should have heard the commotion when she swore she would never marry, because it went against her principles.'

'She is the one who is married to a scholar of some sort, isn't she?'

'Yes,' Sarah smiled. 'I don't think Mama would have tolerated him, were he not better than the alternative— which was Harriet never marrying at all.'

'Did you want to go to school, though?'

'I'm not entirely sure,' she mused. 'I never really cared very strongly about anything, or anyone, except Gideon. Wherever I was, it wouldn't have been with him, because he'd gone to Eton. I reckoned I may as well wait for him to come home to Chalfont as anywhere. The only thing is,' she added wistfully, 'if I had gone to school I may have made some friends, the way Gussie and Harriet did. None of the local girls wanted to come anywhere near. Too scared of what Papa might do, I dare say. Besides which Mama always said they weren't of our class.'

'It always looked to me as though you had plenty of friends. People who admired you. Wanted to be with you.'

She gave a bitter, sad little smile. 'When a girl from my background makes her entrée into society, she will always have crowds of people wanting to get near her. For various reasons. The only trouble was, they were all keen to get husbands, too. So all their talk was of beaus, and fashion, and things I found deadly dull. I suppose they must have found me dreadfully dull. Or cold. I know that some of them whispered that I was cold and haughty. And because I abhorred the prospect of attracting a man's notice, with a view to marriage, prim and proper, to boot.'

'You are none of those things,' he said hotly. 'You are most certainly not dull. Or cold.'

She pulled her hand out from under his, her cheeks warming. 'You have seen a side to me I have never revealed to anyone else.' She frowned. 'So far as anyone else is concerned, I am a demure, rather dull, society miss without two thoughts in her head to rub together and form a spark.'

Though, since she'd done her best to play at being a simpering virgin, too delicate and sensitive to accept the first offer some great brute of a man made her, wasn't it her own fault if people couldn't see who she really was?

'I am honoured, Sarah.'

She lurched to her feet and went to the window.

'The Mayor of Brussels requisitioned all the carriages yesterday, did you hear? They have actually begun going out to the battlefield to search for survivors at long last.'

'Sarah.' Tom's voice sounded pained. He clearly didn't like the way she'd turned the subject. But she couldn't go any further down that road. Or examine too closely why she could tell him things she'd never told another living soul, apart from Gideon.

'Wounded men keep on crawling out of the fields,' she carried on, her back to him, her shoulders tense. 'Half-crazed with thirst and pain. Heaven alone knows where the citizens will put them. Officers have been sent by barge to Antwerp, but as for the ordinary men—'

She broke off and turned to him. 'Now that you are getting better, I really do think I ought to do something. To help. You don't need me so much now, do you? It was different when you had the fever, but now...'

A cold lump formed in his stomach. She was going to leave him. She could already have left him, had he not pretended to be weaker than he actually was. And if Major Flint hadn't tried to bully her into leaving, which had made her dig in her heels to defy him.

Yet he was too proud to beg her to stay.

Too attuned to her views to attempt to forbid her.

'You must do what you think best, of course.'

She stood looking at him for a few seconds, a world of turmoil in her eyes. 'I think, what I will do, right now, is go out riding. Castor will need the exercise.'

And she needed to think.

Somewhere away from the distraction of his handsome face, and his tempting words, and his smouldering eyes.

Chapter Twelve

It had jolted her to realise she'd fallen into the habit of speaking to him the way she'd always spoken to Gideon. Was she using him as a substitute? She had started out feeling that if she couldn't nurse Gideon, doing something for another, seriously injured soldier was a sort of... not compensation, exactly. But something along those lines. The next best thing, then.

Not that anybody could ever take Gideon's place, not completely.

Though she did feel closer to Tom than any other living soul. She valued his opinion. When he said good things about her, it made her feel all warm inside. Like curling up in front of a nursery fire when a storm raged outside.

Was this love? Was she falling in love with Tom?

How could she know?

Though it would explain why it had meant something, to hear him say he loved her. She rather thought she did want Tom to love her. To have been in earnest. She'd always brushed aside any declaration of the sort before, knowing men said all sorts of things they didn't mean.

But Tom's blunt admission that he loved her, coupled with his assumption that nothing could come of it, had sounded genuine. And had touched her. Deeply.

Did that mean she loved him, too?

And if she did, then…

Oh, she couldn't think about that. It was all happening too quickly. And she was still broken up inside about losing Gideon. Thinking of him cut to pieces by cavalry sabres. Worried about whether Justin would survive before she had a chance to mend fences with him. Because as sure as eggs were eggs she would never forgive herself if he died, with the suspicion that she'd somehow been the cause still hanging over her.

Oh, bother Tom for talking about love at a time like this! For making her wonder if her own heart was susceptible, when all her life thus far she'd been immune.

Why should she feel obliged to love him back, simply because he'd said he loved her? She'd never before thought she ought to love a man back, just because he claimed some affection for her.

Not that she'd ever believed any of the others. She probably ought not to believe Tom, either. He'd admitted he was a womaniser. Perhaps he told all his conquests he loved them. Perhaps it was a ruse to get them to become *enthusiastic*. Perhaps that was what made him so successful. For when he said it, with his eyes smouldering the way they did, it had certainly made her want to yield. Oh, not to him, precisely. But to the feelings he was beginning to evoke inside her. That sort of slow burn. The physical, as well as the emotional, pull he exerted over her.

Lord, even in his weakened state he was the most powerfully attractive man she'd ever met. Temptation incarnate.

She still couldn't credit the way she'd felt last night, when she'd been getting ready for bed, knowing she was going to be sharing it with him. Running the soaped washcloth over her skin had made her wonder what it would feel like if he ran his hands over the same places. She'd lingered, her eyes half-closed, until the strange tingles and burning sensations that were mounting had begun to alarm her.

She might tell herself, and him, that she just wanted the comfort of being held in his arms all night, but that wasn't the whole truth. She wanted his hands, too. Touching where they shouldn't. Stroking where she had those tingles. Bringing her the pleasure he'd informed her he always ensured he gave his bed partners.

Whether she loved him or not, she wanted him. Her limbs went so weak with longing, for a moment, that she had a struggle to keep Castor under control. Angry with herself for that lapse in horsemanship, she turned back.

It would be better to exercise Castor first thing tomorrow, when it was cooler. When there were less people about, crowding the streets and providing distractions and alarms in equal measure. So that if her mind did wander, her hands grow slack on the reins, there would be less chance of Castor tossing her over his head and into the canal.

As it was, daylight was fading by the time she returned. She'd been out longer than she'd realised, while her mind had been whirling. Their room was heavily shadowed. Like Tom's expression.

She lifted her chin as she marched in.

'I want to sleep in your arms again tonight, Tom.' She'd decided, as she'd handed over the reins to Pieter, that she wasn't going to fret any longer about the rights and wrongs of it. For once in her life she was just going to do what she wanted.

'I want that, too,' he said gruffly.

'I will go and get ready for bed, then,' she said, a touch defiantly. And flounced out of the room, her heart thudding.

He would just hold her in his arms. Of course he would. She poured water into the basin, and shrugged off her dusty riding habit. Washed herself as quickly as possible, without lingering over the places that were clamouring for his hands.

Doing anything more than just cuddling would be wrong.

And exciting.

And wrong. But then the most enjoyable things always were wrong, weren't they? For girls. Climbing trees or cantering all over the estate on her pony had always held more appeal for her than behaving decorously. It was only because she hated the scenes that followed that she'd moderated her behaviour. Especially since nothing was half as much fun without Gideon to share it.

Also, she'd shrunk inside under both the force of her father's thundering fury, and her mother's tart, stinging words of disappointment alike.

But now her father was gone. And her mother was never anything but disappointed, no matter what she did.

There were going to be scenes, unpleasant scenes, because she'd come to Brussels. Bringing Tom to her room, when she hadn't been able to find Gideon, and nursing him, rather than creeping back to the safety and respectability of the Blanchards's household in Antwerp, had just put the icing on the cake.

So the only question that mattered was what she thought of herself. She hesitated on the threshold, her hand on the door latch. She wasn't an angel, that much she knew. Nor was she a Billingsgate doxy. She might be susceptible to Tom's charm, but so far she was still completely innocent.

She was just a woman. A lonely woman without a friend in the world except the man in that bed. A man the rest of the world said was rotten to the core. Yet he was the only person who understood her. Who really *saw* her.

The only comfort she had.

And she didn't see why she should deny herself that comfort, because of what some mealy-mouthed, judgemental hypocrites might think.

And, yes, he was dangerously attractive. But then a nursery fire could be dangerous, too, couldn't it? If you stuck your hand *into* it. Or allowed your skirts to catch in the embers. Fires could be perfectly safe, as long as all you did was warm your hands at them.

And that was all she would do with Tom. Just warm her cold, lonely heart a little.

Lifting her chin, she opened the latch, and marched into their room.

'You don't look as if your ride did you much good,' said Tom when he caught sight of her mutinous expression. 'You look all hot and bothered.'

'Thank you,' she said tartly. 'That is exactly what every girl wishes to hear. That she is looking far from her best.'

'Would it help,' he said, deliberately ignoring her waspish tone, 'if I were to comb out your hair for you?'

'Comb my hair?'

He indicated the comb she held in her hand. The comb

she didn't even recall picking up. She gazed at it, wondering what category permitting him to act as a sort of lady's maid came under. Would it be the equivalent of warming her hands, or shoving them right into the flames?

'You were about to tackle it yourself, weren't you? And I know how long it takes you. I've watched you wrestling with the tangles often enough. And though you've done without a maid very well,' he said in as calm and rational a tone as he could muster, 'surely, you would appreciate having someone else do it for you?'

Well, there was no harm in asking, was there? The worst she could do would be to refuse his request. But if she let him, ah, then he'd have the memory of sifting all that glorious golden mass through his fingers.

A victorious feeling soared when she plumped herself down on the edge of his bed, her back to him, and handed him the comb with what looked like resignation.

'I used to think having the maid dress my hair was the most tiresome part of the day,' she said as he deftly unbound the braids into which she'd fastened it that morning. A shiver of longing rippled through him as her tresses flowed across her shoulders and down her back in waves. All the way to her waist. 'But at least it wasn't *my* arms that ached with the effort of subduing it.'

It wasn't his arms that were aching, either, just at the prospect of plunging his fingers into all that silken glory.

'It could do with washing, really,' she added, as he started at the tip of one lock and began to tug the comb through. 'It has been getting dustier, and dirtier, every day.'

'Shall we ask Madame if she will bring a bath up here and some hot water? I could wash it for you.'

She sighed. 'Oh, that would be heavenly, Tom, only—' she shook her head '—it would also be disastrous. I haven't any of the special lotion Mama found that helps it take a curl. And nobody to put it in papers. I dare say it is very vain of me, but I have no wish to let you see me looking like a half-drowned waif with a head full of rats' tails.'

'You could never look like that,' he said, laying aside one lock and starting on another. 'A mermaid, perhaps, washed ashore after a storm. Come to steal the heart of the poor fisherman who caught you in his net.'

She shook her head and sighed. 'Tom, you do say the most preposterous things. But you do tempt me to yield. To the idea of washing my hair,' she added hastily. 'Only, don't you think it would be rather improper?'

'You are about to get into bed with me. Spend another night in my arms,' he pointed out. 'Isn't that even more improper?'

She cocked her head to one side. He could almost hear the wheels whirring in her mind as she considered her response.

'No,' she said at length. 'I don't know how it is, but cuddling with you doesn't feel anywhere near as improper as letting you wash my hair.'

He knew why it was. He could just see her closing her eyes and leaning back. He could feel the liquid warmth anointing his fingers as he massaged her scalp. Hear the little moans of pleasure she'd give as he poured warm water from the pitcher to rinse out all the lather. She'd arch her neck, thrusting out her breasts...

The comb slipped from his fingers and clattered to the floor.

She bent to retrieve it. His eyes fixed on the curve of

her bottom where the nightgown stretched over it. He'd become erect at the vision he'd just had, of her getting wetter and soapier as he rhythmically ministered to her. From behind.

Now he was as hard as a ramrod.

He groaned.

She turned swiftly, a concerned frown on her face.

'What is it, Tom? Is something hurting? Oh, I *knew* I shouldn't have let you comb my hair. Lie down and rest.'

She bent over him, laying one hand across his brow.

'I don't need to rest. I need…' He swallowed. Then, pushed to the limits of his endurance, he reached up to cup the back of her neck. 'Don't you know what you make me want, when you speak of intimacy and the impropriety of being in bed together?'

'I'm sorry!' Her face was a picture of contrition. 'I didn't mean to.'

'I know. That's the hell of it,' he gritted. Then, since his soul was bound for hell, anyway, he pulled her down to him and sipped at her lips.

She didn't resist. But nor did she respond. Not with her mouth, anyway, but she was breathing heavily. And he was shaking with the force of desire surging through him.

'Oh, Tom, you're shaking,' she whispered. 'You mustn't exert yourself.'

'It isn't that! It's because I want you so much. Can't you tell?'

'I…' She shook her head. 'I thought it was just because you've been so ill. That whenever you try to do too much, you tremble.'

'No. That's not it.'

He wanted to take her hand and place it over his

arousal. He wanted to put his own hand between her legs. He wanted to tear the ties of her nightgown open with his teeth and devour her breasts.

He shut his eyes and moaned again.

'Tom,' she whispered. 'What should I do? I don't want to torment you.'

And he was a man with a healthy appetite. He'd warned her. She'd even warned herself about the risks of playing with fire. By letting him comb her hair, she'd somehow stoked his simmering urges until they were raging red hot.

And since she was the one who'd fanned the flames, shouldn't she go through with it? She didn't want him to think she was a tease. And he did look so tortured, poor lamb, that…that…

Except—would it be fair to him to let him make love to her, completely? Wouldn't he take that as a sign that she loved him back? That she belonged to him, even? No! She couldn't *belong* to a man. Not even Tom. She'd vowed never to put herself completely in any man's power, the way Mama had done.

Besides, she wasn't completely sure she was ready to commit the sin everyone assumed she and Tom were already enjoying. At the moment, she could still hold her head high, knowing that she was innocent of all their nasty suspicions. She would even be able to face Justin down, knowing she'd done no wrong. But would she be able to look *anyone* in the face, if she really did fall? She'd always been the picture of perfect propriety. How they would all laugh if they knew she'd been tumbled by the English army's most notorious rake.

But worst of all was the dread that Tom might think less of her. It was a bit ridiculous, the way he kept calling her an angel. But the way he always leapt to her defence, whenever anyone assumed she'd been intimate with him, the way he spoke of her purity almost with reverence… A shaft of ice pierced her to the core. Would he still claim to love her if she was no longer innocent? If she admitted she had desires, like all the other women he'd bedded, would he think she was no better than them?

'Perhaps I ought to sleep on the truckle bed, after all.'

'No!' His eyes flew open. 'Oh, no. Please, don't go all the way over there. Behind that screen. It will only make things worse. At least if you are here beside me I can hold you. Smell you.'

She crouched on the bed for a few moments, eyeing him warily.

He grimaced. 'I'm not an animal, Sarah. I won't ravish you.'

'I know,' she replied indignantly. 'I never, not for a moment, thought you would. It's just…' She caught her lower lip between her teeth. 'Won't it be hard for you? Having me in bed, when you want…and not doing anything about it?'

Hard? She had no idea how hard.

'I will be hard all night no matter where you sleep,' he admitted.

She glanced down, saw exactly how hard he was, blushed and looked back at his face.

'Isn't there anything I can do? To ease—' she glanced down at where the sheet tented over his engorged manhood '—your, um, discomfort?'

Oh, yes, there was plenty she could do to ease that. Two or three strokes from her soft white hands, a swipe of her tongue, and he would be done. He was that primed.

'No.' He groaned. She wasn't a whore. She was pure.

Totally pure. And he couldn't debase her by teaching her how to give him relief.

'Just lie down next to me. Let me hold you. And I will be content.'

She did so, though she didn't snuggle up to him the way she'd done the last two nights. She was tense. Almost as tense as him.

Sweat broke out on his brow.

It was going to be a long night.

He'd never claimed to be a good man. Never so much as attempted any form of self-restraint. But he would rather cut his own throat than betray Sarah's trust.

And so, for the third night in a row, he lay sleepless, tortured by the combination of a raging desire, and the presence of the woman who caused it, lying innocent and trusting, in his arms.

But not unaware. He'd destroyed something, by letting her see what she did to him. Of speaking so frankly about all the other women he'd had. Every so often she managed to doze a little and he'd pull her closer. But then she'd jerk awake and stiffen within his hold.

'Shhh,' he murmured, stroking her hair. 'You're perfectly safe. I promise.'

But every time he said it, that promise was harder to keep.

He wasn't sure which of them was the most relieved when it finally started to grow light and she had a valid excuse to get out of bed.

With her purity still intact.

He had precious little to give any woman, but at least he wouldn't rob her of that.

'I promised Castor I would take him out for a gallop

early,' she said, self-consciously flicking her hair over her shoulder. 'Before it gets too hot.'

'And you always keep your promises,' he replied gruffly. That was the kind of woman she was. A woman who should never have got so close to a scoundrel like him.

His vision blurred slightly as he watched her leave, knowing it might be the last time he ever saw her.

He'd made his decision during the night. He wasn't going to be here when she came back.

The moment the door closed behind her, he got out of bed, rang for Gaston and gritted his teeth to do what had to be done.

Major Flint was right. She shouldn't be here with him like this. Every minute her danger grew greater. He was a rake. A rogue. Thus far, he hadn't done her any real damage. People might talk, but Lord Randall was well able to quash any malicious gossip.

But as his physical strength grew, so did his desire for her. He wasn't going to be able to resist her for much longer.

Even worse, she probably wouldn't even resist him, beyond the merest moment's hesitation, either. She was growing increasingly curious about the way her body was starting to respond to his. And the way she'd kissed him two days ago had rung alarm bells in his head. She'd sort of dared herself to see how far she could go. And she was lonely. Susceptible to talk of love.

He grimaced. Love. What right had he to talk of love? What did he even know of that emotion? The only thing he knew for sure was that if he let go, if he seduced Sarah, stole her innocence, then whatever it was she felt for him would curdle. Turn to dislike. Resentment.

He couldn't bear that. Were a few minutes of pleasure worth a lifetime of regret?

He groaned, and clutched the edge of the washbasin as doubt and longing assailed him.

He had to get out of here.

Before the increasing attraction raging between them incinerated the flimsy code of honour by which he lived.

And he dishonoured them both.

He made it as far as the park.

And then realised he should have formulated some sort of plan. He'd left all his things in Sarah's room, thinking he could send for them later. But send for them and have them delivered where? Tourists were starting to flock back to Brussels, which meant that his former lodgings were probably occupied by someone else. He supposed he ought to go there and take a look.

Or perhaps he should report to Major Flint, first. Flint had clearly been left in charge of caring for the wounded. So he could get the company surgeon to look him over and pass him fit for duty. If he *would* be fit for duty by the time Flint finished with him.

They could still give him some sort of light work to do. There was always a mountain of paperwork involved in running a battalion. He could sit at a desk and wield a pen, couldn't he?

Anything, to take his mind off Sarah. To keep him busy and away from her.

Yes, he would report to Flint.

But instead of making his way straight up the Rue de Ruysbrock, misery kept him wandering aimlessly through the Park. He wasn't the only one. Other soldiers loitered in the shady walks, some on crutches, some with arms in slings, and some, like him, with their head swathed in bandages.

'Tom!' Sarah's voice. What the hell was she doing here? And bearing down on him like an avenging fury, brandishing her frivolous little ivory parasol like a battle standard.

'How could you!' Her face was livid. Her voice strident. An officer in a scarlet jacket, who'd been sunning himself on a nearby bench, opened his eyes and frowningly turned his head to see who was disturbing his nap.

'Sarah, please, keep your voice down,' he urged her. He'd left her to protect her reputation. But her words were bound to make people think he'd done the very thing he'd almost killed himself to avoid doing.

'Keep my voice down? Keep my voice down! Ooh, I…' She gathered herself, like a thundercloud about to burst. 'I never thought I'd hear you say anything so utterly mealy-mouthed and…and hypocritical. But then I never thought you'd abandon me, either.'

'I didn't abandon you,' he said, taking her arm and towing her towards a deserted walk. 'I left you a note.' Over which he'd agonised for what felt like hours. 'Explaining.'

'You call that an explanation? Two lines saying Major Flint was right and that you needed to think of duty. *Duty!*' She spat the word as though it was a curse. 'I had no idea where you'd gone.'

He'd had no clear idea where he was going himself.

'When I got back from my ride and saw your things packed, and your note on the pillow…' She shuddered. 'I've just spent the morning scouring Brussels for you. And when I couldn't find you anywhere, I had visions of you lying collapsed in some gutter somewhere. And where do I find you? Strolling about the park as though you haven't a care in the world!'

'I'm not exactly strolling.'

'Don't be so pedantic! You know what I mean! You said—' her lower lip quivered '—you said you loved me! Tom,' she said reproachfully. 'Is this your idea of *love*?' Her eyes grew luminous with burgeoning tears. 'To abandon me, just when I need you the most?'

'Need me the most?' His determination to resist her vanished under a wave of dread. He stopped walking, turned to face her, and seized her arms. 'Has something happened? Your brother? Lord Randall. Is he...'

'I have no idea how he is. It isn't that.' She gulped. 'You said you loved me. I thought you meant it. I actually thought...' Her mouth twisted into a bitter line. 'And then you left. Left me *alone*. I have nobody in Brussels, Tom, don't you realise that? Justin is probably dying and Mary won't let me anywhere near him. Seems to think she has to protect me from him. And Gideon is lying in that revolting coffin, in that hideously cold chapel. Even B-Ben ran off the moment Adam snapped his fingers. I thought at least I could rely on you, Tom.'

'You *can* rely on me,' he said. 'Can't you see that I'm trying to do the right thing by you? If I'd stayed with you any longer, now that I'm getting well, I don't know how long I could have resisted you.' He gave her a little shake. 'Just once in my benighted life, I wanted to do the right thing.'

'I don't *want* you to do the right thing.' She stamped her foot. 'I don't want you trying to behave nobly. It isn't *you*, Tom. And I want *you*. And if...' She lifted her chin, though it was quivering. 'If *you* really did love *me*, you wouldn't dream of leaving me here alone. Knowing I'd have no alternative but to slink back to Antwerp with my tail between my legs and beg everyone's forgiveness. And I *won't*. I won't. I didn't do anything wrong!'

'No. You didn't. You haven't, not yet. But don't you see? If I stay with you any longer, we'll become lovers. I can't resist you any longer. I want you too much. That's why I had to leave. *Because* I love you so much. I want the best for you, Sarah.' He gave her shoulders a gentle squeeze. 'And I'm not it.'

'How do you know what is best for me? Have you ever asked? No.' She gave a bitter little laugh. 'Nobody ever does. Everyone always think they know what is best for me. But they don't. *You* don't.'

'Perhaps you are right.' He let go of her arms and drew himself up. 'But I do know it isn't a cur like me. Sarah, you deserve so much better.'

'No, I don't,' she said defiantly. 'If you knew what I'd done this morning…' She turned her head away briefly and swallowed. 'I was so cross with Adam. So sure it was all his fault.' She shook her head. 'Tom, you keep talking as though you think I'm some sort of paragon. But I'm not. I'm just a woman, that's all. Given to flights of fancy and tantrums, and fits of spite. Not the angel you keep telling me you thought I was when you were in that fever. I started to think…' Her shoulders slumped. 'I thought you knew me, but you don't really. So all your talk of love? It isn't true at all, is it?'

She drew herself up and looked him in the eye, hers flashing with pride.

'Go, then. Leave. After what I've just done to Adam, my own brother, I deserve to be on my own.'

'No, Lady Sarah, you will find someone, one day, who will be worthy of you.'

'I thought I'd found him,' she retorted. 'But I was clearly mistaken. As mistaken as you were when you said you loved me.'

'No!' He took her hand again. 'I do love you. Don't ever think I don't.'

She lifted her chin. 'A fine sort of love,' she said scornfully. 'The sort that leaves me broken and alone.'

An elderly couple who were strolling past caught her words and gave Major Bartlett a scandalised look. Clucked their tongues, and hurried on.

'Sarah,' he said in an urgent undertone, pulling her off the main path and into the shadow of a stone lion, 'the last thing I ever wish to do is hurt you. I didn't think I *could* hurt you. I thought leaving was for the best. It's not as if you care for me all that much.'

'That's all you know.'

'What?' He seized her hand. 'What are you saying? I know you only took me in to prove something to yourself. And then you kept me because you needed the excuse to stay in Brussels so you could find out what happened to your twin. I've been convenient, until now. But—'

'Yes. That's all true. I've been utterly selfish. Until you said you loved me, I *was* only thinking about Gideon. But since then…'

'What?' His heart was banging against his ribs. 'Since then, what?'

'Since then, I started to wish for something I'd never thought I wanted before. To belong to someone, other than Gideon. To belong to *you.*'

'I want that more than anything,' he said, raising her hand to his lips. 'But it cannot be.'

'Oh, for heaven's sake, Tom, stop talking such fustian! So, you've been a rake. So, your background contains a bit of scandal. I don't care. I don't care about any of it. What I do care about is what you think of me. That's all. Because you're the only person never to have condemned me. Or tried to order me about. You might even…' her breath hitched in her throat '…be able to forgive the wicked things I've done,' she ended, gazing up at him with eyes full of hope and longing.

'You couldn't do anything wicked. I don't believe it. If you have done something you *regret*,' he added swiftly when her face fell and he recalled her saying something about deserving punishment because she'd done something dreadful to Major Flint, 'I would know that you didn't mean any harm by it. Or if you did, that you were sorry, afterwards. Sometimes, we all do things, in the heat of the moment, we shouldn't. That doesn't make us bad people. Only human.'

'Well, I suppose at least this has made you stop saying you think I'm an angel,' she said sadly.

His face worked. 'Yes. But that doesn't change what *I* am. Why do you think Lord Randall selected me to become an officer in his unit? It's because I've always been so good at causing trouble wherever I go. And leading others into it.'

'The way you formed those village lads, the ones who taunted you with that horrid song, into a gang who followed you into all sorts of enterprising adventures?' She curled her fingers into his. 'You are a born leader of men, Tom. Why can't you see that it's a good thing? Why do you talk of it as though it is some kind of crime?'

'You speak of me as though I'm some kind of…' He shook his head, unable to find the right word.

'To me, you are, Tom,' she said with a soft smile. 'The best man in the world.'

Her words sucked the breath from his chest. Made his legs start shaking. 'And I can't bear the thought of you leaving. Please, Tom, don't leave me.'

Chapter Thirteen

'I can't fight you,' he said, bowing his head over her hand as he pressed it fervently to his mouth. 'Not as well as my own desire. But it's wrong of me. If I come back with you now…' He looked up at her and what she saw in his eyes made her heart thunder. Naked desire. Agonised longing.

For her.

'Tom,' she breathed, 'I'm already as good as ruined. There is no point in you fighting some sort of rearguard action by leaving me.'

She stepped up to him, slid her arms round his neck and kissed him.

And his brain simply dissolved. He couldn't have formed a rational explanation for why he should stop her from kissing him, had his life depended on it.

'Disgraceful,' he dimly heard somebody say. A swift glance over Sarah's shoulder confirmed it was the same elderly couple who'd walked past a few moments ago. They must have doubled back to make sure they didn't miss anything.

With a low growl, he pulled Sarah closer into his body and gave them something really worth watching.

He stopped kissing her only when his head began to spin.

'Take me home, Tom.'

Home. He lifted his head, eyes closed, and swallowed back what felt like a sob. From now on, wherever she was would be his home. And to think she'd spoken of their little room as home, too.

'I very much fear,' he confessed, once he could breathe steadily again, '*you* are going to have to take *me* home,' he said. 'My legs are shaking so much.'

'Oh, I'm so sorry,' she said, instantly snaking her arm round his waist and wedging her shoulder under his. 'Come on, let's get you back to bed.'

They began to weave their unsteady way back up the slope, and on to the Rue Royale.

They said nothing more during their short walk back to the lodging house in the Rue de Regence. Tom hadn't the breath for it, for one thing. For another, he was too stunned by her declaration she needed him to know what to say.

'You fought for me,' he said as he collapsed to the bed, having only just made it up the stairs. 'You always have done. Right from the first. That is what made me fall in love with you. '

'I will always fight for you, Tom,' she said, bending over him to plant a kiss on his brow. 'Because you are worth fighting for.'

'I'm not. But your faith in me makes me wish I could be the sort of man who was.'

'I don't want you to change,' she said, stroking his cheek tenderly. 'I love you exactly as you are.'

He snaked his arms round her waist. 'You make me feel as if I belong. As if I'm exactly where I ought to be.'

'You are, Tom,' she said softly. 'You're with me.'

'And what,' he said with a rakish smile, 'do you intend to do with me, now you've got me?'

'Do you know, I've been thinking about that,' she said, with a little frown. 'When you left me, one of the things that made me really cross was the fact that I've gained the reputation of being a fallen woman, without actually experiencing any of the pleasure that would have made it worth while. So, Tom, do you think you could show me?'

'Show you?' He swallowed.

'Yes. What is the point of falling in love with a rake, and knowing he's had so many other women, and being the only one to leave his bed still a virgin?'

'Because you're not like any of the others,' he said.

'Are you going to tell me they meant nothing to you?'

'No. Not that. I've been grateful to every one that's been generous enough to share a few moments, or hours of pleasure. I like sex, Sarah. I won't deny it. I like it a lot. It chases away all thoughts of who you are, and where you are, and replaces it with sensation. Glorious sensation. And leaves a sort of peace in its wake. A peace that enables a man to sleep without having to numb his brain with liquor. But this, for me, will be completely different.'

He sat up and clasped her hands. 'I know that you are feeling rebellious, and lonely, and will be seeking comfort and a sort of thrill. And there is nothing wrong with any of that. Those things have driven me to indulge in liaisons, in the past.'

He gazed deep into her eyes.

'But if I make love to you, Sarah, it will be really making love. For the first time in my life.'

She didn't know what to say.

He bowed his head over her hand, and kissed it. 'Lord

Randall would say I'm not worthy of this,' he said, kissing each knuckle in turn. 'And I agree. I don't have the right to claim it.' He slid his tongue between her first and middle finger. She gave a little gasp, because for some reason the slide of his tongue sent sensations spiralling from her stomach to the juncture between her thighs. 'But you have asked me, very politely—' he turned her hand over and bit down on to the mound of flesh at the base of her thumb, turning the spiralling sensations to an insistent throb '—to show you the kind of pleasure that fallen women experience.'

'Are you going to?' Her voice came out like a sigh. He'd already started. And if this was how he could make her feel just kissing her hand, what would it be like when he really got going?

'No power on earth could stop me. Not today,' he growled, surging to his feet and pulling her into his arms.

'Tom, oh, Tom—' she panted between kisses '—you are shaking. You aren't well enough for this. Today was your first time outside since the battle. We should stop.'

'I have strength enough for what I have in mind,' he said, sitting on the edge of the bed and pulling her on to his lap. 'But,' he continued, as he deftly undid the ties at the back of her gown, 'if I need to, I can always lie down, can't I? And you will lie down with me.'

She opened her mouth to agree, when he started kissing his way down her neck to her shoulders, which he could get at easily now that he'd loosened her gown. And all that came out was a little sound halfway between a gasp and a groan.

'I think,' she panted out, when she was able to form thought into words, 'we should lie down right now. Just in case.'

'Not yet,' he pleaded. 'I want to get your clothes off first. May I?' His hand went to her neckline.

'Oh, yes, please.'

The dress fell to her waist. He tugged her breasts free of her chemise. Cupped one gently in his hand, while he kissed and suckled at the other.

'Tom—' she gasped. 'Oh, Tom.' She kneaded at his shoulders, her head rolling back as the delicious sensations he'd already started grew and blossomed, so that she felt full, and ripe, and ready for…something.

He slid his hand up under her skirt, caressing the soft skin he found at the top of her thigh, above her stocking. And then a little higher.

And when his fingers began to work at her there, it was as though he unleashed some kind of storm. As he skilfully removed the rest of her clothing, flashes of lightning flickered up her spine, lit up her blood, dazzled her every sense. And she was naked, on her back, and he was beside her, stroking her, kissing her, nibbling at her neck, her breasts, her belly. Making her gasp with shock, moan with pleasure.

And then he shifted further down the bed, bent over her and fastened his mouth to the spot that was at the very centre of the storm. Pushed his finger into the heart of a maelstrom of sensation. Lashed her with his tongue. Lashed her into a frenzy.

'Tom, I can't, I… Oh, Tom…oh, oh, oh!'

Pleasure exploded through her. Ripped her from her moorings. And gently floated her back to shore.

For a moment or two, she was so stunned that all she could do was breathe. Drag in one breath after another and wait for the world to stop spinning.

But then she managed to just about open her eyes.

To see Tom, crouched over her.

Looking at her not the way she thought a lover should look at all. But like a warrior. A warrior who was about to face a mortal foe.

'Tom,' she breathed, reaching up to cup his cheek with a tender hand. 'What is it? What's wrong?'

What was wrong? He sucked in a sharp, painful breath. There she was, lying there in the afterglow of the pleasure he'd given her. Still virgin.

He'd thought he could do this for her. Thought he could give her the pleasure she'd asked him for—and leave her intact.

But the thought of some faceless man, a man they'd think worthy of marrying her, seeing her like this, having the right to go where he hadn't, it made him want to howl. With rage. With pain. The agony of imagining her with any other man was worse than any physical pain he'd ever suffered.

The temptation to ruin that smug, worthy man's hypothetical wedding night by making sure he wouldn't be her first was almost overwhelming.

He gritted his teeth. It was wrong. It was wicked.

But, hell, when had he ever been anything but wicked?

And hadn't she said that he wasn't any use to her when he tried to be noble? She didn't want him to do the right thing. She wanted him to do the wrong thing. He tore open the fall of his breeches. Had *asked* him to do the wrong thing.

She shifted a little. Parted her legs. Caressed his shoulders.

And the last sliver of resolution melted away. Right now, she was his, utterly his. Whatever happened, tomorrow, or the next day, nobody would ever be able to take *this* from him.

With a shout of defiance, he surged into her. Surged into the only heaven a sinner like him was ever likely to know. The fleeting, carnal paradise of becoming one with the woman he loved.

She rose under him, murmured his name. Shivered with renewed pleasure as he sought his own satisfaction. He slowed down, waiting for her. Wanting to make it last. For as long as he could.

But at length her own rising excitement infected him. When she shuddered round him, gasping out his name, he lost all control. Did the very worst he could have done to her.

Not only did he deflower her, he spent inside her, too.

And he wasn't sorry.

So why were tears streaming down his cheeks? He buried his face in her neck, in her hair, clinging to her as tightly as he could without hurting her. And she, darling that she was, hugged him back. Rocked him as though he was a lost, lonely child.

'Tom,' she murmured. 'What is it?'

'I deserve to be shot,' he growled into her neck. 'For taking your virginity.'

'You didn't take it. I gave it to you.'

'I should have stayed strong. I should have stopped. I should have—'

'Shh, shh. You did exactly what I wanted you to do. You made me feel wonderful. And I don't mean just physically. For the first time in my life, I feel wanted. Really wanted.'

He held her more tightly. If only he could preserve this moment by clinging to it. This moment when everything felt perfect. Just bask in the sensation of her running her hands up and down his back, pressing kisses to his shoulder. His neck. Stroking her foot up and down his calf.

If only he didn't have to burst this perfect bubble with the ugly lance of truth.

'You don't understand,' he forced himself to say. 'I didn't stop when I should have done. I could have dropped a baby inside you. I've ruined everything. I'm sorry,' he said, raising himself up so he could look into her face. 'We'll *have* to get married now.'

For a moment Sarah just froze. But then a stricken look leached her face of colour.

'No.' She shoved him hard, but he didn't move off her. 'For heaven's sake, Tom, haven't you listened to me? I have told you I don't know how many times that I don't want to marry. And nor do you, to judge from that horrid expression on your face.'

'You are right. The thought of marriage—' He swallowed. Before today, he hadn't really thought about it, not in relation to himself. It just hadn't entered his mind that one day he would meet anyone like Sarah. But now, well, even though he hadn't thought beyond the mutual pleasure they could bring each other, it...it made sense.

'But surely, this changes everything?'

'This?'

'The fact that you might be with child. We can't just condemn a child to being labelled a bastard all it's life. I have to give it my name.'

A mutinous expression came over her face. 'No, you don't. My own name is perfectly adequate.'

'Not for my child, it isn't. I don't want it to think I walked away from the responsibility of bringing it up.' The way his own father had done.

'Well, I'll tell it that it was my fault, then, shall I? That should salve your conscience.'

'No, it won't, because—'

'I should have thought you,' she interrupted, 'of all men, would agree that it's better for a child to have no father at all, than a bad, or a reluctant one.'

She didn't think he'd be a good father?

He withdrew. You couldn't have a fight with a woman when you were still inside her, your body still throbbing in the aftermath of release. He had no answer to that clincher. Because he knew it was true. Their own childhoods had been marred by their respective fathers.

She pulled the sheet up to her breasts and scowled at him over the top of it.

To think he'd promised her she'd feel peaceful afterwards. She'd never felt less at peace in her life. And from the looks of it, nor did he.

Marry her just in case there was a baby, indeed! That wasn't a reason to get married. The only reason to get married was if you felt as if you simply couldn't live without the other person. If you wanted to be with them more than you wanted your next breath. If they made you feel as if you didn't care about anyone or anything else but being together.

A little sob caught in her throat. For that was how she felt about Tom. That was why his guilt-ridden proposal had hurt her so much.

A cold fury began to replace the icy stab of hurt. She was almost as bad as Mama—falling for a rake who looked on marriage as the ultimate sacrifice. She'd never understood how Mama could do such a foolish thing, until now, when she'd just had an experienced rake turn her into a puddle of lust and longing.

Except she *had* managed to retain the strength to turn down that half-hearted proposal.

And at least Tom *had* proposed. He wasn't the kind of man to turn his back on a child of his. Not like Papa. Not like Papa at all. Papa had littered the countryside with his own natural children and never cared tuppence what happened to any of them. Or their mothers.

It felt as though someone drew a curtain away, flooding her mind with light. All her life she'd believed marriage was the worst fate that could befall a girl. It had made her reject Tom's proposal in a kind of sick panic, even before she'd registered the reluctance in his voice. She'd always thought marriage meant becoming some man's property, being obliged to watch him have affairs, while bearing him son after son until she was worn to a shadow.

But now she could see why her sisters had been so keen to see her follow them down the aisle. It wouldn't be awful being married to Tom, not if he'd wanted to marry her. Really wanted to. The way Graveney had wanted Harriet. The way Blanchards doted on Gussie.

But he didn't. He'd only proposed because he felt he'd behaved badly and now wished to make amends.

Guilt made her insides squirm. Because Tom had only done what she'd asked him to do. What she'd begged him to do. Why, he'd even tried to escape her and she'd hunted him down and dragged him back to this room.

'None of this is your fault,' she said. 'Even before we came to bed, you warned me that it was only to show me the pleasure a fallen woman could experience. You reminded me that you aren't the man to either ask for, or be granted, my hand in marriage.'

'And you said you would always fight for me,' he

growled back. 'Was that just words? Do you even know what you meant when you said you loved me just as I am?' He gave a bitter sort of laugh.

'I do love you, Tom.'

'But not enough to marry me.'

'Oh, but—'

'No, don't bother saying any more. You're young. This is your first love affair. You're confusing the physical satisfaction for something else.'

Was she? She'd already worked out that it was the physical attraction her mama had for her father that had made her make so many poor judgements. But she wasn't the same as her mother. And Tom wasn't like her father.

'There's nothing to fight about, is there?' he said, flinging himself back into the pillows and staring fixedly at the ceiling. 'We're in agreement. Neither of us wants to marry. We've both been clear about that from the start.'

Yes. They had. Though now she was the only one who thought marriage might not be so bad, if entered into for the right reasons.

Unless—could he have changed his mind, too? Might there be more to his proposal? Was that why he'd seemed so hurt and angry when she'd turned him down flat?

Perhaps she should give him a chance to explain, if that was so.

'It was sweet of you to propose, then, when you really don't want to marry me. All for the sake of a baby that might not even have been made.'

'It wasn't just that.'

Her heart bumped into her throat.

'I shouldn't have gone so far. I know you maintain

you wanted to gift me with your virginity, but I needn't have taken it. I could have given you pleasure, and taken it, without leaving you in no state to marry anyone else.'

Guilt. It was only guilt, after all, that had prompted him.

'I don't want to marry anyone else!' Her eyes were burning so hot she had to blink rapidly. 'I was ruined and facing scandal, just for staying with you here unchaperoned. We talked about it—how I was going to live on a small estate somewhere and withdraw from society. I'm happy to do that. With or without a baby.'

All of a sudden she couldn't bear being so close to him while they were fighting. She rolled out of bed, grabbed her crumpled chemise and dragged it over her head. Then went to pour herself a drink.

So. She thought he was good enough for a quick romp, but not for ever. And any child that might spring from this coupling would be better off living on an estate, somewhere, hidden away in shame, than having him for a legitimate father.

How could she maintain she loved him? She didn't know the meaning of the word.

He watched her pour a drink and tip it down her throat in one go, with a kind of reckless desperation.

He'd done that to her. Not one hour ago, she'd been sweetly purring, anticipating the pleasure he'd promised her, and now she was all stiff and wary again.

Just because he'd suggested they marry.

She was staring into the empty glass now, as though searching for an answer that eluded her.

If only he could be her answer. But she'd been completely honest with him, right from the start. He could understand, really, why she'd refused his proposal. And it wasn't only because of who he was. It was because of who she was. Who she wanted to be.

She wanted to be free. She'd told him she hadn't spent four Seasons avoiding marriage, only to surrender now, when freedom, total freedom, was finally within her grasp. If he persisted in speaking of it, or took some step to force her to comply with his will, for the sake of a child that might not even have been conceived, he'd feel as if he was slamming the prison door shut on her.

It was probably only because he'd said he wasn't the marrying kind that she'd trusted him to become her lover. Maybe giving him her virginity was one more step she'd needed to take, to make sure no other man could shackle her with legal ties.

Maybe he should look on all this as a tremendous honour.

Maybe— Oh, to hell with it. He didn't know what to think. He just hurt so much he wanted to howl with pain.

For Sarah had become his lodestar. His anchor. His every single blessed thing in life that was worth hanging on to. If she didn't want him the way he wanted her, then...

He groaned. God really must want to punish him. He'd spared him eternal damnation only to cast him into a living hell. The hell of falling in love with a woman so elusive she might just as well have been an angel.

Sarah stared down into her wine glass, unable to so much as look at Tom, or the way he was lying there with his eyes screwed shut, as though he couldn't bear to look at her.

How had it all gone so wrong? He did still love her,

didn't he? A chill snaked down her spine, even though the room was as hot as an oven.

She went back to the bed. And found she couldn't just climb in next to him and snuggle into his side. Not while there was all this anger, and hurt, and confusion swirling between them.

'Tom?' She perched on the bedside chair, twirling the glass between her fingers. 'You aren't angry with me, are you?'

He flung his arm to one side and turned to look at her through dulled eyes. 'With you? No,' he said wearily. 'Only with myself.'

With himself? For proposing? For losing control so that he felt he had to propose?

'Please don't be,' she said in a small, rather tremulous voice. 'Don't let anger and regrets spoil this.'

A look of contrition flickered across his face.

He sat up. Reached for her face. Cupped her cheek.

'Forgive me. I have spoiled it already, haven't I? By bringing the spectre of marriage into our bed. Let's forget it, shall we?'

A spectre? She flinched away from his caress. He thought of marriage as something deathly? Then she'd been right to refuse his proposal. She didn't want a husband who looked on marriage as a grisly fate.

Heaven alone knew what she might have said had not someone knocked on the door.

His gaze roamed her body, her tousled hair, in a way that made her feel very conscious of what they'd just been doing together. That made her feel like a...well, a fallen woman.

Well, that was exactly what she was. What she would always be now she'd made him retract his proposal. And she'd better get used to people looking at her like that. With a toss of her head, she marched across the room and flung open the door.

'Yes?'

Standing in the corridor was Robbins. With a letter in his hand.

Looking more than usually grim.

The cold pool in her stomach froze into a solid lump.

'Justin,' she whispered, wrapping her arms round her forebodingly chilled midriff. Something terrible had happened. She could feel it.

Felt as though she deserved it.

Chapter Fourteen

'Is it Justin?' she finally managed to ask. 'What has happened? He hasn't…'

'No, miss, he's on the mend,' said Robbins as she snatched the missive from his fist and tore it open.

The shock of fearing the worst made her instinctively head for the nearest chair and sit down on it. A wave of giddiness assailed her even after she'd scanned the letter that was penned in Mary Endacott's neat, precise hand. Because even though Mary had assured her that Justin was well enough to do without her, she'd ended the letter by wishing her well in the future, just as though they were never going to see each other again.

'What did he do to her to make her leave?' Sarah blinked up at Robbins in bewilderment. 'After all Mary did for him, too.'

'Couldn't rightly say, miss,' said Robbins.

'Won't say, you mean,' Sarah muttered. The man must know why Mary, who had loved Justin enough to go searching for him in the hell that was the aftermath of battle, was leaving him now she knew he was out of danger. But he was loyal to Justin, so Tom had said. So loyal he wasn't going to publish Justin's idiocy abroad.

'Don't know as how this,' said Robbins scathingly, 'is going to affect him, when he finds out.'

He'd come in, shut the door behind him and eyed first the disordered state of the bed, then Tom's insolently lounging nudity and finally her own *déshabillé*.

'Well, it's only what he's been accusing us of getting up to all week,' she retorted.

Tom covered his face with his hands. And groaned.

Which just went to confirm her suspicion that he'd only asked her to marry him because of what others were going to think, not because of what he felt for her at all.

Sarah glared from one to the other. 'No need to worry,' she said to them both. 'Now that Justin is well enough to survive a visit from me, I will come and make a clean breast of it.'

'No! If anyone goes to tell him it should be me,' said Tom.

'It sure as hell ain't going to be me,' muttered Robbins darkly. 'I'll just tell him you will come to see him then, shall I?'

'Yes,' said Sarah.

'No,' said Tom at exactly the same time.

As they squared up to each other, Robbins sighed.

'The note weren't from *him* anyhow. Nor I needn't tell him I've been here. No need to tell him anything at all.'

'Just so. Thank you, Robbins,' said Tom, without taking his eyes off Sarah. 'We need to discuss just how to break it to him that...'

Sarah lifted her chin, though her cheeks went so hot she was sure they must have turned scarlet.

Robbins beat a hasty retreat.

'I'm not afraid of Justin, if you are!'

'It's not a question of being afraid, Sarah. Or not the

way you think.' Tom flung aside the sheet and stalked, naked, across the room to take hold of her shoulders.

'It's just that, once we own up to Colonel Randall that we have become lovers, he is bound to put a stop to it. One way or another.' He'd either split them up altogether, or force them into marriage somehow. Neither of which things were what Sarah truly wanted.

'Sarah, I know you have been anxious about his health. I know you wish to go and see with your own eyes that he is recovering, but, please, I beg of you, don't go right now. Leave it until morning. So we can have tonight. Just one night together, that's all I'm asking.'

One night as lovers who'd chosen each other. Lovers who hadn't been coerced in any way, by anyone or anything but the feelings they had for each other.

Her heart leapt. He still wanted her!

Of course. It wasn't *all* about duty and appearances, or he wouldn't have made love to her in the first place. She'd only slid into that maelstrom of doubt and fear because it was so hard to believe anyone could really love her, after a lifetime of accepting her unimportance in anyone's life.

She bowed her head and rested it on his chest. Tom was the only person—apart from Gideon—who had never made her feel like a duty, or an encumbrance. He might only be asking her for one more night together, but after all, one night was more than anyone else had ever begged her for.

'As your lover,' she said. Marriage was a step too far, for either of them. But hadn't they both kept saying that they should seize the moment? To just live in the present?

'My lover,' he grated. Then closed his arms round her

and held her so tightly she could feel his heart hammering against her cheek.

She bit down on her lower lip. If she'd been more like other women, she would be his fiancée now, not his lover. They could be looking forward to a lifetime together, not just one night. If only she hadn't been so afraid she'd end up like her mother she'd refused his proposal in such terms he'd admitted he hadn't really meant it.

Fortunately the Latymor pride rushed to her rescue. The pride that would never let anyone suspect they'd hurt you. The pride that enabled her to lift her head and give him a saucy smile. 'Well, if one night is all we have, we'd better make the most of it.' Laying the palm of her hand in the centre of his chest, she pushed him towards the bed. 'You are trembling,' she said, tilting her head to one side. 'Does this mean you are not up to the task in hand?'

He sat down heavily, and pulled her on to his lap. Buried his face in her neck. Breathed her in deeply, though tremors kept on running through his magnificently muscled body.

'It means,' he said, at length, 'that I can't believe this is happening. Am I dreaming? Am I in a fever?'

She laid her hand on his forehead. Then placed a kiss where her hand had been.

'This is real, Tom. You are not dreaming. You have no fever.'

'You have really just agreed to postpone visiting your brother, to spend a night in my bed?'

'I really have. And we have all night.' She tiptoed her fingers along his shoulder, then slid them down his beautifully sculpted arm.

His eyes took on a slumberous quality. 'Up to the task, indeed.' he huffed. 'Did I disappoint you last time?'

She pretended to think. Then shrugged. 'I have nothing with which to compare it, as you very well know. So how can I possibly judge?'

For the first time since they'd been intimate, the frown melted from his brow. His mouth curved into a wicked smile. His rakish smile.

'Do I detect a challenge?'

She shrugged with feigned insouciance, though her heart was beating a rapid tattoo.

'Well, I'm always up for a challenge.'

'Ooh,' she murmured with approval, glancing down at his lap. 'Indeed you are.'

'You will have plenty to compare that first time with, before this night is through,' he promised her. 'It will be a night you will never forget.' If she wouldn't marry him, if she only saw him the way other society women did, as fit for a night of pleasure but no more, then he was going to make sure that she would never know pleasure like the pleasure he was going to give her, tonight.

No other man would ever measure up.

Through the gathering shadows of evening, and into the moonlight, he exerted all his strength, and all his considerable expertise, into living up to his vow. He woke her, time and time again throughout the night, sometimes to pleasure her, sometimes to feed her or bring her drinks to replenish her strength.

When she woke the next morning she ached in the most unusual places, but not in a bad way.

On the contrary, she felt a pleasurable lassitude throughout her whole body. For the first time in her life, she was tempted to yield to the heaviness weighing down

her limbs. She had never lain in bed late of a morning.
Even if she'd been dancing all night at a ball, she would
be out in the stables, getting her horse saddled before
anyone else in the house was stirring.

But after one night of Tom's ministrations, she felt
completely undone. If she wasn't so determined to face
Justin, she would have rolled over and gone back to
sleep.

Instead, she yawned and stretched like a cat.

'You are awake?'

She opened her eyes, turned her head on the pillow
and found Tom gazing across at her. He had a lock of her
hair twined round his fist. But he held it so gently she
hadn't even noticed.

'I think the church bells must have woken me,' she
said.

It was Sunday. Exactly one week since she had fled
Antwerp, and the respectable safety she'd known all her
life, to come searching for Gideon. One week that had
changed her into a different person. Gone for ever was
the self-effacing, eager-to-please girl who was scared of
men, of passion, of life itself.

'I should be thinking of going to church,' she mused.
'I missed going last week. But I cannot possibly take
communion.'

'Because you've sinned?'

'Because I can't pretend to repent. Because I'm not
sorry. Not about the time I've had with you, at least. And
I don't think you can make a partial repentance, can you?
Oh, dear.' She sniffed. 'I promised myself I wouldn't cry.
No, don't hug me,' she said, scooting out of his reach and
scrambling out of bed. 'And don't look at me like that.
As though you regret what we did.'

'It isn't that. I just can't bear to think I've made you cry.'

'You haven't,' she said, lifting her chin. 'And you won't. No, don't go being all sympathetic,' she said, stepping further away when he made as though to reach for her again. 'I need to be strong, now, to face Justin. And if you encourage me to lean on you I shall probably go to pieces altogether.'

'You are going to see him, then.' Tom sank back into the pillows, his face drawn.

'Yes. I have to, don't you see? All my life, I've done my best to avoid scenes. I've never let anyone know what I really think, or feel. I've just gone along with what they told me I must do, behaved the way they said I must, so that they would leave me be. My house was one long battleground, growing up. If it wasn't Mama and Papa at daggers drawn, it was Gideon getting into a scrape, or Harriet spouting radical principles. I took delight in being the good girl. It was the only thing about me that was of any comfort to Mama.' She shook her head. 'But now it's time to take a stand. To face Justin. To face life squarely, instead of getting my own way by stealth. And I shan't be able to do it if I'm breaking my heart over you.'

He frowned. 'Breaking your heart?'

'Oh, Tom. Don't you know how much I love you?' Good heavens. Where had her Latymor pride gone this morning? Although, if she was determined to start being honest and forthright with everyone, then where better to start than with the man who'd become the most important person in her life?

'I'm sorry if you don't like it, but I really wish we could have had more than one night. If only there was some way we could be together for longer. If only we…'

She lifted her chin, scurried back to the bed, stooped over and kissed him swiftly on the forehead.

'Even marriage might not be too high a price to pay.'

Having lobbed that grenade at him she went out, presumably to get washed and dressed. Leaving him reeling in shock.

What was all that about him not liking it? Hearing her say she wished they could have one more night made him want to crow with sheer joy.

And when she'd said marriage might not be too high a price to pay?

He sat bolt upright.

There was a chance, then. A slim chance, but a chance, none the less, of persuading her that marriage wouldn't be any kind of penance at all. If only she'd consent, he'd spend his *whole life* making her feel wanted. Treasured.

When she came back…

Hell. By the time she came back, Ramrod Randall would have talked sense back into her.

He flung himself back on to the pillows again, ready to howl with despair.

'Tom?' Sarah poked her head round the door, twisting her hair up out of the way. 'You will still be here when I get back, won't you? You won't go doing anything stupid like trying to report for duty again. Not until I've had a chance to speak to Justin first. Explain that all this has been my fault. I don't want him to punish you. Strip you of your rank or have you cashiered out of the regiment or anything horrid like that. I know that your career is all you have.'

'Don't do anything out of fear for my career, Sarah,' he growled. How many women would have thought of that?

At a time like this, most women would surely be fretting about their own reputation. Their own fate.

But not his Sarah.

'And don't go pleading for mercy on my behalf,' he growled. 'You mustn't worry that Randall might destroy me. He can't. There are always other avenues for a man like me.' He smiled grimly. There were always revolutions going on in distant corners of the world, where men with his experience, his skills, could earn their living. Perhaps not honourably. But if he lost Sarah, he didn't think he'd care about honour any more.

He frowned. *Any more?* Where had that stray thought come from? When had he ever cared about his honour, or what anyone else thought about him? Hadn't he been perversely proud of being picked to hold command in a unit that was so disreputable they'd come to be known as the Rogues?

And yet, somehow, the thought of selling his skills to a foreign power suddenly felt wrong. As though he would be letting Sarah down. As though he would be staining this time for her. If she ever heard news of him, he wouldn't want to have become the kind of man she would regret having taken as her first lover.

Hell's teeth! He was going to have to spend the rest of his life proving he'd been worthy of spending last night in her arms, whether he ever saw her again or not. Making love with her had changed everything. He'd never be the same man again.

She came fully into the room then, though a little hesitantly.

'How do I look?'

She was wearing the least favourite of her three gowns.

It had a high neck and a lot of unnecessary frills. It made her look prim. Over it she'd pulled on her new black coat.

When Sarah saw his expression, her own face fell.

'I really should have bought a black bonnet, as well.' She sighed, pulling on her blue one and deftly tying the ribbons. 'And as for this stupid parasol,' she said, picking it up and looking at it in a puzzled fashion, 'it is of no earthly use, yet I wouldn't feel properly attired for church without it. I don't know why I didn't pick up a black one while I was buying my gloves,' she said, drawing them on.

'Because you have been thinking about things that are more important than your appearance?'

'Sacrilege!' She shot him a brave smile, but didn't approach the bed. 'If Gussie could hear you now, she would rap your knuckles with her fan. Which would, I assure you, complement *her* outfit to a nicety.'

'You don't really care, though, do you? Not deep down?'

She cocked her head to one side. 'Actually, no. I don't. I have found it liberating, not having to consider every single aspect of my dress. Or changing three or four times a day.' She clapped a hand to her mouth. 'Don't tell anyone, will you? That I don't give a fig for my clothes? That, I assure you, would scandalise the *ton* almost as much as discovering that I'd taken a lover.'

Her face wavered. She pressed her lips together as though she was trying to keep them from trembling.

'I am going now, Tom. Wish me luck.'

'I don't think you need luck, Sarah. You are equal to anything.'

'Oh, Tom, don't. Don't say such things. You will make me cry.'

'I shan't apologise. You *are* equal to anything. Even attending service at the Chapel Royal in a mismatched outfit.'

She laughed. Dabbed at her eyes with a handkerchief she pulled out of a little pale-blue reticule and hurried from the room without looking back.

Chapter Fifteen

How much difference a week made. The Sarah of one week ago would have been quaking in her shoes at the prospect of bearding Justin in his den. In fact, she reflected as she knocked on the door of the house in the Rue Ducale where he was staying, she wouldn't have come here at all. She would have stayed hidden away with Tom, hoping that by the time Justin was well enough to get up and come round, something would have happened to avert disaster.

She wasn't even all that nervous. In fact, if anything, she was looking forward to clearing the air.

Robbins said nothing as he showed her to Justin's room. Before she went in, however, she took a large white handkerchief from her reticule and extended it before her, waving it like a flag.

Justin's grim expression didn't falter.

'I hope that ridiculous display signals your unconditional surrender,' he said, in a voice that was so reedy she could barely make out the words.

'Not a bit of it,' she replied firmly, even though his attempt to both breathe, and speak, was clearly something of a struggle. She went across to the bed in which he sat propped against a bank of such snowy-white pillows they made his complexion looked positively grey. No wonder Robbins had been so angry with her.

'I was given to understand that even the bitterest enemies,' she said sadly, 'could conduct negotiations under the flag of truce, though.'

'I am not your enemy, Sarah.' He drew another breath. 'I have your best interests at heart.'

'Yes, well—' she sighed, settling herself on a chair at his bedside '—that is a matter of opinion.'

'No such thing!'

'Justin, don't get yourself into a pucker,' she said, pulling off her gloves with as much nonchalance as she could muster, given the shock his weakened appearance had given her. 'I am aware you *think* you have my best interests at heart. The only trouble is that, like everyone else in my family, you have no real idea what that would be.'

'It most certainly isn't that...' His lip curled. 'That libertine Bartlett.'

'Now, there we shall have to disagree. However—' she raised one hand to stop him when he drew in a sharp breath to remonstrate with her '—I didn't come here to talk about Tom. I know that my taking up with him has upset you and for that I am sorry. Most dreadfully sorry that hearing about our association caused you to become so dangerously ill. Oh, Justin, I never dreamed anything I did could cause you any harm.'

'I know that. But—'

'No. Let us speak no more of it, not today. Please, Justin, if you love me. I know you are angry with me for all sorts of reasons, but when I heard that Gideon had died,

I—' She sucked in a short, sharp breath, blinking rapidly a couple of times in order to stop the tears before they could gain hold.

Justin reached out his hand, his gaunt face softening just a touch.

'You foolish child,' he growled. 'What on earth possessed you to leave the safety of Antwerp? And at such a time. Gussie must be out of her mind with worry.'

'No, oh, no.' She took the hand he offered and held it firmly. 'I have been writing to Blanchards, from the very first, with very carefully worded reports of what I have been doing. And you know how he dotes on Gussie. There is no way he would have let her know I was in any sort of scrape, even if he suspected it.'

'You really are the most cunning creature.' He frowned. 'I would never have suspected you of such duplicity. Or of such reckless behaviour. Gideon was always the reckless twin.'

She smiled at him impishly. 'You should have known that, as a member of the Latymor family, I had it within me to act in the most reprehensible, reckless manner. It was just that, until they told me that Gideon had died, I never had sufficient motive to step beyond the bounds of what is considered proper. I wasn't really interested in anything but what Gideon was doing. I lived for his letters, or for him to come and tell me what he had been doing. It was as if,' she pondered out loud, 'he was the one who went out and lived life for both of us.'

'But what, precisely, did you think you could achieve by coming to Brussels?'

'I don't know.' Her voice wavered. 'It was just that I couldn't believe Gideon was dead. It was too dreadful. He *was* my life. Without him...' She shook her head. 'I don't expect you to understand, but I felt I should have known if what they said was true. We always had this connection, you see. I was sure that if it had been broken, by death, I would have been aware.'

When she saw his lips twist cynically, she added hastily, 'And then again, there was the Duke of Brunswick.'

'The Duke of—?'

'Brunswick. They brought his body to Antwerp. Laid it out in the inn for everyone to see. So I couldn't understand why they hadn't brought Gideon, too. But you all spent so much time telling me not to bother my head about things, whenever I used to ask questions you didn't want to hear, that I got out of the habit of trying. I could see Blanchards patting me on the head, so to speak, and telling me not to make a fuss, because he didn't want Gussie upset. And of course, it would have been unforgivable to have gone and wept all over Gussie and plagued her with all my worries while her own health is so uncertain. So there was nobody. I had nobody. But then I thought *you* would be bound to know the truth. Or would be able to find it out for me. So I came looking for you. Only when I got here nobody knew where you were, either.'

'Did you really have to come right out to the battlefield to look for me, though?'

'No.' She sighed. 'As usual, my presence was pointless. Mary already had the search well in hand.'

His face went carefully blank.

'She couldn't rest until she'd discovered whether you lived or died, you know. Because she loves you as much as I love—loved Gideon.' He turned his face away at that. But she couldn't let the matter rest. Justin had behaved like an idiot where Mary was concerned. She had to at least try to make him see what he'd lost.

'Of course, she is a far better, more sensible woman than I. She even went inside the barn that they told us was full of dead bodies, refusing to believe their report of your death. Though I wasn't brave enough to go in with her. It made me feel so ill that I went over the wall into the orchard to be sick in private. That was the moment when it occurred to me that you might be trying to protect me from distress. If Gideon had been as mangled as some of the poor wretches I saw lying all over the fields, you wouldn't have wanted me to see him like that. For my last memory of him to be so gruesome. It hit me, when I couldn't even bear the thought of seeing *you* dead, or wounded. And we've never been exactly close, have we?'

He looked at her again. 'So you do accept that I act in your best interest.'

She sighed. 'I accept that you *try* to, yes. But as I said, I haven't come here to argue with you. Justin, Tom told me that you were with Gideon, at the end. Will you... will you tell me...?'

If she'd thought he looked ill before, that question made him look positively haggard.

'I know,' she added, 'you cannot tell me all, but I do want to hear as much of the truth as you think I can bear.'

'I can tell you what he wanted you to know,' he replied with a nod. 'His last thoughts were of you. *Tell Sarah I died well, Justin,* were his last words.'

'Oh!' She'd promised herself she wouldn't cry. But discovering that her twin had sent her a message, with his dying breath, was more than her resolve could stand. She reached for the handkerchief she'd brought to use as a flag of truce and held it to her face.

'I promised him,' said Justin more gently, 'that you would know you could be very proud of him.'

'Could I?' She looked up, her stomach lurching with hope and dread and grief. 'I have been so afraid that he threw himself away doing something foolhardy. I'd been so worried about him, in the days before the Duchess of Richmond's ball. I always know when he is planning some mischief and I had this awful presentiment that he was about to do something even worse than usual.'

Justin looked sceptical, but he only said, 'He died bravely. He died well.'

'Can—?' She hiccupped. 'Can you tell me…how?'

He frowned. For a moment she thought he was going to fob her off with the usual excuse of her not needing to trouble her empty little head with the ugly realities that should more properly be taken care of by men.

But then he surprised her by saying, 'Major Sheffield's unit got cut off by a party of French chasseurs. When I came across them, they were penned into a town square.' He paused to draw in a couple of breaths. But she didn't fill the silence with questions. She could see he was gathering his strength to tell her the tale in his own way.

'Bennington Ffog's troop,' he continued, 'were holding off the French, while Lieutenant Rawlins was attempting to get the Rogues to turn the guns round so they could make their escape. Gideon saw him struggling to control the men. They'd lost heart when Major Sheffield was killed. Gideon rallied the Rogues, got the guns turned and then stood and fought a rearguard action. I…' He paused again. There was something in his face that told Sarah he was right back in that town square all over again. With what looked like an effort, he continued.

'For a while, Gideon and I fought side by side, blocking the street so the French couldn't pursue the guns and their crews. We fought until reinforcements came. But by then it was too late for your twin. He was badly hurt.'

'Cavalry sabres,' she said in the ghost of a whisper. 'I've seen what they can do.'

'Yes. I'm sorry. Though if it helps, he didn't take long in dying. I tried to stop the bleeding, but...' He stopped when she gave a choked cry and buried her face in the handkerchief again.

'Sorry, that was tactless of me. I just wanted you to know he didn't suffer for long.'

'Thank you,' she whispered. 'I have been tortured by the thought of him lying out there, slowly dying, like so many of them did. Alone and in pain.'

'He died in my arms. He died bravely. Saving my men, and the guns, to fight the next day. The day we defeated Bonaparte once and for all. He won't come back to tear Europe to pieces again, Sarah. And the way Gideon died made a contribution to that outcome.'

'Thank you,' she said once she'd regained command of her voice. 'For not spinning me some sugary confection to make my grief easier to swallow. For—' She sat up straight, and gave him a searching look. 'You say he actually had command of your men? If only for a short time?'

He nodded.

'Oh, Justin, if only you knew what that would have meant to him.'

'I think I did. We had a chance to speak a little, at the very end. He told me that he wanted me to return to Chalfont and manage the estates. That Mother is struggling, but won't say anything. He even stole the sword, thinking that without it, I wouldn't go into battle—'

'Oh! So *that* was it. I wondered... He'd been acting so very...so very...well, the way he always did when he was planning some mischief.' Thoughts were teeming, nineteen to the dozen, through her brain. 'Yes, of course,' she breathed. 'He saw the chance to prove he could be as good an officer as you. Of course, he had to *steal* the Latymor Luck so that he could wear it into battle.' She shook her head. 'And you blamed Mary for taking it. I heard you. Oh, Justin, how could you?'

'Do you think I don't know what a terrible mistake I made?'

'You made another very grave error, too. About the night of the Duchess of Richmond's Ball. It was entirely my doing that Mary was there. She didn't want to go, you know. I positively compelled her to go with me. I was absolutely determined to see Gideon. And Gussie was too ill to go. So I went straight round to Mary, spinning her such a tale that she felt she had no choice but to go with me. And then you had the gall to accuse her of—what was it?—*ingratiating* herself with your sister?'

Justin's lips firmed as though he was biting back a pithy retort. But before he could utter it, Sarah plunged on.

'It was the very opposite. I tried and tried to make friends with her, but she simply wasn't interested. You were the only Latymor she cared about. Even after you were so beastly to her that night she still came to the battlefield to find you. And wouldn't let anyone else nurse you back to health. What I should like to know,' she said with reproof, 'is what, exactly, you have done now, to drive her away? Surely you know that you'll never find anyone who loves you as much as she does?'

'I thought you came here under a flag of truce. I

thought we were not going to argue about our private affairs.'

'It is not a private *affair*, what you have with Mary. You should marry her.'

'As you plan to marry Bartlett?' His lip curled scornfully. 'The man is a rake. A scoundrel. You know I didn't want you to so much as speak to him, let alone marry him!'

'I didn't say I was going to marry him. But I'm most certainly not marrying anyone else. Not after what—' she lifted her chin, and though her cheeks felt hot, she made sure to look her brother straight in the eye '—not after what we have been to each other.'

'You don't know what you are saying,' he spluttered. 'You cannot ruin your whole life because of one stupid, mad interlude.'

She glared at him. 'Tom has not ruined my life. I will always be grateful to him for what he's shown me this week.'

When Justin looked as though he was about to explode, she laid a restraining hand on his shoulder. 'And I don't mean *that*. Please, try to understand. I told you that I only ever lived through Gideon, before. And, well, it is as if, since he has died, I have started living my own life, at last. This week, for the first time, I have started to ask what I want from life. I've learned more about myself, of what I'm capable of, of what I truly think, than I have in the whole of the preceding twenty-two years, when I was content to just sit at home, like Rapunzel in her tower, watching life through her window.'

'Don't try making Bartlett out to be some prince, climbing up to your turret and setting you free. This is no fairy tale, Sarah.'

'No. It is my life. And I know full well that Tom is just a man. You aren't really listening, are you? You are fixated on Tom.'

'Fixated on *Bartlett*?' He gave her an indignant look. 'Nothing of the kind.'

'Good. Then you do accept that it was Gideon dying that shocked me out of my stupor.'

'I know it was certainly a shock to you, yes,' he conceded. 'But—'

'But nursing Tom,' she interrupted, 'living with him, a life so very different from anything I've ever experienced before, has opened my eyes. I know what I want now.'

'I dare say he can make any woman want *that*.'

'I dare say he can,' she replied loftily. 'But that isn't what I meant. When he asked me to marry him—'

'Do you honestly expect me to give him my permission? And don't forget I have control of your inheritance. Let's see how much he wants to marry you without it.'

'You would cut me off without a penny if I married Tom without your permission? Ooh, you…you…' If he wasn't so ill she would have shaken him. 'You think I'm hen-witted enough to accept a proposal from a rake?' She got to her feet. 'And so unattractive that he wouldn't want me without my fortune?'

'Wait. You haven't accepted his proposal?'

'You can keep my money, Justin,' she cried, ignoring the relief washing the tension from his face when she'd said she'd turned Tom's proposal down. 'I don't need or want it. I can earn my keep.' She could. Surely she could. Somehow. After all, Mary did. And it would mean she wouldn't be dependent on any man, any more, not even to manage her fortune. She really would be able to take control of her life.

'I could become a teacher.'

'Have some sense, Sarah,' he said, with that all-too-familiar tone of exasperation. 'No school would hire a woman who's been ruined and put her in charge of impressionable girls.'

She flinched. She wasn't used to being spoken to like that any longer. Tom never treated her as though she was an idiot. If she'd told *him* she would be a teacher, he would probably…

'Now sit down,' said Justin sternly. 'And calm down. We don't need to fall out, not if you aren't going to marry Major Bartlett.'

'I don't see why you are so against him,' she said huffily, though she did sit down again. Justin had gone alarmingly pale when she'd started talking about marrying Tom and she really didn't want him to suffer another relapse on her account.

'He isn't a bit like Papa, you know. He would never treat me the way Papa treated Mama. Because Papa never pretended to love Mama, not even at the start, did he? It was one of those dynastic unions, arranged by our grandparents, wasn't it? And Tom does love me.'

'Not the way a gentleman should love his wife. Or he wouldn't have ruined you. The man's a rake and a scoundrel.'

'I cannot see that Tom's behaviour has been any worse than yours,' she retorted. 'Or Gideon's. There is a vast difference between a single man enjoying his freedoms, and a married one breaking his vows, is there not?'

'You really think he'd be able to stick to his vows? A man like that?'

'I don't know,' she admitted ruefully. 'But one thing I have learned is that not all men are like our father. Some men do truly fall in love with their wives. And cherish them. You only have to look at the way Blanchards is with Gussie. Or consider how happy Harriet is with Graveney. And she always swore she wouldn't marry, either.'

'Either?'

'That's right, Justin. I swore I wouldn't end up like Mama, chained to a man who treated me with less consideration than his horse or his hounds. In fact—' she gave him a straight look '—I've come to the conclusion it would be much better to be a man's mistress than his wife. And only stay with him as long as he treated me well.'

'No, it wouldn't! Look…' He struggled with himself, as though determined to keep his temper in check. 'I suppose I can understand your aversion to marriage. I have my own reservations, after all. Because of Father. I am his son and I would never be sure…' He grimaced.

'You are not a bit like Papa, Justin. Not in that way.' She stretched out her hand and laid it, briefly, against his gaunt cheek. 'You wouldn't treat Mary badly. You are not that kind of man. So marrying her wouldn't be a disaster. Thank you, Justin.'

'What for?' He eyed her with misgiving.

'For helping me to reach a decision.'

'I don't like the look in your eye. Dear lord, you've never looked more like your twin when he was plotting some mischief.'

She smiled. 'Thank you.'

'It wasn't meant to be a compliment.'

'I know. But you see, when I came here, I didn't know what to do about Tom. And now I do.'

'You agree to leave him? And return to Antwerp?'

'No. I'm not ready to leave him. I love him, you see.' To soften the blow, she bent to kiss his cheek.

'He cannot marry you without my permission,' growled Justin. 'As his commanding officer.'

'He may not want to. As you've taken such pains to point out, marriage isn't for every man.' She stuffed her handkerchief back into her reticule. 'So I shall ask if I can stay with him, on terms he can accept.'

'As his mistress, do you mean? Sarah, you cannot possibly—'

'Well, I'm probably, sort of, his mistress already,' she mused. 'I was certainly ruined the moment his men laid him in my bed, in the eyes of society. And I've been with him for a whole week since then.'

He drew a rasping breath with which to voice a protest.

'I don't think we should discuss this any more,' she cut in. 'I don't wish to make you unwell. And your face is going a most unhealthy shade of puce.'

'Is that surprising? At least Major Bartlett had the decency to propose. Whereas you—'

'I was rash enough to turn him down. I was afraid of marriage then. And worried he wasn't offering because he loved me, but out of guilt.'

'That makes no difference. At least he didn't attempt to get away with sullying your reputation without offering to pay the penalty.'

'Interesting to hear you think of marriage as the price you have to pay for getting a woman into bed. Is that why Mary has left you?'

'We are not talking of me, but of you and that b— Bartlett!'

'We aren't talking about anything, any longer,' she said serenely, getting to her feet. 'Or I shall be late for church.'

* * *

She had been worried about going to church, but she now felt as though she could use a period of reflection before returning to Tom. Her conversation with Justin had made her look at certain aspects of her past in a new light and she wanted to mull over them before dealing with her future.

It hadn't been until Justin had challenged her behaviour, and her motive for coming to Brussels, that she'd seen that while Gideon had lived, she really had behaved like a sort of modern-day Rapunzel, locked up in a tower. A tower that was entirely of her own making. She'd seized on the story their nurse had spun, about how she and Gideon were but one soul, inhabiting two bodies, and used it as an excuse for not struggling to break free of the strictures her parents had placed on her, because she was merely a girl. It hadn't seemed worth the bother of enduring a scene, such as the ones Harriet had caused when she came back from school, to get her own way, when she could tell herself that in some sort of mystical way, she was sharing Gideon's adventures so long as he told her about them.

But now he was gone. He couldn't do all the living for both of them. It was—it was her turn.

If this was Gideon, in love for the first time in his life, would he let fear of potential disaster stop him? No. Why, he hadn't even hesitated to steal the sword, go into battle and lead Justin's men, to prove what he was worth.

He'd always believed life was for living.

And she was in love. Deeply in love with Tom. And just because they both had reservations about marriage, that didn't mean they couldn't be together, in a way that suited them both, did it?

She hesitated on the church steps, noting that only a few people had started arriving. There was just time to go to the vault and visit her brother before the service commenced.

'Gideon,' she whispered, depressed by the gloomy silence that pervaded the vault. 'Gideon.' She reached out and lay one black-gloved hand on his coffin.

She closed her eyes and pictured him stealing the Latymor Luck. Strapping it on to his sword-belt. Taking control of Justin's men, even if it was only for half an hour. Fighting side by side with the big brother he'd alternately adored, and emulated, and chafed against, all his life. Then finally confronting Justin with his choices. *Eldest sons should stay at home, run the estate and set up their nursery,* he'd said, oh, often and often! *It's for the younger sons to go out and become heroes. He has to have it all, damn him! Well, I'll show him, Sarah. You see if I don't.*

Well, he'd shown Justin, right enough. And died in the process.

'Oh, Gideon,' she sobbed. 'Why did you have to prove yourself to him? Why couldn't just being you be enough?'

She was glad, of course, that he hadn't died alone, or in some terribly painful, lingering way, or as the result of some stupid blunder.

But it didn't change the fact that he was still dead.

Sealed inside this coffin. Silenced for ever.

Worse. He'd stolen the Latymor Luck without telling her what he meant to do. And she hadn't known. Hadn't guessed. That stark truth snapped the last frayed thread linking them together.

At the exact moment that the bells began tolling to warn churchgoers that the service was about to start.

She stumbled to her feet, dabbed at her eyes and blew her nose one more time.

And went to sit through a service which was going to be of no solace to her at all.

She wanted Tom. She wanted to run to him and pour her woes into his ears, and have him soothe her with his loving words. Feel the strength of his arms holding her close to his heart.

Because when he held her, she wouldn't feel as if she was all alone in the world any longer.

She raised her head, staring sightlessly straight ahead as the words of the service washed right over her. Talking to Justin had helped her to get some things clear in her mind. She loved Tom. She did. Not just because he was handsome and charming, either. He'd become her friend. Her confidant. The one person she could trust with the secrets of her heart. The man she wanted to live with, grow old with, even have children with.

Even when he'd first warned her he might have got her with child, she hadn't minded. She'd pictured herself bringing up a sturdy little boy with green eyes like Tom's and a thatch of blond hair like hers. And loving him so much it wouldn't matter if his father wasn't around. She would have been all the child needed.

Except—her breath hitched in her throat at a sudden image of Gideon, hanging out of a tree branch, holding out his hand to help her climb up.

If she denied her child a legal father, then it couldn't have any brothers or sisters.

It would grow up alone.

It was all very well thinking she could endure scandal, if it meant she could stay with Tom. But was it fair to condemn her child to a lifetime of loneliness, as well?

She'd have to talk to Tom about marriage, again. In the cool light of day, not in the heat of passion, while he was weltering in guilt and she was reacting from a bone-deep habit of avoiding it at all costs.

She was still a little afraid that he held the same view as Justin—that marriage was the price a man had to pay for taking his pleasures unwisely. But even if that was so, even if he didn't love her the way she loved him now, she was going to have to tell him how she felt. She was going to have to face him, and tell him exactly what she wanted, and why.

And then deal with the consequences like a…like a…

She sat up straighter, and squared her shoulders.

Like a Latymor.

Chapter Sixteen

Tom soon grew tired of alternately pacing and looking out of the window. So he dragged a chair to a vantage point from where he could spot Sarah the moment she turned into the street.

His heart leapt at his first sight of her. Though he couldn't tell anything about her mood from the way she was walking. She might have been any society miss, returning demurely home from church.

Which just went to show how deceptive appearances could be.

'Well?' He fired the question at her the moment she came into their room. 'How did it go?'

'About as well as anyone could expect,' she said with a wry smile as she drew off her gloves.

His heart plunged like a horse refusing a hedge. That little touch of sadness in her brave smile was like an alarm bell, clanging in his head. He wasn't going to like whatever she was about to tell him.

'Justin…well, at least he told me how Gideon died. More or less everything, I think, which was surprising, considering the way he has always brushed me aside before. Oh, not that he was ever actually unkind. It was just that his eyes would always skate over me, as though he had neither the time, nor the patience, to bother with such an insipid little goose.' She smiled wryly as she untied the strings of her bonnet and tossed it carelessly on to a side table.

'And I also managed to speak to Adam after the service, and apologise for what I did to him—or at least,' she corrected herself with a frown, 'the mischief I *tried* to do him yesterday.' She shot him a rueful glance. 'And don't ask me to tell you about it, because I am so deeply ashamed of myself I couldn't bear to repeat it. And by the looks of things, I didn't succeed in my aim, anyway. Though how a man of his calibre has ended up linked to a girl of *that* sort,' she muttered darkly, 'I cannot think.'

His heart was thundering against his breastbone now. 'But what did Colonel Randall say about us? You did talk about us?' He dismissed the cryptic comment about Flint getting tied to some lightskirt. It was what had passed between Sarah and Colonel Randall that concerned him. It had been a risk, letting her go and speak to her brother on her own. Heaven alone knew what arguments the Colonel would have used to induce her to leave him. None of which he could refute, that was the hell of it. Sarah shouldn't have lived on terms of such intimacy with him this week. Let alone actually permitted him to become her lover. If he was her brother, he'd order her to return to Antwerp at once, then do whatever it took to salvage what he could of her reputation.

'Of course I did. Oh, Tom,' she said, before flinging herself on to his chest and wrapping her arms about his waist. He closed his arms round her, hard. Perhaps for the very last time.

'I thought that knowing how Gideon died would help,' she said in a muffled voice, since her face was pressed into his shirtfront. 'And I suppose at least Justin did allay the worst of my fears. But it doesn't really change anything. He's still dead. I don't think I'm ever going to be able to come to terms with that.'

'And why do you think you should? You are always going to feel as if a part of you is missing,' he said, rocking her gently.

'Oh, Tom, I knew you would understand. You always understand,' she said, lifting her head to gaze up at him with her blue eyes full of what looked very much like adoration.

'How is it that you understand, when nobody else does? You don't have a twin. You don't have any family—so how is it that you know what my grief for Gideon is like?'

'Because I know what I will feel like when you leave me,' he grated, past the huge lump that had formed in his throat. 'A part of me will always grieve your loss. There will be a great gaping wound inside me that will never heal. That I will never *want* to heal,' he said fervently. 'Oh, I will wear a smile on my lips so that the world won't know that I'm bleeding inside. I will flirt with women and no doubt, knowing my nature,' he said with a bitter smile, 'I will take fleeting solace in their beds when the loneliness gets too much. But none of them will be you.'

'What are you saying, Tom? Why should I leave you?'

'But—you said you wouldn't marry me.'

'Ah. Well…' She took a deep breath. Turned bright pink. 'Actually, I've changed my mind about that.'

'Have you?' He shook his head, which seemed to be filled with a strange buzzing sensation. 'Are you sure?'

'Yes,' she said firmly. 'If,' she added, looking suddenly very young and vulnerable, 'only if you really do want to. If you really love me. You do love me, don't you Tom?'

'You know I do. I would die for you.'

'Much good that would do me,' she said rather tartly. 'I have no wish for anything but that you should live with me. And,' she added, a bit hesitantly, 'the way you just spoke of what it would be like to live without me gives me hope that you would like it, too.'

'Yes, I would, more than anything.'

'Well, then, I need not be afraid to marry you. Even though you have the reputation of a rake. You wouldn't dream of being unfaithful, or humiliating me by fathering natural children all over the place, would you?'

'Absolutely not!'

She sagged into him with relief. 'Oh, that was so much easier than I'd hoped. I've regretted refusing your proposal ever since the words left my lips.'

'You did?'

'Yes. But you looked so…' She shook her head. 'And I was still so scared, Tom. Or at least, in the habit of being scared of marriage. The refusal came to my mouth without me even thinking about it, really. But when I'd said no, I didn't feel relieved at all, or as though I'd escaped some terrible fate. I just felt as though I'd made the biggest mistake of my life.'

'Why didn't you say so?'

'Oh, Tom…' She sighed up at him. 'It was the way you asked me. As though you were worried about a child, or my reputation. I didn't want to make you marry me for such reasons as those. Marriage is such a big step for both of us to take, we have to go into it for the right reasons.

The kind of reasons that made Harriet marry Graveney, in the end, except without all the books. I want you to love me the way Blanchards loves Gussie—' She gave a swift frown. 'But without all the smothering. I think you do want to marry me for the right reasons, don't you, Tom, or you wouldn't have said all that about no other woman being able to replace me in your heart, even if you did take them to bed, would you?'

'I thought you only wanted to be my mistress. I thought…' He grimaced, swallowed and shook his head.

'I would rather live with you as your mistress than live without you, that is true. But whichever future you choose for us, Tom, I am certainly not going to abandon you to the fate you just spoke to me of. Going around with a brave smile on your face, sleeping with all sorts of women whose names you won't even remember because they won't be me, bleeding inside from a grievous wound.' She clucked her tongue in disapproval. 'So much unnecessary suffering. Besides the guilt you will always bear for breaking my heart.'

'Breaking your heart? No, Sarah, I would die before harming so much as a hair on your head.'

Their eyes held for a moment, and then, on a surge of mutual relief and joy, they kissed.

'There's just one thing you should know,' said Sarah, dragging her lips from his. 'Justin is set against our match. And he's going to cut off my allowance. I don't know if he can stop me from laying claim to the capital when I reach thirty years of age, but I wouldn't be surprised if he doesn't at least try to prevent you from touching one penny of my fortune.'

'Fortune? You have a fortune?'

'Yes. Rather a substantial one. You didn't know?'

'Oh, good God, he's going to think I'm a fortune hunter now on top of everything else.' Tom groaned.

But she began to smile. He hadn't known a thing about it.

'Why are you smiling?'

'Because the thought of my fortune doesn't tempt you. Not one bit. When it is all any of the other suitors got excited about.'

'Well, they were all idiots,' he said gruffly, tightening his arms about her. 'If they couldn't see what a treasure you are,' he added, huffing into the crown of her head.

She hugged him hard.

'Tom? You really do love me, don't you? You don't care about me coming to you without a penny to my name.'

'Well, it won't make any difference to me, will it? I've never had a penny to my name. But you…' He put her away from him a little, so he could look down into her face. 'It's going to be very hard for you, living on my pay. I won't be able to give you any of the things you're used to.'

'You will be giving me things I've never had, though. Like respect. And confidence. And the knowledge that I'm loved, really loved, just as I am.'

'Of course you are.' He cupped her cheek. Gazed into her eyes in such a worshipful manner that she melted with longing.

He kissed her again. With a reverence that made her feel so strong, she could conquer the world.

'You do realise,' he said, after all too brief a time, 'that your brother, as my commanding officer, is not likely to give his permission, don't you? I will have to resign from the British army.'

'Oh…' She pouted. 'Actually, he *did* warn me about

that. But, I wonder…' She glanced up at him through her lashes. 'After the way I threatened to become your mistress if you weren't of a mind to marry me, he might change his mind about that. I should think he will be extremely relieved we intend to make things respectable.'

'Well, that's just where you are out. For one thing, we wouldn't be *respectably* married. The shame of my background would mean you would always be subject to gossip—'

'Pah! Much I care about that.'

He shook his head sadly. 'Tell me, did he look as though he was keen on my marrying you, when you left Lord Randall? Or was he foaming at the mouth and uttering threats of what he'd do when he got his hands on me?'

She looked abashed. 'Well, yes, he *was* very angry whenever I mentioned you, in any capacity. But—'

He shook his head again. 'The only way we are likely to be able to marry is if we elope. Your family may cut you out of their lives, Sarah, for defying them. And I will have to exchange into another regiment. Or even, God forbid, sell my services to some foreign power. And since there has already been one traitor to the crown in the family, we will become notorious, I should think. Could you live like that?' He gripped both her hands in his and looked her straight in the eyes. 'Could you become a disgraced exile from your family, your country? Just so you could be with me?'

She sucked her lower lip between her teeth. 'Are you trying to back out of marrying me, Tom? Is that why you're painting such a bleak picture of our future?'

'No. Goodness, no! But I really would be a rogue,' he bit out, 'of the worst sort, to casually condemn you to such a life. I knew it, the moment I'd proposed. *That* was why I didn't press you,' he said, grasping her shoulders gently. 'Not because I was unwilling, or only proposing out of guilt because I may have made you pregnant, but because I really, truly believed you would be better off without me. I didn't want you to feel trapped and dragged into a future of shame and penury.'

Tears slowly welled up in her eyes. His insides hollowed out. He'd made her see, at last, what the cost of marrying him was going to be. He'd made her face reality. What a foolhardy thing to do! She'd leave him now, for sure.

But then, to his amazement, she flung her arms round his waist again.

'I have lost Gideon.' She sobbed into his chest. 'I absolutely refuse to lose you, too. How could I just walk away, and go back to Chalfont and a life that is no life at all, knowing you are walking around somewhere, smiling bravely, taking other w-women to b-bed? I can't. I can't! And I won't.'

'Then your fate is sealed. For I cannot let you go, Sarah. I cannot break your heart this way.'

No. Instead, the way they would be obliged to live would grind it down, insult by insult. Until the day came when she would look at him with loathing.

He crushed her to his chest and buried his face in her sweet-smelling hair.

At least, until that day came, she would be his.

And even after that, he would always be hers.

He took her to bed. And spent the rest of the day showing her how much he loved her.

And then spent the night, while she slept, watching her. Just watching her beloved face with that sweet, contented look on it, fixing it in his mind against the day when lines of discontent would bracket her mouth and regret would stamp grooves into her forehead.

In the morning, he rose early and went along the passage to the small dressing room, where Gaston shaved him and helped him into his dress uniform.

When he went back to their room, Sarah was sitting up in bed, sipping some hot chocolate, her hair delightfully tousled. Her eyes roved over him appreciatively.

'Tom Bartlett, if I wasn't already in love with you, I declare I would fall for you on the spot. Though—' Her face suddenly fell as comprehension dawned. 'You wouldn't be all dressed up like that if you weren't going out.'

'That's it,' he said, coming to the side of the bed and raising her hand to his lips to kiss it. 'I'm going to visit your brother. Always pays to look one's best when facing a boll— I mean, when about to get a rare trimming.'

'Oh, Tom. Do you want me to come with you?' She made as if to get out of bed.

'No. By no means. I need to speak with him man to man.' When she didn't look at all convinced, he added, 'Apart from anything else, I need to report for duty.'

'You aren't well enough. Don't go. You don't need to visit him today, do you?'

'No sense in putting it off. Best to get it over with quickly. And then we can get on with living our lives, however it turns out. Besides,' he said with a wicked grin, 'you cannot seriously try to persuade me I'm not well enough to report for duty after the shameless use you made of me yesterday afternoon?' He turned her hand and placed a hot kiss on the inside of her wrist. 'And into the night?' He trailed kisses up her arm to the crook of her elbow.

She blushed. 'No, I suppose you are right. You certainly wore me out. I ache all over.'

He gave a quick frown. 'Was I too demanding? I didn't hurt you, did I? I know once or twice I was a bit…'

'You were perfect.' She sighed. 'I wish it could have gone on for much longer. No wonder,' she said with a very sultry look, 'you have gained such a reputation. I only wish I had more stamina.' A sudden look of insecurity flashed across her face. 'It isn't going to be easy for you to be satisfied by just one woman, is it?'

'Now stop right there,' he said sternly. 'If you can't trust me to be faithful, then—'

'No! Oh, no.' She knelt up and flung her arms round his neck. 'It isn't that. I just wish I was more experienced, that was all. That I knew how to please you.'

'Couldn't you tell how much you pleased me?'

She bit on her lower lip and nodded, though a little uncertainly.

'And you will very soon become experienced,' he promised her on a low growl. 'And besides, it isn't the same with you as it has been with any of the others. Because my emotions weren't involved. It was just—' he shrugged '—a sort of appetite that had to be met. The moment I'd finished with them, I left their beds. I have never wanted to hold a woman in my arms all night and just watch over her while she slept.' He brushed a strand of hair from her forehead.

'You just—'

He nodded. 'Did the deed and left. I didn't even want to *speak* to them again. But please don't think of the others, Sarah. They were all before I met you. Just know that from now on there won't, ever, be anyone but you.'

She subsided into the pillow, a frown pleating her brow.

'No, there won't. Because if I ever got so much as a whiff of you betraying me with another, I would…I would…' She crossed her arms. 'Well, I don't know exactly what I'd do, but I most certainly wouldn't turn a blind eye, the way Mama always did.'

'Really?' He grinned at her. 'I must say I'm flattered by this display of jealousy. Even if it is slightly insulting of you to assume I might be so inconstant. Because it means you care.' He sobered as it hit him again what a lucky dog he was. 'You really care.'

'Of course I care. Can't you tell by the way I'm willing to be cut off from my family, and live in some foreign land while you command some revolutionary army? On your wages, too, once Justin cuts me off.'

'Yes.' His face fell. 'Loving me is going to condemn you to a lifetime of penury and disgrace. I wouldn't blame Colonel Randall if he reached for his pistols the moment I set foot in his room.'

'Then take me with you. He won't shoot you in front of me.'

'No.' His face set in harsh lines. 'I'm not going to hide behind your skirts. Nor let him think for a moment I would do so.' He bent and gave her a swift kiss.

And, having set his jaw with determination, strode from the room to face whatever punishment Colonel Randall decided to mete out.

It was awful, being alone in this room, knowing Tom was facing Justin's wrath. Now she knew how he must have felt yesterday, when she'd been the one to go out. She lay in bed, for a while, imagining all the dozens of methods Justin could employ to part them. Though he couldn't, legally, prevent them from marrying. She wasn't under age.

She flung the covers aside in vexation. Tom might have worked himself into such a state that by the time she came home, he'd convinced himself she was going to leave him, but she was a Latymor. She would never, never, fail.

So she would just have to find something to do to keep her mind off Tom's interview with Justin. Though what?

And then she thought of Mary Endacott. Probably breaking her heart somewhere, over Justin. Because it sounded as though, even after all she'd done for him, Justin had been perfectly beastly to her, or she wouldn't have sounded so utterly defeated in that note she'd written. There wasn't much she could do about Mary's broken heart. Only Justin could fix that. But she could at least go and apologise to her, properly, for her part in it.

She rang for some hot water. Apologising probably wouldn't do any good. Mary had never responded to any of her overtures of friendship even before the disaster that had been the Duchess of Richmond's ball. But she wouldn't feel right if she didn't make the attempt to offer what comfort she could. And explain Gideon's motives for stealing the sword that had become such an issue between Mary and Justin.

Besides, if she stayed in this room all morning, wringing her hands and worrying over what Justin was doing to Tom, she'd end up positively demented.

Chapter Seventeen

His collar was too tight. There was a smudge of dust on his left boot. His bandages made him look ridiculous.

Good God. For the first time in his life, Tom actually cared what the person about to give him a trimming thought of him.

'You can go in now,' said Robbins, more dour-faced than usual.

'Well?' Colonel Randall glared at him from a bank of snowy-white pillows. With eyes that were so very much like Sarah's. 'What have you to say for yourself?'

Where to start? He ought to be giving an account of his movements. Report that he was fit for duty.

'I'm in love with your sister, sir,' he blurted, his normal laconic attitude towards superior officers totally deserting him. 'I'm aware you must think it a great piece of impertinence.'

Randall gave a low growl.

'I suppose I'd better resign my commission.'

Randall's eyes narrowed.

'She's already told me you intend to cut off her money,' Tom explained. 'So there's no point in asking for your blessing, is there?'

'None whatever.'

'Even so, I do ask you for it. Oh, not for me. I know I don't deserve it. I know I'm not fit to fasten her boots, let alone marry her. But, have you considered how unhappy it will make her, to be so entirely cut off from her family? She says she doesn't care, but I'm not sure she fully understands what it would mean.'

'There is an obvious solution. Give her up.'

Tom gave a wry smile. 'Do you think I haven't tried? She hunted me down and dragged me back when I tried to do the decent thing. She's even said she'd rather be my mistress than live without me. Naturally, I couldn't treat her so shabbily. No, I'm going to have to marry her, sir. With or without your blessing.'

Randall glowered at him in silence for so long that Tom could hear his heart pounding in his ears.

'She says she needs me, sir,' he added. 'It's because she's lost Gideon, you don't need to tell me that. She clung to the dog to start with. I suppose you might think I've taken its place in her affections. She certainly picked me up out of the mud the same way she rescued that flea-bitten cur. And you may not believe me, given my reputation—' he could feel his cheeks heating '—but I would be as faithful to her as a hound.'

Randall snorted. 'I'd warrant that the dog left her though, didn't it, the moment Major Flint came on the scene?'

'Well, yes, but the dog was always his, more than anyone else's, wasn't it? And I grant you that it wasn't a very good comparison to make, except that, well, the dog may have spread its favours widely, when Major Flint wasn't around, but in the end, it belonged only to him. The way I shall only belong to Sarah, for the rest of my life.'

'You expect me to believe that Tom Cat Bartlett is suddenly going to reform? Because of my sister?'

'Yes, sir.'

'And you fully intend to elope with her if I refuse to grant my permission?'

'Yes, sir.'

'And oblige her to live on your pay?'

'She says she's perfectly happy to do so, sir.'

'She has no notion of what that means. Why, you couldn't keep her in gowns for a month!'

'She doesn't care a rap for gowns. And if you knew her better, sir, you would know she would rather be out on horseback than being dragged from one modiste to another by her mother or her sister.'

'It won't hurt to acquire a wealthy wife, though, will it?'

'It wouldn't if I cared for money. Which you know I don't. I've always contrived to live well within my means. And anyway, she won't be wealthy, will she, not if she marries me. You have said so.'

Colonel Randall made another of those low, sort-of-growling noises.

But—was he imagining it, or had Randall's frown turned a touch less angry, and a tad more thoughtful?

'At least you haven't debts,' he finally conceded. 'Or a gambling addiction.'

'Given the way my father ended, you should know why I abhor gaming of all sorts. Although,' he added thoughtfully, 'in one respect, I believe I am more like my father than I ever knew.'

'Indeed?'

'Yes, sir. It only occurred to me, on my way here, this morning. I know now why he ended so badly. It was because he loved my mother so deeply. When he lost her, nothing else mattered. Not his title, not his position, not even his own son. Without her, his entire life ceased to have meaning. For the first time, I can begin to contemplate what he felt like. For I would feel like that, too, should I ever lose Sarah. And so I regret to inform you, sir,' he said, drawing himself to his full height and looking his commanding officer straight in the eye, 'that nothing you can do, or say, will make me give her up.'

'I suppose you had better marry her, then,' said Randall.

'What?'

'I have not the energy to repeat myself,' he said wearily. 'I have thought of little else since she visited me yesterday.' The line of his mouth softened into something almost resembling a rueful smile. 'The women in my family are strong-willed. Stubborn. Once they get a notion in their heads there is no shaking it. If she's set her heart on you, then have you she will, by hook or by crook. Heaven help you,' he added with a shake of his head.

'Yes, sir. Thank you, sir.'

'Well, then, since you are to become my brother, you may as well be the first to know that I shall be leaving the army. It is past time that I returned to Chalfont and took up my duties there. All of them,' he added, in a rather more determined tone. 'Randall's Rogues may be disbanded. But if they do continue, in whatever form, then I have complete confidence that I may trust them to either you or Major Flint.'

'Sir!' It struck him that it was particularly fitting that the next commanding officer would be either the half-brother or the brother-in-law of the man who'd originally formed the unit.

'It will mean promotion, of course. Better pay.'

'Sir!' He couldn't credit it. He'd come here expecting to get cashiered out of the regiment and instead he was looking at a possible promotion. How on earth would they work out which of them would land the job, though? Normally promotion would have gone to the officer with the most seniority. But it would be devilish hard to work out which of them that was, given the way the unit had been formed. Both had exchanged from other regiments. There was probably some clerk, somewhere, who had a formula for working out such things.

Not that he would object to serving under Flint, if it turned out he was the one who had seniority. On the contrary, he admired Flint for the way he'd worked his way up through the ranks. It took an exceptional man to do that.

'Bartlett!'

'Sir?'

'Stop standing there like a stunned sheep and get out of my sight.'

He just about had the presence of mind to salute, before turning on his heels and leaving.

Sarah was going to be so pleased.

With a broad grin, he skipped down the stairs and out into the bright June sunshine.

'Tom? It's good news, isn't it? I can see by your face.'

'The best,' he said, catching her up and swinging her right round.

'Tom, you lunatic. Put me down this instant!' Even though she was shrieking with laughter, so that he must know she didn't mean it, he complied at once.

'So, Justin gave us his blessing? I don't believe it.'

'He did more than that. He has given me command of the Rogues. At least—'

'What? Is he going to go home, then? Oh!' She clapped her hands to her cheeks. 'It was Gideon's last wish. Mama needs him, you see. And now that Bonaparte is trounced, I dare say he feels he can go back. And oh—' she squealed '—they always hand out honours after such a decisive victory, don't they? I shouldn't be a bit surprised if you got something. A knighthood at the very least.'

He shook his head. 'Only those already in favour get distinctions of that sort. And I won't be in favour. My action, in seducing the sister of my commanding officer, will outweigh any credit I may have gained by whatever small part I played in the battle itself.'

'Nobody will think that. We are going to be married. And once you become his brother-in-law, Justin is bound to put in a good word for you in all the right places. And before you say he is just an artillery officer, he is also an earl and has the ear of some very powerful people. He could even,' she said on a burst of inspiration, 'petition for your grandfather's title to be restored to you.'

'What if I don't get any honours, though, Sarah? You have to face the possibility. Are you sure you will be content to follow the drum? The life of an army wife isn't an easy one, you know.'

'Oh, Tom, how can you say anything so absurd? I've felt more alive these last few days than I ever have done. More…*me*, if you know what I mean? At last, I feel as if my life has some value. Some meaning. I am going to be such a good wife to you. And just to prove it, I have been busy this morning, showing everyone that I am *not* a silly, frippery, fashionable ninny.'

'And just how,' he said with a grin, 'did you do that?'

'I volunteered to help in Mary's hospital. What used to be her school is full to the rafters with wounded men. And Bertrand said I would be a valuable addition to the staff, only think of that!'

'Bertrand?' She thought he stiffened a little. His smile had certainly slipped.

'Yes. The doctor who comes in every day to oversee Mary's work. You need not worry about him. He's in love with Mary. So even if Justin has made a complete mull of it at least she won't be on her own for ever. But never mind them, Tom, the important thing is that this proves I can be a good officer's wife. I will never, never fail you, Tom.'

'You don't need to go working in a hospital to prove anything, Sarah. I don't want you to have to.'

'But *I* want to. I felt so badly for all those poor injured men and wished I could do more for them. Well, now I can.'

He frowned and took a breath, as though about to say something she wasn't going to like.

'You aren't going to be a disagreeable sort of husband, are you? Forbidding me to do things I want to do?'

'No.' He smiled. 'I'm not going to forbid you to do anything. I want you to be happy. But I also want you to be safe. We are going to have to employ a maid for you. And probably some form of male servant to watch over you. I don't like the thought of you wandering about on your own.'

She burst out laughing. 'Oh, Tom, as if I haven't been wandering all over Brussels this week without so much as a groom in attendance. My word, I never dreamt you could say anything so stuffy!'

'It comes of having been a rake, I expect. I know how very bad men can be. So I want to protect you from all the others. I,' he said, pulling her close, 'am going to be the only rake who gets his hands on you from now on.'

'Yes, Tom,' she said demurely. And then ruined the effect by adding, with a twinkle, 'You may put your hands wherever you like.'

* * * * *